HEMINGWAY'S GIRL

Erika Robuck

NEW AMERICAN LIBRARY

New American Library
Published by New American Library, a division of
Penguin Group (USA) Inc., 375 Hudson Street,
New York, New York 10014, USA
Penguin Group (Canada), 90 Eglinton Avenue East, Suite 700, Toronto,
Ontario M4P 2Y3, Canada (a division of Pearson Penguin Canada Inc.)
Penguin Books Ltd., 80 Strand, London WC2R 0RL, England
Penguin Ireland, 25 St. Stephen's Green, Dublin 2,
Ireland (a division of Penguin Books Ltd.)
Penguin Group (Australia), 250 Camberwell Road, Camberwell, Victoria 3124,
Australia (a division of Pearson Australia Group Pty. Ltd.)
Penguin Books India Pvt. Ltd., 11 Community Centre, Panchsheel Park,
New Delhi - 110 017, India
Penguin Group (NZ), 67 Apollo Drive, Rosedale, Auckland 0632,
New Zealand (a division of Pearson New Zealand Ltd.)
Penguin Books (South Africa) (Pty.) Ltd., 24 Sturdee Avenue,
Rosebank, Johannesburg 2196, South Africa

Penguin Books Ltd., Registered Offices:
80 Strand, London WC2R 0RL, England

First published by New American Library,
a division of Penguin Group (USA) Inc.

First Printing, September 2012
10 9 8 7 6 5 4 3 2 1

REGISTERED TRADEMARK—MARCA REGISTRADA

LIBRARY OF CONGRESS CATALOGING-IN-PUBLICATION DATA:

Robuck, Erika.
  Hemingway's girl/Erika Robuck.
    p. cm.
  ISBN 978-0-451-23788-0
  1. Hemingway, Ernest, 1899–1961—Fiction. 2. Women household employees—Fiction. 3. Key West (Fla.)—Fiction. I. Title.
  PS3618.O338H46 2012
  813'.6—dc23 2011053196

Set in Bell MT
Designed by Spring Hoteling

Printed in the United States of America

For my mother, Charlene

Dear Reader,

I fell in love with Ernest Hemingway when I was nineteen years old while reading *A Farewell to Arms*. After reading all of his novels and eventually ending up in his home in Key West, I had a strong desire to tell a piece of his story and inspire others to read his work.

The protagonist of *Hemingway's Girl*, Mariella Bennet, is a product of my imagination. I used her to tell the story of Depression-era Key West, Ernest Hemingway's life at the time, and the major events that took place for the people of that place and time. Any mistakes in the time line or plot are entirely my own.

There are conflicting reports as to whether Hemingway was referred to as "Papa" at the time the book takes place. I chose to make it so to suit my fictional purposes.

Finally, please note that according to several sources, the abundance of polydactyl cats was not a fixture of the Hemingway residence in 1935. I hope their absence does not take away from your enjoyment of the story.

Sincerely,
Erika Robuck

HEMINGWAY'S GIRL

Mariella peered down from the stern at the dark forms below and knew her fish was there if she had the strength to take it.

The urging of the boat on the waves, the arc of the flying fish, and the glints of light on the sea's surface had acted in chorus to bring her here, to this spot. She lifted the pole and scanned the horizon. Moments later, she felt the tug on the line, then the lurch that jerked her forward.

Mariella threw her cigarette over the side of the *Corrida* and backed into the chair anchored to the deck. The line bowed the pole over the edge of the boat and slid back and forth on the railing in response to the fish. She dug her feet into the decking and pushed her graying black hair out of her eyes. She wanted to call Jake, but pride clamped her mouth. It wasn't long before Mariella felt the fatigue in her arms and thought of *The Old Man and the Sea.*

No one could have fought that long, Papa.

Her slender forearms flexed to the pole, and drops of sweat mingled with sprays of seawater, leaving a briny film on her skin. She loved the heat, the wet, and the exertion, because they made her feel alive, but her muscles quivered from the effort. She glanced at her watch and saw that it had been only a half hour. Disgusted with herself, Mariella yelled, "Jake!"

Her son stumbled out of the cabin from his sleep. She'd

insisted he come out on the water to give him respite from his medical residency and put him back in touch with the sea. It had been too long.

"How big?" He ran a hand through his hair.

"Just about took me over."

"No shit?"

He checked her line on the railing and followed it with his hand.

"You ready?" she asked.

"We'll see." He smiled. His eyes crinkled at the corners.

God, he's like his father.

Jake grabbed the pole and sat down once his mother moved away.

It was a dance: one at the pole, the other backing down the boat in response to the marlin's movements on the line. They took turns until their palms bled. In the end, three hours later, they were able to tie the rope around the fish's head, reverse the boat, and pull the water from the gills to drown it. Then they moved like hell to get back before the sharks destroyed it.

Back at the Seaport Harbor dock in Key West, they grabbed a couple of idlers to help haul up the fish and weigh it. When the scale showed three hundred twenty-six pounds, the small crowd that had gathered around them cheered.

"How much, *hermosa?*"

Mariella looked over and smiled at the wrinkled old man who had pushed through the crowd. She gave him a hug.

"Quince, guapo."

"You're givin' it to him," said Jake. "That took me hours."

"Shut up, boy." Nicolas smacked Jake on the back of the head.

Mariella handed Nicolas her camera, and she and Jake stood on either side of the fish. The sun shone in her eyes, making it difficult to discern people's faces in the crowd, but she thought she saw a large man with a white beard and white hair.

Her heart leaped and she started forward, but as quickly as she'd seen him, he was gone. She scanned the area where she thought he'd stood, but he had disappeared.

The flash went off, and Mariella was surprised to feel a lump in her throat.

~⁓⌒

The leaves on the banyan in her front yard hung motionless and nearly indistinguishable from the night sky. She could still feel the banyan's presence, though, its great woody roots strangling some old host tree. She remembered when Hemingway had planted a banyan at his house and told her its parasitic roots were like human desire. At the time she'd thought it romantic. She hadn't understood his warning.

Mariella struck a match and lit her cigarette. Its tip glowed against the darkness, and a sweet burning scent filled the space around her. Duval Street sang from a couple of blocks over, but the bugs outside her door were louder. She leaned on the doorframe and flicked the moths off the screen one by one to clear her view down Whitehead Street.

Bumby and Mouse emerged from the darkness.

"Hello, boys," said Mariella. She fetched the plate of leftover bits of fish from dinner and slid it to the ground outside the door. The cats grabbed morsels and retreated into the shadows.

Her son's mumbling sleep talk drifted in from the couch where she'd sent him to rest. She picked up the *Key West Citizen* rolled up outside her door next to his discarded boat shoes, and lined up her own shoes next to his. It seemed like yesterday that his shoes were smaller than hers. Now, at twenty-five, Jake was a full head taller than Mariella. She went to him on the couch and kissed his hair. It smelled like the sea air.

Mariella walked up the stairs to her room, listening to the

comfortable, creaking sound of the wood responding to her steps. She could smell the aroma of fried fish at the top of the stairs and knew it would sit there for days, reminding her of her time on the boat with her son. In her room she threw the paper on the bed and went to wash up in the bathroom. When she returned, something in the headline caught her eye.

"Papa" Passes
Bell Tolls for Writer
Ernest Hemingway Dies of Gunshot

Moments later, she was vaguely aware of her son's footsteps pounding up the stairs, the door thrown open, and his arms around her as she fell to her knees, screaming. He was unable to console her.

CHAPTER ONE

Key West
January 1935

It was his introduction that caused Mariella to burn her fingertips.

"And the referee, the internationally renowned writer, *millionaire*, and playboy Mr. Ernest Hemingway."

Mariella's eyes jerked up from her cigarette. He sauntered across the ring, hands up to the crowd, his whole face a grin. She'd seen him call before, but it was the first time they had introduced him as a millionaire.

"Ouch!" She dropped the match to the ground and shook her hand as she stepped up to the chain-link fence to get a better look.

"How goes it tonight?" he yelled.

The crowd at Blue Heaven bordello and playhouse roared and stomped their feet. They were a hundred poor, black, out-of-work men, with a smattering of whites and Cubans, and all were his.

"Big Bear from Bahama Village fights visiting opponent Tiny Tim!"

Mariella smiled as Hemingway held up the arm of Tiny Tim, a massive man with coal black skin, bulging biceps, and a neck as wide as Mariella's waist. She knew the newcomers would bet on him, but she also knew that Big Bear never lost, so she'd bet that way. Her sister's doctor bills were piling up and they were late on rent. She needed to win.

A group of noisy, drunken vets pushed by, nearly knocking her over. Mariella straightened up and tightened her father's old baseball cap to make sure that all of her hair remained tucked inside. She had to stop herself from shouting expletives at them, because she didn't want to draw attention to herself. She turned back to the fight, but rather than watch the boxers, she couldn't take her eyes off Hemingway. Key West was a small town, so she'd seen him around, but she'd never much noticed him until tonight. His dark brown hair was a little too long in the back, his shoes were as ratty as hers, and a rope held up his shorts. He certainly didn't look like a millionaire.

Her father, Hal, had mentioned Hemingway from time to time when he saw him at the docks. Hal thought him a decent guy, but her mother had read one of his books and deemed it vulgar. While this intrigued Mariella rather than putting her off, she didn't have time to read. Caring for her sisters and trying to make money consumed her.

More than ever now that Hal was dead.

Big Bear's every punch made contact with Tiny Tim in the first round. Tim was huge but uncoordinated, and he tired quickly. By the second round it looked like he'd lose, and some of the amicable cheers from earlier in the night took on an edge of shock and outrage. Losing money was no joke.

Hemingway sobered, too. He was into the fight and called it with all the intensity of a high-stakes referee. Mariella found it interesting that a man of his stature would participate in a poor men's boxing match and take it so seriously.

She liked that.

When she finished her cigarette, Mariella licked her sore fingertips and blew on them. The suspense was killing her, and in the third round her heart dropped when it looked like Tim would get the better of Big Bear. That meant she'd lose all the money she'd earned the past week from odd jobs at the docks. That meant she'd have to beg the landlord for a few more days, when they were already late on rent. That meant the doctor wouldn't come when they needed him. That meant no money for her secret stash.

Mariella felt her heart pounding and cursed herself for betting so much. She was a damned fool and deserved the tongue-lashing she'd get from her mother. How could she play with money like that?

Tim's strength built like a tidal wave. Bear couldn't get in a punch. Tim had him cornered. He was all over him, and finally, with sickening ease, Tiny Tim knocked out Big Bear.

She grasped the chain-link fence and pushed her face into her arms, listening to the men whoop and holler around her. She felt light-headed and sick, but forced herself away from the fence and toward home. As she passed the ring, she heard a commotion. A small white man from the crowd jumped the rope and tried to attack Big Bear, who sat with his head in his gloved hands.

"You stupid shit," he shouted. "Give me back my money. I bet all my money on you."

Mariella felt her stomach clench. She knew the man from the marina. He used to shortchange and overcharge her father, and she'd always hated him for it. Without thinking, she moved to push him off Bear. Before she got there, Hemingway jumped between Bear and the man and shoved him into the ropes. Hemingway's jaw was clenched tight as a shark's, and he put his face right into the man's face.

"Don't come around here again, asshole," growled Hemingway. "If you don't have the money to lose, you got no business betting it."

With that, Hemingway pushed the man over the side of the ring. He landed at Mariella's feet, quickly righted himself, and ran off cursing into the night. Mariella turned back to the ring and saw the writer crouched down in front of Bear with his hand on Bear's shoulder. She was moved that Hemingway stood up to the guy who lost his bet, but it reminded her of her own loss, and she felt sick.

God, all the money she'd lost.

She felt her head spin, and stumbled with the gait of a drunk toward home before anyone noticed her.

Mariella crept through the front door and closed it as quietly as she could. The room was black except for the moonlight shining through the front window. She was relieved to see that her mother's chair was empty and she'd gone to bed, but it still held the impression of where Eva had doubtlessly sat all evening with her legs tucked into her, teary eyes gazing out the window, shoulders hunched under the weight of her grief.

Mariella reached up and squeezed her own shoulders, tense from the loss, the guilt from gambling, and the strain of watching her mother's pain consume her just a little more each day instead of releasing her. While she and her young sisters had adjusted to Hal's death as best they could, Eva was drowning, and Mariella didn't know how to help her.

The floorboards threatened to expose Mariella with each step, but she made it past her mother's room and into the room she shared with her sisters. The girls slept together on a mattress on the floor—twelve-year-old Estelle curled in a ball, and five-year-old Lulu sprawled with an arm hanging over Estelle on one side and the edge of the bed on the other.

Mariella smiled and felt a surge of love for the girls. She moved Lulu's arm onto the mattress, pulled the threadbare sheet up over both of them, and kissed them each on the head. She considered crawling into bed with them, but instead returned to the front room to try to catch a little sleep on the couch before heading down to the dock before they all woke the next morning.

In spite of her exhaustion, Mariella made it to the dock as the sun rose, warming the sky pink and orange like the inside of a shell. The soft lap of the waves against the pilings soothed her nerves, and she shook off the previous night's loss. The dark forms of the fishermen and their boats already out to sea dotted the horizon, and just arriving at the docks were the tourists and wealthy sailors readying their boats for pleasure cruises.

The sound of an engine turning over and sputtering out broke the stillness. Mariella looked just down the pier to see a man in a crisp white sweater and khaki pants trying to dismantle his boat's engine, while his passengers, two elegant women wearing brightly colored silk kerchiefs on their hair, and another impeccably dressed gentleman, looked on in helpless confusion. The man reached into the engine and jerked back his hand, cursing from the burn.

Mariella could see from the sweat on his brow and his troubled smile that he was embarrassed. She walked over to the boat.

"Sir," she said.

One of the women noticed her first, and ran her eyes over Mariella's hand-me-down men's clothing with distaste. She turned her back to Mariella and pretended she hadn't heard. Mariella felt her cheeks burn with shame, followed by anger, and was about to walk away when the other woman noticed her and smiled kindly.

"May I help you?" she said.

"I might actually be able to help you," said Mariella, "if you let me take a look."

The man working on the engine stepped to the edge of the boat.

"You know a thing or two about boats?" he said, wiping his clean, smooth hands on a towel.

"Yes, sir."

"Good," he said, "because I was about to dismantle the whole thing and make a real ass of myself. Come on up."

Mariella climbed onto the boat, noting the wine and water chilling in the ice bucket, the neatly folded blankets on the plush leather seats, and the oversized picnic basket, no doubt full of fruits and cheeses for a late-morning snack. She ignored the rumbling in her stomach, and her pride, and stepped over to the engine.

It didn't take long for her to see the culprit of the engine troubles—a can was tangled and shredded through it, sucked through machinery a little too powerful for its own good. She knew she couldn't get the can out with her bare hands because of the temperature, but she was able to use a screwdriver and wire cutters from the man's toolbox to disentangle it.

The small party watched in silence while she worked. Though the air still held the pleasant cool of morning, Mariella felt her shirt cling to the sweat on her back. She could feel their eyes on her and wished she'd taken more care with her appearance that morning. She hoped her solution would do the trick.

When she finished, she directed the man to start the boat. He turned the key and the engine started up and settled into a gentle hum. To her pleasure, the group applauded. She nodded and made a move to climb off the boat when the man stopped her and slipped a bill in her hand. She thanked him and climbed onto the dock, where she unwound the lines for them.

As they pulled out of the harbor and into open water, she looked down at the bill and gasped. Ten dollars! It was more than what she'd lost the night before.

She said a silent prayer of thanks, suddenly feeling in her heart that her father was with her.

The glare of the sun on the water told her the fishermen would soon return. Her father's friend Mark Bishop often let her deliver some of his catch to buyers for a small share of the proceeds, and sent her home with good cuts of meat for her family. She stood in front of one of the restaurants and watched the water for Mark.

"*Hermosa!*" Nicolas Oliva called from the second floor of his restaurant, where he lived with his wife and six children.

"*Hola!*" called Mariella.

"You're early!"

"Just trying to keep out of trouble."

"You'd better. I got my eye on you!"

Nicolas disappeared from the window. Inside the house, one of the kids shrieked, her giggles blending with the deeper rumbling of Nicolas's laughter. An image of her own father flashed through her mind, and a hollow spot formed under her breastbone. She turned away.

Mariella rolled up the sleeves of her father's old work shirt and wiped the sweat from her forehead. She lit the cigarette she stole from Mark's boat stand, adding it to the mental tally she knew she owed him. Through the smoke, she smelled a terrible odor, worse than rotting fish. She looked around the top of the pier but couldn't see anything. Then she looked under it. Something was caught in an old net by the pilings. It looked like a shoe. She grabbed a nearby fishing pole and poked at it to pick it up, but when she did she saw that it was the body of a man.

Mariella froze in shock. He was badly bloated and facedown. She worried that he was a friend, but she didn't recognize his clothes. The smell rose in waves, and she covered her mouth to stifle a gag. She threw the cigarette over the side of the pier and ran to get help.

"Shame you had to see that, missy," said Deputy Bowler. "Fool was probably drunk and fell in."

Bowler was there that day, three months earlier, when they'd found her father's boat beating against rocks on the coast near the southernmost point of the island. Hal's body had already been loaded into the coroner's truck by the time the family got word. When Mariella arrived at the scene, the deputy held her back and wouldn't answer her questions or let her see Hal. She still hated Bowler.

All her mother would say after her whispered, tearful meetings with police was that Hal had died of a heart attack and his boat was destroyed. Mariella thought his recent drinking and depression over money troubles must have contributed to his stress and pushed him over the edge, but she still had a hard time accepting it, and the loss of the boat.

Their plans for the future, their dreams of a long row of shiny boats to haul rich tourists on gulf excursions and sunset cruises, their ideas of making a living off the water while helping impart its beauty to the travelers: all gone.

Mariella shook her head, dispersing her dark thoughts. It was time to work, not mourn. Someone had to provide for them all.

"Who was he?" asked Mark Bishop.

"Dunno. No one reported him missing."

As the body was loaded into the truck, Mariella felt a wave of grief at the unwelcome reminder of that terrible day just a few months ago. She wished she remembered her dad as the robust man he'd been, not as a lifeless face in a casket. She clenched her jaw, dug her nails into her palms, and blinked away her tears.

Mark put his hand on Mariella's shoulder. "Come on; I got a decent catch."

They walked to Mark's boat and she helped him unload the

snapper into the iced carts so he could take them to the restaurant owners and barter his way to a few lousy bucks. Mark seemed to sense her need for silence. She liked him because he didn't feel he had to fill the quiet, and because he'd cried at her dad's funeral. She was glad for the simple, monotonous task of filling the carts, because she hoped it would take her mind off her father and the dead man no one cried for or demanded to see.

Mariella hadn't forgiven herself for not going with her dad that morning. Hal would usually wake before daylight and open her door a crack to let her know he was leaving soon. In that time, Mariella would decide to either stay home to help with her sisters or to join him. Most often, she'd slip on Hal's hand-me-down fishing clothes, pull her long black hair into a ponytail, and make their coffee. They'd walk through town in the hush of early morning, meeting other fishermen along the way and exchanging silent nods of greeting. Until the sun rose over the water, they never said a word. That time was sacred.

Before long, Mark returned and didn't have much for her. Just twenty cents and a fish for dinner. Mariella thanked him, sliced up her snapper at the stand, wrapped it in old newspaper, and rinsed her hands in a bucket of seawater. She slipped another cigarette into her pocket and was moving west down the pier when she heard her name.

"Mariella?"

She turned to see Chuck Thompson, the owner of the hardware store, a man who gave her odd jobs for small pay, standing on his boat with Ernest Hemingway, sunburned and smiling. His dark hair was disheveled from the wind, and his white teeth flashed beneath his mustache. She felt a jolt go through her and couldn't help but smile—until she realized what a mess she was, with fish blood on her father's old shirt, rank fish smell on her hands, and dirty, wet hair. She reached up to smooth it away from her face, hoping they wouldn't notice her burning with embarrassment.

"Hi, Mr. Thompson. Mr. Hemingway."

"Call him Papa," said Chuck.

"Papa," said Mariella.

"You look like you've been working hard," said Papa. His eyes traveled over her, and when they met hers she felt the jolt again, in spite of her shame over her appearance.

"Still a beauty," said Chuck.

"Come see what we brought in," said Hemingway.

Mariella stepped over a big roll of rope and walked to the edge of the boat. Hemingway reached down to her and she took his hand as he helped her on board. His hand was big and hot, and she felt a current of electricity run up her arm. She hopped down on the deck and saw, lying there, a gigantic marlin.

"Damn near took my arms off," he said, "but she yielded in the end."

"It's beautiful," said Mariella. Then she felt stupid for calling a big dead fish beautiful, but it was. Its nose was pointed and fierce, but its eyes were big and sad. Its silver-gray skin shone. She ran her hand down its side.

"It is beautiful," he said. "Do you ever go out?"

"Used to, with my dad."

"Ever see a marlin like this?"

She had, but she lied. "No."

"You'll come out with me sometime, huh?"

He winked at her. Was he flirting? Mariella felt her heart race.

"Sure," she said. "I'll teach you a thing or two."

He threw back his head and roared with laughter.

Mariella climbed back onto the pier and started home. She pulled the cigarette out of her pocket, lit it, and turned to wave at the men, but they were already tending to the fish.

Mariella couldn't get used to the hollow woman her mother had become. Eva sat in her chair by the window with a full ashtray at her side and a worn rosary in her hand. She drank watered-down coffee made from the same grounds she'd been using for three days. They had no sugar and the little ones needed the milk, so the thin, dirty liquid must have tasted like someone spit old coffee into hot water.

Eva had once been a beauty—glossy black hair, big brown eyes, small, sharp features. Now she was gaunt. Her hair had gray streaks. Her eyes were perpetually wet and rimmed in shadows.

"I've got dinner," said Mariella.

Eva blinked, pulling herself out of her memories. "From Mark?"

"Yes," said Mariella. "And ten dollars."

She expected Eva would brighten at the amount, and was dismayed to see her mother's eyes darken with suspicion.

Suspicion—the new look that crossed her mother's face now whenever Mariella left the house at night or brought home a decent amount of money. She wasn't used to such scrutiny, and found herself feeling more anger than pity for her mother. Mariella tried to ignore the spark her mother's look had ignited within her, and walked over to the cabinet to pull out a pan, hoping the simple act of cooking would help her simmer down.

Mariella scooped a spoonful of fat from the cup by the sink and heated it on the stove. Once it sizzled, she unwrapped the snapper from the newspaper and placed it in the pan. She sprinkled a pinch of sea salt over the fish and pulled a lime out of her pocket that she had picked up on the way home when the man at the fruit stand wasn't looking. She rolled it over the counter, sliced it open, and squeezed it over the fish. It smoked and filled the air with its tangy smell. Mariella flipped the fish and poured four glasses of water, squeezing the rest of the lime into each glass. She put the water on the table and set out four plates.

There. She felt calmer.

She also felt her mother's eyes on her and wished Eva would offer to help set the table. Mariella couldn't help but think that if Eva would just engage more in day-to-day tasks or even look for a job, she might start to feel better.

"Tomorrow I'll try to find work," Eva said, as though she'd heard the wish.

Eva's words had the opposite effect on Mariella that she knew her mother wanted, because she knew Eva had no intention of trying to find work. Her anger returned in a flash.

"Go find the girls and I'll watch the fish," said Eva.

In spite of her offer to help, Mariella didn't trust her mother to remember to take the fish out on time. The last time Eva offered, Mariella went to find the girls, only to come home to charred, inedible snapper, and her mother, lost in memories, staring out the window.

"It's okay," said Mariella. "I'll get them once the fish is done."

Her mother stubbed out her cigarette in a smash and sat up in her chair.

"*¿Crees que no lo puedo hacer?* Who do you think did the cooking before your father died?"

Mariella was taken aback by her mother's outburst. "I didn't say you couldn't cook. It's just that I'm almost done."

Eva exhaled, looked out the window, and mumbled something in Spanish. Mariella turned her glare to the fish.

The door burst open and her sisters came in, with Lulu leading Estelle by the hand. Before they could start eating, Mariella shooed the girls away to wash up for dinner. Eva walked over and sat down, staring at her food as if she wanted someone to feed it to her.

When the girls returned, Lulu filled the silence with her chatter about the nuns at school, and Estelle, practically mute since Hal had died, hung on her sister's every word as if it were a buoy. Mariella noticed Eva still staring at her plate.

"Better eat before it gets cold," said Mariella.

Mariella tried to remember what it was like to have Hal at the table telling fish stories at night. It had been only months, and already her memory of him at the house grew dim. Memories of her parents' arguments were louder in her mind. She remembered how anxious her dad was when the money got really tight, and how Eva had told Hal to leave fishing.

He said he didn't know anything else. She said to learn. He said their luck would change. She called him a fool. He encouraged her to reach out to her family in Cuba. She argued that they hadn't spoken in years, and contacting them when they needed money wouldn't get her anywhere. He told her how much fishing meant to him and to Mariella, and how well-off they'd be once they started the charter boat business. Eva said there wouldn't be any rich tourists to take on fishing excursions if the depression continued. And on and on.

Mariella remembered that her father started staying away, coming home late, drunk, and then it was as if his light went out.

Then he died.

"Can we go to the Point soon?" asked Lulu, snapping Mariella out of her painful thoughts.

"Of course," she said. "We haven't been to the beach in a while."

Mariella felt the unspoken words that made the silence fall over the room. They hadn't gone to the beach since Hal died.

Eager to end dinner, Mariella stood to clear the plates and walked them over to the sink. She heard Eva's chair scrape over the floor and the door to her room close. Mariella sent Lulu and Estelle to their room to do their homework while she washed dishes. She was relieved to be alone.

~∂⟋

That night, Mariella dreamed of Hemingway.

In the dream, it was a glorious, sparkling day. They were on

Hal's old boat, drinking and fishing. When it got too hot, Hemingway took off his shirt and shoes and jumped in the water. He tried to coax Mariella out of her clothes to join him.

The rest of the dream was fuzzy. She didn't remember taking off her clothes, but suddenly she felt the cool water around her body, his arms pull her into him, and then she awoke, breathless and sweating, troubled and aroused, and unable to fall back asleep.

Mariella thought it strange that someone who had meant so little to her just days ago now invaded her dreams, and she felt guilty for dreaming about a married man. But of course she dreamed of him. He'd been on her mind since the night at the boxing match, and the following day when they were introduced at the dock. The jolt she'd felt when he touched her hand unsettled and confused her.

But her interest in the writer was also practical.

She stared at the window until the pink glow from the morning sunrise filled the panes. Suddenly Mariella sat up, quickly dressed, brushed her hair, and stole out of the house before anyone awoke, headed for Thompson's Hardware Store with an idea.

CHAPTER TWO

The first time Mariella saw Hemingway at his house, he was sitting on a dining room chair on the lawn while his wife, Pauline, cut his curling brown hair. He was big and the chair was small, and he regarded Mariella with the kind of mocking smile that usually runs between old friends. It occurred to Mariella that Pauline was trying to tame that great animal of a man, and the absurdity of it made Mariella smile back at him.

A flash went off and a lithe, lovely woman who resembled Pauline advanced her camera and said, "You look like a lion about to pounce, Papa."

"Don't come too close, Jinny. I bite," he said.

"Honestly," said Pauline. "Keep still for one more minute."

Jinny walked around Mariella, looking her up and down the way a man would. "Are you here for a housekeeping job?" Mariella met her eyes and stared back until Jinny looked away.

"Yes," she said. "I'm Mariella Bennet."

"Chuck Thompson sent her over," said Pauline, not lifting her eyes from the back of Hemingway's head. "She's done work for him at the dock."

"He told me you could use the help," said Mariella.

"Mariella Bennet?" said Papa. "Let me guess: Your mother's Cuban and your daddy's American."

"Yes. And a fisherman."

"Hal Bennet was your dad?" he said, wrinkling his forehead in a mixture of sadness and fondness.

"Yes," said Mariella.

"You're hired!" Papa said.

"I haven't even interviewed her yet," said Pauline.

"Good. Do that and leave my hair alone." The big cat pounced out of his chair, hit Jinny on the backside, winked at Mariella, and ran to the yellow Ford parked on the street. Then he disappeared.

Pauline shook her head without a smile and motioned for Mariella to follow her and Jinny inside. As Mariella passed into the sitting room, she was nearly run over by a boy about six years old, followed by his little brother, followed by a large, sweaty governess.

"Have a seat." Pauline motioned to a formal settee in a pale blue sitting room. Mariella sat and noted a chandelier hanging from the ceiling where she thought a fan should be. Jinny sat down close to Mariella. She smelled of cigarettes and rose water. Suddenly feeling very poor and awkward around these elegant, pretentious women, Mariella squirmed in her dress and tried to figure out whether she should cross her legs at the ankle or the knee.

"Those are your references?" asked Pauline, taking the neat stack of papers from Mariella.

"Yes, ma'am."

"You may call me Mrs. Hemingway."

"Yes, Mrs. Hemingway."

"You're just nineteen?"

"Yes, Mrs. Hemingway."

"Chuck said you need a job closer to home. He spoke highly of you."

"I've known Mr. Thompson for a long time," said Mariella. "He's kept me busy with small jobs at the hardware store and the dock, but I need something permanent."

"Your father was a fisherman?"

"Yes, but he died back in October. I need to support my mom and my two sisters." Mariella looked straight at Pauline. She had practiced saying that aloud, and was pleased with herself for her steady voice.

"I'm sorry to hear that," said Pauline. She shifted in her chair, clearly ill at ease. After shuffling through Mariella's references, she put them on a nearby table, where a nibbled peach lay on a blue plate, browning in the heat. A fly buzzed around it. Next to the plate was a copy of *War and Peace*. Mariella eyed it and wondered whose it was.

"Can you read?" asked Pauline.

"Of course," said Mariella. She sat up straight in her chair, insulted, and badly wishing she could retort, *Can you?* But she kept her tongue in check.

Pauline regarded Mariella for a moment. Mariella could feel the woman testing her, wondering whether she could fight, cry, and live in front of Mariella without actually having to think about her. Mariella relaxed her posture so she wouldn't appear aggressive and folded her hands in her lap.

Something seemed to satisfy Pauline.

"Jinny is my sister," she said. "Her word is as good as mine. Ada Stern is the boys' governess. Stay out of her way if you know what's good for you. And Ernest, always mind him when he's around, but my word is law. The only real house rule is to *never, ever* disturb my husband when he's writing. He gets up very early, at five or six o'clock, and goes to the room over the garage to write. He works until it gets too hot, about ten or so, and then he goes fishing. You've read his work?"

"Yes," she lied.

Pauline sat up, as if anticipating the usual outpouring of sentiments regarding Ernest's talent, but Mariella said nothing. The way the woman then slouched in her chair made Mariella think that Pauline must live vicariously through Hemingway, and that she took compliments to him as praise for herself.

"And does it please you?" asked Jinny.

Mariella looked Jinny in the eye. "Yes, very much."

Only the ticking of the clock and the sound of muffled children's voices outside could be heard. Pauline reached over to Jinny's dress and rifled through a pocket in its side until she found a cigarette. Mariella reached in her own dress and pulled out a book of matches. She lit Pauline's cigarette. Pauline let the smoke drift over her face like a veil and said through it, "You'll start Monday. Be here at seven."

Pauline stood, picked up her book, and left the room. Jinny followed her sister. When the women left, Mariella slipped the peach into her pocket for the girls and stepped out onto the back lawn. She thought how nice it would be to have a full enough stomach to take a bite of a peach and leave the rest of it on a table for the flies. It made her dislike Pauline.

That and the fact that it seemed Pauline knew who Hal was but pretended otherwise so she wouldn't have to talk about him.

And the way Pauline assumed Mariella couldn't read.

Jesus, she didn't know whether this would be worth the money.

As she walked away, she could feel their eyes on her. She turned and looked up to see Pauline and Jinny on the upper balcony, watching her.

"See you 'round," called Jinny.

"Bye," said Mariella. She walked away but could still hear their voices.

"So, what do you think?" said Jinny.

Pauline waited a moment to answer. Mariella strained to hear her reply.

"She's a peach."

CHAPTER THREE

Mariella's stomach dropped when she opened the battered yellow Cuban espresso tin. She could almost hear her father's raspy voice in her ear.

No withdrawals. Only deposits for the business. Pretend it's not even there.

But everything was different now. She'd been bleeding it for rent and food for months, and now all that remained was forty-one dollars and thirteen cents. She'd have to use the rest to keep off the landlord. The doctor would have to wait.

She dropped in her tips and some change from turning in old bottles she found in trash cans. She closed the lid in disgust and shoved it back in the corner under her bed, covering it with an old, threadbare blanket.

Why did she continue to entertain her foolish dream? It would cost her a thousand dollars or more to start the business. Her mother had told her that her father's boat had been battered beyond repair and had been hauled away to a boat graveyard somewhere on Stock Island, or farther north. It was bad enough when they just needed to replace the engine. Now she needed a whole new boat, a slip at the dock, money for fuel, and a million other things.

Mariella stood and put on one of the two identical work

dresses Pauline had sent over—a starchy navy blue smock with white trim. Though she hated the idea of working indoors, away from the water and in a dress all day, she was at least glad she didn't have to do it in any of her ill-fitting, worn clothing.

She crept out of her room, grateful that Eva still slept. They'd fought the night before when Mariella told Eva about her new job with the Hemingways. Mariella could have told her she was working as a prostitute and gotten a better reaction. Eva thought Hemingway wrote filth and had a bad reputation. Mariella said that might be true, but he also paid well and regularly—four dollars a day, and overtime for weekends or parties. That would almost cover rent, and if she could win gambling money and keep up with odd jobs, they could survive.

On her way to the kitchen, Mariella looked into her mother's room. Eva lay asleep, curled around one of Hal's old shirts. It filled Mariella with sadness, and she felt guilty for being hard on her mother, but she just made it so difficult.

Mariella continued to the kitchen and made Estelle and Lulu a quick breakfast. They had only two eggs and a heel of a bread loaf left to split, but it would have to do. They were lucky to have anything for breakfast at all. She knew of many families who didn't, and had herself gone to school and work with an empty stomach plenty of times. Mariella was at least glad the sisters at the free Catholic school would give the girls a good lunch.

After dropping off the girls for morning prayer, Mariella arrived at the Hemingway house. In spite of her nerves, she admired it in the early-morning sun. Twin porches wrapped around the Spanish-styled facade, and its thick, tropical landscaping seemed reminiscent of Eden. She passed two peacocks grazing in the grass and walked up to the front door to knock. She suddenly felt very anxious and out of place while she waited for an answer.

A minute passed, then two. The butterflies in Mariella's stomach now felt like full-on nausea, and she wondered whether she should try another entrance or just leave. She made a move to step off the porch when the door was opened by a heavyset black woman. She took no trouble to hide her impatience and looked Mariella over from head to toe before suddenly breaking into a huge, warm smile.

"The answer to my prayers!" she said. Mariella had an urge to look behind her, but knew that the woman was speaking about her, and smiled.

"You must be Mariella," said the woman, opening the door and thrusting an apron at her. "I'm Isabelle, and I need a pair of young hands around here."

She grabbed Mariella's hands and grunted in approval before hustling her into the kitchen. It didn't take long for Mariella to learn that the household wasn't as peaceful within as it looked from the outside.

Hemingway's boys, six-year-old Patrick and three-year-old Gregory, played an intense game of cowboys and Indians all morning. They jumped on the furniture, slammed the doors, and rattled the china. Pauline shooed them out to the yard, but Jim, the gardener, shooed them back in. Isabelle spanked their hands when they tried to steal food from the kitchen, and Ada spanked their behinds when they fought or cried or yelled.

Pauline pulled Mariella away from Isabelle, much to the cook's dismay, and instructed Mariella on which floors to clean on which days. Then Pauline left to do some shopping in town. Just after she left, as Mariella walked into the family room to sweep, she tripped over Patrick as he dropped a large, struggling peacock on the floor. Mariella used her broom to send the bird back out to the yard, and had just turned back to the house to scold Patrick when she ran into Hemingway himself.

"Jesus, daughter, I hope I never do anything to earn that look from you," he said.

She blushed to her toes and reached up to smooth her hair.

"I guess I'm not used to boys," she said. "I have sisters."

"You're lucky," he said. "I've always wanted a daughter; just don't make 'em, I guess."

She laughed, a little shocked at his reference.

"You're actually just who I was looking for," he said. "Follow me."

Mariella followed, still carrying the broom. He walked her up the stairs and to his bedroom. He stopped for a moment by the bed and gave her a mischievous smile. She broke into a cold sweat.

"Not here," he said.

He turned and opened a door on the side of the room that led to the walkway to his writing cottage. She walked along the narrow walkway and tried not to look down. She hated heights. He pulled a key out of his pocket and opened the door. She followed him into the room.

The cottage was an oasis. Cool from the morning air, it smelled like the books stacked on its shelves around the room. Papa's writing table sat in the middle of the room like an altar—the typewriter some kind of holy instrument of transformation.

"I'd like you to clean in here," he said. "I trust you not to move anything or talk about any of the writing you'll see when you snoop."

Mariella had an impulse to deny that she'd snoop, but thought he'd know better.

"So you're okay with me snooping," she said.

"Snoop away; just never talk about it. You never talk about a book till you're done with it."

Mariella was surprised how easy it was to be herself around him, and how easily he'd taken to her. She thought their meeting at the dock had been the right way to start. It was neutral territory. Now they could just continue on without the formality. Still, she wondered.

"Why do you trust me?" she asked.

"Because you're honest. If you'd have tried to deny you'd snoop, I'd have told you I changed my mind. You passed the test."

Mariella was glad she hadn't tried to lie. It didn't seem like much escaped his notice.

She turned away from him and leaned the broom against the door so she could walk the perimeter of the room. An antelope hung from the wall, and a lion-skin rug splayed across the center of the room. She crouched down to look at its teeth up close.

"Just got these beasts mounted, stuffed, and gutted," he said. "From our Africa trip."

Mariella stood and walked to his desk. A roll of half-typed paper stuck out of the typewriter. She looked at the words and then at him. He nodded, and she leaned in to look at it closer.

"It's when my companion was talking about great writers," he said. "He admired them, but I knew they were a bunch of miserable saps."

Mariella read the words for a moment and then looked at Papa. "And he asked you who was the best writer?"

"My husband," said Pauline. She stood in the doorway regarding Mariella with an icy stare.

"Back so soon?" he asked.

"My stomach's killing me." Pauline looked pale. "Mariella, come draw the curtains and see that the children are kept out of my room. I need to lie down."

"Yes, Mrs. Hemingway."

Mariella walked over to pick up the broom and followed Pauline. As she turned to pull the screen door to the cottage closed, she met Papa's gaze. The way he looked at her made her blush. She turned away so he wouldn't see her burning, and hurried to catch up with Pauline.

CHAPTER FOUR

Mariella's shoulders ached from hanging and folding laundry, and her hands were cracked, but she felt the satisfaction of a good day's work. She pulled the last of the towels off the line and folded it into the basket. It had been a week since she started and she already felt comfortable. Once Jinny left for home and Mariella no longer felt scrutinized, she actually experienced pleasure in keeping up the house. Except for the gruff, distracted governess, the staff was kind to her. The boys were already growing on her, with their vitality and their sweet faces. And as for the Hemingways, Pauline stayed out of her way, and Papa stayed in her way. As much as Mariella hated to admit it to herself, she liked it.

After her first day of work, Mariella had signed up for a library card and checked out *The Sun Also Rises*, figuring she'd see what Hemingway was all about. She was surprised how quickly the book grabbed her. She identified with Jake, the main character—a man who had no patience for phonies—and she wondered how much of himself Hemingway put into the book. It was hard to put down, but she forced herself each night so she wouldn't be too tired for work.

After she finished the novel, she found herself further intrigued by Hemingway, and quite sure that he'd put all of himself into it. Those people he wrote about were, no doubt, real people. His mixture of love and disdain for them fascinated her, as did the complexity of a volatile man like his character Jake. She thought he was like Hemingway in all ways except, of course, his impotence. Mariella contemplated this while she carried a tower of towels up the stairs and into the Hemingways' bedroom, where she ran into the very object of her thoughts. The towels dropped to the floor at their feet. She moved to pick them up, and he bent down to help.

"Don't worry," she said. "I'll get it."

"Let me help you," he said.

They made quick work of the cleanup, and both reached for the last towel at the same time. His hand closed over hers and their faces were inches away. She looked at him when he didn't remove his hand.

"Your hands are raw," he said.

"Laundry day," she said. She went to pull away, but he kept a firm hold on her hand and turned it over in his. He ran his thumb over the dry surface of her palm.

"Pauline's probably got some lotion you could try."

She pulled her hand away. "It's fine."

Mariella felt his eyes on her as she picked up the last towel and folded it. She heard him walk out the door and down the stairs and was surprised to find that she was holding her breath. She caught sight of herself in the mirror across the room and saw the flush on her skin and knew he'd seen it, too.

Mariella knew about the fight in Bahama Village later that night and wanted to see whether she could turn her wages into a small fortune. While she wondered whether Papa would be at the fight, she changed into her father's old shirt and pants, and hung her work dress in the servants' closet next to her apron.

On her way out Mariella called good-bye to Isabelle, walked

down the stone path, and stepped out onto the sidewalk, setting out for Sloppy Joe's for a bite to eat and a beer. She wondered whether she'd see Hemingway there, and whether he'd be as friendly to her in public as he was at home.

The previous evening, Mariella had gone to the market to make sure her mother and sisters had enough for dinner, and told her mother she'd be late on Friday night. Eva had looked as if she wanted to question Mariella, but must have thought she wouldn't like the answer and cut herself off. Eva didn't approve of gambling, and while Mariella felt guilty going against her mother's wishes, she thought it was their best chance to pay down their mounting bills without stealing.

The sky still held the red from the day at the top of Duval Street, but the rest of the street was shadowed. She found a newsstand and bought a pack of cigarettes that she intended to leave at Mark's boat stand, when she heard Hemingway's voice.

"Daughter."

Mariella turned and saw Hemingway in the midst of his mob, stumbling into the bar. He waved them on and joined her in the street. She tried to hide her pleasure at his recognition of her, but it was impossible not to smile at him. She turned away from him to hand her money to the vendor and shoved the pack in her pocket.

"You should quit," he said.

"Why don't you ask me to stop breathing while you're at it?"

"I used to smoke, but it's a dirty, expensive habit."

"It settles my nerves," she said.

He laughed.

"Where you headed tonight?" he asked.

She didn't want to say she'd planned on going to Sloppy's, because it was well-known to be his turf.

"Just looking for a bite to eat before the fight," she said.

"What fights d'you watch?" he asked.

"Yours."

"How'd you know about my Friday-night fights?"

"I live here, don't I?"

"I don't think you should be running around those places," he said. "Not safe for a young, pretty girl like you."

Mariella pulled a baseball cap out of her pocket, twisted up her long hair, and pulled the brim down over her face.

Papa laughed. Then he reached out and pulled off the hat.

"Leave it down for now," he said. "Don't hide that gorgeous head until you have to. Come on; I'll buy you dinner."

She shrugged and followed him into the bar, trying to act cool, though she didn't feel it. When they stepped into Sloppy Joe's, half the bar erupted in a greeting to him. The bartender, Skinner, slapped two scotch-and-sodas on the counter, while Joe kicked a tourist out of Papa's usual chair and slid it out for him. When he saw Mariella at Papa's side he pushed another guy out of the seat next to Papa's and winked at her.

Mariella sat next to Hemingway and felt his leg on hers at the crowded bar. She tried to ignore the heat it caused her and motioned at the drinks before him.

"You're one to talk about bad habits," she said.

He gave her a look out of the corner of his eye, threw back one of the glasses, and smiled at her.

"It settles my nerves," he said.

Chuck Thompson leaned on the bar next to Mariella.

"Is this pig hitting on you already?" said Chuck. "Jesus, Papa, one week and you've got her at the bar."

"Little young for ya," said a thin man with glasses. He held out his hand to Mariella. "They call me Dos, but you may call me John."

Mariella shook it. Hemingway shooed him away like a fly.

"Sorry about bringing you around all the riffraff tonight," said Papa, "though the crowd'll only get worse once we get to the fight."

"Gee, Sloppy's, then a boxing match," said Joe. "How romantic."

Skinner loafed back to the group at the bar. "Romance? Should I mix up some Papa Dobles?"

Papa rolled his eyes. Mariella looked at him with a question in hers.

"Some stupid drink he made up for me," said Hemingway. "I'm happy with my scotch-and-soda, thank you, but get the lady anything she wants."

"Beer's fine," she said.

"Good girl," said Papa. "You can always tell the tourists by the fancy, fruity drinks with umbrellas."

"And the way they come on to Papa," said Skinner. He nodded into the crowd, and a tall, leggy redhead walked over to Hemingway with an unlit cigarette hanging from her mouth. She had on a shade of red lipstick that clashed with her hair, and a black-and-white polka-dot dress that had to have been painted on. She carried a coconut filled with a hot-pink drink, stabbed with an umbrella. She leaned on the bar between Mariella and Papa, her cheap perfume worse than the smell of the booze and bodies around it.

"Got a light?" she asked.

Papa looked at her for a moment, then over at her friends, a trio of equally clownlike tourists smiling, smoking, and nudging one another. He looked back at her without a smile.

"Seems you could have asked one of your friends for a light rather than sticking your ass in my girl's face and bugging me."

She jumped back from the bar as though she'd been slapped, took the cigarette out of her mouth, and looked over at Mariella as if she'd just noticed her. Mariella felt the woman's eyes travel over her dark skin, old work clothes, and dirty fingernails, but she sat up straighter, because she knew Papa was by her side. Besides, she knew that even in her work clothes and with no makeup, she outshone the hussy.

"If I'd'a known that's your type, I wouldn'ta wasted my time," said the tourist. She turned and started back to her table.

As she pivoted, she slipped on the ice melting on the floor around the bar and landed on her rear end. The mob turned and stifled their laughs as the woman stood shakily and glared back at them. Mariella smiled at her and nodded at the floor.

"Mind the ice, there," she said. "They don't call it Sloppy's for nothin'."

It was nine o'clock by the time they finished dinner. Dos and Chuck headed home, and Joe had to stay at the bar, so that left Papa and Mariella on their own.

She'd enjoyed the company of Papa's friends. They were coarse but kind, and accepted her immediately. She understood why her father liked Hemingway, and it made her feel good that he'd stuck up for her in the face of that floozy.

On the way to the fight, they talked about previous champs and knockouts. He didn't know the lineup tonight, but they'd find out soon enough

The Blue Goose was a bordello upstairs, a gambling hall downstairs, and had a yard used for cockfights and boxing. It was populated by a sweaty, surly, poor crowd. Mariella adjusted her hat, rolled down her sleeves, and slouched a little.

"How do I look?" she asked.

"Like a gorgeous little mouse trying to hide in a lion's den. Stick to my side."

He pulled her into him and kept his arm around her waist.

"That's better," he said.

His hand was large and she could feel his strength. She felt her attraction to him slam against her feelings of guilt. All the tension made her dizzy, which forced her to lean into him. They walked up to the ring, where he engaged a large black man in a noisy, enthusiastic conversation.

"Why don't you call tonight?" asked the man.

"You take it, Randall. I'm just here to watch."

"It'll be a good night. Some soldier, Gavin something, is gonna fight Bear."

"How big's the soldier?" asked Papa.

"Not at all. Middleweight, but with a well of strength. He knocked out Shine two weeks ago."

"This I've gotta see."

Mariella forced herself away from Hemingway's side while he talked, and scanned the crowd. She found the soldier. He stood alone, lacing up his gloves with a stern look on his face—if that face could make a stern look. Its boyishness made that impossible, in spite of a deep scar like a line drawn down the right side of it. His dark hair was cut close to his head, and he was sweating. He had a large tattoo on his right forearm of the numbers *11-11-18*, and what looked like a tattoo of a grenade on his left arm—but it was hard to tell because it was also badly scarred. Mariella guessed that he was just under six feet tall and about one hundred eighty pounds. Lean but solid. He caught her looking at him, and she looked away, but he'd seen her. She looked back after a moment, but he was gone.

"Mr. Hemingway." Mariella and Papa turned and the soldier stood at her side. "Gavin Murray."

She crossed her arms over her chest and turned toward the shadows under the ring. "It's good to meet you," said Gavin.

"Pleasure's all mine. You know what you're up against tonight?"

"I've got an idea," said the soldier. "Odds are eight to one against me in there."

"I'll bet against you, too, but I'd love to see an upset," said Hemingway. "Bear took a knockout last week."

"What about your friend? Who's *he* betting on?"

Mariella felt herself sweating. She wanted to keep a low profile so she could come back safely as a boy. She met the boxer's eyes, though, and knew he knew her secret. She felt herself bristle and stood to her full height. What could the boxer do to her, anyway? Women were allowed to be there. They just typically weren't, unless they were working.

"You," said Mariella. They both looked at her, surprised that she made no attempt to disguise her voice. "So you'd better win, 'cause I need the money."

Immediately, she felt upset with herself for being so impulsive. Bear wouldn't lose to this soldier. When would she learn to hold her tongue? She felt the anxiety in flutters in her stomach, but feigned confidence.

The way the boxer looked at her made her think he knew her thoughts. He smiled at her with one corner of his mouth and crinkles around his eyes. She saw that his eyes were blue and looked lit from inside. His eyebrows arched and he didn't show his teeth. She couldn't help but smile back.

"I'll win," he said. "You'll see."

The official called for the boxers to enter the ring, and Gavin disappeared with a nod. Mariella and Hemingway made their way to the bleachers, which looked as if they wouldn't hold the weight of the crowd. They found a seat in the front.

Mariella gasped when she saw Bear step up in the ring. He seemed to have grown since the last fight, but she knew it was because he was standing side by side with Gavin instead of Tiny Tim. His shoulders were massive, and had to be to hold up his neck. His eyes were small slits, and his dark brown skin shone with sweat. Gavin's face was blank. She hated to think of what would happen to his face once Bear finished with him.

"Cocky little son of a bitch," said Hemingway under his breath. Mariella looked at him with surprise and then back at the ring. He sounded jealous, but that couldn't be. She looked at Papa again and he met her eyes. They stared at each other until the official's voice rose. He pointed to Bear and said over the crowd, "This here's four-time champ Big Bear from Bahama Village." The crowd roared. "Six feet, one inch. Two hundred ten pounds." There was more cheering and hooting. Bear rolled his arms and tap-danced his feet. Some of the men in the bleachers started stomping, and Mariella felt the risers sway under her.

"And here we have Gavin Murray. Six feet even, one hundred ninety pounds, Argonne vet, and brigade champ." Booing could be heard over the cheers. Gavin knocked his gloves together. Mariella was relieved that Bear wasn't much bigger than Gavin, but also knew that twenty pounds could make a big difference in force and strength. She wondered why Bear had seemed so much bigger than Gavin, but thought it must have been due to the massive spread of his neck and shoulders.

A bell sounded, and Mariella felt sick. *Why, damn it, why do this again? Why risk the loss?* She wiped the sweat off her forehead and forced all of her concentration behind Gavin, hoping it could somehow seep into him and give him power.

The boxers began a slow, circular dance around the ring, facing each other. Bear moved in and punched, but Gavin slipped his head to the left. Then Bear jabbed with his right hand three times, making contact on the third jab with Gavin's left shoulder.

The crowd cheered.

Gavin continued to circle, and Bear tried an uppercut that made contact with Gavin's chin.

"He's not doing anything," said Mariella.

"He's sizing him up, tiring him out," said Papa. "He's got Bear punching him and moving all around the ring. When Bear's tired, Murray'll destroy him."

He said the last words under his breath and curled his fingers into fists.

One minute passed.

Two minutes.

Bear made contact on a jab, another uppercut, and a straight-handed punch.

"What's he doing?" said Mariella, frantic at the thought of losing a whole week's pay.

The crowd was cheering Bear and booing Gavin, complaining that Gavin wasn't up to the fight. Mariella thought she was going to get sick, but she couldn't tear her eyes off the ring. She stood, and soon the crowd around her was standing.

Then Gavin exploded.

One-two-three-four, jab. Uppercut. One-two-three, straight. One-two-three, jab.

In one final move, Gavin pulled back his arm and brought it forward with the force of a freight train. There was a sickening crunch. Bear's arms went slack at his sides and he dropped to the ring floor.

It was a knockout.

The crowd was silent for a while; then the din began. Everyone got to their feet and began yelling and cheering. Mariella looked at Hemingway with wide eyes. He raised his eyebrows at her. She felt a sudden elation and turned back to the ring to see Gavin looking at her. He nodded. She returned the gesture.

When they got to the ring, Bear was sitting in a chair with his head in his hands. Gavin walked over to him and patted him on the back.

"Good fight, man."

Bear grunted.

Gavin climbed through the ropes and jumped off the ring. Hemingway intercepted him.

"Nice knockout," said Papa, without much enthusiasm.

"Thanks."

"I'd like to fight you sometime," said Papa. "I never lose."

Mariella thought it an odd thing to say to a stranger who had just knocked out a four-time champion, but she didn't dwell on it. She was distracted by the feeling of having won all that money. Rent problems would be solved. At least for this month.

"Sure," said Gavin.

They stared at each other for a moment, sizing each other up. Mariella half expected them to start circling each other. Gavin broke the tension by extending his hand. Papa shook it, hard, then placed his hand on Mariella's back and guided her away.

Gavin counted his money quickly and shoved it in his bag under the hungry eyes of the men collecting.

"Night," he said. None of the men said a thing to him as he walked away, but he could feel their stares hard on his back. His stomach was tight and he was alert in case any crooks wanted to follow, though he doubted they would. They were a tough group, but fair.

He wasn't a fool, though, so he turned and walked down Duval Street, which was heavily populated, even at this hour. Most people just sat and smoked and watched the night pass, but some called out greetings to him. When he turned onto Olivia Street, he passed Beverly's house and saw her sitting alone on the front porch, stroking a cat.

"You win, handsome?"

She sat in the shadows with her legs up on the railing. Her dress slid too far up her thighs, and her feet were bare. He knew he shouldn't stop, but he couldn't help it.

"I won."

"No one's home," she said. "Why don't you come inside?"

He had been inside before and knew Beverly was trouble.

"I'm done with that," he said, and smiled.

She didn't return the smile. "You break my heart."

"You don't have one," he said, not unkindly.

She sighed and waved her hand, as if in dismissal.

"Good night," he said.

She turned her head and looked away.

Gavin smiled and continued down the street. He felt liberated. He had proven to her and to himself that she had no hold over him, and it felt good.

As he continued on, a boy with a baseball cap walked by on the other side of the road. Gavin thought of the beautiful girl at the fight who had pretended to be a boy. He wondered who she was and how she knew Hemingway, and then thought of his exchange with the writer after the fight and found it unsettling. Gavin figured Hemingway was showing off for the girl. He had guided her around with a protective air all night, but Hemingway was married, and this girl looked at least ten years his junior.

It was no matter, he thought. He probably wouldn't see either of them again.

When he arrived at the house, the lights were all out. He pulled the key out of the knot in the wood under the porch and let himself in. Mutt came up to greet him, and Gavin shushed him and scratched him between the ears. He heard deep, regular breathing through the first door and proceeded to the guest room, where he quietly placed his bag on the floor. He went into the bathroom to wash up before bed, and returned to his room to put the money in his lockbox. He took quick inventory of it, pleased to see he nearly had enough to buy into his uncle's business so he could stop risking his neck in the boxing rings and bridges of the Keys.

Bruises and injuries announced themselves in spots of heat on his torso and chin, and Gavin knew sleep would help. He stripped down to nothing, and fell asleep with the girl's face on his mind.

Before Hemingway had placed his hand on her back, Mariella had felt compelled to stay with Gavin. She felt inexplicably drawn to him and wanted to talk about the fight. It was clear, though, that Papa wanted to leave, and she couldn't resist him as he guided her away.

As the noise from the boxing yard faded, Mariella could barely concentrate on walking. The pressure of Papa's hand on her lower back tingled on her skin and sent waves of warmth out over her body. They didn't speak on the walk to her house until they were close to it.

"You're entering the Cuban section," said Mariella.

"I'd better hold on to my wallet," he said, laughing at his own joke.

She gave him a chastising look and ignored the remark.

"My house is actually the dividing line between the white end of the street and the Cuban end of the street," she said.

"Your house is a mix."

"Too bad, huh," she said.

"What happened to your Cuban pride? Cubans are some of the proudest people I know."

"Times have changed," she said. "At least what's left of my family makes people more comfortable now."

"How so?" he asked.

"With my dad gone, we're just Cuban. That makes people feel better. They didn't know how to treat us when they thought of us as mixed."

He was quiet for a moment.

"So now the whites can forget you've got their blood and just demote you to Cuban," said Papa, "and the Cubans can do the same and welcome you."

Mariella nodded. She appreciated his frank talk.

"And you couldn't give a damn either way," he said.

She smiled. "Yup."

They continued on in silence for a few moments; then he said, "You liked that vet."

"I liked how he fought. I'm not ready to marry him."

"Don't get married for a long time. And don't have kids, if you can help it."

"Don't plan on it," she said.

"I will say I've always wanted a daughter. We were so disappointed when Greg came out with a set."

"Is that why you call all the ladies *daughter*?"

"Yes. But you're my favorite."

When they got to her house, he kissed her on the forehead.

"I had fun on our first date," he said.

"Me, too."

He turned to go. "I'm walking away so I'm not tempted to kiss you on the mouth," he called.

"Good thing, or you'd have a black eye," she said.

He laughed and continued walking away, disappearing in the shadows.

Mariella stepped up to the door of her house with a smile on her face, thrilled to have cash for the family and for her secret stash, and warm from something else: the warmth of belonging. Aside from the fishermen at the dock, she hadn't felt the goodness of being part of a group in a long time. She'd watched Papa, his friends, and herself reflected in the mirror behind the bar and thought that to any outsider, she looked like she belonged with them. Hell, she felt like she belonged with them.

But something nagged at her beneath the warmth of new friendships.

The heat of Papa's leg against hers.

The way he'd called her his girl.

The way he'd gotten jealous when she talked to the boxer.

And the shame she felt for wishing he'd given in to the temptation of kissing her on the mouth before he left.

She pushed open the door, stepped into the darkness of the house, and slipped on a shoe lying on the floor. She was annoyed that her mother hadn't tidied the house and hadn't thought to leave on a light. Mariella cursed and caught herself on the wall, and suddenly saw Eva sitting in her chair with only the light from the moon on her face. The shadows on her cheekbones and in her deep-set eyes made her look skeletal.

"What do you have to say for yourself?" said Eva in slow, deliberate English.

Mariella knew that Eva must have seen her and Hemingway through the window, and thought Mariella was drunk because she stumbled into the house. She knew her mother was imagining all sorts of horrible things. She also knew, however, that the smell of alcohol on her breath, the odor of stale cigarettes on her shirt, the wad of cash in her pocket, and the scent of the hussy's perfume, which clung stubbornly to her pants where the dress had touched her, wouldn't help her case.

She tried to keep her temper.

"Kinda hard to walk with stuff all over the floor," said Mariella.

She began to walk down the hallway to her room when she heard her mother mutter, "Your *papa* would be so disappointed."

Mariella felt an urge swell in her to strike Eva. She had never wanted to hurt anyone as badly as she did her mother at that moment. She clenched her fists and strode across the room, kicking toys and junk out of her path, forgetting the way she smelled, wanting only to hurt Eva.

She grabbed the money from her pocket and threw it at her mother.

"Take it," spat Mariella. She surprised even herself with her anger, but she couldn't stop. "Do you not want a roof over your head? Shall we stop calling the doctor? Stop eating? Stop smoking?"

Eva stood and pushed her face into Mariella's.

"*¿Cómo pudiste?*"

"How could I *what?*"

"*¡Se trata de dinero sucio!*" Eva began to sob.

"Dirty money?" She grabbed her mother by the shoulders. "What do you think? Do you think I sold myself to him? Do you think I'm a prostitute?"

Eva shook her head and put her hands over her ears.

"Well, guess what?" shouted Mariella.

Eva backed away and fell into her money-littered chair, still covering her ears. Mariella pulled Eva's hands away so she could hear.

Lulu's sudden cry from the back room caused them both to turn their heads. The child cried for a moment, breaking the spell of their anger, then stopped. Mariella let go of her mother's hands and backed away.

"Do you really think I'd sell my body?"

Eva sniffled but wouldn't look at Mariella.

"Really?" said Mariella.

Eva curled her legs up under her and covered her face with her hands.

Mariella felt her rage boil, leaving a sharp, metallic taste like blood in the back of her throat.

"If you believe that about me, it serves you right to suffer for it."

CHAPTER FIVE

Lower Matecumbe Key
Veterans' work camps, Overseas Highway project

The mosquito beater wasn't fanning hard enough. Gavin slapped the bugs that had found an open area at his neck and turned to the man behind him.

"What the hell are you doing?" he said.

The skinny, pockmarked vet shrugged. "Sorry, Captain. I'm daydreaming about my wife up north."

"Save your daydreaming for night, Bonefish," said Gavin, "or I'll make sure you see her sooner than you'd planned."

"Yes, sir."

Bonefish fanned away the mosquitoes with a cabbage tree branch, and Gavin couldn't decide what was more annoying: the bugs or the slap of the leaves on his back. He decided that he'd rather the temporary annoyance of the branch than a sleepless night of scratching bug bites. He picked up his pace, hacking at the mangroves on the edge of Matecumbe Key to clear the way for the new dock and bridge ramps.

Gavin hated the relentless, coiling branches of the mangroves more than just about anything, but he had assumed the duty of chopping them down when one of the men in his unit had started vomiting and couldn't stop. Gavin had him taken to the doctor immediately in case of contagion. Outbreaks of meningitis and parasitic infections weren't uncommon in the filthy camps. He knew, however, that the vet was probably dehydrated from drinking too much beer and working too long in the hot sun. The men here lived hard and had long suffered from postwar depression and unemployment. He wouldn't begrudge them a drink or two to make the pain go away, but he didn't appreciate when it interfered with their productivity.

A sudden shaking sound made him freeze with his machete aloft. He looked down around his feet and didn't see the dreaded source of the noise, but knew the rattlesnake was nearby.

Bonefish was, of course, relentless in his beating now that Gavin needed stillness, so he reached around and grabbed the branch with his free hand.

"Stop," he hissed. "Rattler!"

Bonefish sucked in his breath and stopped beating.

Gavin slid his eyes over the ground beneath the mangrove and saw the snake, not three feet away, coiled and shaking its tail. He felt a new layer of sweat edge out what had already been there, and his shirt was now drenched. He didn't want to make any sudden movements and have the snake lunge at him, but he didn't think he could get a clean shot through the mangroves with the machete.

Gavin slowly lowered the machete to a better position to strike and took a step back. The snake flinched, Bonefish yelped and ran, and the creature struck. Gavin jumped back, narrowly missing the bite, and brought the machete down hard. In one clean stroke, he severed the rattler's head. Some of the men nearby clapped and whistled, and Gavin felt a surge of pride until their commander, Colonel Ed Sheeran, walked over.

"Get your asses back to work and stop playing with animals," said Sheeran.

Gavin wasn't pleased to be reprimanded like a common vet, but had no energy for confrontation and didn't want to set a bad example for those under him. He nodded, kicked the dead snake out of the way, and continued cutting the mangroves.

The great crane groaned as it lowered the keystone from the quarry at nearby Plantation Key into the bridge piers.

Gavin was relieved to be on crane duty. He preferred operating the heavy machinery to the manual labor involved in bridge building, but he also knew that doing the hard labor made his men respect him. After the rattlesnake encounter, however, he felt he'd earned the high seat for the day.

He kept an eye on Fred, a fellow World War I vet, until he signaled with his shaking hands. Fred's tremors had started sometime during the war and continued to plague him almost two decades later. As the tremors worsened it was getting harder to find work suitable for Fred, but Gavin was determined to keep him busy and on the job.

While he waited for Fred and the men below to help position the stone, he stared out at the great blue-green expanse around him. A welcome breeze slipped through the crane's cabin, and Gavin reveled in a break from the mosquitoes. He imagined steering a boat through the waves, anchoring in the dark blue, and fishing away a lazy afternoon with a beautiful girl at his side.

He thought of the girl from the boxing match. Her deep, dark eyes. Her confidence. The way she'd smiled at him after the fight.

"Murray!" yelled one of the guys below. "Stop dreaming and finish dropping this rock so we can get some grub."

"Sorry, Al. I was just thinking of your sister out with me on a fishing boat."

"Yeah, well, I was just thinking about your mother."

Gavin made a rude hand gesture at Al and resumed his task until the stone was firmly in place.

He climbed down from the crane, ready to smack Al on the back of the head, when he noticed Fred and Al arguing.

"Back off," said Fred.

"Settle down, Shaky; I was just joking with you," said Al.

"I'm not in the mood for jokes."

"You never are, Shakes."

"If you don't stop calling me that, I'll give you a shaking you won't forget."

"Oh, is that so?" said Al. Al looked at the men who'd gathered around and then back at Fred. Then Al wiggled his hands at Fred.

Gavin grabbed Fred's arm just as he was about to punch Al.

Al continued to laugh and shake his hands at Fred.

Fred yanked himself out of Gavin's grip and stormed back to camp.

"Why do you have to be such an asshole?" said Gavin.

"I was just messing with him," said Al. "Come on. I just told him I'd handle the stone positioning, since we didn't want a rumbling bridge."

"This isn't a schoolyard, and I don't want to have to discipline you all like a bunch of kids, so leave him alone unless you want me to get Sheeran involved."

Al waved off Gavin and walked away. Gavin had an urge to follow him and punch Al himself. He was always causing trouble, and Fred was an easy target. Instead he flexed his fingers and thought he'd picture Al's face in the boxing ring at his next fight.

Stock Island, north of Key West

All the abandoned, broken, battered boats left to rot in the sun depressed Gavin.

He ran his hand along the side of an ancient fishing boat and imagined the water lapping against its side during happier days. He thought he felt the sadness in the wood, and then laughed at himself for thinking like a damned fool.

He readjusted the bag of parts on his arm and nodded at the yardmaster—a hefty, toothless man with tobacco running down his chin, which had left a sloppy line down the front of his yellowed sleeveless shirt. The man grunted and went back to the girlie magazine he took no trouble to conceal. Gavin looked forward to the day he wouldn't have to collect spare parts from that disgusting slob for his boss. He envied the fishermen he knew. He wished he could make his living from a boat on the water, instead of dangling over it from one hundred feet up.

Of course, they were all struggling. Plenty of fish, not enough people to buy them. Most of the fishermen he knew had traded their fishing rods for hammers, wrenches, or flasks. It was hard times for everyone.

He pushed all of that out of his head, though. He was just happy to be heading into Key West for the weekend instead of staying up at camp. His buddy in town was glad to have him down, and Gavin was happy he could help him out around the house.

A movement beside the skeleton of a brown fishing boat caught his attention. A girl in rolled-up men's slacks and an old shirt walked around the boat, looked it up and down, and ran her fingers along the bow. As she turned away from the boat she met his eyes and his heart lifted. It was the girl from the boxing match. He couldn't believe it.

She smiled and walked toward him. "Gavin Murray, a boxer and a fisherman," she said.

"Not much of either," he said.

She laughed. "I don't know. You sure filled my pocket last Friday."

"Glad I could help," he said. "Are you a fisherwoman?"

"Yes, though in temporary retirement, unfortunately," she said.

"You got a name, fisherwoman?"

"Mariella Bennet."

"And how do you know Hemingway?"

"I'm his maid."

Gavin was intrigued. Why would Hemingway go to a boxing match with his maid? Judging by her long, dark lashes, full lips, and silky hair, he thought he knew why. An unpleasant and surprising jealousy stirred in his belly. He judged her badly for the relationship he assumed she had with the writer, and didn't know why.

"Well, I guess I'll be on my way," he said.

"I'll walk out with you," she said. "I'm done here, anyway."

His curiosity overcame his negative feelings for a moment.

"What are you doing at the boat graveyard?" he asked.

"Looking for an old boat I knew. Looking for a boat I could fix."

"*You* know how to fix boats?"

"Yes—is that so surprising?"

"Kind of."

"Typical."

Her familiarity relaxed him, and he smiled.

When she reached the old blue bicycle leaning against the chain-link fence, she stopped and pulled it toward her.

"Nice seeing you again," she said. "You fighting anytime soon?"

"Not for a couple of weeks."

"Well, maybe next time."

She swung her leg over and pedaled away. He adjusted the heavy bag to his other shoulder while he watched her ride down the road, hoping he'd see her again in spite of whatever she had with the writer.

Once she'd covered about a hundred yards, Mariella looked over her shoulder. The boxer still stood there, watching her. She turned back toward Key West and felt the pressure of his eyes on her. She felt vaguely annoyed that he didn't think she could fix a boat, and downright aggravated that he assumed she was Hemingway's lover. She'd seen it all over his face.

Why did everyone judge her for spending time with Hemingway? Was it so unusual for a thirty-five-year-old man and an almost twenty-year-old woman to be friends?

Yes.

She knew it was strange, especially because she was his maid. Especially because he was married. And especially because she could feel the electricity between them whenever he was around. She wondered whether others felt it, too.

Part of her wanted to pull away from Papa and not incite gossip. She didn't want to interfere with another woman's husband. She knew he was too old for her, and she certainly meant nothing to him beyond amusement. But another part of her, the part she didn't want to acknowledge, continued to assert itself and didn't care what others thought.

In the meantime, Mariella was thrilled with the bike. She'd seen it collecting rust in the Hemingways' cellar when she was fetching wine for Pauline, and asked whether she could borrow it. Pauline told her it wasn't in good working order because the chain kept coming off, but with a little help from Toby, the Hemingways' handyman, it was up and running in no time.

It took Mariella an afternoon of falling and cursing to teach herself to ride it, but she learned quickly, knowing that the sooner she could ride, the sooner she could get over to Stock Island to see whether her father's boat was salvageable.

As it turned out, it wasn't in the first boat graveyard she found, or the second. The third was clear up on No Name Key, and Mariella couldn't go all that way and get back to town before dark. She was disappointed, but she'd just have to go some other time.

———≈◠———

Mariella felt a tug in her heart when she saw her little sisters on the porch. Lulu sat on the step below Estelle, while Estelle brushed out her knotty hair. Lulu jumped up when Mariella returned, and ran to greet her.

Mariella leaned the bicycle against a tree and hugged her youngest sister, alarmed by her warmth. Mariella put her hands on her little sister's face and saw the flush in her cheeks.

"How do you feel?" asked Mariella, uncertain whether Lulu was warm from the sun or the beginnings of a fever. Lulu's bouts of fever and stomach pain had plagued her most of her young life, but had seemed to get worse within the last few months. The doctor had always treated the symptoms, but he had never been able to come up with a diagnosis.

Lulu pulled away and rolled her eyes with a smile.

"I'm fine," she said.

Mariella checked Lulu's eyes to see whether they looked glassy.

"Are you sure? Let's get you inside in the shade."

That evening, Mariella watched the child's every move, and felt relieved when it was time for bed and Lulu seemed well, though especially tired. Eva went to bed early, leaving Mariella to help the girls wash up. She'd tucked them into the bed they shared in the tiny room and started out the door, when Lulu called her back in.

"Lie with us," she said.

Mariella didn't want to, because she'd had it in the back of her mind that she'd go to Sloppy Joe's once they fell asleep. She'd already chosen a dress from her closet that she rarely wore, and hung it in the bathroom, just in case. She knew that if she lay down with the girls, she might fall asleep.

"It's late," said Mariella.

"Please," said Lulu. "Tell us about the rich house where you work."

Mariella sighed and climbed into the bed. Lulu had asked to hear about the rich house every night since she started work at the Hemingways'. She was pretty sure her younger sisters could tell about it themselves. But she indulged them, taking them into the house in their minds, past the peacocks and huge tropical flowers, past the wrought-iron railings, through the rooms with their fancy chandeliers reflecting off rounded windows and wall mirrors, across the walkway to the writing cottage, where dead animals guarded the words of the famous writer.

"It's the lion that guards the cottage," said Mariella. "Anyone who enters first sees its jaws wide-open on the floor, and dares not disturb it."

"What is a lion?" asked Lulu slowly, drowsily.

"It's a big huge cat, with big huge teeth, and a woolly mane of hair like sun rays around its head."

"Are you scared it will bite you?"

Mariella thought of how the lion reminded her of Hemingway. She felt warm all over and thought of his gaze in the cottage, and his touch on her hand when she'd dropped the towels, and his leg against hers at the bar.

"No."

Soon the sound of the girls' rhythmic breathing filled the room. For a moment, Mariella wanted to melt into the bed with them, but the thought of him pulled her away and into the bathroom, where she put on the dress she was outgrowing, brushed back her hair in barrettes, and ran a tube of her mother's lipstick over her lips. She wouldn't allow herself to think it was the hope of running into Hemingway again that drew her back to the bar.

She told herself it was the camaraderie, the freedom, the friend-ship.

Mariella stepped into Sloppy Joe's and was suddenly filled with dread at the thought of seeing Hemingway. Would he think she'd dressed up for him? Had she dressed up for him? Would he think her too forward? Would he be annoyed? Or would he greet her the same way he did last weekend? Mariella didn't even know whether she'd act like she was looking for him. She didn't know what she wanted from him even if they met.

A buxom, bleached-blond woman with red lips laughed in the midst of a group of soldiers. A bottle shattered on the floor near Mariella, and a drunk knocked her into the wall as he pushed past her to vomit in the street.

Mariella ran her ring finger along her lower lip to smooth the edge of the lipstick and ran her hands down the front of her dress. She looked at his place at the bar and, mercifully, Papa wasn't in his usual seat. Mariella stood on her toes and scanned the crowd, but her limited height gave her a view only of the faces closest to her. The crowd opened and she saw a man who looked familiar, buried in the shadows at the end of the bar. He wore a white shirt tucked into blue dungarees. His dark hair was clipped close to his head. He had a young face, almost feminine. But his eyes were old and blue, and one had a yellowed, fading bruise around it, and a scar like a line. He was smoking, and the tip of the cigarette glowed bright orange when he inhaled.

Gavin.

His gaze met hers, and he stared. She felt self-conscious with-out her baseball cap and work clothes and looked for an exit. Drunken soldiers surrounded her, filling the space leading out of the bar. The only pathway open was the one leading to him. She took a deep breath and started forward. He never took his eyes off her and, as she neared him, broke into a grin.

"We keep running into each other," he said.

"I know. I've never seen you in my life, and now I've seen you three times."

"This look suits you more," he said.

"What—female?"

He laughed, and pulled a pack of cigarettes out of his pocket.

"Smoke?" he said. She took the cigarette he offered and lit it off his. When she leaned into him she could smell the warm, pleasant spice of his aftershave.

"You looking for him?" He nodded down the bar. She turned to see Hemingway slip into his chair. He laughed loudly at something Skinner said. Mariella flushed and was glad for the shadows, hoping Gavin didn't notice her reaction.

Suddenly, a man fell off the chair next to Mariella and into a drunken vet. The vet punched the man in the side of the face and they began to fight, until Skinner came out from behind the bar and dragged them out the door by their necks.

"Kinda rough in here for a lady," said Gavin.

"There are plenty of women in here."

"Not like you."

Mariella looked at the crowd and saw that most of the women there were clearly trying to earn a living. She felt more pity for them than disgust. She knew she was lucky to have found steady, honest employment.

"So what's it like working for him?" asked Gavin.

"It's . . . interesting. They have a lot of visitors. I'm very busy."

"What about him?"

"I don't see him much. He writes early, goes fishing when it gets hot, and goes to the bar in the evening. How about you? Are you working on the Overseas Highway?"

"Yeah. I live on Matecumbe Key."

"You vets have a bad reputation around here."

"Hemingway has a bad reputation around here."

"I'm surrounded by thugs."

Gavin laughed.

Mariella looked back in Papa's direction, and he raised his glass to her and pointed at her dress. Then he raised his eyebrows and nodded at Gavin. Papa probably thought she was on a date with the boxer. At first she hoped he didn't think that, but then stopped herself. Hemingway was married. She didn't want another woman's husband. She didn't know whether she wanted any kind of man right now. Relationships led to trouble. She knew that from her parents.

Gavin's voice in her ear drew her attention back to him.

"Wanna dance?"

Mariella looked at the sign over the door: no vulgar dancing. She looked at the dance floor and saw sailors gyrating all over drunken women in low-cut shirts and tight dresses. She raised her eyebrow and pointed to the sign. He laughed and grabbed her hand. She pulled away.

"No, really," she said. "I'm terrible."

"Who cares," he said. "I am, too."

Her eyes flicked over to Hemingway, and she saw that he was watching them with interest, maybe even jealousy. She turned back to Gavin and took his hand.

He pulled her close to the band, and they started a messy Lindy to the music pounding through the bar. The next time she tried to get a glimpse of Hemingway, he was gone. Her heart sank. She wondered whether she'd made him jealous, but then realized the madness of the whole thing, from her dressing up, to coming out, to trying to anger him. This behavior scared her, because it was purposeful and had a note of desperation. She didn't know who she was.

A couple ran into Mariella's back and pushed her into Gavin. They bumped heads, and laughed at each other's absurdity. The drummer began banging out a solo that had soldiers throwing their girls all over the dance floor. Gavin grabbed Mariella and flipped her over his arm, and when she landed, she fell on her backside. He picked her up and apologized, but then they laughed until they couldn't catch their breath.

He pulled her over to a corner and touched her forehead.

"You really are a terrible dancer," he said.

"I don't know why you didn't believe me," she said.

"I thought you were just trying to put me off."

She looked him in the eye squarely for the first time that night and saw all the intensity she'd seen the first night they'd met. She grew warm and hoped he hadn't noticed her divided attention. The strains of the slow and sultry "All Through the Night" began. Gavin reached for her hand.

"Let's try this one," he said. "If we knock heads now, we can cross dancing off the list forever."

She smiled and allowed him to lead her back to the dance floor, enjoying the way she fit into his arms and the weight of his hands on her back. She looked up at his face and stared at his scar and the shadows under his eyes. It didn't seem as if he could look her in the eye from this close, and she wondered why he was suddenly so shy. She thought he tried to turn his face so his scar was away from her, and she wished she could tell him that it didn't bother her, but she didn't want to make him uncomfortable. When the song ended they walked back to the bar. Hemingway wasn't there. She was satisfied with herself that she'd gone a whole five minutes without thinking of him.

"Where do you live?" Gavin asked.

"Whitehead and Louisa. Where are you staying?"

"At a friend's house on Olivia Street. How about I walk you home? It's getting ugly in here."

Mariella hesitated. What if he was just trying to get her alone? She looked at his face and decided that she trusted him.

Besides, if he tried anything, she knew all the hidden alleys and escapes and had friends on every corner. He wouldn't get away with anything.

"Okay. Let's go," she said.

They stepped out onto Greene Street and enjoyed the change from the stuffy, noisy bar to the fresh air and the night. He led her to Duval to look into the bars and listen to music. The people were getting sloppy, and Gavin put his hand on Mariella's back in a protective gesture. She looked at him with her eyebrows raised.

"Sorry," he said. "Can't help it. I know how these vets get."

"Last week one of them took off his clothes in my neighbors' yard and had to be taken to jail."

"That was me."

Mariella punched him in the arm, and he laughed.

Before long, they'd ended up on her street. She could see her house and saw Lulu's doctor pulling open the screen door.

"Oh, no!"

Mariella took off running, a thousand guilty thoughts going through her head, followed by prayers to the Blessed Virgin, to her father, to Saint Theresa—everyone but God himself, since she was too ashamed for running around to apply to him directly. She was home in minutes, with Gavin at her heels. When she got to the house, she pressed him to go.

"I don't know how my mother will take you," she said. "Go, please." She ran through the door without waiting for a response.

Estelle wrung her hands in the corner. Mariella heard water filling the tub in the bathroom where Eva stood at the open door— her hair and eyes wild, and her hands fumbling over the beads of her rosary. She looked Mariella up and down, and then looked over Mariella's shoulder as if she expected to see Hemingway.

The doctor came out of Lulu's room.

"What's her temperature?" asked Mariella.

"One-oh-three," said the doctor. "I just gave her aspirin."

"And her stomach?"

"Horrible," said Eva.

Dr. Wilson smelled like booze, wore a wrinkled shirt, and looked as if he'd just been woken up. Mariella thought he must hate living around the corner from them. She ran to her room, pulled three dollars out of the can, and hurried back out to the doctor, thrusting the money into his hands. He took it, but he looked ashamed. He started to pass it back to Mariella, but she stopped him.

"No, you do so much for us," she said.

He mumbled a thank-you, stuffed the bills in his pocket, and stepped around Mariella to carry Lulu to the bathroom. The child thrashed her body and wailed in shock as he lowered her into the ice-cold water.

"Shh, shh. I know," said Dr. Wilson.

After a moment, she seemed stunned by the cold and stopped moving. He lifted Lulu, wrapped her in a towel, and walked her to the bed. While Eva came in to dress the child, Mariella slipped over to hug Estelle, who was growing increasingly frantic. She led her into her mother's room, where she sat Estelle on the bed and wiped her tears.

"She's going to be okay."

Estelle looked down at her hands, which continued to crawl over each other. Mariella placed her hands over the girl's and touched her forehead to her sister's.

"I know," said Mariella. But she didn't know. She didn't know whether Lulu would be all right. She didn't know whether her mother could take much more strain. She didn't know whether Estelle was going to come through this time without lasting scars. Her middle sister had grown so withdrawn. The week before,

Mariella had seen Estelle playing with dolls that she hadn't touched for years.

After Estelle calmed, Mariella led her back to the room where Lulu slept. Dr. Wilson talked softly to her mother in the kitchen, while she helped Estelle back to bed and crawled in next to her.

Mariella's guilt returned. If she hadn't gone out, she could have helped earlier. Maybe Lulu's fever wouldn't have gotten so high. Maybe she could have summoned the doctor sooner, or could have talked Estelle through her attack of anxiety. It was another case of her not being there to help her family.

Gavin circled the block and came back to stand in front of Mariella's house. A doctor stepped off the porch and brushed by him.

"Keep moving, soldier," he said. Gavin ignored him and looked in the window. No one was in the front of the house, but he didn't want them to find him and think he was a peeping Tom, so he lit a cigarette and continued on his way.

He wondered how old Mariella was. She couldn't be older than twenty, but then again, he looked young for thirty three. He thought she was beautiful and spirited. He also had to admit to himself that he was intrigued that she might be Hemingway's girl.

Suddenly he tripped on a hole in the sidewalk and ran into someone.

"Sorry," said Gavin.

"Been drinking, sailor?" A thin old man with small glasses and a heavy German accent stood before him. He carried a bouquet of flowers in one hand and a paper bag in the other. He smelled of formaldehyde, and something else that Gavin couldn't identify, but which caused him to recoil.

"No, sir, just clumsy."

"Your mind on a girl, no doubt."

Gavin smiled and rubbed the back of his neck. The man extended his hand.

"Count Von Cosel."

The name rang a bell, but Gavin wasn't sure why. Gavin shook his hand. He looked at the flowers and the bag. "For your lady?"

Cosel grew dead serious. "Yes. Everything for my love." He stared at Gavin until Gavin felt uncomfortable and excused himself. He walked down the street for a bit and then turned back to watch the count move away into the shadows.

CHAPTER SIX

Mariella stood on a stepladder in the front parlor, polishing Pauline's chandelier. She rubbed the soft cloth over each crystal until it sparkled. It hung over the room like a fat, useless diamond.

Pauline had gone out for some lunch and shopping with Chuck Thompson's wife, Lorine, and Ada had taken the boys somewhere. Mariella enjoyed the stillness, but it didn't last. She soon heard Papa's footsteps on the stairs and on the floor behind her.

"What time do you get off?" he asked.

"Five." She feigned disinterest, but she had to use her will to keep her body from turning toward him. She knew these feelings for him were wrong and wanted to do everything she could to suppress them.

"It's only three o'clock! What am I supposed to do until then?"

"Don't you have some fish to catch, or a book to write or something?"

"I wrote for four hours this morning and I had to stop. It was getting really good."

"You stopped when it was getting really good?" she asked.

"I always stop when it gets good. Then I can pick right up the next day. If I stop during a lull, there are no guarantees."

Mariella raised her eyebrows.

"Wouldn't that be like leaving a fish on the line before you pulled it all the way in?" she asked.

"No, it's like leaving a woman in bed before she's—"

A dish slammed the sink in the kitchen. Isabelle must have heard him. Mariella turned red.

"She'll want more, right?" he said.

Mariella couldn't look at him. She kept polishing the chandelier.

"Sorry—that was out of line," he said.

Isabelle snorted from the other room.

"Come on, daughter. Get down off that ladder. Let's go get some lemonade and watch people. I'm the boss. You're done for today."

Mariella looked at him. He leaned his arm on the ladder and looked up at her pleadingly. She badly wanted to join him, but she knew Isabelle was listening and didn't want to sound too eager.

"I need to get this done today, because I have to do the rug tomorrow, and I like to work from the top down. You go on. I'll catch up later."

"No. I'll wait here until you're done. You only have a bit more to do anyway."

He smiled at her and walked over to the couch, where the paper that he'd been reading earlier lay folded over the arm. He picked it up, shook it out, and watched her over the top of it.

Mariella concentrated on the chandelier so she wouldn't be tempted to look at him. She knew she'd blush from head to toe if she met his gaze. She was almost finished and she'd already done so much. Knocking off early wouldn't be such a sin. And he was the boss.

"Who in the hell replaces fans with chandeliers in a house in the damned tropics," he said.

He had stolen the thought from Mariella's head.

"I'm not here to judge, just to clean," she said.

He made a grunting noise and shuffled the paper.

After she finished, she stepped down the ladder. He was immediately at her side and had the ladder folded up, hanging from his hand like it weighed nothing, and out the French doors before she could blink. He was back in a flash.

"Let's go."

The fragrance of a great magnolia drifted past on the afternoon air. The streets were noisy with children who had just gotten out of school and fishermen who just finished at the dock. Hemingway walked her to the café, got a table, and ordered two lemonades and two slices of key lime pie. A cat walked up to the table and rubbed against Ernest's leg while they waited. He reached down and rubbed the back of its neck.

"She's like you," he said. *"Mi pequeña gata."*

Mariella looked down at the soft black cat.

"Your little cat? *You* are the cat. A lion."

He laughed. "I've been told that before."

The drinks and food came quickly, and Mariella tried not to shove the whole pie in her mouth in one bite so she could save some for her sisters. It was delicious and tangy, and the sour lemonade was the perfect complement to it.

They watched the people walk by for a little while and then he asked her if she would mind if he jotted down some character ideas in his notebook. She said she didn't and continued working on her pie. After a few minutes, a tall, thin man with thick glasses stopped on the street in front of their table.

"Hemingway? Ernest Hemingway?"

The lion looked up without a hint of friendliness or welcome.

"Jesus H. Christ, it is you?" asked the man. "How the hell are ya?"

Hemingway didn't say anything. Mariella watched.

"Mike—Mike Johansen, from Josie's bar. We shot pool one night with Larry and his girl, and saw a big bar brawl with some soldiers. Holy shit, that was something else, wasn't it?"

"I think you'd better watch your mouth in the presence of a lady," said Hemingway. "And can't you see I'm working here?"

"Jeez, Hem, sorry."

"Good. Get the hell outta here."

Mariella squirmed in her seat while the man walked away, shoulders slumped and humiliated. Hemingway went right back to scribbling away in his notebook. She stared at him. After a few minutes, he stopped writing and looked up at her. His face was friendly and open. Her brows were knitted together. His smile faded.

"What?" he asked.

"That wasn't very nice."

"Do you think it was very nice for that loser to come over and interrupt me at work with his foul language and his stupid memories from some night I can't even place?"

"No, but you shot him down pretty hard."

"And it's a good thing. Otherwise he'd have pulled up a chair and driven us crazy with his ridiculous ramblings. Can't a man sit and write without being aggravated?"

"You're in a public place, Papa."

"But I'm doing a private thing."

"You're a famous writer. You can't expect to sit in public, unnoticed, doing the very thing you're famous for."

"But I need to watch people for ideas."

"Then expect to get interrupted every now and then."

"You could sit here without interrupting me," he said. He stopped to take a long drink of his lemonade.

"That's because I had my pie to keep me occupied. I'd probably interrupt you if I didn't have my pie."

He broke into a grin and shook his head. She went back to her pie, and he went back to his notebook. He stopped after a few minutes and reached into his pocket.

"I just remembered, I have something for you," he said.

He placed a black rabbit's foot on a key chain in her hand.

"For luck," he said.

"Where's the rest of it?" she asked.

"How the hell should I know? The foot's the only lucky part of the rabbit."

"Wasn't so lucky for him," she said.

He laughed loudly and took another drink. "You know, I'm going to write a story about you, Mariella."

"Please don't," she said.

"Why?"

"I won't be used."

"Used?"

"When you put people on your pages, you take something away from them."

He looked at her closely, and then at his notebook. "I don't want to share you with anyone, anyway." He drew a long, diagonal line over everything he'd written, and turned to a clean page.

She felt chills rise on her arms when he crossed the pencil down the paper.

There. Gone.

After another bite of pie, she put down her fork and sipped at her lemonade. He looked up again.

"What's wrong with the pie?"

"Nothing. I just want to save some for my little sisters."

He stared at her for a moment and then stood and disappeared inside the café. She wondered what he was doing and started to get uncomfortable sitting alone, with people at neighboring tables looking her up and down and surely wondering why Ernest Hemingway was sitting in a café with his housekeeper.

He was back in a few minutes.

"Go ahead and finish that," he said.

"But my sisters," she said.

He raised his hand at her, and the waiter suddenly appeared with a brown bag he set heavily on the table.

"A pie for the family," said Papa. "There are also some sandwiches in there."

Mariella was embarrassed to feel tears well up in her eyes. He winked at her and went back to his work. She willed herself not to cry and finished her pie, basking in his generosity and attention, until a shadow fell over them.

Pauline.

"Hello, Mama," said Hemingway with enthusiasm.

Too much, Mariella thought.

He jumped up from the table and wrapped Pauline in a big embrace. She never took her eyes off Mariella.

"Where's Lor?" he asked.

Pauline glanced at her watch and ignored the question. Mariella burned, knowing it was earlier than five and Pauline would be upset that Mariella had knocked off before quitting time.

"I didn't know you weren't putting in a full day today," said Pauline.

Mariella started to stammer an apology when Papa cut her off.

"I insisted she come keep me company," he said. "She'd finished, anyway."

"She doesn't work by the chore," said Pauline. "She works by the day."

"It's really not your concern," said Papa.

"It actually is," said Pauline.

Some of the people at the nearby tables started to stare. Mariella wished she could just melt away into her chair. She could see Papa's temper flare in the red on his face.

"Why don't you sit down and join us instead of making a scene," said Papa.

"I'm just fine where I am—"

"Sit."

Pauline stared at him for a moment, and then took a seat at the table, placing her shopping bags at her feet.

Mariella felt responsible for the trouble, and worried that Pauline would dock her pay. She found her voice. "I'll go back to the house and do some more work. I shouldn't have left early."

"Absolutely not," said Papa. "I told you to leave. Now let's just drop it."

"Yes," said Pauline, closing her eyes and rubbing her temples. "Let's drop it. I want to go home, anyway. I'm exhausted."

The waiter came and asked Pauline whether she'd like anything, and she shooed him off.

"I'm going home," said Pauline. "Mariella, be a dear and help me with my bags. We'll leave Papa here so he can finish his work."

Mariella felt her cheeks burn and thought she'd like to lay Pauline out with a right hook to her smug face. It took every ounce of self-control in her to stand and pick up Pauline's bags. She was aware that her own bag of food that Papa had bought for her sat on the table. She didn't want to pick it up, feeling that it would somehow make all this worse in Pauline's eyes, but she hated to leave it.

Pauline kissed Papa on the head and started out to the sidewalk. While her back was turned, Mariella looked at Papa and then the bag. He shook his head and mouthed, *I got it*. She turned back to Pauline and hurried to catch up with her, mentally coaching herself not to respond to any insults.

Pauline didn't say a word on the way home, and her silence unnerved Mariella more than shouting would have. Pauline walked several paces ahead, with perfect posture and the grace of a queen. Mariella tried to walk a little straighter herself. Pauline's poise and confidence made her attractive, and Mariella recognized the power in that.

When they got to the great wall bordering the Hemingway house, Pauline turned and took the bags from Mariella's hands, her face flushed from the brisk pace she'd set. Mariella suppressed her pride and spoke. "I'm sorry I left before I should have. I'll come over early tomorrow to make up for it."

"Fine." Pauline started through the gate but stopped herself and turned back. She looked like she badly wanted to say something. Mariella prepared herself for the tongue-lashing, the reprimand, the *stay away from my husband* talk she thought she'd get, but Pauline's face just looked tired.

"He's incorrigible," she said. "He wants playmates like a child, but you *can* say no."

Mariella nodded and looked down at her feet.

"In fact," said Pauline, her voice steel, "I insist."

<hr />

The bag of food was sitting on Mariella's front porch when she got home. It was good of him to drop it off, and she marveled that they'd been able to read each other's minds like Catherine and Henry in *A Farewell to Arms*. But these were the thoughts she had to stop thinking. They made Pauline suspicious, Mariella blush, and others judge her harshly.

When she stepped through the door with the bag and opened it on the table, Lulu clapped. It cheered Mariella to see Lulu looking so much better since her fever had broken.

"Where did you get this?" asked Eva.

"Papa bought it for us," said Mariella, instantly regretting referring to Hemingway as Papa.

They spread the food out on the table and began eating. Her mother didn't say a word and tried to leave the table without dessert. Mariella put her hand on her mother's arm.

"You have to eat a slice of pie," said Mariella.

"*¿Por qué?*"

"It would be wrong not to," said Mariella. "It will go bad if you don't eat it. You don't want to be wasteful."

Eva looked at Mariella and then at the pie. She sat down, and Lulu spooned a bite from her own plate into Eva's mouth. Eva looked at Lulu with wide eyes and then closed them, savoring the tangy perfection.

"Isn't it heaven, Mama?" asked Lulu.

Eva nodded, her eyes still closed, and a smile slowly spread on her lips. Estelle smiled a little, too. They took turns feeding one another with spoonfuls of the pie, going in for seconds until only one slice remained. They agreed to give it to the old man across the street. Lulu and Estelle volunteered to deliver it, leaving Mariella and her mother alone in the kitchen.

Mariella felt sedated by the delicious dinner and hoped her mother did, too. She started taking dishes to the sink when Eva said, "That was a big gesture, don't you think?"

Mariella felt her heart sink. Somewhere inside she'd suspected that her mother would find a way to twist Papa's gift, but she hoped she wouldn't. "He's a generous person," she said, resolving not to take the bait. She wanted to enjoy her full belly.

"I just hope he doesn't expect anything of you," said Eva. "You need to be on guard about that. Men like him don't give something away for *nada*."

Mariella squeezed the dish towel in her hands and clenched her teeth to keep herself from responding. Her mother placed the rest of the plates next to the sink and went to her chair. Mariella could feel Eva's eyes on the back of her head and had just about worked herself up enough to respond when Lulu and Estelle ran back in the door, Lulu chattering about the good food, the good rich people, and the happy old man with his pie. Mariella suppressed her anger for the second time that day and forced a smile.

That night, Mariella couldn't sleep and lay in bed brooding over her mother. She fantasized about finding her dad's old boat, fixing it up, and cruising out to the Gulf Stream. When she finally drifted off to sleep, she dreamed of a boat on the sea at night. There was a man behind her with his arms wrapped around her waist, but she couldn't see his face.

Chapter Seven

Mariella shoved the last of the ice into a tub on the yacht, pocketed the money, and thanked the men for the tip. She watched the boat slip out of the harbor and felt the pull long after they were out of view. She ached for the water and closed her eyes, imagining she was at the wheel of her own boat, cruising around the gulf.

"Daughter."

She opened her eyes, and he stood before her.

"You miss the water," he said.

"Terribly," she said.

"Then today's your lucky day."

"Why?"

"Because I'm just heading out and I want you to go with me."

"No, I couldn't."

"Why not?"

Mariella fumbled for an answer. "I didn't tell my mother I'd be out that long."

"So what? Are you six years old?"

"No, but my sisters," she protested.

"—have their mother."

"It could take a while."

"They'll survive."

"But you don't want to take *me*."

"I asked you, didn't I? I don't do anything I don't want to do."

A cloud threw them in shadows, and Mariella looked around, half expecting to see Pauline, and remembering her words about saying no to Papa.

But it was Mariella's day off. She'd made a little money.

She glanced back at the water and felt dizzy with longing.

"You're coming," he said. "As your employer, I insist."

As they pulled away from the dock, Mariella looked back and saw Nicolas in front of his restaurant. He watched her with a scowl and had his arms crossed. Mariella smiled and waved. He raised his arm but didn't smile. Papa saw.

"He's just looking out for you," he said. "Nicolas is a good man. A lot of these guys around the dock are good men."

"Just down on their luck," she said.

"I've been there," he said. Mariella looked at him out of the corner of her eye as if to say, *Bullshit.*

"What?" he said. "I was poor as a dog in Paris. Hadley and I didn't eat some days. And I've never been happier than I was at that time."

"You can't argue that it's better to be poor than it is to be rich," said Mariella.

He grew quiet for a moment.

"If you are true to yourself and your wife and your son and your work, and you eat and drink with people who are the same, yes, it's better to be poor," he said.

Mariella shook her head. "You're just remembering the good times. You forget the ache in your belly, never knowing if you'll have enough to keep a roof over your head, the sleeplessness."

"I didn't say I was comfortable. I said I was happy and true."

"You're not now?"

He was quiet again. They pulled farther out and faced the open water. A cruiser moved over their path ahead and threw a big swell at them. It caught Mariella off guard, and she fell into Papa. He grinned at her from inches away.

"It's early for that, but I'm game," he said.

Mariella tried to control her skin from burning and fumbled for a retort.

"Please, you're too old," she said.

Papa laughed his big, booming laugh.

They took turns at the wheel, moving the *Pilar* slowly out to sea. Mariella had never driven a thirty-eight-foot yacht before and was pleased that it felt as natural to her as her father's small fishing boat. Papa pointed out the specialized features: the live fish well, dual motors, and giant fuel tanks so he could stay out as long as he wanted.

As they pulled away from the no-wake zone, Mariella increased their speed.

"You're a natural," he said.

"This is heaven to me. There's nothing I'd rather be doing."

"So why don't you?"

"I'd need a boat for that."

"Your dad's?"

"Wrecked. Ruined. Missing."

He was quiet.

"Someday," she said.

"Will you be a fisherwoman?"

She hesitated a moment. She feared she wouldn't be taken seriously, or worse, that she would, and naming it out loud for someone else meant she needed to get serious about it.

"A charter boat captain with a shiny fleet."

There. She had said it.

"Now you're talking," he said.

He'd taken her seriously.

"So, where to?" he asked.

And moved on. That was good. She didn't want to dwell on it.

"South of the Tortugas has the best fish running this time of year," she said.

"Take us there, Captain."

As she drove the boat, she stole glances at Papa, admiring his profile against the waves and alternating between feelings of gratitude, attraction, and guilt. She wondered whether what her mother had said about owing him something was true. She also couldn't help but wonder whether she was just an amusement for him—a diversion from boredom or routine. She didn't like being used, but when he chose to dole out his attention she knew of none who could refuse. Certainly not herself. She also reasoned that as long as they didn't cross the line, it couldn't hurt to play his little game.

"You never answered my question," said Mariella.

"What's that?"

"Are you happy?"

"I don't know how to answer it to someone who's poor without sounding like a piece of shit."

"Just say what's on your mind."

He looked at her and she stared back at him, unflinching. She wanted him to know that he could be straight with her.

"I'm not all that rich, myself," he said.

"What do you mean?"

"I mean Pauline's uncle bought us our house. She's rich. It's her money."

"You're a successful author."

"I am, and I do well enough, but I couldn't afford all this without her money. And sometimes I feel dirty for it."

Mariella was quiet. She'd always assumed that his writing funded their lifestyle. She didn't realize how much Pauline had brought to the marriage. Mariella started to understand what he meant about being rich not always being better. She thought of the

ways Pauline and Papa were different. Pauline with her chandeliers. Papa with his bohemian haircut and toothless fisherman
friends. Pauline with her shopping excursions. Papa with his boxing matches in Bahama Village. Pauline with her fancy, well-bred
sister. Papa with his maid on a fishing boat.

"I'm going to show you something you're gonna love." He
broke her line of thinking when he disappeared into the cabin and
returned moments later carrying a Mannlicher rifle.

"Jesus, Papa."

"I know. It's beautiful, isn't it? I'm so sick of those goddamned
sharks. One nearly took off my hand last time I was out."

"You're gonna kill yourself with that thing."

He grew quiet. "No." He ran his hands over the barrel. "I'm
not like my father."

Mariella looked at the floor of the boat. She'd had no idea.

"Do you know about him?" he asked.

Mariella looked at him. He had creases on his forehead. His
eyes were sad. He looked like he wanted to talk about it.

"No," she said.

"Sometimes I think it's the way to go. He was sick. He knew
he wasn't getting any better. My mother had worn him down."

"Were you close to him?"

"At times, yes—yes, I'd say I was."

Mariella felt an opening to talk about Hal with someone who
might understand—someone who also loved his father, sometimes
hated his mother, and understood the loss.

"My dad and I were close, too," she said.

"I was sorry to hear about him."

"I just can't believe I wasn't with him that day," said Mariella.

"Thank God you weren't."

"But maybe I could have saved him."

Hemingway didn't say anything but gave her a look of troubled confusion.

"I mean, I'm no doctor," she continued, "but maybe I would have seen how pale he was. Maybe I could have encouraged him to go to the hospital, and he wouldn't have had the heart attack, and our boat wouldn't have been wrecked."

He continued to stare at her, making her feel uncomfortable and like she wished she'd kept her thoughts to herself.

Finally he cleared his throat. "How old are you?"

"Nineteen. Almost twenty."

"And you still live with your mom?"

"I've got to be there for the girls."

He stared hard at her.

"Doesn't your mother know you're an adult, for Christ's sake?"

Mariella didn't understand why he was suddenly so angry and wanted the conversation to return to small things, but he wasn't ready to move on.

"Sometimes I think my father was such a coward," he said. "You just don't do that when you have kids. I wouldn't do that, if for nothing else but my kids."

"Maybe he thought you would understand, or maybe he wasn't thinking at all. A person can't be thinking right to do a thing like that and leave his family to pick up the pieces."

Papa laughed bitterly, and Mariella covered her face. "Sorry."

"It's only him who should be sorry."

A lock of hair curled into Mariella's mouth, and she brushed it away. She shifted her attention to the water to stop this conversation she didn't like, and to watch for signs of fish.

She found that she had a harder time connecting to the sea from such a large boat. It felt different from being in a small boat, closer to the surface. She had to concentrate more deeply on the feel of the boat in the waves, but before long, she was able to imagine the yacht disappearing and the water rising up to guide her.

"Beer?" he asked.

"Thanks."

Papa handed Mariella the beer, then opened one for himself. They clinked bottles and drank together. It tasted bitter and delicious.

"Your boxer's at Joe's a lot," he said.

Mariella blushed and cursed herself for her weakness while he laughed.

"That's a sweet blush. Don't be ashamed. Soon you'll be a woman and you'll forget how to do that."

Mariella didn't like him downgrading her from an adult to less than a woman in a matter of minutes. She downed the rest of her beer in one gulp.

"Another," he said. He passed her a bottle and their fingers touched. Mariella felt a current run up her arm. He didn't pull away, and neither did she. She was suddenly aware that he had taken off his shirt and now stood very close to her. He smelled like salt and alcohol. She closed her hand on the bottle and he ran his fingers over hers. His face was deadly serious.

A splash broke his concentration.

"Shark," said Mariella.

Papa looked overboard as the gray fin waved from side to side along the surface of the water. He jumped to grab the gun and fired over the side. The water exploded and splashed up high. The shark dropped to the right and resurfaced.

"Bastard," he said.

"He doesn't even care," said Mariella in disbelief.

"Look at the line," said Papa. Mariella saw the fishing line jerking back and forth, and wondered how she hadn't noticed it before. Then she realized why she hadn't noticed, and blushed again.

"Their hunger trumps all of their other instincts," he said. "Those sons of bitches chew up every fish I bring in. Just once, I'm bringing in a fish without a single shark bite."

Mariella saw the shark circle around the back of the boat, intoxicated by the blood from the fish. She looked at the gun. He saw her.

"You wanna try?"

Marialla shrugged, but inside she was screaming, *Yes!*

"You need a lotta strength to keep it down and controlled. It goes *bam-bam-bam*, and it'll kick up in the air. Ever fired one?"

"No."

"A virgin."

She looked at him straight in the eyes and used every ounce of concentration she had not to blush.

"Yes."

He seemed at a loss for words. Mariella's heart pounded so hard she thought he must see it behind her shirt. A loud splash drew their attention back to the water. Papa handed Mariella the gun.

It was heavier than she thought it would be and strangely cold on the hot day. He gave her a few quiet instructions, but it felt natural in her hands — like an extension of her emotion toward the shark.

She lifted it up and aimed it at the shark, adjusting herself so the gun pointed just ahead of where it swam. Her shirt clung to her back. She had never killed anything with a gun before, and it gave her pause for a moment. It was a lot of life to take. The shark had needs, too. God knew she knew what hunger felt like. But she was overthinking this. A cloud covered the sun and she could see the whole dark outline of the shark.

She fired.

The gun wanted to point up, but she kept it down.

A spray of blood and water shot into the air.

Papa howled, "Holy shit! You got it!"

The sun came back out.

He looked at her and laughed, shaking his head as he took the gun. Mariella smiled and rubbed her hands—still white from clenching it so hard. She looked back at the red stain in the water. It seeped down and dissolved on the waves.

"Pfeiff could shoot pretty well," said Papa as he rebaited the line. "In Africa she was a pretty good shot. And a good sport."

It was the first kind thing Mariella had ever heard him say about Pauline. He said it with regret and longing.

"But she just did it to please me, which took something away from it," he said. "When you picked up the gun, you wanted it. I like that."

"It's okay to want to do something because someone you love does it."

"Of course it is," he said, "but the irony is that it gives the one you love more pleasure when you want to do it also for yourself."

"I see."

"I know you do," he said.

Mariella looked into the live fish well, pleased with the assort-ment of fish they'd already caught in such a short time. They still wanted a big one, though. The line moved back and forth, but not hard enough to indicate that a fish was hooked.

"It's a drug, you know," he said.

"What?"

"Wealth. Money. Power."

"I'll let you know what I think if I ever have any."

"I hope you always have enough to keep your belly full and a roof over your head," he said. "Everything beyond that's trouble."

Before Mariella could respond, the line jerked hard, once, then twice.

"Here we go!" he shouted.

He rose up from the chair, knocking over his beer. Mariella

picked it up. But not before it slid in a quick line to wet his shirt, which he had thrown in a heap on the deck. She picked up the shirt, shook it out, and placed it over the back of his chair to dry.

"It's a good one," he shouted.

Mariella turned and saw the great beast leap fully out of the water.

———⌒———

When they docked, a small crowd loitered along the pier. The old locals, wrinkled beyond their years by sun and hard living, lined the dock and waved to them as they pulled in. Mariella thought they were beautiful.

"They have a thousand fish stories to tell, and I never get tired of hearing them," said Mariella.

"I'm going to write a fish story one day."

"Do."

"But it won't be as pretty as what we did today."

Mariella turned and looked at the fish they brought in. She'd cleaned the snapper on the way in and was pleased to have fresh fish for dinner. As they pulled into the dock, Papa called the men over to see a marlin free of shark bites. When Mariella saw the poor men, she thought of her father and then her mother, and suddenly felt guilty for not earning more that day.

It was early evening. Hemingway instructed some locals to string up the fish for a picture. She looked off toward home and back at the big fish and felt pulled away.

"I've got to go," said Mariella.

"Wait—I want you to be in the picture," he said.

"No, you did all the work," she said. "I'll see you on Monday."

"Stay," he said.

"I can't," she said.

He gave her a scowl, like a sulking child. She laughed.

"Next time," she said, taking her fish and starting down the dock. She made it to the road and then turned back. He was still watching her.

Thank you, she thought. He nodded and kept watching her.

~⌒◯

The ambivalent sky settled on rain, and Mariella was running by the time she got home. The girls were on the porch. Lulu filled soup cans with rainwater that dripped through holes in the sagging roof. Estelle sat on the bottom step, staring across the road at nothing, letting the water run over her without flinching.

"You're soaked," said Mariella, helping Estelle stand. The girl looked down at her clothing and back at Mariella in surprise. Mariella led her into the house, past her mother sleeping in her chair, and into the bathroom, where she wrapped a towel around her sister and kissed her cheek. "Go change, *cariña.*"

Estelle walked into their room and closed the door. Mariella hoped Estelle would be able to manage on her own and felt a familiar flutter of worry for her younger sister. Every day Estelle seemed more and more detached, but Mariella tried to convince herself that such behavior was a normal grieving response. It did not escape her notice or irritation that her mother slept while Estelle sat in the rain, but guilt slapped that thought away. After all, she had been on a boat all day with Papa.

A sudden fatigue gripped Mariella from the weight of her physical and emotional burdens. She looked into the mirror and pulled her long dark hair out of its tie, letting it spill around her face. She smelled her own stink from the day on the boat, and her stomach growled. Her head pulsed from a lack of food and too much beer and sun. She started the water in the tub. It was ice-cold, because there was no money to heat it. Mariella peeled off her dirty clothes, stepped into the tub, and washed herself. Before long, her body became accustomed to the chill, and she sat still, mindful of how alive the sharply cold water made her feel.

In the quiet, Hemingway crept into her thoughts—the touch of his fingers on hers and his kiss on her forehead. She knew he'd wanted to kiss her mouth, and was surprised at how unafraid she'd been. He was going to be her undoing.

When she heard the front door slam and Lulu come babbling into the house, Mariella stood and stepped out of the tub. She dropped her dirty clothes in the water to soak, dried off, reached for her dress hanging on the back of the door, combed her wet hair, and walked down the hallway in bare feet to start dinner.

"You got dark today," said her mother from her chair. "Were you at the dock?"

Mariella debated whether to tell her mother that she went out on the boat with Hemingway and decided to tell the truth. Lying about it would have meant there was something to hide.

"At first, yes, but then I went out on Mr. Hemingway's boat."

"Was anyone else with the two of you?"

Estelle came out of the room wearing a dry dress, and she and Lulu watched her with large, brown eyes.

"No," said Mariella.

Eva looked at the ceiling and started mumbling in Spanish.

"Did you catch a fish?" asked Lulu. Someone's stomach growled, and Mariella smiled.

"Yes, many, many fish. Even a big marlin. I brought home snapper for dinner."

"What did you talk about all day long?" asked Eva. "*If* you talked."

Mariella turned to glare at her mother, but she had her face turned away, staring out the window. Thunder rumbled.

"Sounds like the sky's hungry, too," said Lulu.

They laughed, and Mariella kissed Lulu on the cheek, again thankful that she was there to lighten the mood. Even Eva couldn't help but smile.

"We talked about fishing, and sharks," said Mariella. "And Dad."

Eva looked over sharply. "What about *tu padre?*"

"Nothing much, just that his father had died, too, and that he was sad when he heard about Dad."

Mariella felt the air leave the room. She knew her father's death was a constant source of tension, but this quiet felt different. It felt like something holding its breath. The thunder rumbled again, more loudly.

No one said much during dinner. The tension remained, and lingered after she'd done the dishes and put the girls to bed. When Mariella stepped into the living room, Eva turned and gave her a dark look that made her stomach flip. But then Mariella remembered that she was an adult, and straightened her posture. She crossed her arms and leaned on the doorframe. Her mother stubbed out her cigarette and smoothed a lock of hair off her forehead.

"I don't think you should be spending so much time with him."

"Why?"

"Do I have to spell it out?"

"You do, because as far as I can see, it's innocent."

"*¿De verdad?* When his name's brought up you flush from head to toe. You're out late at night and all day with him. He's married, and he's trouble."

"I'm not a child."

"It doesn't matter that you're not a child. I'm older than you, and you can benefit from what I know."

"When I want your opinion, I'll ask for it."

Eva turned her head to look out the front window and put her forehead in her hands.

"If Dad was still alive, you wouldn't notice me," said Mariella. "Just pay attention to the girls and don't worry about me."

"How can I not worry about you? Do you want to end up with a baby of your own? Do you want to end up like me?"

"I'm not stupid."

Her mother snapped back as if she'd been struck.

"I'm sorry," said Mariella. "I didn't mean that the way it came out."

The rain started up hard again, and the thunder growled after each flash of lightning.

"It's not about *estupidez*," said Eva. "It's about desire. Desire wins, Mariella."

Mariella didn't want to talk about desire with her mother.

"Not for me," said Mariella.

She went to the room she shared with her sisters and shut the door. She took off her clothes, put on a nightshirt, and crawled into the pallet she slept on near her sisters' mattress. Mariella could hear her mother put on Ponce's *Suite in A Minor*. Hal had bought Eva a portable windup phonograph several years ago, in spite of the fact that they could barely afford their house. He used to bring her records whenever he could. The melancholy guitar sounds depressed Mariella and made her miss her father.

At the end of the song, she heard the needle scratch and saw the light go out in the hallway. She heard her mother feel along the wall and stop outside her door. Eva opened it and stood there for a few minutes. Then she walked to her room and shut the door.

Mariella was tense. It was hot so she took off her nightshirt and lay naked in her bed. The sheet stuck to her, but she didn't want to pull it down and expose herself in a room with her sisters. The cloth settled around the contours of her body with a pleasant weight, and Mariella started to relax into the bed.

It was on hot, frustrating nights like these that Mariella wished she lived alone, or maybe with a lover or a husband. Her mind played at what it would be like to marry Papa. She thought of their fishing trip together and imagined what it would be like to take him right there on the boat. Her mind couldn't wander too far, however. Guilt caused the fantasy to recoil, suppressing the coveting.

She turned her thoughts to Gavin. Now, *he* was within the realm of possibility. So possible, in fact, that it suddenly scared Mariella more than her flirtation with Hemingway. She knew the barrier of Papa's marriage was there, but there were no outside barriers with Gavin. Well, no barriers except her mother.

When they had danced, she'd felt the attraction. It made her heart race. He was as tall as Hemingway, but not as thick. She liked the feel of his lean, muscular body. She liked the smell of tobacco and aftershave on him.

She ran her hands down the sheet and felt her body soften.

But her mother's words snapped into her mind. *You don't want to end up like me.* And how right she was. Three daughters, poor, widowed—no, Mariella would not end up like Eva.

Lulu's voice pulled her from her thoughts.

Mariella listened to see whether she'd go back to sleep, but the minutes passed and the child kept whining. Mariella threw off the sheet, pulled her nightshirt over her head, and tiptoed to the bed to quiet her sister so she wouldn't wake Estelle.

"What is it, Lu?"

Her soft, dark curls were wet on her forehead. "I'm hot."

Mariella felt her head and was thankful Lulu didn't feel feverish, just sweaty.

"How's your belly?" whispered Mariella.

"It's fine," said Lulu.

"Good. I'll be right back."

Mariella went to the kitchen to get a cold rag and a cup of water, because a drink would be Lulu's next request. She went back to the room and sat on the edge of the bed. She took the cool rag and ran it over Lulu's head. Then she blew on her softly. Lulu closed her eyes and smiled and after a little while said, "I'm thirsty." Mariella produced the cup and gave it to her. She helped her drink, allowing her to spill a little down the front of her. Mariella ran the wet towel over Lulu's chest and blew on her again. In the moonlight coming through the window, she could see the girl's skin rise in tiny goose bumps.

Once Lulu was comfortable, Mariella tiptoed back to her bed. She left on her nightshirt and lay brooding over her mother, and finally decided she wouldn't be able to sleep. She reached under her pillow, pulled out the book she'd picked up at the library, and went out to the living room to finish it.

A Farewell to Arms.

She'd read the part where the priest came to visit Frederic Henry and spoke with him about God and love. The priest told Henry that he would love someday, and that love would make Henry want to make sacrifices.

Mariella knew she'd never been in love. She felt something in her belly more and more each time she was around Hemingway, but that couldn't be love, could it? It must be that other thing. Then she thought of Gavin and how good it felt in his arms when they danced. She didn't know him well enough to love him, and she thought she'd probably never see him again—especially after the way she'd run off.

Her thoughts returned to Lulu, Estelle, and her parents, and her spirits sank. She tried to pray but thought that she was a little afraid of God, like Frederic Henry, and was also unconvinced that she would ever truly love.

Chapter Eight

Mariella felt as if she was being watched.

She opened one eye and Lulu was in her face.

"Sister Theresa says it's a mortal sin not to go to church."

Mariella groaned and rolled over, covering her head with a pillow. She'd stayed up way too late reading.

"You don't want to go to hell, do you?" said Lulu.

Mariella groaned again, feeling as though she were the five-year-old child with the adult standing over her.

"Don't you want to see Daddy when you die?"

Mariella removed the pillow from her face and looked at Lulu, troubled that such words came out of a child's mouth. Mariella didn't know whether she believed them, but it didn't feel right for her sister to speak that way.

"Did Mama send you to wake me up?" asked Mariella.

"Yes," said Lulu. "She said you wouldn't say no if I asked."

No, Eva wasn't stupid at all. Mariella smiled and gently pushed Lulu off the bed.

"All right, all right. Give me a little privacy while I get dressed, would ya?"

Lulu ran out the door, telling Eva that Mariella was getting ready.

Church was the one place Eva ventured all week. She even

made a halfhearted attempt to dress up for mass. Since Hal's death, Mariella had mixed feelings about the whole thing. The only place that felt really holy to her was the sea. If there was a God, Mariella felt that he or she or it must be out there.

Mariella forced herself out of bed, washed her face, combed her hair, and put on a little makeup, but when she pulled her only church dress out of the closet and tried to put it on, it got stuck on her hips and barely zipped over her chest. She walked to the kitchen to show Eva.

"I can't go," said Mariella, pointing to her dress.

Eva ran her eyes over her, widened them, then said, "No, that dress isn't going to work."

"Say a prayer for me," said Mariella, as she turned back to her room.

"You can borrow one from me," said Eva. Mariella stopped and turned back, surprised by the suggestion. Her mother didn't usually think of ways to solve problems lately, especially when they had to do with other people. Mariella nodded and went to her mother's room.

In the closet, there were a few shirts and a pair of slacks that had belonged to her father. His only pair of dress shoes stood with the toes pointing out under the pants. The rest of the closet was filled with Eva's dresses. It was hard to believe that just months ago Eva had dressed and made herself up every day for Hal. Now the only things she ever wore were a dingy, stained housedress that looked like prison-issue, and her black, shapeless church frock.

Mariella knew which dress she wanted—the one from the picture of Eva and Hal on the dresser as newlyweds, staring at each other with open longing. In the picture, Eva had her hand on Hal's chest. It was so intimate that it embarrassed Mariella to look at it and made her wonder who had taken it. The dress was white with large red flowers and had a low neckline. It was a dress that wanted to be danced in.

Mariella slipped it out of the closet, closed the door to the room, and peeled off the dress she was wearing, careful not to rip it so her sisters could wear it when they got older. Her mother's dress slid on easily. The white and red were a perfect contrast to Mariella's dark skin and hair. She checked her reflection in the mirror in her parents' room and went back to the kitchen, unsure why her heart was pounding.

The girls stopped what they were doing and stared at Mariella. "You're pretty," Lulu said.

Estelle's face turned red, and she looked down. Mariella knew Estelle remembered the dress and probably feared her mother's response. Eva looked over Mariella from head to toe, but didn't tell her to take it off. Mariella didn't know whether her mother's frown was over the dress being worn to church or the memories it must have stirred up about Hal, and she suddenly wished she'd chosen something different.

"I can pick another one," said Mariella.

"No," said Eva. "It's too late. *Vámonos.*"

As Mariella entered the church, she saw the crucifix behind the altar and bowed her head. If she was being honest with herself, her avoidance of church lately had to do with the rush of her weekly misdeeds hitting her in the face when she stepped through the door. She thought of the gambling, the stealing, the back talk to her mother, and now lusting after a married man. She wondered whether she should get communion in the state that she was in, but determined that it would be a scandal not to do so. She felt the presence of the Blessed Mother and dared to look up at the massive, stained-glass rendering of her. Mary's face was so gentle that Mariella relaxed.

Mass had started just before they arrived, and the church was full. She couldn't find a space in the row with Eva and the girls, so Mariella sat on the end of the row behind them. She knelt, crossed herself, and put down her head to pray.

Please, God, forgive me, for I have sinned. I'm sorry to make this confession to you this way, but I don't want to tell a priest. I've been lusting after and coveting Mr. Hemingway. I've also been gambling, swearing a lot, and stealing cigarettes from Mark and limes from the fruit stand. Please forgive me and help me to be a better person. Please bless my mother, and Lulu, and Estelle, and the Hemingways, and Nicolas and his family, and Mark Bishop, and the man who died at the dock, and Gavin, and most of all, my father's poor dead soul. Mother Mary, please help me to be a good daughter and sister and woman, like you. In Jesus' name I pray.

"Amen."

She made the sign of the cross and stood to sing the opening hymn. Mariella was reaching for a hymnal when she felt the heat of someone at her side. She looked to her right and saw that there was barely any room in the pew, but that there was plenty of space behind where she sat. She summoned the most annoyed look she could and turned to face the man squeezing into the pew.

It was Gavin.

Her annoyance quickly turned to a smile.

"There's plenty of room in the row behind us, Murray," she whispered.

He leaned close to her ear. "I know." She could feel his breath on the side of her neck, and it made her light-headed.

Gavin and Mariella stole glances and smiles at each other throughout the opening song, and when it came time to sit, he put himself right next to her with his arm touching hers. She leaned back and saw that though he had a bit of room on his other side he stayed pushed up against her. She narrowed her eyes at him and nodded for him to scoot over, and he smiled back and shook his head slightly.

The mass was a blur. She tried to concentrate, but she could only see his tattoo jutting out from under his rolled-up sleeve, feel the heat from the side of his body on hers, and smell the sweet tobacco smell that hung around him. When it was time to kneel he pressed his leg against hers. She felt his hand against her dress and nearly fainted; then she realized he had put something in her pocket. When mass ended, Gavin smiled at her and slipped away before they could talk. She pulled the crumpled paper out of her pocket and read it.

Mallory Square, sunset.

Mariella put the paper back in her dress, wondering whether she'd go. She needed to concentrate on making money for her business. She also knew part of her reluctance had to do with a man she was drawn to who wasn't hers. Hemingway and Gavin got her pulse racing in the same way. The difference, she thought, was how she felt afterward. Guilt after flirtations with one, warmth after the other.

Yes, she'd meet Gavin.

Eva went to light candles for Hal, but Lulu was getting restless. Mariella picked up her little sister and moved outside, where she found a new reason to blush. Standing under the statue of the Virgin in the window of the church's facade was Hemingway, smiling his Cheshire cat smile. His boys ran in circles around him. Pauline saw Mariella and called her name.

"Good to see you," said Pauline, her face alight with approval. "Do you usually attend mass here?"

"It's been a while," said Mariella. "I should come more."

"I wish *he* would come more, too," said Pauline, nodding at Papa.

"Did you ever hear how I became a Catholic?" he asked.

Pauline smacked him on the arm. He laughed his loud, wicked

laugh, looked Mariella up and down, and walked down the street. Mariella watched after him, her emotions a whirlpool that threatened to drown her.

Storms rolled in through the afternoon, keeping Mariella indoors with the girls, reading and drawing. Unlike Estelle, Lulu cared nothing for the product and only for the process of shading and blending the pastels Mariella had bought for them with her recent pay. Many color-smudged papers littered the floor around her, and Lulu's dimpled hands were a mess of rainbow dust when they'd finished. Estelle spent the entire time on one picture, meticulous in her depiction of Hal's boat on the water at sunset. It made Mariella pause, and when she noticed all five of the family members on the boat, she felt like she'd cry. The family had rarely gone out together, and when they did, Estelle and Lulu were much younger. Mariella swallowed the lump in her throat and spoke.

"This is beautiful," she said.

Estelle stared at the paper, but didn't say a word.

"This is my wish, too," said Mariella.

Estelle stayed quiet, so Mariella just squeezed her hand and hung the girls' drawings around the kitchen with penny nails.

When they finished, she glanced at the wall clock for the millionth time and hoped the rain would clear so she could meet Gavin. Her joyful anticipation of seeing him grew throughout the afternoon. It occurred to her that he was a good distraction from all the things that made her feel guilty, like Hemingway, her mother, gambling. He felt like an answer to a prayer she hadn't realized she made.

To Mariella's relief, the rain slowed and the clouds drew back to let in the evening. Mariella got the girls fed and ready for bed early. She felt guilty leaving them with her mother, who sat chain-smoking and listening to classical guitar music, but she needed a life, too. She told Estelle to put herself and Lulu to bed at eight o'clock and told Eva that she was going to Mallory Square. She left out the part about meeting Gavin, guessing that Eva would have something unkind to say about vets.

Mariella walked up Whitehead Street, passing the lighthouse and Hemingway's house. A group of gawking tourists stood by the gate. The house was quiet, so the family must have gone out. Mariella wondered whether they were dining with the Thompsons or out at a bar. She wondered whether she'd run into them.

As she passed a café, she stopped to check her reflection in the glass. She pushed her hair out of her eyes and smoothed it back away from her face. She reached in her pocket and put on a little more red lipstick she'd found in the bathroom medicine cabinet. She was nervous and wished she had a cigarette.

At the top of Whitehead, Mariella stepped onto the dock at Mallory Square. The presunset carnival had begun. Jugglers, singers, magicians, and vendors converged to celebrate the sun and start the party on Duval Street. What had started as a small event had become a pagan celebration and tourist beacon in spite of the depression that weighed so heavily on the rest of the city. Everyone needed an escape.

The sun was still fat over Sunset Key. Mariella thought back to second grade in Catholic school, when Sister Theresa told her of the Son's all-consuming love for his children, and her seven-year-old ears had heard *sun*, and had associated the sun with God. Her childish imaginings had been reinforced throughout her schooling—the burning bush, the transfiguration, visions where God was too bright to look upon. The all-consuming love of God was like fire. Then she had read that the angels were the wind that moved the trees, and she felt what she did on the water, and became convinced that the veil between this earth and the other was thin, but people just lost the ability to recognize it as they got older.

She felt a hand on her back.

Gavin.

He hugged her, and she inhaled the faint smell of his after-shave and the traces of his last cigarette. He held out his hand and they started walking.

"I didn't think you'd meet me," he said.

"Why? Too many hopes dashed in the past?"

"Something like that."

"I've never seen you in church before this morning," said Mariella.

"I'm not usually in Key West. I stay up on Matecumbe most weekends."

"You stay with your friend on Olivia Street?"

"Yeah. I'm gonna have to start paying him rent. I've been down here a lot more lately." Mariella liked the way he said that—as if she were the reason.

The jugglers on Mallory Square separated as Mariella and Gavin walked among them. The sun was going down. A wisp of a boy brushed by the woman in front of Gavin, and reached for the wallet in her purse. Mariella grabbed the kid by the arm and saw it was her neighbor Manuel. He looked up at her in shock and then screwed up his forehead and shook his arm out of hers.

"Put it back," she said.

The boy dropped the wallet into the woman's purse without her noticing any of the exchange. Then he looked at Gavin's and Mariella's clasped hands and his face darkened. Manuel turned and disappeared as fast as he'd arrived. Gavin raised his eyebrows. Mariella shook her head.

"He's a neighbor and a thief," she said.

"And an admirer of yours," said Gavin.

"Probably, and he doesn't like people mixing."

"He's not alone."

"I guess it doesn't bother you or you wouldn't be here," she said.

"Not a bit," he said. "Why'd you give him a hard time about stealing? You never steal?"

"I never get caught."

"That was the lesson you wanted to teach him?"

Mariella smiled and kept walking.

"So, why are you such a well-behaved vet?" asked Mariella. "All the other guys stir up trouble around here on the weekends, while you go to church and invite girls for sunset walks."

"I can hold my liquor," he said. "It wasn't always that way."

"What changed?"

"Maturity. Fatigue."

"Fatigue? At your age?"

"I'm probably old enough to be your father."

"Hardly. I'm almost twenty. How old are you?" asked Mariella.

"I'm thirty-three."

"Why aren't you married?"

"The war screwed things up. I'm just getting around to fixing them." He was quiet for a moment. "Does my age bother you?"

"No," she said. "Does my skin bother you?"

"No. Do my scars bother you?" he asked.

She ran her hand over the scar on his arm, and he flinched. She immediately pulled away, regretting the intimacy of the gesture. He turned to her so she could see the scar on his face. He took her hand and ran it over the scar.

"I'm not a monster to you?" he said.

"It goes away the longer I look at you, but I want to brush it off. It's like a smudge on a painting. You look like you're lucky to have that eye."

"The cut from the shrapnel was so deep the doctors couldn't believe I kept it. I wouldn't be able to box without it."

Mariella removed her hand from his face. The crowd clapped while the sun sank into the ocean—curtain drawn, or, rather, opened for the night. She watched as the sun slipped into the waves. He turned her face back to his own. He brushed a lock of her hair off her forehead and tucked it behind her ear.

He leaned in to kiss her and she responded. My God, she felt as if she were melting into him. How much time passed? Two minutes, five, ten? She pulled back and turned from him to look where the sun had left the sky. She put her hand to her mouth.

"I'm sorry," he said, breathless. "Too much?"

She looked back at him without any restraint. "No." She had only stopped to make it a moment she wouldn't forget, framed by the passage of the sun.

⁓ ❧ ⁓

They walked down Duval, arms laced, past bars pouring music and laughter into the street. It was too early for the drunken overflow, so it was nice passing bars as each song spilled into another in a continuous, energetic sound track. Gavin stopped to buy them both ice cream, and they moved along in silence. He kept stealing glances at her, taking quiet pleasure in the cool refreshment and in her company.

"When the road's done, I'm going up to Miami to get my mom," said Gavin. "I'm going to work up there. I've saved up a decent amount, all things considered."

"What'll you do?" she asked.

"My uncle's got a construction business that's been around awhile. Once his partner retires, I'll buy in. My dad passed while I was in the war, and Mom's been pretty bad off with her health."

"What's wrong with her?"

"She's got a disease in her nervous system called ALS. She was doing okay for a while, but she's gotten really bad recently."

"Can she come live down here?"

"I thought about it. But my uncle's business is up there, and my aunt helps care for her now, so I'll have her stay put."

"Do you see her often?"

"About once a month. I wish I could see her more. How about your family?"

Gavin thought he saw Mariella stiffen, and he wondered whether he shouldn't have asked about them. She hesitated a moment, but then replied.

"My dad died a few months ago," she said.

"God, I'm sorry," he said as he stopped walking. "How have you been holding up?"

"It's always there," she said. "Lurking behind everything, you know?"

"I do," he said, and pulled her into him. He held her for a moment; then they continued walking.

"You know what I miss most?" she asked. "My parents were really great together. They danced around the kitchen when their favorite songs came on the radio. They sat on the front porch swing talking long into the night after they thought my sisters and I were asleep. During thunderstorms, she read to him while they shared an apple on the couch."

Gavin was touched by Mariella's memories. "That's sweet," he said.

"I feel bad, too," said Mariella.

"Why?"

"My dad had this great, deep, raspy voice, and he used to sing all the time. It didn't matter if we were in public, at church, at home—he loved to sing. And when we were out I used to tell him to stop, and I'd get so embarrassed. But now I'd give anything to hear that scratchy voice singing his out-of-tune songs."

"I'm sure he understood."

Mariella nodded.

When they arrived back at the house, Gavin asked, "Would you and your sisters like to go to the Point next Saturday? I'm going back to Matecumbe tonight, but I'd love to see you again."

"All right," she said. "The girls would like that."

"What about you?"

"I'd like it, too," she said. "But we can't go too late. I have to work a party at the Hemingways' house next Saturday night."

"We can go in the morning," he said.

Mariella stood before him, close enough to kiss, and he badly wanted to. He also wanted her to know how much he respected her. When he looked into her eyes, he was overcome with emotion, but he didn't want to overwhelm her, so he kissed her hand and walked off into the shadows.

CHAPTER NINE

The morning sunlight revealed all the things Mariella's house was able to conceal in the night—broken shutters, peeling paint, holes in the screen door. Gavin thought it was like waking up with a woman you'd met drunk the night before, and hoped the feeling wouldn't extend beyond the house.

He flicked his cigarette into the road and walked up to the porch. The thin, wrinkled Cuban man across the street watched him. Gavin raised his hand in a wave, but the man just narrowed his eyes and exhaled his cigar.

The beach outing filled Gavin with apprehension. He worried that he had come on too strong with the kiss in Mallory Square, then not strong enough at the end of the evening. He didn't want to overwhelm Mariella after they'd talked about their fathers, but it had taken everything he had not to kiss her again.

Before Gavin got to the door, Mariella opened it and stepped out with her two sisters in a line behind her, suited up and ready to go. His apprehension disappeared as soon as he saw her. The sun lit up her face, turning her brown eyes gold, and she smiled warmly at him. Forgetting himself, he hugged her, but she broke off quickly and hurried them onto the sidewalk.

"Introductions?" said Gavin.

"Sorry," she said. "This is Estelle. This is Lulu. Girls, this is Gavin. Let's go."

"Is your mother home?" asked Gavin. "Doesn't she want to meet the guy taking all of her girls to the beach?"

Mariella looked back at the house for a moment. "I thought about it, but I don't know how that would go."

"You won't know until you try," said Gavin. "What did you tell her?"

"That we were going to the beach with a friend."

"That all?"

She broke into a grin at him and he smiled back. Then he reached out and took her beach bag from her.

"We'll introduce you when we get home," she said. "That way, if there's a problem, we'll have had our fun."

Gavin thought that probably wasn't a good idea, but Mariella had already picked up Lulu and started quickly away from the house, with Estelle following. Gavin looked at the old man, who continued to regard him with suspicion. He turned back and saw Mariella and her sisters crossing the street to the next block, and he jogged to catch them.

Under the shade of a palm tree, Mariella watched Gavin pull a floppy hat out of her bag and crouch down in front of Lulu to put it on her head. Lulu brushed her dark curls out of her eyes and Gavin tied the hat under her chin, careful not to pinch her. Gavin's tenderness with her sister touched Mariella.

Gavin stood and looked at Estelle, who watched Mariella for a cue.

"Are we all going to stare at each other, or are we going to have fun?" Mariella asked. She grabbed Lulu and tickled her, and then ran down to the water with the girls, Gavin trailing behind them.

The Point was at the southernmost tip of the island where the Atlantic Ocean met the Gulf of Mexico. The landscape was littered with driftwood, palms, and sea grapes, and a pleasant breeze moved over them, taking the edge off the heat and rustling the palm leaves in a whisper.

The water was rough, so Mariella and Gavin started Lulu on a sand castle. He asked Estelle to join them, but she shook her head. They piled heaps of sand into a mound that Lulu started to form into a drippy castle, complete with fringes of seaweed and bits of shells. Estelle walked to the water and faced the horizon.

"Is it me?" asked Gavin.

"No. She's been like this since Dad died."

Gavin looked at Estelle and then back at Lulu.

"Her?" he asked, nodding toward the little one dripping sand over the peak of a large mound.

"She's already stopped asking about him."

They watched Lulu, lost in her task. Mariella thought of how strange it was that a father could become so insignificant to his child once he was gone. It depressed her.

"Dolphins!" Estelle called to them in a moment of childish abandon, and Mariella and Gavin were quick to respond, eager to acknowledge her attempt at communication. Gavin picked up Lulu and ran her down to the water's edge. They watched the pod work its way west into the gulf waters.

"Do they notice the change?" asked Mariella. "They go from wide-open waters to enclosed." She thought of the wild, unpredictable currents of the ocean, the warm, still flow of the Gulf, and then of Hemingway and Gavin. She thought Gavin might be like the Gulf. She turned toward him and saw him holding her girl and smiled. She shielded her eyes to see them more clearly.

A sudden shouting called their attention to the water. A man of about fifty waved from a few dozen yards offshore. He was trying to get their attention, but kept disappearing behind high waves.

Mariella stepped toward him. "He needs help!" She started into the water, but Gavin held her back.

"Mari, wait. It's not going to do him any good for you to go out there and drown with him."

She knew he was right, but she couldn't just stand there watching him die.

"We need a rope," he said.

"We can't throw it to him; he's too far."

"No. I'll swim out; you hold the rope, and pull us in when I signal."

Mariella told Estelle to watch Lulu and stay out of the water. She and Gavin ran around the beach trying to find a line. Mariella spotted a fishing boat on the other side of a rock formation, untied it, and pulled the boat onto the shore. She ran with the rope to Gavin. He threw his shirt in the sand, grabbed the rope, and rushed into the water.

Mariella could see how Gavin fought against the current. She held her breath, knowing how rough the water must be for a young, healthy guy like Gavin to struggle. After she saw him pass the fourth set of waves, Mariella lost sight of both Gavin and the man and broke into a cold sweat. The rope hung limp in her hand.

"I can't see them," said Lulu.

"I can't, either," said Mariella.

The seconds felt like hours, and panic crept into her heart. Mariella stepped into the surf up to her calves. She looked down at the water and silently implored it to carry them back safely. Finally, just when she thought she'd burst, she felt the sharp tug on the line.

"He's on!" she said.

Mariella pulled with all her strength and felt the tide helping her. Estelle surprised Mariella and grabbed the rope behind her.

She was strong and they made quick work of hauling them in. When the men were safely onshore, they collapsed on the sand, panting hard.

"You saved my life," said the man. "All of you. I wouldn't have made it back."

Mariella helped him up and Gavin shook his hand. The man shuddered and walked over to a nearby picnic table to gather his things. He picked up a towel and turned to face the sea. Mariella watched him as he walked away. She thought about how quickly disaster slipped into life, and didn't know whether it made her want to wring the energy out of every moment of every day, or curl up in her bed covered with a blanket.

"I'm hungry," said Lulu. Mariella looked at her and shook her head while Gavin laughed. She couldn't help but smile.

"I guess that's that," said Mariella.

Gavin put his arm around her and squeezed her shoulder, then went to grab a towel to dry off. Mariella watched him shake the sand out of his shirt, and admired his broad shoulders and muscled chest as he put it back on. Then she forced herself to turn her attention back to spreading out the blanket and setting it for lunch. Mariella had packed cheese and bread, and Gavin had brought papaya and some lemonade. During lunch, without a word, Lulu got up and walked over to the other side of the tree to relieve herself in the sand. Even Estelle laughed as Mariella scolded her little sister for her immodesty.

"And you said the vets have bad manners," said Gavin.

Lulu clapped and danced around, enjoying the commotion she'd caused, and then ran off to chase seagulls. Estelle trailed her. Soon they settled in the sand to add to the castle, with their backs to Mariella and Gavin.

"I wish we could stay out here all day," said Mariella, enjoying the way the day had turned out. "I hate that I have to work that Hemingway party tonight."

"I wish I could go with you," he said.

"Maybe you could. They pay well for overtime. Maybe they'll need an extra bartender."

"Let me know. I planned on staying in Key West for the night."

Mariella felt a sudden anxiety at having Gavin and Hemingway in the same room. She thought they didn't like each other and that had to do with her. She hoped she hadn't just created a world of trouble for herself.

She watched the water, and its rhythm calmed her. After a moment, she stretched and lay on her back with her legs crossed at her ankles, drinking in the sun. Gavin started to clean up lunch, so Mariella pushed up on her elbows and moved to stand.

"No, stay," he said.

"And leave you to do all the work?" she asked.

"You deserve a rest," he said. "And I like to watch you."

Mariella looked at him, and he didn't break her gaze. She gave him a sly smile.

"You just watch the mess, Murray, or I'll report you to the proper authorities."

She lowered herself to her back and closed her eyes, inching her dress a little higher up her legs. She heard him whistle and she laughed from the blanket. Mariella could tell that Gavin made slow work of lunch cleanup so he could watch her. She turned over onto her stomach and leaned up on her elbows. She swung her feet up and grinned at him. Her face was flushed from the sun.

"I like you," she said.

He laughed. "That's a start," he said. "I might love you."

"You don't know me."

"I know enough."

"Like what?" she asked.

"I like that you have balls."

She wrinkled her forehead in a question. He sat next to her on the blanket and leaned back on his elbows.

"You showed up at a bordello for a boxing match in a rough neighborhood, dressed as a guy."

"What else?" she asked.

"You have a good heart," he said. "You take care of your sisters. You're comfortable in a smelly fishing boat, a bar, or a church. You have religion."

She laughed. "I don't know about all that, but go on."

He moved closer to her on the blanket, until their arms touched, but kept his eyes straight ahead on the girls at work on the sand castle.

"You make me laugh," he said, "and there aren't many who can do that. Am I getting sappy?"

"No, go on."

He looked at her with his face deadly serious, and her smile left. She kept her eyes on his and leaned closer to him. They stared at each other a moment longer. It took everything she had in her not to kiss him.

"There's one more thing," he said.

"Yes," she said, nearly breathless.

His eyes traveled down her back, and goose bumps rose on her legs in spite of the heat of the sun. He moved his gaze back up her body to her eyes.

"You've got the best ass I've ever seen."

She gasped and punched him in the side. He laughed and shielded himself from her until he was able to grab her arms and pin her down on the blanket. He looked quickly over at the girls and saw that they weren't facing them. When he turned back, Mariella leaned up and kissed him.

She felt everything around them fall away while they kissed. She tasted the salt still on his lips from the seawater, and felt the warmth of his weight and the sun on her. He took his hands from her arms and ran them down her sides. Chills rose on her skin.

Suddenly, a shadow fell over them.

Eva.

Gavin jumped to a standing position and Mariella joined him, brushing sand off her dress. The girls ran over to the blanket.

"Mrs. Bennet," said Gavin.

"Mama!" said Lulu. "Come swimming."

Eva glared at Mariella until the girls reached her.

"Put on your shoes," hissed Eva.

"I don't want to," yelled Lulu.

"*Ahora!*"

"Mama," said Mariella. "The girls are having fun; please don't. I'm sorry."

"No," said Eva. "You'll have more fun if they're gone, *¿sí?*"

"It's not like that," said Mariella.

She could see the rage building in her mother and knew it would be best if they left, so she turned and helped Gavin, who had leaned down to help Lulu with her shoes.

Lulu cried, "I don't want to leave."

Gavin held her face in his hands. "We had a good day. Maybe we can do it again."

"Ha!" said Eva as she grabbed Lulu by the hand and started dragging the child down the street. Lulu wailed. Estelle followed with her head down.

"I'm so sorry," said Gavin.

"I'm not," said Mariella. She picked up her beach bag and started after her mother. Then she stopped, turned back, and kissed Gavin on the mouth. After a moment he gently pushed her away.

"You should go after her," he said. "Do you think it will help if I go with you?"

"No," said Mariella. "But I will come to you later."

"It's okay," he said.

"Later," said Mariella. She stole one more kiss and then hurried down the street in her mother's wake.

Mariella had almost caught up by the time they reached the house. Eva was several paces ahead of Mariella, and let the door slam in her face. Mariella threw open the door and slammed it shut behind her. Eva put Lulu down and turned on Mariella.

"Is *he* why you're always running off at night? He's a soldier! Do you have any idea how dangerous they are?"

"How dare you!" shouted Mariella. Estelle crept back to her room, pulling Lulu behind her. "I'm an adult. You can't decide to parent me now that I'm grown."

"*No me importa* how old you are. It's my job to protect you. He's probably *treinta*, with one thing on his mind."

"He's thirty-three, and that's never even come up. I'm safer with him than I am hanging around the dock, or Duval, or even Hemingway's."

"You shouldn't be doing all that, either."

"That's my life. Like it or not. You didn't object when Dad was alive—you can't just wake up and decide to take charge of something you've never paid attention to until now."

"It was different then. Now you've got to watch out. There are a lot of poor, desperate people around here."

"We *are* the poor and desperate."

"Then you should stick to your own kind," said Eva.

Mariella thought Eva must be mad. Had she forgotten her marriage to Hal—an American-born man as white as she was dark?

"What—like you?" said Mariella. "My God, you left your entire family in Cuba for Dad. I'm just going down the street, and Gavin and I aren't so different."

"You are to them!" said Eva, pointing out the door. "Your father and I suffered for it—the nasty looks, the stares, the comments."

"Christ, you know I don't care what people say about me," said Mariella.

Eva gasped at Mariella's language, but she didn't care. She was enraged that Eva would choose to interject her opinion now—after all that had happened, now that she was finally finding joy. And it hit her that she *was* finding joy. She loved being around Gavin. She loved being around Papa. She didn't know which she loved more, but she wanted to find out. And she wasn't going to take any parenting now that it was too late.

"You're still living *en mi casa*, so I'm still in charge," said Eva.

"*Your* house? My job keeps us in this house!"

"How can you say these things to me?" said Eva as she began to cry. "When all I do is try to love you."

"Jesus, now the holy martyr speech," said Mariella. "Please spare me."

Eva gasped again and ran to her room, slamming the door behind her. Mariella felt a stab of guilt for her last line. She knew it was hateful, and now she'd have to apologize. Her blood was boiling, though, so she couldn't yet.

She went to Eva's chair, pulled a cigarette from the pack, and lit it. Mariella sank into the chair and looked out the window, then laughed bitterly at the irony of assuming her mother's position in the house. She inhaled and stared across the street at the old man's house and the house next to it. A garden separated the two, and large pink roses of every shade crept over the latticework. Birds and butterflies slipped in and out of the bushes, and a statue of the Blessed Virgin rested in the middle of it all. Her arms were open and she looked out at the world—her marble face a mixture of tranquillity and acceptance.

Tranquil and accepting—Mariella thought she was neither.

As her nerves calmed, Mariella realized why her mother enjoyed the view. She put out her cigarette and rubbed her face in her hands. When she looked up, Lulu was before her, yawning.

"Sleepy?" asked Mariella.

Lulu nodded.

Mariella stood and carried Lulu to her room. Estelle was sitting on her bed lining up her dolls. She didn't turn when Mariella came in, which made her feel even guiltier for the fight with Eva. That was the last thing she needed to do around Estelle.

Mariella put Lulu in bed and crawled in beside her. She rubbed the child's hair while stewing over her mother's anger. Punctuating her own frustration, however, was her guilt. Maybe she should have told her mother about Gavin before they left. And Eva did find him on *top* of her while the girls played on the beach. But Mariella suppressed those thoughts. Eva would have found fault with them even if they'd just been sitting together on the blanket. She was sure of it.

Once Lulu was sleeping soundly, Mariella motioned for Estelle to get into the bed and she got out. Estelle crawled in and wrapped herself around her little sister. Mariella covered the window with a sheet to block out the light and crept out the door.

After putting on her work dress and freshening up, Mariella walked to her mother's door and raised her hand to knock. She thought she heard her mother crying. Mariella knew she should go to Eva and make it better, but stubbornness fixed her in her place. If Mariella went to Eva now, she would be condoning her interference.

She cleared her throat. "The girls are napping," she said through the door.

No response.

"I have to go to work at the Hemingways' this evening. They're having a party."

She heard sniffling on the other side.

"There's beans and rice for dinner."

She stood there a moment more, trying to decide whether to open the door. Ultimately, she knew her anger outweighed her compassion at the moment, and she didn't want another fight, so she turned and left the house.

CHAPTER TEN

The sun was high and hot, but Mariella had a chill from her sunburn. It made her think of the beach with Gavin. She pushed her fight with her mother out of her head and started for Olivia Street, where Gavin said his friend lived.

She waved to the old man on his porch smoking cigars and took in the scent. He nodded. She smelled fish frying nearby and heard a dog barking in the distance. When she got to Olivia Street she looked for the pale blue cottage Gavin told her he stayed in with his friend. She heard classical guitar music on the breeze. It was the suite her mother liked, and it filled her with a sudden and deep melancholy.

The blue house was just where he said it was. The lawn around the house was trim and tidy, the white fence had a fresh coat of paint, and the flower garden around the perimeter of the yard was well cared for. The roof looked new. Mariella noticed the contrast of the cottage to the surrounding homes in various levels of poverty and disrepair—peeling grayed paint, overgrown vegetation, vines breaking through cinder blocks, cracked windows, dirty children idle around the edges of the street. And then this house— warm and well tended, gleaming on the street as a reminder of good times past and, hopefully, what was to come.

The guitar music was coming from the house. Mariella stopped to hear the piece finish when a hammer started pounding loudly and regularly. She thought its operator was hitting it in time to the music.

An old brown mutt came around the edge of the house and broke into a gallop when it saw her. Its tail was wagging and its mouth was open like a smile. She crouched down to meet it. The dog ran faster, and before Mariella could stand to brace herself for the impact, she was on her back getting licked. She laughed, pushed the dog off her, and stood up to brush off her clothes.

"Mariella?" She looked up and saw Gavin appear at the edge of the roof. He had a hammer in his hand and a tool belt around his waist. He wasn't wearing a shirt. Mariella admired the view.

"Are you earning your keep?" she asked.

"You could say so," he said. "Hold on; I'll be right down."

He disappeared down the back of the roof and was out in the front yard with her in a moment.

"I see you met Mutt."

"He's friendly."

Gavin reached for Mariella's hand.

"Come on in," he said. "Meet my friend. He'll love you."

Mariella felt butterflies in her stomach. She didn't know what to expect. She didn't know whether she should be going into a house with two men she barely knew, and thought her mother was justified in worrying about her.

They stepped onto the white covered porch with well-trimmed vines hanging over its edges. The music from inside stopped briefly and then started again. The heaviness of the last piece ended and was replaced with a light melody.

Inside, the house was painted blue. It was a shade of blue Mariella had never seen before on walls, but she thought it was beautiful. It reminded her of the ocean and Mary's robes on the statue at church. There were watercolor paintings on the walls of beaches and boats and places in town she knew. Mutt followed them in the

door and thumped over to a man sitting on a conch-colored couch
with a sheet over his legs. He looked a little older than Gavin, with
creased eyes and brown hair graying along the temples. He continued picking the guitar as they walked into the room. He smiled at
her and nodded for her to sit on the chair nearest to him, as if he had
been expecting her. She noticed a wheelchair next to him, and then
looked back at the sheet and noticed it covered two stumps.

The music stopped.

"Mariella," said the man. He took his hand from the guitar
and reached for Mariella's. She shook it and was surprised at its
strength. "John Bates Jr."

"It's a pleasure to meet you, John Bates Jr.," said Mariella.

"How's Lulu feeling today?" asked John. Mariella smiled. He
knew all about her.

"She's doing better. She's always been a sickly kid, though.
Thanks for asking."

John gestured to the couch next to him and grabbed a pack of
cigarettes from the end table. He offered one to Mariella and lit
hers for her. Gavin disappeared down the hallway.

"So you're the reason Gavin's been spending so much time
down here?" asked Mariella.

"No. I believe *you* have something to do with that," he said, to
Mariella's pleasure.

Gavin returned wearing black pants and pulling a white
T-shirt over his head. "Uh, I'll go get us something to drink," he
said, and walked into the kitchen.

"I can manage fine without him," said John. "He's a real pain
in the ass with all his hammering and fixing."

"Kiss my ass, you cripple," yelled Gavin from the kitchen.

Mariella winced and shot a look at John. He was smiling.

"You'd better watch out," John said, "or I'll start telling her
what a lovesick puppy dog you are over her."

Mariella looked down at her hands, trying to suppress a smile.

The dog pawed over to her from the kitchen and put his face on her lap. His beard was wet with water. She ran her hand over his back, and Gavin walked in with three beers.

"Please excuse him, Mariella," said Gavin. "John's brain was injured in the shelling. Just tell me when you want me to tape his mouth shut."

"I'd like to hear more of what he has to say," she said.

Before John could reply, there was a commotion on the street. Gavin and John exchanged glances, and Gavin got up and walked out the door. Mutt followed.

"Stay here," he said on the way out.

Mariella watched him leave, but then got up to go to the window and see what was happening. There was a small crowd of men yelling at one another. She recognized two of them from around town, and the other three were vets who had clearly been drinking. A pretty girl with bleached-blond hair stood off to the side looking at the ground while the locals pushed the vets. They were all shouting and cursing at one another, but Mariella could make out only bits of what they were saying.

From what she could guess, one of the vets had insulted the sister of one of the locals. The girl smiled to herself. Mariella could tell she was enjoying the commotion. A vet punched a local in the face and a brawl erupted. Gavin, who had been walking toward the gang, broke into a run. He yelled something at Mutt that made him stop and sit by the street, but the dog looked like he badly wanted to join him.

Mariella put her beer down and clutched the windowsill, worried that Gavin would end up with another scar on his face.

"What's going on?" asked John. "Wait—drunken vets?"

"Yes. It sounds like one of them was getting fresh with the sister of a local and her brother didn't appreciate it."

"And so it goes, again and again."

Mariella looked back out the window and saw Gavin separating the group and calming them down. He pushed the drunks down onto the curb and used his hand to keep the locals away from them. Mariella saw the girl openly admiring Gavin, and clenched her own fists.

Gavin and the girl's brother shouted back and forth a bit, but then, gradually, the arguing stopped. He shook hands with Gavin, shouted something nasty to the vets sitting on the side of the road, and walked down the street, pulling his sister by the arm. She looked back over her shoulder at Gavin and winked, and Mariella had to fight the urge to go punch the girl herself. Gavin turned back to the vets, slapped one of them on the head, and walked back toward the house with the dog following him.

The sun came out from behind the clouds and lit him up. He saw Mariella in the window and smiled out of the side of his mouth. John started playing the guitar again, and Mariella took a long drink of her beer, feeling warm and completely at ease.

Gavin could barely breathe.

Having a woman in the house, a woman as beautiful, alive, and interesting as Mariella, overwhelmed him. It was the feeling soldiers often experienced after having been surrounded by male company for long periods. A woman was like a drug. Her softness, her smell, her lightness—it was magnetic, hypnotic. It balanced the atmosphere. He ached to touch her.

Gavin excused himself to the kitchen and tried to contain his agitation so he could finish supper and they could get to the Hemingways' on time. He still didn't know whether he'd be able to help out, but he was interested to go and see her interaction with the writer. Whenever Hemingway's name came up, Mariella's attitude was so casual it felt forced. Gavin thought he'd be able to tell a lot by watching them together.

He didn't want to think too much about that, though, because having her here felt so good. Gavin could tell John approved of Mariella, and that meant a lot to him. He basked in the sound of her voice as it came in through the open door.

"So we're on the beach with the girls," she said, "and a man starts yelling from about fifty feet out in the water. He's drowning and he can't swim back."

"And Mariella marches into the water like she's gonna save him," called Gavin from the kitchen.

"I could have done it," said Mariella. "The sea and I have an understanding."

"Is that so," said Gavin, walking to the door.

"We speak each other's language."

"That may be true," said Gavin, "but I reminded her that she had the girls to take care of, so luckily she came to her senses."

"So, did you let him drown?" asked John.

"No, we found a rope. I swam out and Mariella and her sisters helped pull us in."

"No shit," said John. "That guy was lucky you all were there."

"He was lucky Gavin was there," said Mariella. "I'll never go to the beach without him again."

Gavin smiled and disappeared back into the kitchen. He heard Mariella come in behind him. She started cleaning the shrimp that were lying in a bowl in the sink. Gavin stood next to her, slicing potatoes. He felt the air shiver between them.

"I'm really glad you came over," said Gavin as he threw a potato peel at Mutt.

"I'm really sorry about earlier," she said, "with my mother."

"I understand why she would be upset."

"I guess I do, too," said Mariella. "She did find us rolling around on the blanket."

They looked at each other and laughed as guitar music started from the other room. Gavin couldn't stand it any longer and leaned in to kiss Mariella. Her hands were covered in raw shrimp, so she held them away from her body. Gavin ran his hands down Mariella's sides and rested them just above her hips. She responded to him like she'd been waiting for his kiss all afternoon.

He tickled her waist and she jumped away from him, laughing, and the music stopped. John yelled, "Less kissing, more cooking. I'm starving."

Mariella opened her mouth in surprise. "How did he do that?" she said.

"My other senses are stronger since I lost my legs," called John.

"I don't think it works that way," said Gavin, throwing the potatoes into the stew simmering on the stove.

Gavin insisted on washing the dishes and left Mariella to talk to John, who'd clearly become a little drunk. Mariella watched him run his hands down what was left of his legs and out past the stumps. It was as if he were trying to draw what was left of them down to fill the empty space below his knees. He still took up a surprising amount of space, even without half of his legs. It was easy to see he had been a large man. He had a great expanse of shoulders, a thick neck, and arms that were still well toned. He, too, had the Argonne date tattoo.

"Forgive me for saying this," said John, "but you're too smart to clean houses for a living and too pretty to wear a maid's uniform."

"Thanks, I think," she said. "It's a means to an end."

"What end?"

She hesitated. She'd already voiced it to Hemingway. To say it to John, a virtual stranger, was serious and somehow more frightening. Papa understood her connection to the water. John did not. She swallowed a large gulp of beer.

"The water. My own boating business. Charter fishing, sunset cruises—you know, tourist diversions."

"I can see that," he said to her relief. "You saving for a boat?"

"Yes, and at this rate, I'll be about fifty before I've got enough cash."

He was quiet for a moment. "Did you know that Gavin wants to do the same thing?"

She did not know that, and for some reason it shook her. How could her dream belong to someone else? How was Gavin connected to the water? Her independence surged and she bristled.

"What about his uncle's business?"

She heard Gavin turn on the water to rinse the dishes.

"A means to an end," said John.

"Well, he'll just have to find another dock, because Key West is mine."

He laughed and finished his beer, adding it to the mess of bottles cluttering the table in front of them.

"There's room enough for both of you," said John. "You could partner." He winked.

"We'll see," she said. "He'll have to prove himself to me before I even consider it."

John's face grew pale and serious. He closed his eyes and she worried he'd pass out, but then he opened them.

"You couldn't get a better partner," he said. "Gavin saved my life."

The water turned off in the kitchen, and John leaned closer to Mariella and spoke in a low voice.

"He wouldn't want me talking about it to you, but Gavin was almost blown up dragging me and our friend Jordan out of enemy fire. Jordan didn't make it. He bled out. All I can remember from that day is watching my legs get farther away from me as Gavin pulled me through Jordan's blood all the way to a hole by a tree. It was a dark red line over the charred grass. Like a dividing line between us and them."

John's voice trailed off, and Mariella saw tears form in his eyes. Seeing him so moved put a lump in her throat and made her feel sick. She couldn't imagine Gavin and John anywhere but here in this small blue place, eating stew and smoking cigarettes. She understood that they'd had a whole lifetime before this one. She felt small and young—especially when she realized that Gavin and John had been around her age, or younger, when they went through the war.

"Jesus, Mariella, I'm sorry," said John as he put a hand over hers. She hadn't realized that she'd been clenching her fists. "I don't know why I had to tell you that."

His face was close to hers. He had the same old-looking eyes that Gavin had. She blinked back her own tears, and couldn't speak, so she reached for his hand. Gavin appeared in the doorway.

"Christ, John, I leave you alone with her for one minute and you've already stolen my girl."

Mariella and John laughed and wiped their eyes.

"Would you like me to scoot off so you two can continue?" asked Gavin.

"No, this girl's killing me," said John "You all had better get outta here. You're gonna be late."

Mariella hugged John, then stood and joined Gavin. As she and Gavin stepped out of the house and walked away, John started playing his guitar. The lonely sounds followed them until they turned up the street.

⁓ↄ

Gavin wished John hadn't gotten drunk on his first meeting with Mariella. He suspected he'd told the Argonne story, and Gavin wasn't ready for that to be shared just yet.

"What did he say to upset you?" asked Gavin.

"He didn't want me to tell you," said Mariella.

"Was it about the war?"

"Of course."

Gavin sighed and looked away. He worried she'd never want to come back to the house.

"I wish he didn't tell you," said Gavin.

"Why?"

"Because it upset you."

"I want to know."

"Why?" asked Gavin.

"The same reason you want to know about me. You want a clear picture."

"There are some things best kept secret."

"You can't believe that," said Mariella.

Gavin stopped and waited for a line of chicks following a hen to move out of his path. He resumed walking.

"You're right," he said. "I just want to protect you from that."

Mariella dropped Gavin's hand. "I don't need your protection."

He knew that he had angered her and should have known better. Her mother treated her the same way. She walked a little ahead of him. They were almost at the Hemingway house. He jogged to catch her and grabbed her by the arm.

"Hey, wait up," he said as she turned to him. "I'm sorry. You don't need protecting."

She looked at him with mistrust in her eyes. "I only need honesty," she said.

"That's fair. But I need time."

"Time?"

"Time to tell you things at my own pace. I'll tell you everything, but it's not going to be over shrimp stew with John around, when we have to leave in five minutes. A piece of me died that day. It was a whole other lifetime. It's not something I can just give away."

Mariella looked down, and he could see that she felt ashamed.

He didn't want that. He lifted her chin so she looked him in the eye. Her eyes were dark. He kissed her and the tension dissolved.

"Hey, this is a public street." Papa pulled up next to them in his car with Toby at the wheel. Mariella jumped away from Gavin. Papa smiled, but it wasn't friendly. "Get in, daughter. I'll get you away from this riffraff."

Gavin saw Mariella look from the car to him. She was immobilized.

The Hemingway boys came running up and climbed into the car, saving her from having to choose. Ada was huffing along behind them. Her hair had escaped its pins, and her portly chest rose and fell heavily.

"We want a ride!" cried Patrick.

They piled into the car, and Ada started back to the house on foot. Papa looked at Gavin. "Mind yourselves, kids," he said. Gavin clenched his jaw at Papa's condescending tone. Toby drove them toward the house, and Papa never took his eyes off them.

Gavin decided that he didn't want to be around Papa that night. He wasn't in the mood to be talked down to, and he thought Mariella's indecision over whether to stay with him or go with Hemingway showed him all he needed to know.

"You know what?" said Gavin. "I think I'll leave you to the party tonight."

Mariella started to protest, but he cut her off.

"I'll catch you later," he said, and walked away. He kept listening for her feet on the sidewalk behind him, hoping she'd come after him, but she let him go—just like that. When he got to the corner and looked back, she was gone.

When Mariella got to the house, Papa was nowhere in sight. She didn't have time to worry about Gavin or Papa, though, since

Isabelle dropped an apron over her head and pushed her toward the bisque.

"Don't let that stick. Keep stirring!"

Mariella looked into the dining room over her shoulder and watched Pauline give Ada money and instructions to keep the boys in town until eight o'clock and then bring them back and put them straight to bed.

"And no drinking for you until you get home," Pauline added.

Ada made a gruff noise and pushed the boys out the door.

Pauline went to the window and watched them walk away. Mariella thought Pauline looked lovely with the evening light on her slim form, a drink poised in her hand. Her silhouette was like a fashion spread in *Vogue*, where Mariella knew Pauline used to work before Papa and the boys. Pauline turned and looked at Mariella. A smile touched her lips but not her eyes. She looked back out the window for a moment and then turned and walked out to the foyer.

Mariella turned back to her bisque, trying to imagine what had drawn Papa to Pauline. Was it her graceful form in contrast to his first, athletic wife? Her haughty worldliness? Pauline was open to no one except him. She met everyone with cool regard except him. Her whole being lit up when he was around.

The more sinister issue of Pauline's money struck Mariella. Was Papa so sick of his poverty that he'd seen Pauline as a way out? Mariella felt sure Papa would never have admitted to himself at the time that Pauline's money and lifestyle attracted him to her. But maybe it had. Or maybe he was just Pauline's target. The rich were used to getting what they wanted.

Mariella did find it strange that whenever Papa's first wife, Hadley, was brought up, everyone had kind things to say about her. Even Pauline didn't say unkind things. Mariella thought she must have a lot to learn about men and women.

Her thoughts returned to Gavin, and her stomach roiled. She

tried to think of when the afternoon with him had turned sour. Was it the thought of him as a charter fishing boat captain? His reluctance to share his past? Or the exchange with Hemingway at the car? She decided that Papa was the tipping point, or rather, her reaction to Papa. She felt guilty for her indecision and abandonment of Gavin, but she had to get to work, didn't she?

"Okay, turn that down," said Isabelle. "Help me get these shrimp peeled, honey."

"What's the occasion tonight?"

"Just a meeting with friends. The Thompsons will be here. John and Katy Dos Passos. Sara Murphy's in town, though her husband couldn't come for some reason. Jane and Grant Mason." Isabelle raised her eyebrows.

"Who are the Masons?"

"Some fancy couple who live over in Cuba. She used to be a model. He's got money from some airline. They used to spend a lot of time with Papa and missus, but they haven't seen them for a while. Mrs. Papa doesn't like her much." Isabelle raised her eyebrows as if to say, *You'll see why.*

"It sounds like there's more to that story," said Mariella.

Isabelle crept to the hallway and looked both ways. Then she came back in, peeked through the door to the dining room, and returned to Mariella's side. She leaned in close and spoke in a whisper.

"Mrs. Mason went out the window of her house in Cuba a while ago and broke her back, supposedly after a fight with Papa."

Mariella gasped. "She tried to kill herself?"

"Don't know. Some say so."

"What's with her husband?" asked Mariella. "Does he know?"

"They have a strange marriage," said Isabelle.

A noise in the hall sent Isabelle and Mariella scurrying to finish their preparations. Isabelle finished peeling and deveining the shrimp, while Mariella went to the bar they'd set up in the living room to cut lemons and limes. Papa was in there with Pauline. They got quiet when she entered. The air in the room felt heavy with their argument.

Mariella made herself as small as she could. She watched only the fruit while she cut it. Its sour fragrance and sticky juice masked the smell of shrimp on her hands. She heard Papa's voice from the other end of the room.

"Don't start," he said.

"Do you invite Jane to torture me?"

"Jealousy doesn't become you."

"You didn't answer my question."

"Why should I? She's a dear friend and has been to you, so don't treat her ill tonight."

"You correspond more with her than you ever did with me."

"You know that's not true."

"Do I?"

"She's a friend."

"She's a harlot."

"That's a pretty sharp judgment from a woman who stole another's husband. Or does it take one to know one?"

Pauline recoiled as if she'd been slapped. Mariella burned inwardly for her. She flicked up her eyes and saw that he'd changed his posture. His shoulders slumped and he looked at Pauline with remorse. He pulled her into him. Mariella looked back at the lemons.

"I don't mean that. You know you're my one true girl." Mariella couldn't help but look up again, and saw him lean in and kiss her on the neck. She saw Pauline soften and put her arms around him.

"She's just so beautiful," said Pauline. "It's hard not to feel like an ugly duckling around her."

"I swear I only have eyes for you. She only flirts to torture her husband, poor bastard."

Pauline kissed Ernest, and Mariella thought that if she was

ever in a position in her life to have servants, they wouldn't know her private life. It was such a strange thing to be a living, breathing, feeling fly on the wall—in plain view but entirely unnoticed. It made her skin crawl to be a witness to such intimacy and have no connection to it. She derived no voyeuristic pleasure from the scene, only a mixture of emotions that left her unsettled—jealousy, anger, and guilt.

If only Gavin were here.

But then what? He would be a witness to her unease, and she would be exposed for coveting another woman's husband. And Gavin probably wouldn't be able to see her longing for him, which was every bit as strong as her longing for Hemingway, but so much simpler. No, it was best he wasn't here.

Mariella felt small and dark next to Jane Mason's bright, strawberry-gold beauty. It radiated from her as she slipped through the guests and their conversations. Her hair was pulled back in a tight chignon at the base of her neck. She wore an airy dress in pale green that contrasted beautifully with her tanned skin. She made the women slouch and the men stiffen. She was wholly fascinating to watch.

Mariella wanted to get close to Jane Mason. She wanted to hear her talk. She knew that from behind the bar she wouldn't get a chance—the men ordered the drinks.

Mariella watched Papa watching Jane when Pauline was otherwise occupied. His desire seemed to burn, growing hotter with each drink. Pauline lost her grace around Jane, and Mariella found herself feeling strangely protective of Pauline. She wouldn't necessarily call Pauline a friend, but a line was being crossed, and Mariella wanted to protect Pauline's family. This simpering beauty was a threat.

It was Jane's familiarity with the men that put Mariella on edge. Jane knew she was the most beautiful woman in the room and shamelessly lorded it over the men. They were helpless to her charms. She laughed too loud. She talked about shooting and fishing too much. She was never without her hand or arm on one of the men, but never her husband. He stood at the bar with a bland, vacant smile, watching Jane with indifference.

Papa, at least, seemed to respect Pauline by keeping himself out of Jane's hands. But contact or not, his eyes did the talking. Mariella saw Pauline excuse herself when the boys got home. She helped Ada get them off to bed, leaving Papa to openly admire Jane. The look Jane gave him caused Mariella to blush. Papa looked toward the bar at Mariella and she turned a deeper shade of red. He walked over to her.

"Daughter, why are you so red?"

Mariella wiped off the counter in slow circles. She looked at him with open hostility. "It's too hot in here."

He sipped his drink and squinted his eyes. "Step out with me for a breath of fresh air."

Mariella scanned the crowd. Everyone's drinks were full, so she walked out from behind the bar and toward the open French doors. The contrast of the party with the night was acute. Palms rustled in the breeze and the lawn was dark with shadows.

"I don't need two women judging me all night," he said.

"Why would you worry about my judgment?" asked Mariella.

"I wish I knew. You're the help, for chrissake."

Mariella flinched. He continued. "Jane's harmless. She just needs every guy panting after her, but that's it."

"How do you think that makes the wives feel?"

"Their insecurities are to blame for the way they feel, not Jane."

"Why does her husband put up with that?"

"What would you do if you were him?" he asked.

"I'd tell her to knock it off."

"Do *you* respond well to coaching?"

"No, but I would never carry on that way."

"What way?"

"Interfering with other women's men."

"Really?" The question hung in the space between them until Mariella grasped its meaning. Her face burned; then the very object of their discussion saved her from the moment. Jane walked out holding a bottle in one hand and a spoon in the other.

"Darling, the Green Fairy has arrived."

Hemingway leaned in and kissed Mariella on the cheek. Jane looped her arm through his and led him back into the house. Mariella stepped into the doorway and watched Jane set the bottle on the bar.

Absinthe.

Jane placed a sugar cube on a slotted spoon she balanced over the rim of a martini glass. She poured a shot of the green liquid over the sugar cube and into the glass and then used a match to set the cube on fire. The party grew silent and watched as the little white cube was consumed by the fluid blue flame and dripped into the absinthe. She topped it off with a shot of water and stirred the concoction. She handed the first to Hemingway and then made one for herself. Jane looked over to Mariella in the doorway and held up her drink.

"Cheers."

Absinthe took the crowd to a new level of intoxication, and things went downhill fast. John and Katy left in a huff over a rude remark from Papa. The Thompsons followed shortly thereafter. Sara Murphy left to call and check on her boys back home because one had been sick. Jane and Papa grew intolerable, and Pauline left the party, slamming her bedroom door. Grant Mason sat at the bar sipping his cocktail and looking around the room in confusion. Mariella kept his glass full and watched Papa make a fool of himself.

When Jane and Papa started to dance seductively, Grant finally intervened and ushered his wife out the door. Papa threw a fit because everyone had abandoned his party, and then he said he needed to write. Mariella heard him pound up the stairs, through the master bedroom, and out to the walkway to his studio. She cringed at the thought of him navigating the high walkway in his inebriated state, and said a silent prayer that he wouldn't fall.

She walked out to the yard and watched his dark form struggle with the door to the cottage. He kicked it and tried to punch it in, mumbling something about his missing keys. She watched him stagger back into his room, heard him yell at Pauline and then stagger back to the cottage. He fumbled with the door for a while and nearly fell in when it opened. He slammed it hard.

Mariella walked back into the house, her heart pounding. Isabelle came in. "Go home."

"I'm sure he's passed out," said Mariella. "Let's get this place straight."

Isabelle nodded and returned to the kitchen with a tray of discarded plates and napkins. Mariella righted the bar, moved the chairs back into the dining room, and fluffed the pillows on the couch. She swept the living room and collected the remaining glasses. She stopped when she reached a half-full glass of absinthe. She looked around the room to make sure she was alone and picked up the glass. It smelled like a mixture of flowers and herbs. She looked around again and took a sip. It tasted like black licorice, and was not at all unpleasant. It was refreshing and opened up her chest. She wanted to drain the glass, but thought better of it, and took it to the kitchen to dump down the sink. When she went back into the living room, she saw that a quarter of the bottle remained.

As she went to place it on the shelf, she thought that she could hear crying. Mariella went to the bottom of the stairs and heard Pauline crying in the room upstairs. Pity made her start to climb the stairs, but she stopped halfway up. What could she say? Surely Pauline would want to be left alone. Surely she wouldn't want the help to intervene.

Mariella went back into the living room. The absinthe sat in the middle of the bar, glittering in the light of the chandelier. She watched the sheers blowing gently in the night breeze and heard Pauline's muffled anguish. She walked over to the bottle of absinthe, carried it out to the yard, and poured it over the grass.

Chapter Eleven

Mariella tossed and turned all night, and when morning came, she dressed eagerly for church, where she hoped to apologize to Gavin. She was ashamed of herself for her hesitation the evening before. Seeing Papa and his crowd at what she thought was their worst last night had shaken Papa's hold on her a bit. She wanted to show Gavin that he meant a lot to her.

Her disappointment was acute when Gavin didn't show up. She held out hope until the readings were over, but once the homily started she knew he wouldn't come. She didn't know whether it was because he was upset with her or because he had to get back to work, but either way, it would be a long time before she'd see him again.

When she got home, ten cans of lavender paint waited on the porch. They'd been delivered earlier in the week as part of the government's dole out to spruce up the town in hopes of making Key West a great tourist destination. She put on her work clothes, found some old paintbrushes in her father's toolbox, and started on the front of the house. Lulu and Estelle thought they wanted to help, so she let them paint the low siding they could reach, until they realized that slapping on smelly paint in stifling heat wasn't a great way to spend the afternoon.

She was soon left alone, clearing dust off the siding and sand-ing away rough spots before running the brush, thick with lavender paint, over her house. In spite of the heat and the smell, she found the action of painting therapeutic and was pleased with her progress by sunset. She'd finished the front of the tiny house and thought it would almost look charming to tourists from afar. Good thing they couldn't see inside.

As Mariella hammered the lid onto one of the cans, Eva stepped outside and looked over the work Mariella had completed. Eva walked out to the lawn and looked at it from afar, inhaling her cigarette and letting the smoke drift out of her mouth.

"Do you know this is almost the exact shade of *mi abuela*'s house in Cuba?"

Mariella stood and looked out at Eva. She could see her mother's eyes glistening in the disappearing light. She stepped off the porch and stood next to her, eager for her mother to elaborate on her family and her past.

"*Abuela* was a strong woman," said Eva, almost to herself. "She raised six children without a husband. He died of a heart attack at a very young age."

"What a terrible coincidence," said Mariella, thinking of her father.

Eva looked at her and blinked as if she didn't understand what Mariella meant. Then her face grew dark. "*Sí.*"

"Do you ever wish to go back?" asked Mariella.

Eva looked pained at the question.

"Even if I wanted to, my family would never accept me back. I abandoned them."

"Are they so cold?"

"I made the choice," said Eva. "I need to deal with the consequences."

"You should write to them. They must miss you."

Eva shook her head. "I'm dead to them." She walked back into the house and closed the door. Mariella was surprised how much

Eva had shared with her. Her mother had never opened up so much. In spite of the weight of her words, it lifted Mariella to have a civil conversation with her mother.

Her frustration over Gavin continued, however, and once she finished dinner with the girls she asked her mother whether she'd mind if she went out to visit a friend. Eva looked Mariella over and must have determined she wasn't meeting a man while dressed in her lavender-splattered work clothes. She said she didn't mind.

Mariella got to John's house just as the night fully arrived. The house wasn't as cheerful in the shadows as it was during the day, and only a small light burned from the front room. She worried that John might want to be left alone and thought of leaving before she knocked, but Mutt saw her through the screen. He heaved himself up and thumped his tail on the ground in greeting. John called, "Who's there?"

There was no going back now.

"It's me—Mariella." She heard a rustling sound inside and a grunt. Then he appeared in the doorway in his wheelchair. He looked tired, but Mariella was relieved to see him smiling, clearly happy to see her.

"I'm sorry, but Gavin took the morning ferry back up to Matecumbe," said John. "I'm afraid he won't be back for at least a week."

"I can visit you, too, right?" she asked.

His smile widened, and Mariella warmed. John must not get many visitors. He seemed at a loss for what to say.

"Unless you'd rather I go," said Mariella.

"No, no, I'm glad you're here," he said. "Come on in. I'll grab some beer."

He wheeled over to the kitchen while she opened the door, and he returned with four beers on his lap.

"Let's sit on the porch," he said. "It's a nice night."

Mariella helped John get settled and filled Mutt's water bowl at the hose. When she got back up to the porch, John had a beer opened for her. She thanked him and took a long drink. Mutt nudged her, so she kicked off her shoes and stroked his back with her feet.

"What happened last night?" asked John. "Gavin obviously didn't help at the party, and he was a moody son of a bitch when he got home."

Mariella felt a stab of remorse. She should have gone after him. "I was given a choice and I couldn't make a decision," she said.

"Between Gavin and Hemingway?"

"Yes."

"Ah."

"But I'm employed by Papa, so I obviously had to follow him."

"Obviously," said John. She didn't miss his sarcasm.

"What would you have me do?" she asked as she lit a cigarette. "In case you didn't notice, times are tough right now."

"The thing is," he said, "you know as well as I do, and I'm sure as well as Gavin does, that there was more to that choice than your job."

She looked at his profile in the shadows, inhaled her cigarette, and blew the smoke at him.

"Don't be angry at me for making you face facts," he said. "Give me one of those."

She passed him a cigarette.

"Do you know that I bought these cigarettes with my own money?" she said. "Didn't steal 'em."

John looked at her and smiled. "Is that something to celebrate?"

"Yes," she said. "I've been known to steal things."

"Cigarettes?" he asked.

"Yes."

"Beer?"

"Yes."

"Husbands?"

She punched him in the arm. He raised his hands in surrender.

"Just curious?" he asked.

"No."

"Gonna start?"

She inhaled again and turned away.

"Good thing you're Catholic," he said.

"Good thing," she said.

Mutt sighed heavily and readjusted his position under Mariella's bare feet. She changed the subject.

"Do you get out much?" she asked.

"Sure I do," he said. "I have a place at the dock where I like to sit and paint. I go to Sloppy's sometimes. We have a friend in town who takes us out fishing. Why do you ask?"

"Just making sure."

"Don't worry," he said. "I don't sit here drinking and smoking all day by myself."

He put out another cigarette.

"Back to you," he said. "How much do you need to start your business?"

"By my calculations, at least nine hundred to a thousand to do it right."

John whistled through his teeth.

"I know," she said.

"And what's your experience on the water?"

Mariella told John about her father, their joint dream, and his death. It was easy to talk in the dark, and John didn't say a word. He chain-smoked and listened, shaking his head when she finished.

"You've gotta find that boat," said John.

"I've looked up on Stock Island in a few places, but I haven't had much luck yet. It's hard to get away."

"How about the marinas in town?"

"They don't have space for junk boats."

"Maybe Gavin could check the yards on the way up to Matecumbe sometime."

"I'm afraid he's too angry with me to care."

John laughed. "No. If he didn't care, he wouldn't be angry."

"If he weren't so judgmental, he wouldn't have to be angry."

"If you didn't give him cause to be judgmental, you wouldn't have to worry about that."

Mariella didn't have an answer.

"You know what I see?" said John. "I see you and Gavin running a boat business together. Married. Five or six kids."

"Slow down, there, Sergeant."

"Tourists lined up on the dock, waiting on your sunset cruise—the finest off Key West. The best booze, the best eats, the best views, the prettiest captain."

"Now you're talking," she said.

"Can you see it?" he asked.

The smile left her face. She tried but she couldn't. All she could see was the half-empty tin under her bed. Gavin's face, red with resentment over Hemingway's treatment of him. Her father's boat crashing into the rocks.

A dog barked in the distance, and Mutt raised his head for a moment. Then he slumped back down, too lazy to respond.

It wasn't easy to talk anymore, thought Mariella. Shadows or not.

"I'm gonna get going," she said. "It's getting late and I have to be at work bright and early tomorrow. It's silver-polishing day!"

John rolled his eyes.

"I shouldn't joke," said Mariella. "These rich people with their silver are keeping a roof over my head."

"Amen," said John.

She wheeled him into the house and helped him onto the

couch. He seemed embarrassed by the contact, and Mariella thought how little he must get touched. At home Lulu hung off her neck, Estelle leaned on her, and even her mother hugged her at church during the sign of peace. Hemingway stroked her like a pet. Gavin kissed her and held her hand. John was alone day in and day out, with only a buddy on the weekends. She felt a wave of pity for him but tried to hide it.

"Will you be okay?" she asked.

"Of course," he said. "Christ, you're as bad as Gavin. I manage without you guys all week long."

She kissed his cheek and started to leave, but John called to her to stop.

"You never answered my question," he said.

"What's that?"

"Can you see it?"

He looked as desperate as she felt about her future. He must have wanted something good to happen to someone to prove to him that good existed. She knew he wanted it to work out well for her.

"I can see it," she lied.

⁂

The Hemingway house was unnaturally quiet.

No one was downstairs, the door to the Hemingways' room was closed, and the boys were playing marbles in silence on the lower porch. It was a stark contrast to the noisy, angry days of the previous week, with Papa raging through the house about Scribners, and *Cosmo*, and his editor, Max Perkins, and being undervalued. But today's silence was more unsettling than the yelling of the previous days, so Mariella went to Isabelle.

"What's going on?"

"Sara Murphy had to rush home to New York," said Isabelle,

running the soapy cloth over the breakfast dishes. Mariella stepped in and took the towel from Isabelle to give her scalded hands a break. Isabelle picked up a cloth and switched to drying. "Her son's mighty sick."

"I heard her mention him at the party," said Mariella. "She left early to call home."

"He's bad," said Isabelle.

"Is this the one who's had tuberculosis?" asked Mariella.

"No, the older. He's got the measles or meningitis, or something like it."

Mariella shook her head. She passed a plate to Isabelle and started washing the next dish. The water was almost too hot to stand. She understood why Isabelle's hands looked like tree bark.

"Where's Papa?" asked Mariella.

"Bowels acting up again. Not right since he caught dysentery on that African safari."

Mariella heard Pauline come down the stairs and into the kitchen. Her forehead was tense and her eyes dark.

"Why must everything go wrong at once?" she said to everyone and no one.

"Can I make you some tea, Mrs. Pauline?" asked Isabelle.

"No, thank you," said Pauline. "Mariella, will you shake out the cushions on the patio furniture? I'd like to sit outside and wait for Sara's call. Then go ahead and water the houseplants."

Mariella nodded, rinsed the last plate, and handed it to Isabelle. She wiped her hands on her apron and crossed the living room to the porch.

The palms rustled and Mariella felt a chill rise on her arms. It was cool for the Keys. She untied the cushions and beat them over the lawn, and then arranged them and tied them back down so Pauline could sit by the phone. Pauline had her book in her hands but she didn't open it. She just stared at the boys and their marbles while she chewed her nails.

Mariella went in to get the watering can and returned to soak the plants on the porch. Patrick crawled into Pauline's lap and she stroked his hair. Gregory came over to Mariella and tugged on her uniform.

"Can I do it?" he asked.

"Sure, Gig," said Mariella.

She crouched down and helped the small boy hold the heavy watering can.

"I can do it," he said. "I'm a big boy."

Mariella smiled at him and allowed him to tip the watering can. He sneezed and ended up spilling it all over the patio. Ada stood from the nearby patio chair and slapped Greg on the hand, and he started crying.

"It's okay," said Mariella, feeling bad that she let him spill the water and got Ada in a huff. "I'll get it."

"Just put the marbles away and stop making a mess," said Ada to the child. Greg whimpered a little while he put the marbles in the bag.

The phone rang.

Pauline lifted Patrick off her lap and gave Ada a look that sent her indoors with both boys. Mariella followed with the watering can and to get a towel, but was back in time to listen to Pauline's conversation.

"Sara," she said. It was quiet for a moment before Pauline began crying. "Oh, no, I'm so sorry. Oh, God, I'm so sorry."

Papa came outside looking pale, rubbing his hand across Mariella's shoulders as he stepped onto the porch. He ran his hands through his hair and sat on a nearby chair. When Pauline got off the phone, she went over to him and climbed into his lap. He rubbed her hair and stared over her shoulder, his tired eyes meeting Mariella's. She looked at him a moment, then turned and left him and Pauline alone, touched by his care of her.

When she got back to the kitchen, she emptied what was left

in the watering can into the herbs in the windowsill and placed it under the sink. Her chest felt heavy at the thought of the Murphys' loss, though she barely knew them. All loss fed into the ache still left from Hal's death, and she felt tears burning in her eyes. She looked up at the ceiling, willing them away. She had no use for tears.

As she took off her apron and hung it in the closet, Mariella felt as if there were signs all around her that losing what you loved was worse than never having it to begin with.

Chapter Twelve

Lower Matecumbe Key

Gavin turned the boy's face and pointed at the shadowed shallow waters on the starboard side of the rowboat. The boy gasped when he saw the lobster slip under a nearby rock in the water, the moonlight reflecting off its shell.

"Can I try?" asked Teddy Morrow, the six-year-old son of a vet who'd moved his family down to the Keys. His dad was home helping his mom with the new baby, so Gavin had offered to take Teddy out to catch Florida lobsters in the night.

"Sure, Ted," said Gavin. "Do you want to hold the net or the spear?"

"Spear," said Teddy.

"That's fine," said Gavin, "but make sure you don't kill it. We want to steam that thing alive. Just coax it out from under the rock and guide it into the net."

Teddy nodded and stood. The boat rocked with the boy's sudden movement, so he waited until she settled before putting the spear in the water.

Gavin enjoyed these fishing excursions at the north end of the key, where the mosquitoes weren't as bad, and the sweet coolness of the night almost made you forget about the day. He found himself thinking of Mariella and how he'd like to bring her fishing at night here sometime. He had replayed their kiss on the beach in his head a thousand times, and hated how they'd parted ways the night of the Hemingway party.

"Now?" asked Teddy.

"Whenever you're ready."

The boy nodded, and Gavin lowered the net to the seafloor. Teddy slipped the spear into the water and slowly slid it under the rock.

"I can feel him," said Teddy. "He doesn't want to come out."

"Of course he doesn't," said Gavin. "He knows we're gonna eat him."

Teddy pulled a bit and the legs of the lobster poked out from under the rock, then its head. Gavin waited with the net until its body was mostly out.

"Okay, give him a hard nudge," said Gavin.

Teddy pulled at the lobster with one final motion, and as it scurried out from under the rock, Gavin scooped it up and pulled it out of the water. It twisted and squirmed in the net.

"We got it!" said Teddy.

"I'll be damned," said Gavin. "You're a natural. This guy must weigh ten pounds."

He could see the boy beaming in the moonlight.

Gavin shook the lobster out of the net and into the pot of water where the other lobster they'd caught waited for its death.

"Come on," said Gavin. "These things are huge. Let's get back so we can steam them up for your family before bedtime."

⁓⌒

When Gavin opened the door, Teddy's father, Henry, was dozing on the couch with the baby sleeping on his chest. His eyes snapped open when they walked in.

"Catch any good ones?" he whispered.

"Yeah, Pop," said Teddy. "A ten-pounder!"

"I'm proud of you. You're like the man of the house, providing food for us."

Teddy smiled, and Henry reached out to ruffle the boy's hair as his mom, Lorraine, walked out from the bedroom, yawning. Her brown hair was tousled, and she had stains on the front of her dress, but Gavin thought she'd be pretty if she didn't have to live in squalor.

"What time is it?" she asked, rubbing the sleep out of her eyes.

"It's about eight o'clock," said Henry.

"I'm sorry we woke you," said Gavin.

"Oh, no, don't worry. I have to feed Janie soon, anyway," said Lorraine.

Gavin carried the plate over to the table and pulled off a towel to reveal two perfectly steamed lobsters, cracked open and ready to eat. Lorraine gasped.

"Those are beautiful," she said.

"Teddy caught 'em," said Henry.

Lorraine gave Teddy a squeeze and turned to Gavin.

"Thank you so much for taking Teddy out," she said. "I've been so busy with Janie, poor Teddy hasn't gotten a lot of attention. Will you stay and eat with us?"

Gavin considered the question. He enjoyed being around the Morrows. They were a nice family and a welcome change from the others in his camp, and he would have loved to stay. But he also knew that Lorraine would need privacy to feed Janie, it was almost bedtime for the boy, and they could use the nutrition without having to share it.

"No, thank you, ma'am," said Gavin. "I'm just the delivery boy. I told Bonefish I'd meet him at the canteen for a drink."

"Well, thanks again," said Lorraine.

Gavin nodded at Lorraine and Henry, and saluted Teddy. Teddy returned the salute.

"Next week?" asked Gavin. "Same time, same coast?"

"Yes, sir," said Teddy.

Gavin turned and left, careful not to slam the door and wake the baby.

Gavin surveyed the completed lines of wood cabins, the sports fields, and the tidy landscaping through the morning rain. After numerous complaints about the living conditions and poor vet behavior, FERA had sent in an engineer to reorganize the camps. Gavin believed that treating the vets more like human beings and giving them decent food and shelter would elicit better behavior and morale. He hoped he was right.

He didn't know whether anything was going to help Fred, however.

It seemed the man retreated more and more into himself these days. His eyes were shadowed, and his hands shook worse than ever. He lashed out at the others or ignored them. He was easily confused and didn't complete assigned tasks. Gavin had been trying to cover for him, but didn't know whether it would work much longer.

Gavin walked to Fred's cabin and gave the door a hard knock. Fred had never shown up to work that morning, and Gavin wanted to fetch him before Sheeran noticed.

He thought of the night before, after fishing, when he had sat smoking by the water and saw Fred walk out into the gulf and start swimming. He thought the man must be crazy to swim in shark- and barracuda-infested water at night, but had no mind to get nibbled himself, so he just watched and prayed he wouldn't have to go on any lifesaving missions.

In truth, Gavin was starting to resent Fred for his detachment and lack of gratitude. Gavin didn't want a handwritten thank-you, but at least Fred could acknowledge his efforts at keeping him afloat on the job.

Gavin knew he was just brooding because of what had happened with Mariella the last time he saw her, and it was making his mood sour. He wiped the rain off his face and knocked again, harder this time, and Fred pulled the door open. He reeked of stale beer and cigarettes and his eyes were bloodshot. His hair was a mess, and his trousers hung loose on his emaciated frame. Gavin tried to ignore his irritation at the man and attempted humor.

"Morning," said Gavin. "Would you like some coffee and the paper with your wake-up call?"

Fred muttered something, said he'd be along in a minute, and disappeared into the dark cabin. Gavin waited on the porch while Fred readied himself and then started walking with him to the work site.

"I can't keep covering for you," said Gavin. "I think you're a good guy and I know you still have war demons, but it's about the bottom line to them."

Fred looked ahead and didn't respond.

"We're getting enough shit from up north about being a bunch of lazy good-for-nothings. We shouldn't do anything to reinforce that image."

Fred coughed and kept walking without speaking.

"Hey, man," said Gavin. "You can start by responding to me."

"You don't need to make me your project," said Fred.

Gavin felt anger rise inside him. He'd been breaking his neck covering for Fred, clearing the guy's mangroves, giving him personal wake-up calls, and he had the nerve to give him some flip response.

"Why don't you try that again," said Gavin, putting his hand on Fred's arm and stopping him. "How about a thank-you for covering for your ass all the time? How about a little gratitude for fighting off the guys who pick on you?"

"Gee, thanks, Murray," said Fred. "I don't know what I'd do without you."

Gavin clenched his jaw. He'd never wanted someone in a boxing ring so bad. He'd have loved to lay Fred out for his bad attitude and sarcasm. He fought the urge to cuss the guy out, shook his head, and left Fred standing by the side of the road.

CHAPTER THIRTEEN

Key West

A letter arrived for Mariella that got her pulse racing and helped thaw the chill that had crept over her. It was from Gavin, and it was full of apologies for his awkward departure, fond memories of their time together, and wishes to see her again. He wrote that he had to spend most of March up on Matecumbe. His supervisors were laying into them about finishing their segment of road before hurricane season, and Gavin, who was in charge of his unit, had to oversee the workers. In addition to dealing with the troubles of laying road in sweltering, bug-infested heat over miles of water, he also had to deal with depressed vets, drunks, and fights among the idle, tired, and shell-shocked men. He told her that the thought of seeing her again kept him going.

She smiled and slipped the letter that had grown soft with handling into her pocket, mentally planning her response and eager to get off work so she could write it. There were many hours left, however, and the mood in the house kept her subdued in spite of Gavin's letter.

Papa had lately been intolerable—stuck in bed with his recurring throat infection, grumpy about his writing, and insistent that everyone wait on him hand and foot. He was nasty and demanding with Pauline, John and Katy, and the boys, and lost his playfulness with Mariella. As much as she wanted to hate him, though, Mariella still couldn't help but feel drawn to her brooding patient.

One afternoon when John and Katy were away and Pauline was at Lorine Thompson's house, Papa called Mariella to his room. He was sitting in his bed in the same disheveled state he'd been in for days. His dark hair was greasy, he needed a shave, and he had papers strewn about the blankets. An empty teacup sat on a tray at the foot of the bed, next to a partially drained glass of whiskey. The Spanish gate that Pauline had shipped to the house as a headboard for the bed gave the whole scene the appearance of a sloppy throne. The grumpy king nestled amid its pillows caused Mariella to stifle a laugh as she walked into the room.

"Daughter, read this out loud to me. My throat is killing me, and I have to hear it out loud to see if it makes sense."

Mariella sat on the bed. He smelled of whiskey and like he needed a bath. He wore his glasses, which made him look vulnerable and erudite at the same time. His eyebrows were knotted and his mouth was turned into a frown.

Mariella smiled. "You're pouting and feeling sorry for yourself."

His scowl deepened. "How would you like to have a throat infection, and the shits, and a bunch of elitist asshole critics tearing you apart every day?"

"Poor Papa," she said as she took the papers from him.

"Don't you feel sorry for me?"

Mariella covered her smile with the papers and nodded her head heavily. "Yes, you are pitiful."

He finally broke into a smile. "I'm a real pain in the ass, aren't I?"

"It would be improper for the help to criticize the boss."

She turned her attention to the manuscript and began reading about the African country, the storks, and the old man who was their guide.

"What's this called?" asked Mariella.

"I think I'll call it *Green Hills of Africa*, but I haven't settled yet."

"That has a nice ring to it."

"Thanks," he said. "Now skip ahead. There's some haggling over money; we passed out pay, but the old African who'd been hunting with us and guiding us couldn't let go," said Papa.

Mariella scanned the page and started reading again. She got lost in the words that took her to the African night, where a native begged the hunting party to take him with them, even chasing their car, calling and pleading after them. It filled Mariella with great sadness to imagine the old African man chasing them down the road.

"Good," said Papa. "You're upset. It was a good image."

"Is there more about him?"

"Not after that point."

Mariella wondered whether Papa cared about the old man at all, or just the impression he left. She wondered whether the people surrounding him were worth more to him than just characters in his stories.

"Why are *you* pouting now?" he asked.

Mariella shook her head. "Do you ever think about the old man?"

"I think about him always. He's a major figure in the book."

"But is he more than that to you?"

"What could be more than that? To be immortalized on the page? He left a major impression on me."

"But is he useful to you beyond the part he plays in your story?"

"Yes. He haunts me. But that's life. You can't take them all with you."

Mariella didn't know whether she believed him, and she wanted to be done with him for the time being. She stood from the bed and Gavin's latest letter slipped from her pocket. Papa's hand shot out, and he opened it up and started reading.

"Give that back to me," she said. She didn't want to appear frantic, so she stood there with her hands in fists, willing herself not to reach for the letter. Papa read over it, first with curiosity, then with contempt.

"I'll read aloud to you," he said with a cruel edge to his voice. He began without her answer: "'Dearest M. The only thing that gets me through the night here in these miserable, mosquito-filled shacks is the thought of you.'

"Oh, God," said Papa. "This is terrible." Mariella's face burned as he continued.

"'I dream of a time when we can spend days on end together, without interruption.'"

Mariella put out her hand. "Give me the letter," she said.

"Wait, it's getting good. 'It felt so right with you in John's house. It would have been even more perfect if it could just be us two.'"

Mariella grabbed the letter. A piece of it tore off in Papa's hand. She grabbed that, too. He laughed, mocking her.

"Do you get off on those cheap, clichéd proclamations of love?" he sneered. "Is that what excites you?"

Mariella threw his manuscript papers over her shoulder, and they dropped to the floor in a mess.

"Those weren't numbered yet!" he yelled.

"Go to hell," she said, and walked out of the room.

He spent the next day holed up in his writing cottage, and Mariella was glad not to have to see him. She brooded about his nerve while she shook out the laundry and carried the basket up to the master bedroom. She placed it on the bed and began folding clothes when Pauline called her from the bathroom in a tremulous voice, utterly different from her usual haughty tone. Mariella walked to the door of the bathroom and stopped short. Light from the open window illuminated an empty bottle of peroxide and Pauline's newly gilded hair. Mariella couldn't hide her horror.

"It will look better once it's dried, won't it?" asked Pauline.

Mariella was speechless.

Pauline's hair was gold. Her once-beautiful dark hair was a dried, brassy crown. It was worse than the hair on the working girls in Bahama Village. Worse because it had to have been inspired by Jane's hair. Worse because it was for him.

Mariella stepped forward and took the towel from Pauline's hands, which were dry from the peroxide. Pauline sat in the stool and looked in the mirror. Mariella stood behind Pauline, working the towel gently through her ruined hair. She wrung the wetness from it over and over, squeezing sections of it with the towel, wishing she could absorb the gold and restore the warm, brown, silky hair that had preceded it. Once Pauline's hair was almost dry, Mariella picked up a wide-toothed comb from the vanity and began combing it in small sections and pinning it in curls around Pauline's face. She was careful not to pull too hard.

Pauline closed her eyes, and tears leaked out of them, but she didn't make a sound. It mortified Mariella, and she didn't know what to say. She put all her energy into gentle, tender brushing and pinning. When she finished, Mariella picked up the towel and handed it to Pauline to wipe her tears.

"Am I like Jane?" Pauline asked.

Mariella couldn't lie. "Better," she said.

Pauline's mouth formed a smile, but her eyes were still sad. Pauline pulled herself out of the seat and looked out the window at the lighthouse.

"I have to try," she said.

Mariella didn't have an answer. She felt a wave of pity, and thought she might hate Hemingway.

Mariella had wrestled the floor polishing from Isabelle that afternoon to save the fifty-year-old woman's knees, but now regretted it. She made big circles over the floor and shined it until she could see her reflection. Her knees cracked when she stood, and she massaged her lower back.

After finishing the floor, Mariella went up to the writer's cottage. She'd saved the cottage for last, since she knew Papa worked only early in the morning. She didn't want to run into him, because she was still fuming mad at the way he'd treated her and the way he treated Pauline.

Mariella walked into the cottage and closed the door. She placed her broom against the wall and headed over to the bookshelf to start wiping it. As she passed the writing table she stopped short. There was a half-empty glass of bourbon next to his typewriter. He never left a glass of booze unfinished.

He was here.

She felt the hair on the back of her neck rise and turned to leave, running right into him as he stepped out of the bathroom.

He held her by the shoulders. She turned her face toward his. His forehead was wrinkled with worry, his eyes were sad, and he shook his head. The bourbon smelled good on his mouth.

"I'm a shit," he said.

"You really are," she said.

"I deserve everything you give me. Call me every name in the book."

She was aware of how close they stood, and of the heat between them. That damned persistent desire she felt for him was there, but attached to it were fear and revulsion. She'd never been so confused.

"I'm jealous; that's all," he said.

The fear and revulsion dissolved, leaving only the burn and the guilt from them.

"Why?" she asked.

He tilted his head to the side and gave her a look that said, *You know,* and she was rent in two. After she felt a bond with Pauline. After her resolution to focus on Gavin. Her mother's words came back to her: *Desire wins.*

He was waiting for her, but she knew that if she started, they wouldn't stop. She felt dirty and ashamed, but couldn't tear herself away. She hated her indecision and was angry at him for taking it so close to the line. She needed to leave.

"I don't belong to you," she said.

Suddenly she heard someone on the walkway and pulled herself out of Papa's grip. As Mariella stepped away, Pauline walked in. Mariella busied herself at the bookcase so Pauline wouldn't see her face.

"Pfeiff, you're a vision," he said. Mariella was amazed at his smooth reaction and turned to the side to watch them out of the corner of her eye. He lifted Pauline and swung her around before placing her on her feet. She looked at Mariella, and the smile on Pauline's face pained her and made her feel even worse. Pauline believed him.

"Isn't it grand," said Pauline. "Mariella helped me set it."

"I love it," he said.

Mariella thought she'd better say something. She found her voice and filled it with an enthusiasm she didn't feel. "You look like a model, Mrs. Hemingway."

Pauline beamed.

"I feel absolutely youthful," she said. "And just in time for summer and vacations and Bimini."

Mariella's heart pounded at the mention of the island. She'd known they were planning on spending much of the summer in the Bahamas and was terrified of being left behind, not only because she worried about her job, but because it would mean separation from him. Of course, going meant separation from Gavin, and that felt bad, too. After what had just happened, though, separation from Papa would clearly be a good thing.

"It's good you're here, Mari," said Pauline. "We'd like you to join us in Bimini if your family can spare you. We'll still need help with housekeeping, food, and organization."

Mariella couldn't believe it. She couldn't believe Pauline wasn't suspicious of her and Papa. All it took for Pauline to glow was attention from him. It blinded her to everything else.

"I'll have to talk to my mother," said Mariella.

"Please do," said Pauline. "I don't know how we got along without you."

Mariella thought she'd burst if she stayed in the cottage a minute longer. When Pauline had her back to Mariella, she shot Papa a look of severe reprimand and excused herself back to the house. At least he had the decency to look ashamed.

She was a bundle of nerves all evening, eager to get off work and away from that house, and miserable at the thought of telling Eva about Bimini. When it was time to go home she thought of stealing some of Pauline's letter paper to write to Gavin, but thought she'd taken too much from the woman already and asked her for the paper. To her surprise, Pauline agreed with a smile, still high from Papa's attention. At least Mariella didn't have to add personal property theft to her growing list of misdeeds.

Eva was in a dark mood when Mariella got home. She seemed catatonic again, and Mariella wondered whether her mother's grief was a cloak she'd wear forever. She hated the nights Eva couldn't cope, because they reminded her of her own pain and cast a shadow over the house.

She sat up that night long after the girls were in bed, working on her letter to Gavin. She used one whole piece of paper, front and back, for all the starts and stops she knew she'd need, and then copied what she finally wanted to say on a fresh piece. She hoped he couldn't read her turmoil between the lines. She hoped he'd just see her feelings for him and not all the darkness that lingered from the grief and hopelessness and now lust for Hemingway that she felt pursuing her and threatening to overtake her, especially in the night.

Chapter Fourteen

Mariella walked in from the yard she'd just mowed and went to the kitchen for a glass of water. She drank in long, thirsty gulps, then put her fingers in the glass and flicked the cool water on her face and neck. She walked over to the door into the living room and watched John paint and wondered what it would be like living alone, accountable to no one and perfectly free. She envied his solitude.

The red paint sliced through the browns and yellows of the dead grass on the canvas. The brush was drying, so it left rough edges on the sides of the line. It was effective for showing how the blood would have looked on the ground.

"You're a morbid son of a bitch," said Mariella as she walked over to where John sat painting in watercolors the scene from Argonne that still haunted him, when he left his legs in another country.

"I do *dwell*, don't I?" said John.

"With good reason, I suppose."

John put the painting on the floor beside the couch. A sketch of the lighthouse on Whitehead was behind it on the easel. John dipped the red-tipped brush into an old soup can, and the color was absorbed by the murky water.

"I'll replace that for you," said Mariella. She picked up the water and walked it to the kitchen, where she dumped it down the sink and rinsed it out. The color stained her fingers and slipped down the drain as she ran her hand along the lip of the cup under the water. Her eyes scanned the counter and she saw a line of dirty plates like orderly soldiers waiting to be washed. Behind the plates was a broken coffee cup. She saw where it used to hang with three other cups in a row under the cabinet. It was the third one missing. She pictured John reaching for it, knocking it down, and it shattering along the counter.

Mariella filled the can with cold, fresh water and returned to John. She set it down on the table next to a half-empty bottle of whiskey with a half-full tumbler and an ashtray full of butts next to it. Her romanticized notions of being alone didn't include scenes of maimed veterans smoking and drinking without company. She shook the image from her mind.

"Did you forget Gavin's not here this weekend?" he said.

"I know he's not here," she said. "Why do you think I only want to come here when Gavin's around? I can visit you, too, can't I?"

"You can do anything you'd like with me. Just so we're clear." Mariella laughed.

"Actually, you'll have to get over me," he said. "I've never seen Gavin so crazy over a girl."

This was good for Mariella to hear. She was trying to focus on Gavin to stop thinking of the other one. But underlying that thought was how much easier life would be if she stayed solitary. If you didn't put all of yourself into loving someone else, you could never get hurt by them. Her mother, Pauline— both depended on their husbands too much. One was left a widow, and the other's future marital happiness wasn't looking good.

"Is this worth getting into?" she suddenly asked. "With Gavin?"

Mariella didn't like the look John gave her in reply. It looked like pity.

"Of course," he said. "What—you think being alone is better?"

"I don't know," she said. "I just see you in your house, painted the way you want, full of your hobbies, with the beer you like in the fridge. You've got no one to answer to, no one to check with, no one to judge you, no one to take care of."

"No one to touch me, share dinner with me, no one for me to play my guitar for—you fail to mention the rest and, I'd argue, the most important."

"I don't know. Maybe the pain of losing is worse than not having it to begin with."

"Really?" he said. "So you wish you never knew your father?"

She had no response.

"I didn't think so," he said.

She thought of the way Gavin made her feel the first night at Sloppy Joe's when he made her dance. She thought of the day he took her and the girls to the beach, and when they hung out at John's house. It was undeniable that it felt good and that she wanted to feel that way again.

John dabbed the wet brush on a rag and dipped it into a smudge of black paint. He turned away from her and began filling in the top of the lighthouse.

"I never had anyone to dote on me," he said. "My parents were cold and distant before, and now don't know what to make of half a son. My girl sent me a 'Dear John' letter the week before I got blown up. I know *alone*, Mari, and believe me, it's not better."

He dipped the brush into the water again and dabbed it on the cloth. He mixed some blue and white and began work on the sky in the background. They were quiet for a while; then Mariella spoke.

"I'm sorry about your parents and the girl."

"Me, too," he said. "We were engaged."

"Where is she now?"

"Married to my best friend from high school. He couldn't

fight in the war on account of his poor eyesight. They have two kids."

"If it makes you feel any better," said Mariella, "I'll bash her face with a bat if I ever meet her."

John laughed and shook his head.

"Gee, thanks, Mari. I'm glad you're on my side."

Mariella stood to go.

"Hey, let's just talk about the weather the next time you stop by," said John. "You know, small talk. I don't know how it always gets to this stuff."

"Deal," said Mariella.

"Thanks for cutting my grass," he said.

"Anytime."

On her way to the door, she saw Gavin's tool belt hanging off the couch and felt a sudden longing to see him.

"Hey, how do you think Gavin would take it if I showed up on Matecumbe?"

"I think that's like asking how a beached marlin would like a drink of seawater," said John. "If you go up to Matecumbe tomorrow, there's a pickup baseball game. Gavin plays when he stays up there. You should go watch him."

"Watch?"

Mariella stepped outside, enjoying the sound of John's laugh behind her.

Lower Matecumbe Key

Mariella tilted her head so the brim of her baseball cap shielded her eyes from the glare of the sun. She wore her dad's old cutoff fishing pants and shirt—the same outfit she'd worn the night she met Gavin at the boxing match.

"I wonder if he'll recognize you," said Bonefish, a tall, lanky vet with a slow Southern drawl. John had set her up with Bonefish by telegram to meet her at the ferry and drive her to the game so she could surprise Gavin.

"I hope not at first," she said. "I want to watch him when he doesn't know I'm here."

Bonefish smiled at her. "You're kinda hard to miss," he said. "In spite of the getup you got on, there."

She smiled back and then looked out the window.

"It's nice to see a lady around here," he said. "Even if you are dressed up like a guy. The kind of females usually hangin' around here are . . ." His voice trailed off and he looked embarrassed.

"Gotcha," she said.

As the pickup bumped along, Mariella stared out the window. The flimsy shacks and crude wooden buildings provided a stark contrast to the beautiful tropical scenery. The water stretched for miles in every direction, and mangroves and palms dotted the sand.

She glanced back at Bonefish, and noticed that he wore a wedding band.

"Your wife down here with you?" she asked, nodding at his finger.

"Naw," he said. "My wife and two boys live up in Macon with her parents. I'm tryin' to make some money to get us back on our feet. I miss 'em bad. I've actually got a job up there startin' in October. It's in maintenance at the school where my boys'll go. It's a new school and they're a little behind schedule. They were supposed to open in August, but you know how that goes."

"That's great," she said. "You're lucky to be getting out of here."

"Don't I know it?"

When they arrived at the ball field, Mariella got butterflies in her stomach. She stepped out of the car and immediately spotted Gavin. He was talking to a man who looked like the umpire; then he went back to the dugout and told his team something. She could tell he was in charge by the way the men responded to him.

It took all she had in her not to run toward him, but she wanted to prolong her anonymity. Bonefish walked her over to the other team's dugout and told the captain he had a walk-on. She walked over to the end of the bench and sat in the shadows so no one would be able to tell that she was a girl.

Her team was first at bat, but since she was last, her turn didn't come up. Bonefish sat between her and the guys so she wouldn't be found out, though judging by the state most of them were in, Mariella didn't think they'd notice her either way. They were a rowdy, drunken, foulmouthed group, and were getting rowdier by the minute. Bonefish apologized to her after one of the men made a particularly disgusting comment about the whores on the floating brothels that serviced the men, but she assured him she'd heard as bad at the docks in town. He seemed to relax after that.

Gavin seemed a different breed from the crude men around them. It reminded her of the conversation in *A Farewell to Arms* between Frederic Henry and the priest about the difference between men who were meant to lead as officers and men who were meant to follow and fight. Gavin was certainly cut from the former, but seemed compelled to the latter.

Suddenly they were switching sides.

Mariella ran close to Gavin on the way out, but he didn't notice her. It gave her a thrill to be so close to him without his knowing it. He was first at bat, and she was on second base.

His first hit was a foul, but the second flew high over her head. Bonefish was behind Mariella in the outfield. It went over his head, too, so he had to chase it. When he got the ball, he threw it to Mariella. It landed square in her glove, stinging her hand with its force. She turned just in time to tag Gavin out as he slid into second base.

As she tagged him, she was thrilled to see how his face lit up when he recognized her. He jumped up, took her in his arms, and kissed her. All the cheering and yelling on the field got deadly quiet until Gavin pulled off her hat, and her long black hair spilled down her back. A roar of catcalls and applause began, and he led her off the field. He waved to his team to show them that he was leaving. Then she jumped on his back and he carried her over to his truck.

On the ride through camp to the beach near Gavin's place, he kept staring at her with a look of complete shock and pleasure.

"You have to watch the road a little, too," she said with a smile.

"I don't want to take my eyes off you," he said.

When they stopped, he came around to her door and opened it for her. He led her around a clump of mangroves to a shack built of plywood. It sat on the sand next to three other shacks and wasn't much bigger than a large outhouse. He could see her shock at his modest living arrangements.

"I know," he said. "It's not much, but it has a great view."

She looked out at the water stretching for miles in each direction and agreed.

"Come on," he said. He held her hand and led her along the beach to a mess hall. In its back room was a gym. It had several punching bags, some weights, and a crude ring. It was dark and hot in the room, and thus empty.

"I practice at night," he said. "That keeps me away from the bugs outside, and it isn't so hot. It's like an oven in here in the daytime."

They stood and stared at each other for a moment. He felt his heart pounding and still couldn't believe she'd come up here to him. She looked a little nervous and out of her element. He pulled her into him.

"So we'll be left alone in here," he said.

He leaned in and kissed her as though he'd missed her. She sank into him and wrapped her arms around his neck. Voices in the mess hall caused her to jump back. He laughed and walked her over to the ring. They sat down on the edge.

"You seem a little shy today," he said. "Not at all in character for you."

"I'm just thinking through some things I talked about with John."

"Oh, great," said Gavin. "Do I have him to contend with, too?"

"No," she said. "We talked about you."

"Good, keep it that way."

He followed her gaze to the hanging bags and boxing gloves.

"I wish I'd sneaked up on you boxing," she said. "I like to watch you do that."

"We can arrange that another time," he said.

He pulled her onto his lap and kissed her neck. She closed her eyes and put her head back.

"It's nice with just the two of us," he said into her collarbone.

"No distractions," she said. "We should do this more often."

"Yeah, but you have to watch yourself around here. There're a lot of men. A lot of fights. A lot of drunkenness."

"That's not so different from Key West."

"But here it's men without women," he said, "and it's early in the day. It gets much worse at night."

"I can take care of myself," she said.

He smiled. He leaned in to kiss her again, but they were interrupted by Bonefish.

"I'm sorry," he said. "You've got a telegram, Gavin. It's your mom."

Gavin looked at Mariella, gently moved her off his lap, and hurried out of the mess hall and over to the post office with her following.

When they got there he ran his hands through his hair as he read the telegram, and started pacing around the room.

"What is it?" she asked.

"My uncle says I need to come quick," said Gavin. "She's not well."

"I'm so sorry."

"No, I'm sorry," he said. "After all you did to come here."

"Don't apologize," she said. "It was perfect. Go to your mother."

Gavin walked over to Mariella, took her face in his hands, and pressed his forehead to hers.

"Thank you for coming here," he said. He kissed her, but she quickly pulled away.

"Go," she said, surprised to find a lump in her throat. "Go," she said a little louder. She turned him around and smacked him on the behind. He smiled over his shoulder, rushed back at her with a kiss, and then left.

When Mariella returned to Key West, she saw her father's friend Mark Bishop out unusually late, arguing with Nicolas. When they saw her coming toward them, Mark grabbed his fish cart and dragged it toward his boat. Nicolas shook his head sadly.

"*¿Qué está mal?*" asked Mariella.

"He's trying to sell me fish I don't need. I'm overflowing. I know he needs the money, but I do, too."

"Did he just get in from the gulf?"

"*Sí.*"

"This late?"

"*Sí.* Second time out today. Very sad. Too many fishermen, not enough market for them."

Mariella watched Mark stop at the end of the pier and begin hurling the fish back into the water.

"I can't watch," said Nicolas.

"Go," said Mariella. "I'll talk to him."

Nicolas shook his head again and turned back to his restaurant.

Mariella walked out to Mark. When he turned back to grab a handful of fish, she took his hands.

"Stop," she said. "Let me help you find another restaurant."

Mark's chest was heaving. He looked much older than his forty years. She thought she saw tears in his eyes and understood his pain.

"I've been to every one," he said. "Same story."

"They're on ice. Why don't we ferry them up the Keys and see if you have any luck?"

"It doesn't matter, Mari. It's no use."

"Can I buy some off you? I have to feed my girls tonight."

He shook his head. "You've got mouths to feed and you're offering to give me money," he said. "No, but thank you. You take what you need. I'll take this as a sign."

"What do you mean?"

He looked down at the fish and shook his head again, as if struggling to put into words what he was trying to say.

"I'm leaving."

"What? For where?"

"Going north. I hear there are jobs in Baltimore, Philly, New York. I gotta do something, 'cause this isn't working."

"But this is what you love," said Mariella. "You've been here most of your life. It's going to get better. If tourism picks up, the restaurants will need a bigger supply—"

He cut her off. "I've been going off of that since well before Hal died. It's not getting better. I've got to get out of here."

Mariella's mind raced. She couldn't stand the thought of Mark giving up. He had that same terrible expression her father had had before he died. She couldn't bear to look at him, and she didn't know what to say. Maybe he was right. Maybe it would never get better. He must have seen the panic in her face, because he smiled sadly and reached for her hand.

"I'm sorry you had to see me having a fit," he said. "Don't worry about me. I just have myself to take care of. I'll be all right."

He gave her the fish but refused to take her money. She started for home feeling as low as she had in a long time. She turned back to glance at Mark once more. He stood with his shoulders slumped, facing the water, a dark form against the shimmering surface.

Mariella felt exposed and raw.

She sat on a blanket at the edge of the water on the beach where Gavin had asked her to meet him, having arrived early to be with the water and herself. She held his telegram telling of his mother's death. It had stirred up all of her feelings about her father, and she was trying hard not to cry so that she could be strong for him. It wasn't working, so she just wiped her eyes and hoped it was dark enough by the time he arrived that he wouldn't see.

Just before the sun sank into the sea, Mariella saw him walking toward her on the beach. He was covered in shadows, but she knew it was him. She stood and tried to walk to meet him, but her feet started running, and then he was running, and then they met and held on to each other for a long time.

When they let go, Mariella cupped his face in her hands. Even in the evening's shadows she could see the darkness under his eyes. She kissed him on each cheek and then found his mouth. He held her for a while, and then they walked over to the blanket to sit.

"When did it happen?" asked Mariella.

"A few nights ago, I was sitting up with her at the hospital because she couldn't sleep. She wanted me to read to her, and all I could find in the waiting room was *A Farewell to Arms*." He laughed with contempt. "I was so tired I started slurring words. She told me to stop and said she'd see me in the morning. I kissed her, went to my uncle's, fell asleep, and the next morning when I got back, she was gone."

"I'm so sorry," said Mariella.

"I know it's for the best. She was getting frantic as she grew weaker. She hated relying on my uncle and his wife for everything and didn't want to burden me. I just wish I would have moved in with her sooner so I could have cared more for her. I wish she could have met you."

It made Mariella feel good to hear him say that, and she felt the same about him with her father.

"I also found out my uncle's partner has no intention of leaving the business," continued Gavin. "I've been saving up for nothing."

"I'm so sorry," she said.

He was quiet for a moment and then spoke. "You know what? I'm not."

She looked at him with a question in her eyes. But it dawned on her as soon as he said it.

"My ties to the mainland are cut," he said.

"So I get to keep you?"

"Yes. At least on the weekends I don't have to work."

She leaned in closer to him and wrapped her arms around his waist. He kissed her forehead and looked back out toward the water.

Mariella wiped her eyes again. Her father, his parents, his friend from the war—they couldn't escape the loss. It seemed that always, after the joyful times, the pain was there waiting to reassert itself. It exhausted her, but still she held on to him.

CHAPTER FIFTEEN

The air of the Hemingway house quivered with unspent energy and expectation. The building excitement over the summer trip to Bimini island in the Bahamas was a welcome change. Visitors came and went even more than usual. Patrick and Gregory were restless and made trouble. Pauline was impatient with them and the staff, but glad that Papa was singing songs again, instead of being a miserable patient, barking orders from his bed. He was euphoric at the thought of a summer in a remote paradise with friends and fish.

Mariella couldn't fully embrace the joy in the household. She still hadn't told her mother she was leaving, and avoided her as much as possible. The Hemingways acted under the assumption that she was going, and she didn't do anything to dissuade them.

Pauline had asked Mariella to come over on Sunday after church to wash Papa's clothes and help her pack him up for the trip. He'd be taking the *Pilar* on fishing trips to Bimini and back with the Dos Passoses and his friend Mike Strater until June, when they'd all set up camp there and vacation for the summer months. Reports of spectacular tuna fishing and mounting frustration over aggressive tourists in Key West made Papa anxious to leave.

When Mariella arrived, she found that Pauline and the boys

were going to the later mass to leave her to the chores. This
pleased her, because the children would have gotten in the way.
Also, in spite of the moment she'd shared with Pauline over her
hair, her employer had returned to her haughty, condescending
ways and seemed embarrassed that she'd allowed herself to show
her vulnerability.

. Mariella rolled her eyes at the boys as they ran all over the
house pretending to shoot each other. They climbed over the dining room table, hammered up and down the stairs, were slapped
and punished by Ada, and had started the game over again by the
time Pauline was able to round them all up and drag them out the
door.

In all the madness, Papa was hooting and laughing with John
and Katy in the living room, oblivious to the chaos going on
around him. Pauline left in a huff without saying good-bye to the
guests—clearly angry that Papa wasn't going with her. She nearly
ran into a tall, handsome man on her way out the door.

"Hey, Pauline!" He turned back and stepped into the doorway.
"Anybody home?" he called. Papa ran into the hallway and grabbed
the man in a full embrace. Mariella was walking down the stairs
carrying a basket to fetch the laundry that had been hanging outside, and slipped on a toy gun that was lying on the third step. She
dropped the basket and caught herself before she landed on the
floor.

"Whoa! Easy there!" said Papa as he stepped over to help.
Mariella felt her face burn with embarrassment as Papa introduced her to the strapping man who had just walked in the door.

"Mariella, this is my best friend from Paris, Mike. He's a hell
of a boxer. He might even be able to beat your boxer."

Mariella glared at Hemingway, annoyed that he tried to be-
little Gavin in front of her every chance he got.

"Mike, this is our gorgeous housekeeper, Mariella. She's a
feisty one and she's all mine, so keep your hands off."

Mike smiled at Mariella. "Watch out for this one, Mariella," he said. The men laughed and went into the family room. Mariella was irritated that Papa felt the need to claim her like a piece of property, but she was growing used to it. She wondered whether she took him too seriously.

Mariella walked through the group assembled in the living room to go to the side yard. They were packed and ready for the fishing they'd planned that day. Katy carried a cooler, John carried a video camera, Mike carried tackle and bait, and Papa had a .22-caliber pistol.

Katy rolled her eyes.

"That's cheating, Papa," she said.

Hemingway slapped her on the backside and told her to mind her own business. He turned back to Mariella, winked at her, and then they were all out the door.

The evening shadows seeped into the room. Mariella flicked on the light in the master bedroom and walked over to the bed. Her hands were raw from washing, and her back ached. She stuffed the last of Papa's clothes into the bag. He'd requested only fishing clothes, which meant the bag was full of clean, dry khaki pants, shorts, his lucky striped shirt, and some linen collared shirts. All had fish bloodstains and rips, would be filthy after an hour on the island, and could probably crawl home at the end of the trip, but it was nice to at least start out with them laundered. As she zipped the bag shut she heard the front door slam open and yelling downstairs.

She raced to the top of the stairs and gasped as she saw Mike and John carrying Papa into the living room with his legs wrapped in bloodstained bandages, singing drunken nonsense at the top of his lungs.

Pauline and the boys ran in from the kitchen, and Mariella ran down the stairs. They met and entered the living room as the men heaved Papa onto the couch. He groaned and touched the bandages.

"What happened?" shouted Pauline. "Oh, God, are you okay?"

"Funny story," said Papa with slurred words.

"He was trying to shoot a shark he had stuck on the gaff," said Mike. "It jerked and the gun went off."

"Bullets hit the railing and then his leg," said John.

Pauline covered her mouth, "My God! He could have been killed. Anyone could have been killed."

"'S not deep!" said Papa. "Stop your worryin'."

The boys crowded around Papa, fascinated by his injury. He was a legend even to them.

Mariella looked around the room, acutely aware of the absence in it. "Where's Katy?" she asked.

Mike looked at John, who looked away.

"Mad, mad, mad," said Papa.

"She won't speak to him," said Mike. "After she lectured him about nearly killing himself and other people, she barely said two words the whole way home."

"She's at the bungalow," said John.

"You'll have to call her when you're sober," said Pauline.

The room was quiet; then it filled with Papa's snores.

"I'll come back to check on him tomorrow," said Mike.

"I'll talk to Katy," said John.

Once they left, Pauline put her hands on her face and exhaled. Ada came into the room and took the boys upstairs to get them ready for bed.

"Now he'll be down again," said Pauline.

Mariella had just thought the same thing. His moods changed like the weather, and when he was down, he threatened to bring them all down with him.

"Go get a towel to put under his legs, and a blanket," said Pauline. "He'll sleep down here tonight, and I don't want him bleeding on the furniture."

Mariella got the towel and blanket upstairs, and when she returned, Pauline was smoking on the porch. Papa continued to snore, and Mariella covered him. He looked boyish while he slept, and she said a silent prayer of thanks that he hadn't been killed on the boat.

"You can go now," called Pauline from the porch.

Mariella didn't like Pauline's tone. It sounded accusatory. It was as if Pauline somehow blamed Mariella for his injury. As if Pauline seemed to think Mariella was amused by Papa's daring behavior, which further encouraged it.

She supposed it wasn't far from the truth.

Eager to get out of the line of Pauline's fire, Mariella took off her apron, hung it in the kitchen closet as quickly as possible, and left.

Mariella knew she couldn't avoid the talk with her mother any longer. She pushed her dinner away and cleared her throat. "Something we have to talk about."

All eyes were on her.

"The Hemingways need me to go with them to Bimini for the summer. They won't need me in their house back here, since they'll all be gone, and if I want to get paid for those months, I'll need to go with them."

Estelle looked from Mariella to her mother. Lulu spoke first. "Can we go?"

"Why didn't you discuss this with me sooner?" asked Eva.

"I'm discussing it now," said Mariella.

"It doesn't sound like a discussion. It sounds like you've made up your mind." Eva pointed to the door. "Estelle, take Lulu outside to play."

"I'm not finished!" said Lulu.

"*¡Fuera!*" said Eva.

Estelle stood and carried the two plates out to the front porch, with her little sister complaining behind her.

"So you want my blessing to send you off to some half-deserted island with Hemingway and his rich male friends?" said Eva.

"Pauline and the kids are going, too. And no, I'm not asking for your blessing. I'm telling you that you are going to have to care for the girls while I'm gone."

Eva slammed the table and the dishes jumped.

"As long as you live with me, you have to answer to me. I don't care how old you are."

"My income keeps us here," shouted Mariella. "We won't have a house if I lose my job. What do you do to contribute to the rent?"

Eva started crying. "I'm in mourning, *por el amor de Dios!*"

"And I'm not?"

Eva stood from the table, and the chair scraped the floor and fell over backward. She ran to her room and slammed the door. Mariella put her hands on the table and hung her head.

The door opened and Estelle and Lulu walked in. She heard the clink of the dishes as Estelle started to wash them. Mariella picked up the rest of the plates and brought them over to the sink. Estelle placed her hand on Mariella's arm. Mariella looked at her younger sister, whose face was knotted with worry. Estelle's eyes pleaded with her.

"She won't listen," said Mariella.

Estelle looked at her a moment longer and then turned back to the dishes. Mariella sighed and kissed her sister on the cheek. She turned and walked down the hall to her mother's room, not knowing what she'd say. She felt an invisible resistance pressing her back, but she fought it. At her mother's door, she stood outside holding the handle. Lulu appeared in the hallway and shooed her forward with her hands.

The room was dark, and she could see her mother's form on the bed with her back to the door. The sound of Eva's crying defused Mariella's anger, and she walked over to the bed and sat down.

"I'm sorry," said Mariella.

Silence.

"I understand that you're worried about me," she continued. "I wish I could be two places at once to help you with the girls, but I have to go with the Hemingways. I promise I'll be okay."

"You can't make that promise."

"If I don't go and I lose that job, I won't be able to get one anywhere else. No one can get a job right now. It was a gift that Mr. Thompson was able to get me in at the Hemingway house to begin with."

Silence.

"It's safer than other ways of making money."

Eva turned on the bed and sat up next to Mariella.

"You just have so much ahead of you," said Eva. "I'm so worried you'll ruin it for yourself."

"I can take care of myself."

"But he's a rich, powerful man. I'm worried he'll take advantage of you."

"He's married," said Mariella, "and his wife will be there on the island. Besides, I have a boyfriend."

"The soldier?"

"Yes."

Eva rolled her eyes and put her face in her hands.

"Stop," said Mariella. "You need to trust me. I don't want to sneak around. I'm not a child, and I shouldn't have to. I want to tell you these things. I want friendship from you, not judgment. The time for that has passed. If our relationship is going to work, it has to change."

Eva was quiet for a moment, but then reached for Mariella's hand. Mariella reached for her and they hugged. Mariella felt gratitude for Estelle's silently encouraging her to go to Eva. It was suddenly clear that she should have done it a long time ago. Sneaking around and telling half-truths only perpetuated her childishness in her mother's eyes.

Mariella still didn't fully trust herself with Papa, but that was almost too much to admit, even to herself. Going with him and his family felt like a dare, but she wanted to take it.

"I trust you," said Eva.

It felt as if a weight that she'd been carrying for a long time lifted from her shoulders. She hated that she had taken this long to talk openly with her mother.

Mariella and Eva stood and went back out to the kitchen with their arms around each other, and the girls smiled broadly when they came out. They hugged in the kitchen until they were crying. Then they started laughing, and the girls looked at them as if they were crazy, until they started laughing, too.

CHAPTER SIXTEEN

Mariella admired Gavin in the late-afternoon sun. He was shirtless and sweating as he leaned over the bow of the boat and loos-
ened the ropes that held it to the pier.

She walked down the dock where he had told her to meet him
for her birthday present. She wore a striped boatneck shirt Pauline
had given her, and a pair of khaki pants she had rolled up to her
knees. She carried her fishing pole and a paper bag of bait. She
enjoyed watching him when he couldn't see her, and hoped she'd
be able to behave herself.

"Hey, soldier!" she called. "Is that any way to dress for a date?"

He stood up and broke into a smile. "I'm sorry; that's the rule:
No shirts allowed." He grabbed a towel and wiped himself off.

"Ha," she said as she climbed into the boat. He swept her into
his arms and kissed her, then took her supplies to the cabin. She
reached for the line to help loosen the boat, but he insisted she
sit. "You look too pretty to do dirty work. Just relax. Have a
beer."

Mariella stepped into the cabin and saw that Gavin had set
some beer on ice in a tub. He also had a box of spices for the fish,
a lemon, and a loaf of bread.

"Wow, you really prepared for this," called Mariella. "Are you
going to ask me to marry you?"

He laughed from the front of the boat. "Yes, damn it. Now, don't spoil it."

She smiled and cracked open two beers. Gavin walked to the steering wheel and started to motor the boat away from the dock. She kissed him on the side of the neck and put his beer down next to him.

"I'm really touched that you did all this," she said.

He smiled at her and took a long drink of his beer. They pulled away from the dock and out to open water.

Gavin went straight out to the sun and then headed west into the gulf. The sun was hot and glaring on the surface of the water, but they knew it would sink fast and then they'd be chilled, so neither complained about it. And their attraction to each other made everything around them shine with goodness. The sun wasn't scorching them; it warmed them. The wind wasn't rough; it was brisk. Their hunger didn't weigh them down; it reminded them of the fish they'd fry in a little while. Their poverty was merely simplicity, and living simply was good.

Now she understood what Papa meant.

They found a place where the tuna were running and dropped anchor. The swells rolled under the boat in regular patterns as they bobbed on the surface of the water. Gavin set their chairs together, and they leaned on each other while they held their own fishing lines.

Mariella closed her eyes to firmly place the moment in her memory: the smell of the salt water mingled with Gavin's aftershave, the feel of his skin on her arm, the soothing lull of the boat. When she opened her eyes, he was smiling at her from inches away.

"What?" she said.

"I will always think of you here, like this."

"This is a perfect moment," she said.

"Rare and beautiful," he said. "It's hard to believe that moments like this exist after loss and war."

Marielle knew he was ready to tell her about his past, and she stayed quiet and looked back out at the water to make it easier for him.

Gavin spoke of Argonne. He was a sixteen-year-old kid from Pittsburgh who'd enlisted under the lie that he was eighteen. His father worked coal; his mother stayed home with him. His time in France was his first time out of Pennsylvania. He'd broken up with his girlfriend when he went to war to save himself the trouble of her doing it once he was gone. He, John, and Jordan became tight and planned to move to Florida after the war to build their lives under sunny skies. John had told them about his parents' place in Key West, and they all decided they'd rent there until they could afford their own places.

"The winter came on quick and miserable that October," he said.

Mariella looked over at him and saw his face drained of color and his eyes blank. The change alarmed her, and she had to look back at the water.

"It was freezing outside, but not cold enough to snow, so we were soaked through by frigid rain with scratchy, cold, wet wool on our skin week after week. I thought influenza would kill us all before the Germans could. With the big battle looming we were all pretty edgy. Then I got the telegram that Dad died. I couldn't even go to his funeral."

Mariella felt numb. She couldn't imagine not being able to bury her dad and get that chance to honor him. There were no words of comfort she could offer him, and it made her feel small and inadequate.

Gavin stood suddenly and started reeling. After a few moments his reel spun out and the line went slack. He lifted it out of the water and set the pole in the holder. He looked back at her and shrugged. She smiled at him and motioned for him to come over to her chair, where she stood, eased him into the chair, and sat on his lap. He wrapped his arms around her and helped her hold the pole.

"Do you want me to keep going, or am I ruining everything?" he asked.

She turned until she faced him. "You could never ruin anything. Please keep talking."

He kissed her nose and continued.

"Our general, Pershing, began an offensive that most of the guys thought was crazy. He just kept pushing and plowing us through the Germans. It ended in November, when we finally crushed the enemy, but we lost twenty-six thousand guys in the process."

Mariella felt her mouth go dry. She knew it had been a bloodbath, but hadn't realized exactly how many Americans had lost their lives.

"It's an out-of-body experience at that point," said Gavin. "You're inhuman. You haven't slept or eaten properly in weeks. You're soaked to the bone. You're killing and killing, and crawling over the dead and dying. Your mind is blank. Purely fixed on a target. No emotion. No fear. Until your guys—your close buddies— go down. Then your mind turns on and you can't think of the target, only of getting them out of there. Only of helping preserve them so you can get to that sunny place and start your business together, and raise your kids together, and tell your war stories.

"I kept thinking of all that when the shell went off. I saw Jordan fly backward, and when I got to him the whole front of his body was gone—just gone. His face was gone. But I wanted to pull his body to a safe place, because I knew he had a girl at home—a girl who loved him, who'd want that body to bury—so I got him to a ditch. I pulled him perpendicular to all the action—they were all going forward and I was pulling this body sideways, and I had a hell of a time getting him to a safe place.

"But then I heard John screaming and knew he was alive, and I should have found him first. When I got to him, he was hyperventilating over his missing legs. There they were—severed almost neatly above the knee—but there were explosions everywhere, so I couldn't save the legs, too. I just pulled what was left of John along the same path I'd pulled Jordan. When I got us there, something exploded in the path we'd just come from and everything went black."

Mariella turned her head so she could see his profile, and reached up to run her hand down the scar on his face. He flinched, but didn't move her hand away. She leaned in to kiss where it ended near his lip, and he closed his eyes. After a few moments, he started again.

"The next thing I remembered, I was in a hospital. Then the war was over. While John recovered in the vet hospital, I went home to Mom. I had some bad times. I was drinking too much to hold down a job, and the insomnia was killing me. I was edgy and mean and I knew I was hurting her, but I didn't know how to stop. Then she was diagnosed with ALS and something clicked for me. I realized I needed to take care of her and grow up. Lots of guys went through what I went through. Without my dad, I had to support us.

"We stayed there for a while, but I was getting claustrophobic in that small town. All the girls I'd grown up with got married. I had a few girlfriends, but I was still no good in the head. I didn't trust anyone. I mostly just worked in the steel mill, ate dinner with Mom, and kept to myself. Then the crash came, and Mom started getting really bad off. I lost my job at the steel mill and couldn't find another job.

"Winters in PA are bad, and I'd been writing John all along.

He'd since moved to Key West. Mom didn't want to go that far south, but she said she'd go live near my uncle in Miami. So we packed up and left. My uncle's business was struggling, so he couldn't hire me, so I got a job working on the Overseas Highway."

"And then you met me," said Mariella.

"And I lived happily ever after," said Gavin.

Mariella let him hold the pole and ran her hands over the tattoo on his forearm. Then she saw the line jerk. Mariella grabbed the pole and started reeling. He let her go and cheered her on while she struggled with the fish. It dived down hard several times before she felt the control shift to her hands. She stood up and reeled faster until she could pull it up. Finally, with a great tug and a splat, she pulled in a fat, flipping grouper. She pulled the hook out of the grouper and tossed it into a bucket of salt water next to a baby tarpon Gavin had caught earlier.

"Perfect distraction," he said. "I'm done talking now. It's your turn."

He wrapped his arms around her waist and she reached up around his neck.

"Let's find a little island all to ourselves first," she said, "and then I'll start talking. I know a good one near here."

"Deal," he said, kissing her full on the mouth.

Mariella opened the throttle and led them to an island near a stretch of the old railroad, where her father used to take the family. The Keys were made up of hundreds of tiny islands surrounding the larger islands. Some were only thirty feet from tip to tip. Many locals enjoyed using the islands for fun. Others were rumored to be used for more sinister purposes, including the hiding of drugs and weapons.

It wasn't long before they anchored the boat and splashed through the shallows to the beach of the small, uninhabited island. They gathered dry wood and made a fire. Gavin cleaned and seasoned the fish, and they baked it and toasted the bread over the flame. They rubbed the smell of fish off their hands with wet beach sand and lemon and rinsed their hands in the water. When the fish and bread were ready, they ate and drank beer.

While the sun slipped into the horizon, Mariella told Gavin about her family. She spoke of her mother's family disowning Eva when she married Hal. She spoke of never having met her grandparents, her parents' close relationship, her sisters, and her father's death. She regretted that she hadn't gone out on the boat with Hal that day, and wondered aloud whether, if she had, her father would still be alive.

"I always wonder things like that," said Gavin. "If I hadn't tripped when we started out, I'd have been in front of Jordan and blown to pieces. Then he'd have been able to come home to his girl."

"But then the man on the beach would have died," said Mariella.

"Who?"

"The man you saved when we went to the beach with the girls," she said. "Maybe he had a wife and six kids. If you'd died in the war, he'd have died here."

"I guess we could go on all night with ifs and thens," he said. "We just have to accept what happened."

"And move on."

It was easier to talk of these things in the dark, with only the firelight and the starlight. It felt good to get it all out. Then Papa came up.

"I know you don't want to hear this from me," said Gavin, "but watch yourself with him."

Mariella was glad he couldn't see her roll her eyes.

"I'm not sure why everyone feels the need to tell me that," said Mariella. "I'm a grown woman. He's a married man."

"Surely you aren't naive enough to think marriage stops people from pursuing relationships."

"He loves his wife."

"I'm sure he does."

"And more important, I don't love him."

"Then what is it?"

Mariella poked the fire with a stick and felt the heat seeping off its embers and warming her. She thought of Papa on the boat, tanned and windblown. She thought of him hopping into his car or sitting at the bar at Sloppy's, holding court.

"I'm drawn to him," she said. "He's like a character from one of his books. He demands attention."

"It's the celebrity," said Gavin.

"It's more than that. It's his whole lifestyle. You know; you've met him."

"Yeah, I do know what you mean," said Gavin. "I feel good when he gives me the time of day. Like I'm part of his mob."

Mariella didn't want to talk about Papa with Gavin anymore. "Enough about him," she said.

"Yeah, I don't want to talk about him while I'm on a date with you."

Gavin pulled Mariella back on the blanket and began to kiss her. She lifted her leg and let it rest over his body. He ran his hands over her, and she reached up and felt his chest. His heart was pounding. He pulled back and looked at her.

"I don't know if this was a good idea," he said.

"Is there a problem?"

"Yes."

Mariella's brow creased with a sudden uncertainty. He ran his hand down her neck and onto her collarbone, and then kissed her there.

"I don't know if I can stop," he mumbled into her chest. She let the air out of it, relieved that there wasn't a problem with her, and ran her hands over his hair.

"I don't know if I can, either," she said.

He groaned. "You're supposed to be the strong one here."

She laughed and kissed his neck. "You're clouding my judgment!"

He turned her over on her back. She felt a catch at her heart, and a mixture of fear and longing. She knew that they couldn't—not yet. She didn't want to end up like her mother. He'd been kissing her hard, but must have felt her stiffen. He kissed her more softly, then stopped and rested his head on his hand.

"This isn't the right time," he said, as he traced the outline of her face. She reached for his hand and kissed his fingertips.

"No," she said. "But not because every inch of my body doesn't want to."

"I know," he said.

He rolled off her and onto his back, letting out a deep sigh. They both lay looking up at the stars. Their hands fell together on the blanket between them.

CHAPTER SEVENTEEN

Mariella sulked.

It was the third straight day of rain. She felt like a caged animal in the small house listening to her mother play Ponce's *Suite* over and over again on this day, her father's birthday. No one mentioned it out loud, but his absence took up more space than if he'd actually been there. It didn't help that Lulu was getting over another bout of fever and stomach troubles, which left Mariella second-guessing her decision to go to Bimini. Or that they ran out of cigarettes. Or that Mariella felt guilty for not visiting John in days. Mariella thought she'd go mad when her mother started the record over again, so she opened the screen door and sat on the porch.

Small rivers of water had formed on either side of the road, washing up into the front yard and turning it into a great, sopping mud puddle. She felt Gavin's letter in her pocket poke her side, and pulled it out to reread it, missing him acutely and moody about his words.

I wish I could be happy for you, but the thought of being separated from you while you're on the beach with him all day and night for weeks on end makes me miserable. I wish I knew if I could join you, but I'm afraid I won't know until the time gets closer, and it's not looking good, since we need to finish our stretch of road before hurricane season. . . .

Mariella shoved the letter back in its envelope, put it in her pocket, and rubbed her eyes. A dribble of water hit her on the ear and slid down to wet her shirt. She moved to a drier spot on the porch, determined to stay outside, avoiding her mother's grief and the memories of her father.

Even before today, it had been a tough week. Papa had already left for Bimini on board the *Pilar*, and the house felt dead without him. His gunshot wounds were superficial, so he'd healed quickly. He had made amends to Katy and was able to charm her back to loving him, as he could anyone. Knowing it would be a while before she could see Papa again left Mariella cold and disappointed.

Pauline had to travel to St. Louis to pick up Ernest's oldest son, Jack—or "Bumby," as he was nicknamed—where he was spending his summer vacation with Ernest's former in-laws, and then wait for Jinny to arrive in Key West before taking them all over to Bimini. Mariella's sense of adventure was piqued at the thought of taking her first airplane flight to a primitive island to live with the Hemingways. She was both eager to go and anxious about leaving.

She turned her mind back to Gavin and felt the real ache of missing him. The time they'd spent together on her birthday meant a lot to her, and she was afraid that all the progress they'd made would fade over the weeks of their separation.

The sound of footsteps splashing in the rain drew her out of her thoughts. She stood and looked down the road in the direction she had heard the noise, but couldn't see anything through the sheets of rain. Finally a figure came into view moving toward her house.

Gavin!

He ran up to the porch—his military T-shirt and shorts stuck to his body—and picked Mariella up, swinging her around and soaking her. She laughed and swatted at him to put her down. Then she held his wet face in her hands for a moment and kissed him.

"My God, I've missed you," she said.

"I know; it's been awful," he said.

"Why are you out running in the rain?"

"I had to see you."

She grinned and kissed him again, reveling in the surprise of his presence.

Suddenly the music inside the house stopped. Mariella pulled away.

"Mari," called her mother. *"¿Quién está ahí?"*

The warmth in her body from Gavin's kiss vanished and she felt her nerves start to jump. The last time Eva had met Gavin she'd been a harried maniac. Mariella's instinct was to shoo him away. Her relationship with Eva was improving and they were learning to communicate better, but Mariella still wasn't confident in Eva's stability and didn't want any setbacks.

"Are you worried she isn't up for it yet?" he whispered.

She was worried, but she was also aware that Eva might surprise her. She had to give her a chance. Mariella looked over her shoulder into the house and felt her confidence return. It was now or never.

"Let's find out," said Mariella.

Mariella led Gavin into the house by the hand. Eva stood by her chair and, when she saw Gavin, looked down at her feet and wrung her hands. Mariella knew Eva must feel embarrassed for how she'd behaved when they first met. Lulu saved the awkward moment by leaping into Gavin's arms. He grunted and laughed. "Whoa, Lu!"

Eva watched for a moment, her eyes darting back and forth from Gavin to Mariella to Lulu. Mariella saw Eva take a deep breath and walk over to Gavin with her hand extended. He held on to Lulu with one arm and reached for Eva's hand with the other.

"Let me start over with you," said Eva. "I'm sorry for the first time we met."

Gavin shook his head and placed Lulu gently on the ground. "No, I'm the one who should have apologized. I should have introduced myself properly before taking the girls to the beach."

"You tried," said Mariella. "It was my fault."

"No more apologies," said Eva. "It's nice to meet you. My girls love you, so I'm sure I will, too."

Mariella felt relief wash over her.

"I'm actually here on a mission," said Gavin, unable to contain his grin. "John and I would like you girls to join us for dinner tonight, since it's Mariella's last night before she leaves for Bimini."

A smile crossed Eva's face, and Mariella felt her approval. It thrilled her.

"If it wouldn't be too much trouble, we would love to," said Eva. "May I bring something?"

"No, just yourselves."

"I'll make a pie," said Eva.

Mariella looked at her mother with surprise. She couldn't remember Eva ever making pie.

"That's great," said Gavin. "Now I'd better get home and make myself presentable."

And almost as fast as he'd come, he was gone.

Though she was excited about dinner, Mariella felt uneasy. She hoped her mother wouldn't regret saying yes. She worried about how the girls would respond to John and his missing legs. It felt too good to be true, and she prayed they could have a peaceful night.

Gavin wiped the sweat from his forehead and cursed as he cleaned up the second beer he'd dropped on the floor. The rain had miraculously stopped, but it left sticky, humid air that felt almost as wet as the rain itself.

"Relax," said John as he wheeled to the door. "You said she was nice."

"I just want to make a good impression," said Gavin. "Mariella says her mother's up and down with her emotions. On the beach, she was definitely down. I don't want to see that again."

"Well, keep spilling beer all over the place. It'll make a real nice impression if it smells like Sloppy Joe's in here."

Gavin glared at him over the shards of glass. John grinned and threw him a towel hanging from a knob on a nearby cabinet. He wheeled back to the living room to watch for the girls.

Gavin wrung out the soaked towel in the sink and washed his hands. The water on the stove started hissing and boiling over.

"Shit!" He crossed the kitchen and turned down the water. Once he got the potatoes in without incident, he opened another beer and drained half of it in one long gulp.

"They're here," called John.

Gavin felt his heart pound and ran out to the front hall to look out the screen. The sight of all of them—dark, pretty, and laughing—made him smile. He looked down at John and saw he was smiling, too.

Before Gavin could hold him back, Mutt pushed through them and out the screen door. Lulu was carrying the pie, and sure enough, the dog jumped on her and caused her to drop it. She began to cry. John wheeled down the ramp after the dog. Lulu stopped crying when she saw him. He spoke sternly to Mutt, who'd begun eating the pie, and the dog hung its head and licked Lulu. She laughed when she saw that his nose was covered with pie.

"I'm sorry, Miss Lulu," said John. "He can't help himself."

"You know my name," she said.

"Of course I do," he said. "Mariella and Gavin have told me all about you and Estelle, and your mom."

"And you still invited me to dinner?" said Eva.

John looked up at her and smiled. "I've only heard good things."

Eva beamed back at him.

John turned back to Lulu. "Would you like a ride?"

She looked at his legs. "Will I hurt you?"

He laughed. "No, but thanks for checking." He opened his arms and Lulu climbed up. Mariella stepped behind the chair to push them, since John's arms were full.

"Hold on tight," she said, and zoomed them across the front yard and up the ramp to the house. Gavin held the door open, and Mariella kissed him as she walked through the doorway. He opened his eyes wide at her as if to say, *Your mother!* but she just laughed and walked into the house. Estelle followed Mariella, smiling shyly at Gavin as she walked by. Eva was the last in the door.

"I'm so glad you could come, Mrs. Bennet," said Gavin.

"Call me Eva," she said. She reached for his hands and took them in hers. "Thank you for having us."

Gavin watched Eva enter the living room, and was struck by her warmth and beauty. Her hair was loose around her face and wavy from the humidity. Her features were softened by the smile that played at her lips. She wore makeup, and her black dress was pressed and flattered her small frame. It was amazing to see her transformation from the woman wild-eyed with depression and anger on the beach. He relaxed for the first time all day and closed the front door.

When he stepped into the living room, he stopped to look at the roomful of people. Lulu skipped around touching everything. John talked to Estelle about the guitar when he saw her looking at it. Mariella showed Eva the paintings on the walls and by the easel. The scene filled him with an emotion he hadn't expected. He felt a lump form in his throat and blinked back tears. He thought that everything he loved and would love was in this room, and he wanted to freeze the moment forever.

~⟋⟍◯

In spite of her happiness, Mariella's stomach rumbled in nervous anticipation. So many heartbreaks left her wary of moments of pure happiness.

Mariella watched Gavin as he instructed everyone to fix their plates in the kitchen and take them out to the living room to eat. Her eyes traveled over his starched white shirt, ironed pants, and fresh haircut. She could see from his creased forehead and tidy appearance how important it was to him to make a good impression, and she loved him for it.

Dinner was delicious. Gavin served roasted chicken, boiled potatoes, and carrots, and he'd seasoned everything with sea salt he'd picked up at the market. The pie was unsalvageable, but they were all too full from dinner to contemplate dessert.

When dinner ended, the girls helped Gavin clean the dishes while John patiently answered Lulu's questions about his legs. Mariella finally intervened when she asked to see them, and the rest of the group came to sit in the living room. Eva sat on the couch next to John's chair, and Mariella sat at her side. Estelle sat on the floor near John, while Gavin sat on the floor leaning on Mariella's legs. Lulu crawled into Gavin's lap.

Their talk of the Keys and the Overseas Highway led to a discussion of Mariella's trip to Bimini.

"Mama is worried about me," said Mariella. She reached for Eva's hand. "She's worried about all of the rich men drinking and gambling."

"I can't help it," said Eva.

"I'll do everything I can to go for a long weekend," said Gavin.

"I would be so relieved if you did," said Eva.

Mariella tried to hide her smile. She never could have pre-dicted that the Eva from the beach would want a soldier to spend a weekend on a faraway island with Mariella for her protection.

It was quiet for a moment, until Estelle asked John to play something on the guitar. He said he'd play Satie's *Gymnopedie No. 1.* It sounded like a lullaby. Gavin leaned in closer to Mariella, and Lulu crawled into Eva's lap. When the song ended, the room was silent.

"Where did you learn to play?" asked Eva.

"My mother was a classical pianist," said John. "She taught me the piano, and I taught myself guitar from that. I wanted to go to Peabody in Baltimore, but the war came and I felt called to fight. I thought I'd pursue music when I got home."

"You still could," she said.

"I don't think the Sloppy Joe's crowd would be interested in classical guitar," he said.

"No, but you could give lessons or teach classes."

"I'd love to do that, but I'm afraid not many could afford a luxury like that now."

What he said was true. Mariella knew that John hated living off of his parents' money, but he had no choice. She saved the awk-ward moment by requesting another song. Incredibly, John started playing Ponce's *Suite.* Mariella shot a look at her mother, cringing at the response she anticipated. Mariella started to ask John to play something else, but Eva placed her hand on Mariella's arm to stop her. She shook her head and smiled.

Estelle watched her mother for a reaction, too, but Eva seemed lost in the music. When it ended Lulu said, "That's my daddy's song." Mariella was surprised Lulu remembered.

"I'm sorry," said John. "I hope that didn't upset you."

"No, it made me happy," said Eva. "It might sound silly, but it brought Hal here to this, and it felt right."

The room was quiet until Lulu yawned.

Eva stood and picked her up.

"We should probably get going," said Mariella.

"If you'd like to stay," said Eva, "I could take the girls home."

Mariella loved the idea, but she didn't want her mother walking home alone with the girls, and she knew she had to wake up early to go to Bimini.

"I'd love to," she said, "but I should get home to rest before tomorrow."

"I'll walk you home," said Gavin.

As they all started out, Mariella hesitated. She hated to go. The evening had been so perfect.

Eva put Lulu down and she walked over to kiss John's cheek. She stared for a moment at the blanket that hid his missing legs.

"Well, I hope you grow those back," she said.

Eva buried her face in her hands. Mariella gasped and mouthed an apology to John. He laughed and shook his head to dismiss the apology.

"Me, too," he said.

Amid the chaos, Estelle crept over to John.

"Thank you for playing the guitar for us," she said.

Mariella was moved to see Estelle open up to John. Gavin met her eyes and smiled.

"If you ever want lessons," John said, "I'll teach you for free."

Estelle beamed and even leaned down to hug him before running out the door.

Eva stepped up to his chair and took his hands.

"Thank you for your patience with them, and for playing for us," she said. She leaned down to hug John, and when she stood Mariella saw that John blushed. She thought that he wasn't used to so much female attention and that it must feel good for him.

After she kissed John's burning cheek, Mariella joined Gavin and her family on the porch. Lulu was almost asleep in Gavin's arms, and he told Eva he'd be happy to carry her home and put her to bed.

Mariella trailed Gavin and the girls as they started down the stairs, but turned for one last wave at John. When she looked back at him, all she could see was his dark shape in the door with the light behind him. His shoulders sagged, he held his head in his hands, and he appeared to be crying.

CHAPTER EIGHTEEN

Bimini, Bahamas

The seaplane descended and Mariella felt her stomach in her throat. As excited as she'd been for her first airplane ride, she quickly learned that flying did not agree with her. It took every ounce of self-control she had not to get sick, especially when Ada got sick. Jinny sang songs with the boys, told jokes, and created a general uproar on board the small aircraft. Pauline sat with her back to them, watching the water. Mariella could feel her willing the island to come into view.

The silhouette of the island appeared. Mariella held her stomach as the plane dropped and lifted erratically before making a swift landing in the water. Mariella settled as the plane drifted toward the dock. She nearly forgot her sickness when she saw the crew welcoming them. Papa stood on the pilings above them, a bronzed god waving furiously and pretending to shoot at the boys. They loved the show and bounced up and down, eager to board the little rowboat. Carlos, Papa's first mate on board the *Pilar*, brought it out to them. He helped them each down into the boat and they bobbed through the choppy surf toward the dock.

Hemingway radiated happiness. Never before had Mariella seen him so completely in his element. He wore only a pair of fish-blood-splattered pants rolled to the knee. His hand had a bandage from some new injury, and his face had grown enough stubble to make a respectable beard. His white teeth flashed at them with every smile.

Pauline was leaning forward at the bow of the ship like a figurehead, looking eager enough to jump into the water and swim to the dock. As they pulled in, Hemingway helped them out of the boat. He kissed Pauline passionately and they embraced. Bumby, Patrick, and Gregory jumped out and bounced around while Papa ruffled their hair and hugged them. He nodded curtly at Ada, and kissed Jinny. Mariella started to climb out of the boat on her own when she felt his hand on her arm. He lifted her as if she weighed nothing.

"Daughter, you have made my vacation." He put his hands on the sides of her face, and she thought he was going to kiss her. Instead, he just gazed at her until Patrick pulled his arms and dragged him down the pier.

Mariella helped Carlos unload the bags from the boat, then started after the Hemingways, still flushed from his touch.

A seagull flew across the white sand and out over the surf. Mariella followed its line to the sandbar about fifty yards offshore. Just past it, the water suddenly became deep blue-green in a channel. Mariella knew it was teeming with fish swimming north on the Gulf Stream. The blue of the sky and the water were almost the same, and the breeze blew the fresh saltwater smell over her. She understood Papa's euphoria.

She started back to the Compleat Angler—the only "big" hotel on the island. It had twelve rooms, wraparound porches on each level, and a noisy rum bar. Pauline and Ernest were in room one, the boys and Ada in room two, and Mariella in room three.

The rest of their friends and staff filled the place like Papa's subjects traveling in his court.

Mariella pushed open the door of the dark-paneled room and stepped inside. It smelled of damp wood and seawater. There were paintings of big fish on the walls, and the bed and curtains had cream-colored lace overlays. She walked to the window and looked out over the beach. The sand was white as sugar. It was nearly sunset, and the evening light warmed the landscape. A large fish leaped out of the waves. The boys saw the fish, too. They jumped off the deck and ran down to the beach. Ada stood on the deck yelling after them, but they knew she couldn't possibly catch them and danced like shirtless savages in the waves.

Mariella turned back to the room and realized she was without her mother and sisters for the first time in her life. She'd always longed for this kind of freedom and privacy, and now she had it. She didn't know what to make of it.

She hung her dress in the closet and put her bathing suit and beach clothes in the drawers in the bureau. She peeked into a small bathroom and was happy to see that it was clean. When she turned back to face the room, she smiled broadly. She ran toward the bed and leaped onto it, rolling around on the cool, soft comforter. She smiled at the fan over her on the ceiling.

At last!

The men were very much what her mother and Gavin had feared.

Mariella stepped through the smoke into the rum bar to a chorus of catcalls from the tanned, rich, drunken crowd. Papa emerged from them and put his arm around her. There was a general uproar as he led her to the end of the bar.

The room jumped with the music of the singing bartenders, glasses hitting wet wood, and random bursts of laughter. Mariella soon realized she was the only woman in the room and thought she probably should have gone to bed when the others did. Then again, why not stay up and have fun? How many opportunities in her lifetime would she have in such company?

Papa ordered her something fruity and delicious, and sat so close to her that she could smell the booze and the outdoors on him.

"This is a tourist drink," she said.

"Well, you are a tourist, aren't you," he said.

"True."

He downed a shot from a line of three and hiccuped loudly.

"The fishing's been shit; Jane's quack therapist, Kubie, has written a libelous article I intend to sue him over; and the *Pilar*'s been acting up," said Papa.

"Then why are you so happy?" asked Mariella.

"Because all my loves are here."

He leaned into Mariella and clinked the shot glass on hers before he drained it.

"Of course," she said. "And this is paradise. You couldn't be unhappy here."

"Never."

"Who's this Kubie?"

"Some shrink who claims I have disdain for women through my overmasculine protagonists—among other things."

"You do make us out pretty bad."

He looked at her with suspicion.

"I've read your books," she said.

"Which ones?"

"All of them."

"I'm flattered."

"You should be," she said. "I haven't cracked a book since my school days."

"And you think the guys are dicks?"

"It's more about how you make the dames look."

"How's that?"

"Weak."

"Damn it—no!" He slammed his glass on the bar. "It's the men who look like assholes; don't you see?"

"Explain."

"The women are there to highlight what macho jackasses the men are."

"You don't believe that."

"I do," he said. "But they, too, are flawed. My characters are flawed and deeply human, and I'm sorry if that makes them not look so good, but have you ever considered humanity?"

She looked around the room at the sunburned, drunken men falling all over one another, smoking and slapping one another on the back. Mariella pulled a cigarette out of her pack and lit it. She inhaled and then blew the smoke away from Papa.

"That'll kill you one day," he said after downing his third shot.

She sent him and his empty glasses a look.

"Touché," he said.

"Back to your characters," said Mariella, emboldened by the alcohol. "Can you even call them characters? It seems as if you just change the names to protect the innocent—or guilty."

He smiled at her out of the corner of his eye while he motioned to the bartender.

"You're onto me," he said.

Mariella took another sip of her drink and felt her head spin. She looked around the room and couldn't help but feel that all these people would show up somewhere in his stories to serve some purpose—not for their own good, but for his.

"You have to stop collecting them," she said.

"'Scuse me?" he said.

"They're human beings."

"Not this again," he said.

"They deserve their dignity."

He regarded her with a furrowed brow. "I will always collect them."

"Not me," she said.

"I know. Not you," he said. "I told you that when we ate pie in Key West."

The bartender brought him a whiskey. He slowly swirled the liquid in his glass, not meeting her eyes. She wondered whether he'd already done it—whether he'd already used her in his work. She wondered whether he would take it back.

She also knew she'd regret it if she continued drinking, so she stood to go.

"Where are you going?" he asked, turning on the stool to face her.

"I'm going to bed. To my *own* space, for the first time *ever.*"

His face settled into a sad smile, as if it hadn't before occurred to him that Mariella was poor.

"Thank you for bringing me here," she said. "I know you didn't need me, so it was a gift."

He put his hands on her waist and she moved a step closer to him.

"To me," he said, looking into her eyes.

His desire was palpable. Mariella felt an urge to kiss him, but she closed her eyes and fought it.

"To you," she said. She reached around him, raised her glass, and drained it. She stepped back from him. "Good night, Papa."

"Good night, daughter."

She walked by the men at the bar as they called to her and begged her to come back. She smiled from under her long eyelashes and raised her hand in farewell as she walked out the door. Their pleading followed her into the night, and she laughed and felt good from the attention.

She walked unsteadily back to her room, closed the door, and leaned against it. Her heart pounded. She walked over to the window and opened it to let in the fresh air. The sound of the surf came in on the wind, but she could hear the noise of the men at the rum bar in bursts over it. She heard Papa laugh, and smiled to herself. She walked over to the bed and lay on top of the covers, listening to the night. It wasn't long before she fell asleep.

Mariella awoke in the middle of the night with a headache. She rolled out of bed and felt her way to the bathroom, where she filled a cup with water from the faucet and drained it. She drained another cup and filled it once more to put on the bedside table.

She sat on the end of the bed and rubbed her temples with her hands. The night breeze came in through the open window. The beach was lit by the full moon. Mariella moved to the window and stared out, mesmerized by the haunting beauty of the night landscape.

She had a sudden urge to walk in the sand in her bare feet. The freedom of being alone on Bimini at night was almost too much for her to bear, and she didn't want the magic of the moment to dissolve. She opened the door and stepped out onto the porch. The wind caught her off guard. She didn't expect it to be as strong as it was, but she was glad that it blew as it did. It would keep away the mosquitoes.

The sand felt cool under her feet, but the water was warm. She thought about a night swim, but realized that would be foolish without anyone else around, so she just stood there taking in the night. She looked in the direction of Key West and thought of her family and of Gavin. She imagined them all sleeping, and she was filled with love for them.

After standing there for a while, Mariella walked back to the hotel. She knew she'd better get to bed if she didn't want her headache to get worse. She crept up the stairs and down the porch to her room. As she walked by Papa's room, a sudden noise stopped her. She turned toward his window and saw that it was open and that the curtains were blowing out in the wind. The pain in her head reasserted itself, almost as if to urge her back to her own room, but she couldn't resist looking into his room. She just wanted to see him sleeping.

Moving against the outside wall, she slid until she was right next to the window. She reached, held the curtain flat against the wall, and peered around its edge.

Her eyes took a moment to adjust to the darkness in the room, but the moonlight helped illuminate Hemingway and Pauline moving together under the sheets. When Mariella realized what she was seeing, her heart began to pound, but she couldn't tear her eyes away. She felt a mixture of revulsion, arousal, and jealousy.

The bed was parallel to the window, so she could see a side view of the lovers. Hemingway had his head buried in Pauline's neck, and her face wore a look of ecstasy. He had her arms pinned above her head, and it was clear that Pauline liked it.

Suddenly he turned his head toward the window. Mariella sucked in her breath and pivoted flat against the wall. Her heart pounded. *My God.* Had he seen her? She didn't want to move, but she was afraid that if she didn't, he'd come out and find her there, and— *Oh, God.* Mariella crouched down and crept under the window as quietly as she could. She raced to her room, went in, locked the door, and leaned against it to catch her breath. She could swear that she heard footsteps on the porch, so she ran to her bed and jumped under the covers.

Mariella didn't sleep for the rest of the night.

The next morning, Mariella was terrified at the thought of seeing Papa, and obsessed over whether or not he'd seen her. She knew that she'd be able to tell whether he'd seen her by the way he greeted her. She stayed in her room as long as she could, but once she heard everyone's voices as they congregated on the front porch, she knew she had to join them.

The men stood on the porch talking, smoking, and drinking coffee. They were bleary eyed but happy. They planned to go out fishing and felt lucky already. Papa's hair was rumpled and his stained shorts were held up with a rope. He wore his green fishing cap and a white button-down shirt.

The boys ran up the steps, jumped off the porch, and started over again. Pauline watched them from a rocking chair. She wore a housedress, had a cup of tea on the small table next to her, and pressed against the banister with her bare foot to rock herself. She was talking with Jinny and Katy and Dos, and they all burst into laughter at the same time.

Mariella could see Pauline's ease and the happiness of the guests. She thought that wealth must be so freeing —to be able to spend weeks on holiday, without a care in the world. It was easy to forget about the rest of the world in exchange for your own comfort. Mariella understood why Papa called it a drug.

"Will you fish with us today, Mari?" called Papa. He smiled at her warmly, without any mockery. Relief washed over her.

"Not today," she said. Pauline had instructed her that today was market day, and they'd go into Alice Town and find food. Papa told her that their diet on vacation would be his catch. "Man hunt. Wife cook."

"Wife not eat fish every meal. Man get out of here," said Pauline. They laughed.

"I hope you can cook, Mariella," said Katy. "The food has been terrible here. We are all hopeless in the kitchen."

"I'm not bad," said Mariella. "Isabelle's taught me a lot."

"Bad food that someone else cooks is better than good food that I have to cook," said Katy. "I can't wait."

"Jane just sent over a nice package of caviar and fine things," said Papa. "Eat that."

Pauline stopped rocking, visibly tense at the mention of Jane and her fine things.

Katy rolled her eyes. "Please, I'd rather eat nothing than that."

Jinny assumed the posture of a model and held her cigarette out from her. She put on a voice imitating Jane. "Oh, *dahling*, I just thought everyone would want fine food like me. And I do want you all to think highly of me, because I'm *so* very special, and you're all *so* very lucky to know me."

Pauline relaxed a little. Katy and Dos laughed. Ernest rolled his eyes and stepped off the porch.

"Look forward to our return, fine people," said Papa. "Meet us at the dock at happy hour." He blew Pauline a kiss and started walking. Then he stopped, looked back at Mariella, and waved. "You're coming with me on my birthday," he called.

The mood of the men pulling into the dock was much darker than when they'd left, particularly Papa's. His face was black with a scowl, and he complained about the lack of big fish. He spouted off about how all the rich sons of bitches had overfished the island, apparently excluding himself from the notorious group of which he spoke. Most of the guys were amused by Papa's tantrum, but Joe Knapp—a publisher from New York—was becoming increasingly irritated by it. Cocktail hour on the dock was tense. So were dinner and drinks at the bar afterward.

Mariella wanted to go to bed early, but couldn't tear herself away from the action. While Papa bragged about his usual fishing prowess, Knapp became more and more hostile. It was clear that the teasing had gone from good-natured to mean-spirited, and people were beginning to emit bursts of nervous laughter while the men argued openly.

Finally, Mariella heard Knapp call Papa a "phony, fat slob," saw Papa's fists fly, and before she knew it, Knapp was laid out on his back on the floor. It was deadly quiet until the island men working the bar burst out in a ridiculous song about the knockout. Knapp's friends pulled him up and out to his boat while the song followed them into the night.

Pauline shook her head at Papa. "I don't understand you men, but I can't take any more," she said. "Wife go sleep." She walked out of the bar.

"Husband come for wife later," called Papa, much to the amusement of his peers.

Mariella blushed. She finished her drink and turned to leave the room. Then Papa was at her side.

"You didn't say good night," he said.

"I was afraid I'd get knocked out."

He smiled and kissed her on the forehead. "Good night, daughter."

"Night," she said. She turned to walk out, but he stopped her again.

"You might want to lock your door," he said.

"Why?"

"Sleepwalking's dangerous." He winked at her and turned back to the bar.

CHAPTER NINETEEN

Based on Papa's comment about sleepwalking, Mariella knew he'd seen her at the window that night, and she'd spent the following days trying to avoid him. When his birthday arrived, however, he insisted she join him on a fishing excursion.

She helped Carlos load the *Pilar* that morning, while Ernest went to fetch his oldest son, Bumby, from the beach, where he and the younger boys were turning over rocks in search of sea creatures.

Once he had the boy, Papa walked down the dock toward the boat, wearing his straw hat and glasses. Patrick and Gregory chased him, begging to come. Bumby trailed with what appeared to be a toy gun on his shoulder like a soldier.

"You're too young," said Papa to the little boys. "When you're big like Bumby, you'll come with us."

Patrick's eyes darkened and he kicked at the dock. Gregory began to have a tantrum.

"I want to shoot the big gun," said Gregory between sobs.

Papa ignored him and climbed onto the boat, followed by Bumby.

Mariella wondered why Papa didn't just tell Bumby to give Gregory the toy gun. He didn't need a toy on the boat all day. On closer look, however, she realized it was a real machine gun.

Gregory had his eyes closed and began to stomp his feet so hard, Mariella feared he'd fall off the dock. She glanced down the pier, but Ada was nowhere in sight. She was probably nursing a hangover.

While Papa and Carlos tested the lines and inventoried the fishing gear, Mariella climbed back onto the dock and knelt down in front of Gregory, gently holding his arms. He opened his eyes and quieted.

"If you're a big boy and you stop crying, I'll take you spearfishing when we get back," she said.

He thought about this for a moment and then nodded, suddenly overtaken by a bout of hiccups.

"Promise," he said.

"I promise."

He smiled a little smile at Mariella, and looked at the boat one last time. Once Papa was turned safely away from him, Gregory stuck out his tongue and ran to catch up with Patrick, who was already back on the beach. Mariella smiled after him and returned to the boat.

"Where did you get that?" asked Mariella, pointing at the gun.

"Bought it off some rich bastard," said Papa.

"When?"

"Couple months back."

"How come I've never seen it?"

"It's the first time you've gone fishing with me here."

"I can't believe I haven't heard you mention it."

"Well, I pissed off Strater before he left," he said. "He'd hooked a big marlin and I was shooting the sharks to keep them away. The blood made them go nuts and they chewed up his fish."

"So you didn't want to rub it in around him."

"Bingo."

"That showed an amazing amount of sensitivity on your part," said Mariella, impressed.

"I can be sensitive," he said.

There was a splash off the starboard side of the boat, and Bumby swung the gun around toward it, passing Carlos in the arc. Mariella gasped, but Papa just knocked the boy on the head. "Watch it."

"Sorry, Papa," he said.

Mariella looked at Carlos and raised her eyebrows, shocked that that was all the reprimand the boy got for being careless with a gun. He could have killed Carlos. Carlos just shook his head back at her and started the boat out toward the Gulf Stream.

Papa sat holding a tumbler of whiskey in one hand, a gun leaning against his chest, and his son resting against his legs on the floor. Mariella found a camera on board and snapped a picture of the man, his boy, his booze, and his gun.

"Should I send this to *Life* magazine?" said Mariella.

Papa snorted.

"I can see the caption," she said. "'Legendary Author Balks at Safety for Sport.'"

"Just don't let Mama see it," said Papa.

"Mama wouldn't mind," said Bumby.

"I mean Mama Pauline, not Mama Hadley," he said.

"Ah," said the boy. "Mama P would mind very much."

Papa ruffled the boy's hair and stared out at sea.

"Too many people trying to make damned sissies out of boys nowadays," said Papa moodily. "Don't teach 'em to hunt, don't teach 'em to swear—hell, we'll all be wearing skirts when they're done with us."

"Not me!" said Bumby. "I want to be just like you."

Mariella looked at Papa, and he smiled at the boy with great affection. "You're better than me, Bumby, because you've got a lot of your mother in you."

The boy didn't know what to say to that, but he looked up at his father with adoring eyes. Mariella again found herself confused over Papa's continued esteem for his first wife, Hadley. It sometimes seemed that he had more kindness and affection for her than he did for Pauline.

A tug on the line jerked Mariella from her thoughts.

Papa jumped and grabbed the pole just as a great marlin jumped from the water. Carlos ran to the edge of the boat with Mariella and Bumby.

"¡Puta madre!" said Carlos.

Mariella laughed at the expletive from the slight, sweet man while he shrugged sheepishly. She was taken aback when Papa yelled to Bumby to grab the gun and shoot the sharks while he tried to control the pole. She didn't feel comfortable with the boy in charge of the gun, but didn't think it was her place to interfere.

As Papa reeled and pulled, reeled and pulled, his white shirt stuck to his body, outlining his back muscles. Mariella admired his strength and wished she could handle such a feat.

Bumby wasn't a bad aim, and his shots appeared to deter the sharks, but also spooked the fish. It leaped fully out of the water again, and Mariella gasped at the sheer magnificence of it.

It took a tremendous effort on Papa's part, but he was finally able to pull it close to the boat. When he got it near enough, Papa handed the pole to Carlos. Against such a slight man, the weight and strength of the fish were clear, and Mariella was glad she hadn't made an attempt. If she had lost the fish, she couldn't have stood it.

It took Carlos everything he had in him to hold the marlin close to the boat. Papa picked up a harpoon and raised it high in the air, pausing for a moment while the sun gleamed on the dart. With a sudden flash of movement, Papa brought the harpoon down into the heart of the fish. It twitched and shuddered, and then it died.

They all stood in awe of it—its great silver belly facing the sky. Its gills were open and the light in its eyes had gone. They gave it respect through a moment of silence. Finally, Papa spoke up.

"Let's get this thing back before the sharks find out about it," he said.

⟋⟍⟋ ⟍

The idlers at the dock buzzed like flies around the fish while Carlos and some of the stronger men strung it up. It weighed 540 pounds—a record size. It hung next to the other marlin Papa had caught over the last few days, and they all took turns posing for photos with it.

When Papa found out that the locals didn't want the meat, his mood soured. He complained that he didn't like killing for killing's sake, and that they didn't have proper respect for the animal. He insulted the men at the dock with racial slurs that made Mariella cringe and darkened the men's eyes. She could tell that Papa was no longer in their good graces, though he didn't seem to care.

That night at the rum bar, Mariella watched Papa while she smoked. He still complained about the locals, but spent more time entertaining his audience with tales of the fish that grew more dramatic with each retelling. As she stubbed out her third cigarette, she acknowledged her increasing disdain for him. His endless boasting around the rich men; his foul, racist language; his complaints about critics; his overblown stories of game hunting in Africa; his flirtation with Jinny. The way he got off on Mariella's attraction for him around his wife. It diminished him. He used to seem so authentic, but lately she found him replaced by a sunburned, overfed legend of his own making. She felt strongly that he was in character, forever trying to hold up his image for the men around him.

Katy called to Mariella, motioning for her to join her and Dos on the outside porch, and Mariella was happy to do so. They sat drinking in the shadows, watching the boys play in the sand. Mariella passed around her cigarettes and lit one while she regarded the children, who were clearly enjoying the thrill of staying up past their bedtimes.

"Why aren't you two inside listening to fish stories?" asked Mariella, a wry smile on her lips. She enjoyed the companionship of the Dos Passoses and that they could speak openly with one another.

"Please," said Katy. "I'm about worn-out on Papa for the summer."

"Yes," said John. "Katy can only take him in small doses these days."

Mariella nodded. She knew what he meant.

"He doesn't seem to wear *you* out," said Katy to Mariella.

Mariella flicked her eyes to Katy and then back to the boys. Though her tone was playful, what was under it troubled Mariella. She didn't want anyone to notice her interest in Papa.

"I'm about at my limit," said Mariella, her voice lighter than she felt. "He takes up a lot of space."

John chuckled and nodded his head.

"Where's Ada?" asked Mariella.

"She passed out a while ago," said Katy.

"We sent Pauline to bed and told her we'd watch the boys," said Dos. "The little ones drove her crazy all day until you took them spearfishing."

"It's kind of you to look after them with all of the other chores you've got to do," said Katy.

"I don't consider it a chore to play with the boys," said Mariella. "It's nice to have them around. I miss my little sisters."

Mariella missed them terribly—more than she ever would

have anticipated. Papa's boys' voices, laughter, and play reminded her of Lulu and Estelle, and Mariella couldn't wait to see them again. She wished she could have brought them with her.

"Look! Look!" Patrick was suddenly yelling from the beach, calling for Mariella and the Dos Passoses to join them. They jumped up and hurried down the stairs to the sand to see what had excited him so much. The moon was bright and lit the beach, but it took Mariella a moment for her eyes to adjust. She saw a lot of movement in the sand.

"Turtles!" shrieked Gregory.

They all crowded around to watch the little creatures digging out of a depression in the sand and flopping around.

"Look—they're heading to the water," said Mariella. She picked up Greg so he wouldn't step on them, and carried him along as the turtles struggled over mounds in the sand to get to the sea.

Bumby told Patrick to make the sand smooth so the turtles wouldn't have to climb over the "sand mountains." Dos grabbed an oar and helped them smooth a runway to the surf, while Katy helped the tiny stragglers and wanderers back to the path.

Greg put his arms around Mariella's neck and his head on her shoulder. She could smell the wind in his salty hair and feel his plump cheek nestled against her neck.

God, how she missed the girls.

She stood for a while, facing Key West, sending her thoughts to her family on the night breezes. Then she turned back to the moonlit path, and the turtles, and her company, and embraced the beauty and the gift of the moment.

All night she dreamed of Gavin.

They were good dreams. Dreams that made her blush. She thought of them all that morning as she went about her chores, and nearly ran into Pauline as she carried the beach towels in from the line. Pauline frowned and regarded Mariella suspiciously, grounding her in the moment.

"Does everyone have to be out of sorts today?" asked Pauline.

"I'm sorry," said Mariella. "I was daydreaming. Who else is out of sorts?"

Pauline moved the brassy hair out of her eyes and turned her gaze in the direction of the dock.

"Papa's been grumbling all morning about the *Pilar*," she said. "I think he's getting bored. He just challenged the local champ to a boxing match."

Mariella's interest was piqued. Over the past few days, Papa had bet the locals that none of them could go three three-minute rounds with him. He'd pay two hundred and fifty dollars to the guy who could, and no one had beaten him yet. Mariella would enjoy watching a match, and turned her face eagerly to the dock. When she looked back at Pauline, however, she could see Pauline's disapproval. Mariella wiped the eager look off her face.

"Are you worried he'll lose?" asked Mariella.

"Yes! His opponent can carry a piano on his back."

Mariella gasped and raised her eyebrows.

"I can't watch," said Pauline. With that, she went to her room, slamming the door behind her. Mariella could certainly watch. She hurried the towels to her room for folding later and ran down to the dock. When she got there, she'd already missed the fight. All she saw was an enormous island man laid out on the dock and a crowd around Papa, cheering and slapping him on the back. When he noticed Mariella, he grinned and walked over to her.

"That guy could carry a piano on his back," he said.

"Impressive," said Mariella.

"When's your soldier coming?" asked Papa. "I'd like to knock him out."

Mariella narrowed her eyes at Papa.

"My soldier never loses," she said.

"I don't, either, so it should be a hell of a match."

Mariella ignored his remark and turned to leave. She was dying for Gavin to come over and give Papa a taste of defeat. She still didn't know whether he'd make it, and their separation was killing her. Gavin hadn't sent a telegram in weeks, and Mariella was beginning to worry that he'd forgotten her.

Finally, the next afternoon, there was a knock at her door. When she opened it, one of the cleaning staff of the hotel handed her a telegram. She quickly unfolded it, and her hands shook as she read it.

First weekend in August. Love, Gavin.

Mariella whooped and jumped up and down in her room. She couldn't believe the good news.

She ran out her door and toward the dock, where she knew Papa was working on the *Pilar,* with every intention of teasing him about being scared for the boxing match. Breathless and sweating by the time she reached him, Mariella was startled to see Papa outside of the boat and gazing down the dock at the small plane that had just pulled in.

Jane Mason had arrived.

CHAPTER TWENTY

Mariella stood on the dock watching Jane in the center of the group of men. Her hair stood out like a crown of red-gold in the midst of her brown suitors. She'd been out fishing with them all day, and had killed a shark and hooked a tuna—an amazing feat, since they hadn't been biting thus far. To Mariella's surprise, however, Papa wasn't among her attendants. He wasn't hanging on her every word, and he even appeared put out around her.

At the bar that night, after a few drinks, he seemed to warm up to Jane, much to Pauline's displeasure. Pauline maneuvered the seating so Papa was in the corner blocked by her, but when she got up to go to the bathroom, Jane took her place. Mariella cringed when Pauline returned to the bar.

"Oh, honey, is this your seat?" asked Jane.

"Take it," said Pauline. "We were just getting ready to go to bed."

Mariella raised her eyebrows. It wasn't like Pauline to assert herself that way. Papa laughed a little and pulled Pauline over to his lap.

"Let's stay, Mama," he said. "One more drink."

Mariella exhaled her cigarette and shook her head. That was the wrong thing for him to say.

Pauline pulled herself from his grasp and straightened her dress. "Let's go."

The bartender must have heard Papa's suggestion for one more drink, because he appeared with another overflowing glass and placed it in front of Papa at the bar.

"Look, see," said Papa. "I can't waste a perfectly full drink." He picked up the drink and sipped it.

Pauline left without a word, but she didn't need to say anything. Her look said it all.

Mariella stubbed out her cigarette and sat a few seats down from Papa and Jane. She wasn't quite ready to leave, either.

"You're going to get in trouble for that," said Jane.

"Nah, it'll be fine," he said.

Jane laughed and ordered a daiquiri.

"I enjoyed our hunt today, darling," she said.

"Like the good old days," he said.

"I wish you would have come on safari with us this year."

He didn't answer her. Mariella looked down the bar at him and saw that his face suddenly turned very dark. Dangerously dark.

"Mr. Cooper's a fine sportsman," Jane continued.

Papa drained his glass and looked ahead. Mariella could feel the tension oozing out of him. She wondered whether Jane could sense the change.

"Africa was such an adventure with him, *darling*, but you would have made it better."

"I wouldn't want to have been anywhere but here," he said.

"Even not with me?" she asked.

"You had *Mr. Cooper* to entertain you," he said through clenched teeth.

Jane grew quiet. She must have realized that he was angry. Mariella wondered who this Mr. Cooper was, but it didn't take a genius to understand that Papa was jealous.

"How's your back these days?" he asked. "Keeping the windows closed around the house?"

Jane looked as if she'd been slapped. Mariella gasped.

God, he could be cruel.

Jane's chair scraped against the floor and she walked out of the bar. He looked after her and caught Mariella's eyes in Jane's wake. Mariella showed her disdain. He held her gaze for a minute, his face as blank as white paper. She chastised him in her mind and thought she could hear his thoughts justifying himself. Finally, he looked away from her.

⁂

Mariella looked into her pack of cigarettes. Only one left. She'd smoked three on the dock while waiting for Gavin's plane. She searched the sky from every direction, but couldn't see a thing except high cirrus clouds in wisps over the deep blue of the water. She paced up and down the dock a bit and finally lit the last one.

Great, dark forms glided under the surface of the water. She shivered, knowing the sharks were only biding their time before nightfall, when they'd hunt. She saw smaller fish leaping out of the waves and wished them luck outrunning the predators.

Then she heard the low buzz of the engine and the seaplane appeared.

She jumped up and down, waving like a madwoman. The local man waiting in the boat to pick up Gavin laughed at her.

"That's a good welcome," he said.

She beamed and watched the plane land smoothly in the water. The man rowed out to meet Gavin in the plane. She could see Gavin wave and she almost jumped into the water to swim out to him. The boat brought him to the dock, and he threw his bag to the pier, leaped onto it, and picked up Mariella, swinging her around and kissing her.

He held her face in his hands.

"I'd forgotten how beautiful you are," he said. "I'd never have let you leave if I'd realized."

She laughed and kissed him again.

"I can tell you're happy to see me, too, so I haven't lost you to him," said Gavin.

Mariella rolled her eyes. "Oh, please," she said. "I'm more yours than ever before."

"Then it sounds like my prayers were answered," he said. He picked up his bag, and they started down the dock, hand in hand.

Gavin wasn't staying at the hotel. He'd rented a small, inexpensive room by the harbor. He was insistent that he pay his own way.

Mrs. Duncombe, who owned the Compleat Angler, organized a big dinner at the hotel that night. Everyone was invited, from Mariella and Gavin, to Ada Stern, to Jane Mason.

While Gavin left to wash and rest, Mariella helped the kitchen staff at the hotel with the cooking. She had learned how to make conch stew and johnnycake, a pan-fried bread the locals enjoyed. They made crabs and rice and several varieties of fried fish. Mariella didn't stay to join in the dessert preparation, because Pauline needed help with her hair and Mariella wanted time to wash and dress.

When Mariella got to the Hemingways' room, she could hear arguing inside. She rolled her eyes, annoyed that she had managed to intrude on another private moment between Pauline and Papa, and unsure of how to proceed. She stood outside the door trying to make up her mind.

"I just feel she takes what's mine," said Pauline. "I wish she hadn't come."

"You encouraged me to invite her," said Papa, clearly irritated.

"I know, but it seems as if she wants to edge me out of my own life," said Pauline.

"How ridiculous. To insinuate that she's somehow taken me. Jesus, I might as well screw her. I'm being accused anyway."

The room grew silent.

"What kind of sadist are you to invite someone who makes you miserable?" he said.

"I just thought I needed to deal with my feelings toward her."

"Well, you're not dealing with them. And you're making it my problem, and I resent the hell out of that. Christ, I came here to relax."

Mariella could hear Pauline start to cry. She didn't want to pass the Hemingways' window, so she crept down the stairs and walked along the beach to the other staircase on the porch and went to her room from that direction.

Mariella thought about what she had heard and that Papa had been cruel. But she also knew that Pauline's insecurities were making it worse. If Pauline could show some confidence around Jane and Papa, she could take control of the situation. Based on what Mariella had heard Papa say to Jane at the bar, she knew that even if they had once been lovers, they certainly weren't now. It sounded like Jane and this "Mr. Cooper" were lovers.

Mariella felt disgust that a married woman would carry on with other men. Why would Mr. Mason stand by and let his wife run around on him? Why even bother getting married in the first place? Did the rich play by a different set of rules? And did Pauline deserve it? After all, hadn't she started her relationship with Papa while he was married to Hadley?

Mariella felt a wave of shame that she had allowed herself to flirt so dangerously with Papa. She was glad their relationship had never fully crossed a physical line. It had been a dangerous game she'd been playing.

When Mariella reached her room, Papa slammed his door and started toward the dock. He didn't notice Mariella. She waited until he was out of sight before going into her own room.

When she got inside, she found her red and white flowered dress and put it on. Then she pinned up the sides of her hair and applied her red lipstick. It was dramatic against her tan skin, and she was pleased with the effect. The last thing she did was put on the perfume she'd made with one of the kitchen staff. The woman had shown her how to crush marlberry flowers and mix them with water and vodka to make a light, sweet-smelling fragrance.

Mariella stepped out of her room and walked over to the Hemingways' room. She listened for a moment and then knocked. Mariella heard the bedsprings creak and then Pauline opened the door. Her eyes were still swollen and she looked disheveled.

"Come in," she said.

Mariella went into the room, which was as dark as a tomb, and smelled like a man who had fished all day and bathed by swimming in the ocean. She made a mental note to relieve the hotel cleaning staff so she could take over cleaning it.

"We need to open up this place and get in some fresh air," said Mariella.

Pauline nodded.

Mariella opened the door and both sets of windows. She picked up the wet towels on the floor, shook them out, and hung them on the side of the railing on the porch. Then she walked the ashtray outside, emptied it into the sand, and put it on the table. She walked back in and saw that there was sand and bits of dried seaweed on the bedspread. She carried it out to the porch and shook it hard over the railing. Then she went back in, opened it over the bed, and smoothed out the creases.

Pauline watched her like a helpless child, and Mariella realized the situation was more dire than she'd thought. She instructed Pauline to dress in the bathroom and then sit by the mirror on the dresser. While Pauline dressed for dinner, Mariella picked up the dirty clothes off the floor, dumped the half-empty glasses of alcohol scattered throughout the room, and lined up Papa's moccasins and Pauline's espadrilles by the door. She surveyed the room with her hands on her hips and was satisfied that it looked better for now. The sea air was also flushing the room of its mustiness, and soon the pleasant ocean aroma was the strongest fragrance in the room.

Pauline came out of the bathroom improved in appearance. She had changed from her housedress to a pretty dinner dress with capped, wavy sleeves and a tea-length skirt. She had washed her face and combed water through her hair. She walked over to the chair and sat, looking at Mariella in the mirror. Mariella began forming curls and securing them with bobby pins.

"I don't know how I've become so helpless," said Pauline.

Mariella thought it sounded more like an address to the universe than a conversation starter, so she stayed quiet.

"It's because of how we started, me and Papa," said Pauline. She now looked at Mariella, directly addressing her.

"And how's that?" asked Mariella—fully aware of how *that* was.

"He was married to Hadley when we fell in love," she said. "And now I'll always worry that he'll fall in love with another once he's tired of me. You're lucky to have your soldier, Mariella."

Mariella continued setting Pauline's hair in silence. She didn't wish to discuss Gavin with Pauline. She didn't want to discuss Papa with Pauline, either. She didn't know what to say, but Pauline was obviously looking for some comfort.

"You've seen them," said Pauline. "Do you think he loves Jane?"

Mariella needed to choose her words carefully, without letting on too much. If she told Pauline about what she'd overheard at the bar, it would confirm that there had been *something* between Jane and Papa at some time. But she also wanted to assure Pauline that it appeared over.

"I think Jane forces herself on people," said Mariella. "I think she's charming and beautiful and people respond to that, but I don't think that Papa loves her. He loves you."

"I know he does," said Pauline. "I don't know why I wanted to invite Jane to the island. I think I was trying to pretend that everything was okay. But I can't handle it."

"When does she leave?" asked Mariella.

"Next weekend, thank God."

"Good. Then you won't have to worry anymore."

Mariella walked around the front of Pauline.

"Would you like me to put on your makeup?" asked Mariella.

"No, dear, you go find your beau," said Pauline. "Enjoy your time together."

Mariella felt a wave of gratitude for her dismissal. "Thank you, Mrs. Hemingway," she said. "Let your hair dry for a bit before you take out the bobby pins."

Pauline nodded and Mariella stepped to the door. Pauline's voice stopped her.

"You know, Mariella," said Pauline, "I need to apologize. I used to think you and Papa had something going on."

Mariella looked at her shoes and felt the shame burning in her face. She hoped she was shadowed enough for Pauline not to notice.

"Now I think that my jealousy has been making me see crazy things," she said. "I hope you'll forgive me."

Unable to find her voice, Mariella nodded. She turned and left the room.

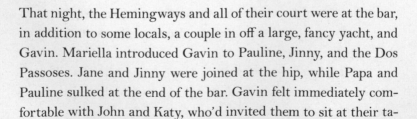

That night, the Hemingways and all of their court were at the bar, in addition to some locals, a couple in off a large, fancy yacht, and Gavin. Mariella introduced Gavin to Pauline, Jinny, and the Dos Passoses. Jane and Jinny were joined at the hip, while Papa and Pauline sulked at the end of the bar. Gavin felt immediately comfortable with John and Katy, who'd invited them to sit at their table. John was interested in hearing about Gavin's work on the Overseas Highway.

"I used to love taking the train down to Key West," said John. "There's nothing like looking down over the water from twenty feet up. Felt like flying."

"We're trying to use the rail beds from the old railroad where we can," said Gavin, "but not all of them are salvageable."

"It just seems like madness to think those roads will last with the storms that come through the Keys," said Katy. "I worry that you all are being worked to death for nothing."

"At least it's work," said Gavin. "There's nothing for me up north. Though the men down here are pretty difficult to deal with."

"The vets have been causing a lot of trouble in town," said Katy.

"I found a good one," said Mariella.

Gavin reached for her hand and kissed her on the cheek.

"I'm afraid there are a lot of us with big problems," said Gavin. "The drinking's pretty bad, the fights, shell shock."

"Still, all these years later," said Katy. "It's very sad."

Papa came around, turned a chair backward, and squeezed between Gavin and Katy. He was drunk.

"Far too serious over here," he said, slamming his drink between them.

"We were discussing the vets on Matecumbe," said John.

"Ah," said Papa. "How's Uncle Sam treating you up there?"

"Like they're glad we're out of Washington, as far away as possible."

"That's what I thought," said Papa. "Never trust the government. But enough of all this heavy talk. Let's talk about boxing."

At the word, the men crowded around, and Katy walked away. She went and sat next to Pauline, who was nursing a glass of gin and glaring at Jane, while Jane talked to Jinny.

Gavin saw two crisp tens land on the table.

Then a twenty.

They were betting on him and Papa. The men were calling out all kinds of combinations of rounds and minutes.

"Papa never loses," said John.

"Neither does Gavin," said Papa.

"Papa just laid out an island guy who could carry a piano on his back."

"Winner take all," said the yachtsman, dropping in twenty. "One round, knockout, Papa."

"When's the fight?" asked Mariella.

"Tomorrow morning. Nine o'clock," said Papa. "At the dock where you came in."

Gavin nodded soberly and took a swig of his drink.

"I'll go easy on your face," said Papa.

"Don't worry about that," said Gavin. "Damage is done there."

Gavin saw Mariella looking at the scar that ran down his face, then back at Papa.

"You could have one of those by the time he's done with you," she said.

The men "oohed."

Papa scowled. "You think he'll win?"

"I'm sure of it," said Mariella, to another chorus of "oohs."

"What'll you wager?" he asked.

Gavin thought Mariella shouldn't be betting on the fight. He knew Papa was trying to embarrass her for not choosing him. She pulled her wages out of her pocket and dropped them in the middle of the table.

"That's all my pay from working this month," she said, glaring at him. "Three rounds, knockout, Gavin."

Gavin reached out and tried to push the money back to Mariella. "No, don't do that."

"It's done," said Papa. "She can't take it back."

He stood and slammed his drink over the money on the table. He stared down at Mariella, breathing fast. His fists were clenched. Gavin didn't like the posture Hemingway had taken with Mariella and stood eye-to-eye with him. The room became quiet and all eyes were on the two men.

"Can you wait until morning, soldier?" asked Papa, quivering with agitation.

"If you can," said Gavin, his voice steady and calm.

Hemingway curled his lips in an ugly sneer. He stepped away from Gavin and left the room. Shortly after his exit, the bartenders sneaked around the corner and started with one of their ridiculous songs: "Big Man and Soldier, gonna throw down, gonna throw down." The room started to breathe again, and Gavin sat down next to Mariella while the crowd dispersed. Jane stood with Jinny, walked by the table, and threw down twenty dollars.

"Three rounds. Knockout. *Papa*."

John left and returned with an envelope in which he put the money, and wrote all the bets, times, rounds, and picks. He sealed it and shoved it in his back pocket. He and Katy left, followed by Pauline.

"Why did you do that?" asked Gavin. "He's never lost."

"I know you'll win," she said.

"That was foolish," he said. "Now you'll lose your whole summer. Shit, I didn't need that added pressure."

"I'm sorry," said Mariella. "I just couldn't take his arrogance."

"And now those rich people will take all your money."

"Don't think that way," she said.

"Do you know why he'll win?" said Gavin. "Because now he has to prove something. Because he hates me and he wants to impress you. You challenged his manhood, and you just don't do that to Ernest Hemingway without consequences."

Mariella pulled a cigarette from the pack Gavin had brought her. She lit it, handed it to him, and lit another for herself.

"You're wrong, love," she said. He shook his head and reached for her hand. She took it and they stood and walked out to the porch.

Jinny sat on a bench, with Jane leaning up against her side. Jane smoked with one hand and rubbed Jinny's leg with the other. Jinny leaned into Jane and whispered something in her ear that made Jane laugh. She looked as if she would kiss her, but turned toward Mariella and Gavin when their shadows fell over them.

"Girl," said Jane.

"Mar-i-el-la," said Jinny, giggling through the smoke that drifted around her face.

"Mariella," said Jane. "You have balls. I love that."

Gavin looked at Mariella and saw that she was taken aback.

"You're the only woman I've ever seen who could scare him," said Jane. She looked at Gavin, inhaling deeply. "Kick his ass for me, darling, and for your girl."

"I'll do my best," said Gavin.

"I bet against you, but I want you to win," she said.

"Mar-i-el-la," said Jinny again, laughing to herself, and draining the glass.

"Good night," said Gavin, guiding Mariella away from the women. As they walked down the stairs, they could hear Jinny saying Mariella's name in that teasing way.

Gavin and Mariella stepped off the porch and into the sand. They both left their shoes on the bottom step, and Gavin rolled up the bottom of his pants. He took Mariella's hand and they walked to the water.

"What was that all about with Jane and Jinny?" said Mariella.

Gavin just looked at her and smiled.

The moon winked off the crest of the waves, which were often broken by the large fins of hunting sharks.

"So I guess there's no nighttime skinny-dipping on the island," he said.

"Not unless you want to come back missing essential parts," said Mariella.

He laughed.

"That's a good sound," she said. "You don't laugh out loud much."

"Not usually much to laugh about," he said. "But, God, now, aside from getting my face broken tomorrow, I feel so good to be with you."

She leaned in closer to his side. "I'm so glad you're here. I'm afraid this weekend will be gone before we know it."

"It will," he said, "but then you'll come home in a couple of weeks and we'll be together again."

"I miss my sisters," said Mariella. "And my mom. Have you been to see them while I've been gone?"

"I have."

"How are they? Mama was never good at letter writing."

He was quiet for a moment, and Mariella sensed tension. She didn't know what to make of that and stopped walking.

"What is it?" she asked.

"I'm not going to lie. It was bad at first."

"Why? What happened?"

"Lulu had a fever and your mom wanted to call you. Estelle convinced her to look for me at John's, and luckily I was there."

"What did you do?"

"I just calmed your mom down and talked her through the usual procedure. We ended up calling the doctor, and he helped. Her fever broke in a day."

Mariella felt guilt rumbling in her belly.

"I shouldn't have left them," she said.

"Yes, you should," he said. "Your mom needs to learn how to be a mom again."

Mariella was quiet.

"And she's doing better," said Gavin. "Keeping it together. Making some positive changes . . ." His voice trailed off. Mariella sensed more trouble.

"What is it?"

"I'm going to tell you something that I'm fifty percent convinced you'll love and fifty percent convinced you'll hate," he said.

"God, what is it?"

"Let me preface this by saying I love it and see only good coming from it."

"Tell me!"

"I've wanted to tell you, but I just didn't want to put it in a telegram or letter."

"Gavin, if you don't tell me right now, *I'll* break your nose."

He looked down at her and laughed.

"Okay. I think your mom and John are falling in love."

Mariella fell silent and looked away from him at the water. She felt uneasy at the thought of her mother dating. It felt like a betrayal of her father. She didn't want to lose her mother just as she'd found her. But then she thought of John, and her heart filled with love. She wanted him to be happy, she wanted Eva to be happy, and the girls loved him. John would have someone to take care of him besides Gavin, and her family wouldn't need her as much as they did now.

She turned back to Gavin and smiled.

"That night at your house," she said, "I saw it. When we were leaving. When they hugged."

Gavin nodded.

"I think that may be the best thing that's happened to my family in a long time," she said.

He reached down and hugged her, lifting her a little off the ground and swinging her from side to side. He put her down and kissed her softly, first on the lips, then on the neck. She tipped her head back and saw the moon high over them and thought she'd never been happier.

"You know what Lulu said when your mom brought the girls to lunch at John's house?"

"What?" asked Mariella.

"She said your mom and John could get married, and you and I could get married, and we could switch houses."

Mariella laughed. "Lulu said that?"

"Yes."

"And how did everyone respond?"

"I think John and your mom were too busy trying to hide their blushes to speak. I said it was a swell idea."

"Gavin Murray, are you asking me to marry you?"

"Not yet," he said.

Mariella opened her mouth as if in shock and punched his chest.

"Easy! Don't beat me up before tomorrow," he said.

"Then why are you teasing me?"

"I just wanted to see your response," he said. "And I need to make some more money before I can support you."

"Don't be so practical," she said, leaning in to kiss the hollow at the base of his neck. "I can't wait much longer for you."

He groaned and kissed her hard. "Me neither."

They walked over to the dock where the *Pilar* was tied and rocking in the water to the rhythm of the waves. Mariella put her hand on the side of the boat and closed her eyes.

"You miss being out on the water," said Gavin.

"To my bones," she said.

"John told me what you want to do," said Gavin.

Mariella opened her eyes and looked at Gavin, waiting for his thoughts on the charter boat business.

"I think it's a great idea," he said. "It will work."

When he said it, she suddenly knew it would. For the first

time she could see it. Clearly. It would work. It made her feel too emotional to speak, so she turned back to the *Pilar.*

He came up behind her, slipped his hands around her waist, and kissed the side of her neck. She felt every nerve in her body quiver and turned back to him to wrap herself up in his arms.

"Why don't you do it with me?" she said.

He laughed deeply in her ear. "Here?"

She gave him a punch in the side and he pretended it hurt.

"I'd love to do it with you, but we'd get splinters," he said.

She punched him again and pulled away. He pulled her back and kissed her.

"Seriously, I was hoping you'd ask," he said. "I've always wanted to work on the water, but I thought it was hopeless, with the fishermen in the state they're in right now. With your connections to these richies through Hem, even with the state of the economy, it would work."

"There's just one small problem," she said.

"A boat."

"I've been trying to save since my dad was alive, but rent and taking care of my family drains us. I only have about thirty bucks. Until you beat Fat Slob tomorrow, that is."

He laughed.

"I've got a little money saved," he said. "We'll keep saving and we'll do it."

The sound of drunken voices arguing called their attention to the beach.

"We'd better get back," she said. "Big day tomorrow."

He took her hand and walked her back to the hotel. He dropped her off at her room with another kiss that made it difficult for her to send him away, but she did. She closed her door and went to the open window. He stuck his head through and kissed her again, then started down the porch stairs. She watched him walk away, but he ran back up and kissed her again. She laughed and he shushed her and she pushed him. He walked back down the stairs, watching her, and tripping down the bottom steps. She laughed and he put his hand over his heart. He finally turned and walked down the beach, toward the road that would take him to his hotel. She watched him until he was lost in the shadows.

Thunder rumbled over the water, and the wind picked up. Mariella rubbed the chill from her arms and went to bed.

Chapter Twenty-one

It was cloudy and threatened rain that morning. Mariella woke early, pulled up her hair, and went to the dining room to help with breakfast. She had settled in fast with the hotel staff, and could envision herself working there if she didn't have so much back in Key West. Mrs. Duncombe, the hotel owner, was very kind and accommodating. She didn't seem to find it at all strange that the Hemingways would fly their housekeeper to Bimini with them and put her to work for the hotel.

"Big fight this morning?" asked the cook, Laney, a large Bahamian with a deep voice.

"Oh, yes," said Mariella.

"Your beau and Fat Slob?"

Mariella laughed. The staff had been calling Papa that, much to his and everyone's amusement, since he had knocked out Knapp.

"Any chance of Beau winning?" asked Laney.

"He's never lost a fight," said Mariella, "so the odds are good."

"But neither has Fat Slob, and he knocked out the piano man."

"Don't remind me," said Mariella.

She helped Laney with the coffee and eggs and sliced a pineapple.

The breakfast crowd arrived early and the room buzzed. Papa came in off the beach from an early swim, pulling on his Basque shirt and running his hands through his hair. He winked at Mariella and sat down with the Dos Passoses. He laughed loudly at something Katy said. He appeared to be in high spirits.

Mariella was too nervous to eat, so she left to head over to the dock to give Gavin some encouragement. He was there when she arrived, along with a larger than usual crew of locals. They were gambling with dice on the end of the pier and laughing raucously. The air was charged from the weather and the anticipation of the fight.

"Jeez, news travels fast," said Gavin as he gestured to the crowd.

Mariella rolled her eyes and reached into her pocket. She passed Gavin the rabbit's foot.

"For good luck," she said.

"I didn't know you were superstitious."

"I'm not, but Papa gave this to me and told me it was lucky."

"I don't believe in luck—good or bad," said Gavin.

Mariella shrugged. She put it back into her pocket.

"Wait," he said. "I do remember hearing something about good-luck kisses."

She smiled and kissed him. Some of the locals began clapping, and Mariella pulled away as she felt the dock shake. She looked over her shoulder and saw Papa walking ahead of his entourage. He looked like the happy king this morning. Mariella felt the confidence drain out of her.

Papa reached out and shook Gavin's hand. "I'm sorry about last night," he said.

"No apologies," said Gavin.

"If you'd like to forget all this silliness, we can just go have a drink and call it a day."

Mariella felt her confidence rise. Was Papa nervous?

"It's your call," said Gavin.

Mariella thought it was smart of him to put it back in Papa's hands. Now, if Papa backed out, he would look like a coward.

"Then we'll fight," he said. "Gloves or no?"

"No."

A nervous twitter went through the crowd, and Mariella cringed. Papa raised his hands as if to say he tried.

The group spread into a ring around the men. Mariella looked over the crowd and her eyes found Jane's. Jane winked at her and inhaled her cigarette. Mariella wished she hadn't left hers in the room. Pauline also locked eyes with Mariella and looked anxious. Mariella looked away and down at the beach by the pier. The Hemingway boys were boxing in the sand, knocking each other over and wrestling in the surf under the disapproving gaze of Ada. John pulled out his watch and announced he'd keep time. They'd fight three-minute rounds. Katy stood next to him biting her nails.

The fight began.

Papa and Gavin circled each other slowly, each one willing the other to make the first move. They circled so long, the crowd started jeering them. That prompted Papa to action, and he took a heavy swing at Gavin's face. Gavin ducked and landed an uppercut on Papa's left side. He groaned and so did the crowd.

Papa backed off, then stepped forward and aimed for Gavin's stomach, making strong contact and knocking the wind out of him. Gavin recovered and dodged a near miss to his right cheek. The men started circling again, and Gavin went in for a jab to Papa's face. Papa moved his head too slowly and got clipped on the right cheek. It swelled immediately.

The boys had stopped boxing now, and were watching, cheering their papa on loudly. The rest of the crowd shouted and cheered for no one and each one. She thought they all would have wanted to see Papa knocked out, with the exception of Pauline, but no one would dare voice it.

John called time and the boxers rested. Mariella gave Gavin some water she'd brought. Pauline mopped the blood off Papa's cheek. The men turned quickly back to each other, and the next round began.

Papa was mad. The red blood on the white towel must have ignited something in him, and he realized the seriousness of the situation. He looked like a bull struck by a sword at a bullfight, emblazoned with anger and ready to maul.

He came at Gavin with a quick, right-handed one-two-three, followed by a left jab that missed its target. Papa was back on him with a right uppercut that made soft contact with Gavin's side and gave Gavin time to get in a left hook to Papa's face. It opened the cut even more and infuriated Papa. He pulled back and struck Gavin's chest with a straight jab. Gavin stumbled back, but regained his footing and quickly circled around Papa. Papa had thrown a lot of hard punches and was breathing heavily. They spent the remainder of the round circling each other and throwing small punches. Then John called time.

The clouds, which had been threatening for a while, opened up in a downpour. Gavin put his head back and shook the rain off his face. Mariella gave him some more water and followed it with a kiss.

"Get his cheek again," she said. Gavin nodded and turned back toward Papa.

The crowd was in a frenzy. They sensed Papa's anger and lack of control and felt that Gavin might be able to finish him. Mariella felt butterflies in her stomach and couldn't help but smile.

John called to start the round, and Gavin stepped forward. Papa again came at Gavin fast. His feet were heavy, but his fists were sure. Gavin dodged the punches and swung around quickly. He landed a jab in Papa's side, but Papa got in a punch on Gavin's chin. It slid off Gavin's face in the rain.

Papa looked exhausted, but to Mariella's dismay, so did Gavin. She wished he would come on stronger or would at least go for the wound. As if in response to her thoughts, Gavin stepped forward with a quick one-two from his left, followed by a right that again made contact with Papa's bloody cheek. The crowd groaned and shouted.

With a loud growl Papa pulled back and knocked Gavin square in the face.

Mariella saw the knockout in slow motion. She heard the sickening crunch of Gavin's nose and watched him fall back. Her legs felt too heavy to move, and she heard his head hit the pier with a terrible thud. The noise silenced the crowd. They could hear only the lapping of the water against the pilings and the shush of the rain.

Mariella ran to Gavin and lifted his head into her lap, terrified that Papa had killed him. Blood ran out of Gavin's nose, and his eyes were closed. Papa shook his hand and dropped down next to Gavin. He was worried, too. The crowd closed in on them. Mariella felt tears hot on her face.

"Is he okay?" asked Papa.

Mariella felt for a pulse and found one. Gavin's eyes fluttered open. The crowd released their breath, and Gavin smiled.

"Fat Slob," he said. Papa and Mariella smiled and the crowd cheered. Papa picked up Gavin and slapped him on the back.

"Let's never do that again," said Papa.

Pauline ran over with the towel and gave it to Gavin to stop the bleeding from his nose. He was unsteady, so he sat on the bottom of an upside-down dinghy.

The boys were hooting and hollering on the beach, clearly thrilled with their magnificent father and being able to play in the rain. Mariella saw Ada push through the crowd. Ada grabbed the towel and passed Gavin her flask.

"Drink," she commanded.

He took a long gulp and shuddered.

"You'll thank me for this later," she said as she pushed the towel roughly onto his face, covered his nose, and jerked the bone back into place. The crowd gasped and Gavin nearly passed out, but Mariella and Papa propped him up. Ada skulked away and Gavin looked at her, whispering, "Fat Slob."

Papa threw back his head with a roar of laughter. Mariella finally allowed herself to laugh, too.

"Come on," said Papa. "Let's get out of this rain."

The sound of the rain and its fresh smell drifted in through the open window. Gavin lay on Mariella's bed facing the ceiling. His nose throbbed and he felt nauseated. He hoped the aspirin Papa had brought over after the fight would kick in soon. Mariella lay with her head touching Gavin's and held a towel full of ice chips on his nose. She pulled back the towel and looked at his nose.

"The swelling's going down already," she said. "Would you like me to fetch Ada so you can thank her?"

Gavin looked sideways at Mariella and then back at the ceiling.

"I'd like to knock her out," he said.

"I'm sorry, but you have a better chance of beating Papa than her."

Gavin laughed, then grimaced and reached for his nose. Mariella put the ice back on.

"She really did you a favor," said Mariella.

"I know," said Gavin. "At least it will heal straight. You'd leave me if I had a crooked nose to add to my hideous scar."

Mariella put the ice on the bedside table and leaned over Gavin's face. She ran her finger down the scar and softly kissed the area by his lip where it ended. "No, it makes you look tougher," she said. "We can't have you looking prettier than me."

He reached up and pushed a lock of hair out of her eyes and put it behind her ear. His face grew serious.

"I'm so sorry I lost you your money," he said.

"Stop," she said. "That turned out exactly as it should have."

"What?"

"Really," she said. "First, this trip has been a joke. I've barely worked. I'm sorry I can't send the money home, but I'll work over-time once I get back. Second, imagine if you had beaten Papa. Do you think he would have taken that well?"

"No, but ultimately, what do I care?"

"You should care, because now he likes you and feels a sense of responsibility to you. He respects you for not backing down. He respects you for almost beating him. Now he'll always buy you a drink at the bar and sing your praises in front of others. If you had beaten him, he'd be mean as a snake."

"I guess you're right. But what a shitty way for a person to be."

"Shitty or not, that's the way he is."

Thunder rumbled outside of the window. Mariella turned to watch it, and Gavin wrapped himself around the back of her. They lay like that, watching the rain, until they slipped off to sleep.

At dinner that night, the weather had cleared and Papa was in high spirits, so the crowd was, too. There was laughter, food, drinking, smoking, and more drinking. Everyone congratulated Jane for winning the money on the fight. Papa bragged about the knockout, but also admitted that Gavin was a formidable oppo-nent. He followed with stories of Gavin's boxing in Key West. The sports talk soon turned to war talk, and Papa sobered the crowd by predicting that the U.S. would be involved in a second world war sooner rather than later. Mariella shivered at the thought and listened intently to what he said about the Germans. When talk of the Spanish Civil War began, Mariella felt a gentle tug on her arm. It was Jane.

Jane motioned with her head for Mariella to follow her outside. She handed Mariella a cigarette when they got out there and leaned against the balcony with her. They stood for a while, not speaking, until Mariella felt uncomfortable. Finally, Jane spoke.

"I hope we can be friends," said Jane.

Mariella wasn't sure how to take the offer, but smiled anyway.

"I know you don't like me," said Jane. "But I want you to know I'm not Papa's lover."

Mariella thought Jane would say, "now," but Jane cut herself off at that.

"I would hate for people to think that," said Jane.

Mariella thought that by "people" Jane meant Pauline. She wanted Mariella to tell Pauline what she was saying.

"I do love him, but not the way you think," said Jane. "I suppose I love him the way that . . . *you* do."

Mariella turned away. She was upset that Jane saw her feelings for Papa, whether they remained or not. She didn't want to be judged by Jane.

"Why are you telling me this?" asked Mariella. "I'm just the help."

"No," said Jane. "No, you are much more than that. You can control him."

"I don't think anyone can do that."

"I don't mean it in a literal way. I mean that he respects you and cares for you in a good and healthy way. I would just ask one thing of you."

"Yes," said Mariella.

Jane took a long drag of her cigarette and looked out at the water. The noise from the dinner party inside increased, and the bartenders were singing the "Phony Fat Slob" song again. Jane smiled to herself.

"You know, we used to be that way, once," said Jane. "But I let it cross a line."

Jane turned and faced Mariella.

"Don't let that happen to you," said Jane. "Keep him always at arm's length. And not just for you or for Pauline, but for him. He needs good, true friends. And he's going to need them more as the years go on. I don't see age treating Papa well."

"Why do you say that?" asked Mariella.

"His physique, his writing, his strength—they're how he defines himself—and when they go away one day, he will have nothing. He alienates too many and relies too much on himself. I wish I could be his friend, but that chance is lost."

Jane's words chilled Mariella, and, truthfully, she couldn't imagine Papa ever less than the bronze god on the dock.

"Will you just be his friend, Mariella?" asked Jane.

Mariella heard a tremor in Jane's voice and was moved by her emotion. She wasn't sure whether she completely understood what Jane meant, but she understood the gravity of her words and the good place they came from.

"I will," she said.

Jane smiled and wiped away a tear.

"You are a good girl, Mariella."

Mariella felt a lump in her throat she didn't understand. She wanted to get back to Gavin. Jane stepped forward and kissed Mariella on the forehead. Then Jane threw her cigarette in the sand and walked back to her room. Mariella watched her go, then returned to the party. She scanned the crowd and saw Gavin and Papa leaned into each other at the bar, earnestly discussing something—probably war or politics. Pauline and Jinny laughed and danced to the music with the boys jumping around them. John and Katy slow danced in the corner.

Mariella looked at the people in the room and loved them deeply. In a rush, she felt the physical melancholy of vacation's end settle over her. Its shadow fell over everyone in the room. She knew all these people would start leaving, and they would have to go back to work, and she would be without Gavin during the week, and hurricane season would rush into full swing. Instead of the joy and expectation of time left on holiday, she felt the dread of numbered days, and even though she missed her family greatly, she knew that these people would never again be together, like this, on an island at the edge of the world.

Gavin and Mariella built a fire down the beach from the hotel so they could have some privacy. They spent most of the time kissing on the blanket, wrapped up in each other, and watching stars move over the sky. They fell asleep for a short time, but the bugs were biting, so they parted with reluctance.

When Mariella arrived back at her room she put on a night-shirt, combed out her hair, and crawled into bed. While she lay waiting for sleep to come, she noticed an envelope on the night-stand with a red hibiscus flower on it. Mariella sat up, pushed the flower off the envelope, and opened it.

Inside was all the money she'd bet on the fight.

CHAPTER TWENTY-TWO

Mariella felt a wave of sadness as she watched the seaplane take off and get smaller and smaller in the blue sky, taking Gavin away from her, back to the place she craved. She dreaded all of their return flights home and knew she'd worry about Gavin until she got word he was safe. She stood alone at the end of the pier for a long time after he left, imagining his kiss and desperately wishing she could go with him.

The ache of missing her mother and sisters had grown to real, physical pain. She was worried that her mother might have regressed again. She missed taking the girls to the beach. She missed reading to Estelle and drawing pictures with Lulu. She missed John.

The mood on Bimini had changed. After Gavin's departure, Jinny left. Then Jane left.

They all walked down to the pier to see Jane off.

"I can't wait to see you all in Cuba later this summer," said Jane. "And I hope you'll come, too, Mariella."

Mariella thought she'd love to go to Cuba. Maybe she could even find out about her mother's family. She didn't have much time to think about this, however, because Pauline's face turned red and she shot a look at Papa. "What do you mean?"

"Jane was kind enough to extend us an invitation to Cuba at

the end of August for marlin fishing," he said. "Then I can leave
Pilar with Carlos for hurricane season."

Suddenly everything seemed silent. The waves didn't even
dare make noise.

"Were you planning on discussing this with me?" asked Pauline. "I've got organizing to do for the boys' schooling. I have to
figure out when we'll visit my family in Arkansas. I have to plan
for our trip to New York."

"Well, you don't need to go to Cuba," said Papa.

Mariella cringed and her heart started racing. Papa clearly
didn't care whether he hurt Pauline. It even seemed as if he tried
to upset her.

Pauline stared at him for a moment and then looked at Jane.
Jane crossed the dock and squeezed Pauline's shoulders.

"I really hope you'll join us," said Jane with sincerity in her
voice. "It wouldn't be the same without you." She leaned in,
kissed Pauline on the cheek, then turned and climbed aboard her
plane.

Jane tied a kerchief around her hair and gave Mariella a wink.
She waved at them with the grace and elegance of a movie star as
the plane took off. It was out of sight within minutes.

Mariella started to walk back to the hotel. She wanted to get
away from Pauline and Papa as soon as she could. She hadn't gone
far before she heard the hisses and shouts beginning. She couldn't
make out their words, but she didn't need to hear to know what
Pauline was saying.

～⌒

The days became intolerably long and hot. Record temperature
highs, little to no wind, and the biting flies and mosquitoes made
everyone grumpy. The island's charm waned, and they were all
short with one another. Pauline barely spoke to Papa, and he was

especially moody without a manuscript to occupy him, with poor fishing, and with the *Pilar* acting up.

Then a letter came from Gavin that haunted Mariella almost more than she could stand.

August 7, 1935

Dear Mariella,

It makes me sick to write this to you, but I need someone to talk to. Last week while I was off enjoying myself in a tropical paradise, one of the men in my unit walked out onto the track in the path of a train traveling to Key West. Most of my men were eyewitnesses. They said he waited for the train, stepped onto the track when it was clear the train could not slow down in time, raised his arm, and was killed instantly.

His name was Fred, and I knew he'd been troubled for some time. He was shell-shocked and miserable from the war, but I didn't understand how serious it was. Or rather, in spite of understanding how serious it was, I left him alone. I should have gotten him help when I saw the warning signs, and now it's too late. Every time I close my eyes, I see horrible images of what the accident must have looked like. I can't get it out of my head.

I debated whether or not to send you this letter, but I thought you needed to know before you came home and found me a mess. While I prayed for Fred's soul you kept jumping into my mind, like God was trying to tell me what I already know: You are the way to goodness and peace. When you get home I'll never let you forget it and how much you mean to me.

I'll tell you every hour of the day until we're old and gray and you can't stand it anymore.

I love you,
Gavin

Mariella folded the letter back into the envelope and placed it on her bedside table. She crawled into bed with her hands shaking, and barely slept that night.

What finally pushed her into near-hysteria was the telegram she received the next day.

Lulu's sick. Please come home. Mama.

Mariella burst into Papa and Pauline's room without knocking. Pauline stopped painting her nails. Papa looked up over his glasses at Mariella.

"I've got to go home," said Mariella. "Lulu's sick. My mother sent for me."

Papa put down his paper. "But the next plane doesn't leave until Friday. That's days away. Did the telegram say anything else?"

"No," said Mariella, thrusting the paper into Papa's hands. She fought the urge to cry.

Papa read it. He took off his glasses and rubbed his eyes. He looked up at Mariella.

"Then we'll go."

Pauline looked at him sharply. "Today?"

"That's not possible," said Papa. "I've got to do some work on the *Pilar*, and I hope to God she'll make the return trip. But we can't wait until Friday. This appears urgent. We'll go tomorrow."

Mariella lunged into Papa with a hug that nearly knocked him over in his chair. Pauline walked over to the window and looked out at the boys fishing in the surf.

"I don't know how we'll all pack up our entire summer in such a short time," said Pauline. "Surely a few days won't make a difference. This happens all the time to your sister, doesn't it?"

Panic rose in Mariella. Something felt different this time. She didn't want to beg, but she had to get home. Papa saved her from humiliating herself.

"'Tell Ada to start packing the boys' things," said Papa. "You get our stuff ready once your nails have dried. If it's not too much trouble," he added with sarcasm.

Mariella was filled with gratitude, and relief washed over her. It all left her, though, when she saw Pauline glare at her. The last time she'd seen that venomous stare it had been directed at Jane Mason.

After Mariella helped Ada pack for the boys and for herself, she sent a return telegram to Gavin. She asked him to check in on Eva and the girls, and assure them she'd get home as soon as possible. She sent him some words of condolence about the vet's suicide and told him she would be there for him when she returned.

It didn't take Mariella long to get ready, so waiting on the island was agonizing, especially with Pauline's open hostility. Mariella found it ironic that when she felt least attracted to Hemingway, Pauline was angriest at her. She decided to stay out of Pauline's way, and hoped that her mood would improve once they returned to Key West.

That night Mariella couldn't sleep. She prayed earnestly to God that Lulu would be okay. She prayed that they'd make quick time on the *Pilar*, and that Pauline didn't hate her. Sleep finally came, but was plagued with nightmares.

Mariella dreamed that Gavin was sick. He was feverish and his nose was bleeding. His arm hung over the side of the bed, the

11-11-18 tattoo showing like an exclamation on his arm. Then she turned and saw Lulu in another bed, sick and feverish. Mariella looked down and saw a white uniform. She was a nurse in a war hospital. Moaning coming from behind her caused her to turn. It was John. His severed legs bled on the bed. They were angry red stumps, and he cried and grabbed at them while a doctor tried to restrain him. Mariella turned to run and saw her father—wet, blue, and cold on a stretcher. A nurse covered him, and two men carried him away.

Thunder rumbled outside and jerked Mariella awake. She was wet with her own sweat from the dream and the heat. The window was open like a mouth gasping for air, but all that came into the room was the sound of the crashing waves.

Mariella lay in bed, trying to blot the bad dream from her mind, but it was still vividly before her. She got up and went into the bathroom to splash her face with cold water, then walked over to the window. She saw heat lightning far out over the Gulf Stream, followed by thunder, rolling in a slow growl toward the island. In front of the waves was a solitary figure. She strained her eyes and saw that it was Papa. He stood staring out at the lightning and the water. His shoulders sagged and his arms were crossed over himself. He looked so lonely.

Mariella opened her door and went out to him.

The stairs down to the beach were still warm with the sun's daytime heat, and there was no breeze for relief. Mariella felt a mosquito on her neck and slapped it. Papa heard the noise as she approached and turned to the side and nodded at her. She stood next to him, looking out over the water.

"Can't sleep?" he said.

She shook her head. "Terrible dreams. You?"

"I can't manage to fall asleep to even try at nightmares. The moonlight tortures me."

"Everything is worse at night," she said.

"It is," he said. "Don't trouble about Lulu. We'll get you back to her."

"It just must be really bad if my mother sent a telegram."

"She needs you, Mari. We shouldn't have taken you for so long."

"It's been a great trip. I don't know if I've properly thanked you. You didn't have to bring me."

"I know," he said. "But I wouldn't have enjoyed it as much without you."

He sighed and ran his hands through his hair.

"What is it?" she asked.

"The words are starting to back up, but when I sit down I can't get them on paper."

"Once we're home and you're back to your routine, they'll come."

"What if they don't?'

"Then you write about Key West and what you do there and see if a story comes from it."

"I am tossing a lot of things around in my head for a story about a rumrunner. I'll guess I'll see where that goes."

"Does it end well?"

"No."

"Why not?"

"I don't know if I believe in it."

"Jesus, Papa, I came out here to feel better. This isn't helping."

He chuckled and put his arm around her. "I could love you, Mari."

A shark surfaced near the shore, its dorsal fin drawing a lazy, wavy line over the surface of the water. A warm wave broke and washed up around their feet.

"I'm tired of the summer and the heat," he said suddenly. "Have you ever seen the change of seasons?"

"No," said Mariella. "I've never lived anywhere but Key West."

"God, you haven't lived till you've seen the leaves change color up north. I need to see that this fall. I wish you could see it with me."

"Someday I'll see it," she said. "There's a lot I want to see. I can't even imagine snow."

"The best part of the snow is the silence. It muffles the world. You've never heard such silence as a nice batch of snow makes."

Mariella tried to imagine it, but could hear only the whisper of the ocean. She rested her head on his shoulder and thought that if she'd imagined this scene before her trip, her heart would have raced. Now she felt only a warm, familial connection to him. She thought of Jane's words and fully understood now. And she knew that he'd be her friend, always.

CHAPTER TWENTY-THREE

Key West

The *Pilar* came into the dock with a gasp after the twenty-six-hour trip that began at nearly midnight the day before. The *Pilar* had needed more work than Papa had anticipated, but he had pushed and sweated all day with Carlos and Mariella at his side until they got her into shape for the trip. Pauline said they should wait until the next day to leave, but Papa saw Mariella's face and wouldn't hear of it. He told her to put the boys to bed and they'd wake them up when it was time to go.

It was time to go at midnight.

The *Pilar* was burning oil fast and would need extensive work when they got home. Papa grew moody and angry during the trip, and everyone tried to stay away from him the best they could on the cramped boat. The boys were restless, they were hot, and they all needed sleep. Mariella was beside herself with worry, and her tension had made the rest of them uneasy. She also sensed Pauline's disdain for her and hoped it would dissipate soon.

Pauline immediately dismissed Mariella when they arrived in Key West. Papa protested that she shouldn't be wandering the streets at one o'clock in the morning, but Mariella was gone before he could win the argument.

She ran through the streets with her bag slapping her side as she went. She felt overjoyed to be home, but also out of place. For the first time in her life, Mariella felt uneasy on the streets of Key West. The shacks were covered in shadows. Very few lights burned in windows. It had the look of an abandoned town, and a chill rose on her arms.

Finally, her house appeared, and she sprinted to it as fast as she could. With her heart racing and sweat pouring off her, she burst over the lawn and up the ramp that went to the front door. She looked down and registered that John had, indeed, been spending some time here, but couldn't dwell on it in her need to see Lulu.

Mariella dropped her bag by the door and slowed to catch her breath. There was no one in the front room or the kitchen, and the house was a mess. The curtains were drawn and the air was stale. Old dishes with dry, crusty food littered the countertop and table, and dirty clothes lay in limp piles on the floor. The plants in the window were dead and dried, and the ashtray by her mother's chair spilled over with cigarette butts.

Mariella's heart sank.

She walked to her room and only Estelle was there, sitting on the mattress, rocking back and forth. Estelle jumped when she saw Mariella, and Mariella crossed the room and embraced her sister, taking in the sweet smell of her plaited hair.

"I missed you so much," whispered Mariella. "How's Lulu?"

Estelle didn't say anything, but based on her behavior, Lulu wasn't well. Mariella eased Estelle down on the mattress and covered her with a blanket. Then she went to her mother's room.

It was dark, but Mariella could see Eva kneeling in prayer by the side of the bed. She mumbled her rosary at the bedside where Lulu lay, her wet, ragged breathing the only other sound in the house. Eva hadn't registered Mariella's presence.

Mariella didn't want to scare her mother, so she gently touched her shoulder. Eva jumped and, when she saw Mariella, pulled herself into her daughter's arms and sobbed.

"She's dying," said Eva. "There's nothing we can do. The doctor said there's nothing we can do."

Mariella was filled with a surge of anger—at the doctor and at Eva. Mariella pushed her mother aside and sat on the bed. She put her hands on Lulu's head. It was burning hot.

"Why isn't she in the cold water?" said Mariella. "You've got to put her in cold water."

"She shakes so bad when we do that."

"It's the only way. Her body needs help getting her temperature down."

Mariella stormed past her mother and into the bathroom, where she turned on the cold water. She went back into the room and tried to gently rouse her sister. Lulu moaned while Mariella undressed her.

"Get me some ice," said Mariella. Eva went to the kitchen to chip some.

Mariella carried Lulu into the bathroom and lowered her into the tub. The child screamed and thrashed when she hit the water, and Mariella blew a sigh of relief. It seemed good to her that Lulu was so responsive. She tried to calm Lulu and forced her to sit in the water until she calmed down. Lulu's eyes opened. They were darkly rimmed and bloodshot, but they focused on Mariella. She blinked and then a smile flickered over her lips.

"Mari's home," she said, and again closed her eyes. Mariella exhaled a laugh and tears came to her eyes. Eva walked into the bathroom.

"Did she just say something?" said Eva.

Mariella nodded.

"She hasn't spoken in days," said Eva.

When Lulu's shivering became violent, Mariella lifted her out of the tub and wrapped her in a towel she found on the floor. It was still damp from someone else's use, and she looked at her mother with reproof.

"I've been at her side for days," said Eva. "I didn't have time for housekeeping."

Mariella thought from the state of the house that it hadn't been cleaned or kept for more than a few days, but she didn't say anything. She carried Lulu back to her mother's room and placed her under the sheets in the bed. She wet a small towel and laid it over Lulu's forehead while she spooned ice chips into her mouth. In a few minutes, Lulu had fallen asleep.

"What exactly did the doctor say?" asked Mariella.

"That there was nothing he could do."

"That there was nothing *we* could do or nothing *he* could do?"

Eva looked confused. Mariella groaned, aggravated that she had spent days in a state of agony over Lulu's well-being when it was the same problem the child always had. She was frustrated that she had made the Hemingways leave Bimini early and ride twenty-six hours on a boat in a state of anxiety when the matter wasn't pressing.

"I'm so sorry, Mariella," said Eva.

Mariella was too exhausted to fight. She rubbed her temples and shook her head, then looked at her mother. Eva looked as if she hadn't showered in days. Her housedress was soiled and her hair was stringy. Her eyes were dark. Mariella could see the worry and pain on her mother's face and was moved with pity. Mariella was used to dealing with Lulu's fevers and should have left better instructions for her mother. She also knew that she was so, so glad to be home, and lunged at her mother with a hug.

"I'm so happy you're home," said Eva.

Mariella pulled back and smiled. "Me, too."

Eva cupped Mariella's face in her hands. "Island living suits you. Was it a wonderful trip?"

"It was," said Mariella. She yawned.

"You must be exhausted," said Eva. "Let's go to bed. You sleep here and I'll sleep out in my chair. You can tell me all about Bimini tomorrow."

Mariella didn't argue. Her fatigue made her dizzy. She went over to the bed and crawled in beside Lulu. Lulu didn't feel quite as hot as she did before, but still seemed warmer than she should be. Mariella listened to the sound of Lulu's breathing. It was less ragged, but still didn't sound healthy. She watched the little girl's chest rise and fall and was soon sleeping beside her.

Mariella jerked awake. Something had changed. The room was too quiet. She couldn't hear the raspy breathing.

She turned over on the bed to face her sister, terrified at what she'd see.

The light was creeping into the room with the sunrise, but Mariella could see only Lulu's outline. She couldn't hear her breathing. Her arm felt cool against Mariella's.

Mariella felt the tears hot and fast and started praying, "Oh, God, no, no, no, no, please, no."

She reached her hand over and felt under the blanket. She placed her hand over Lulu's heart.

And there it was. The soft pounding of her little heart. The gentle rise and fall of her chest.

The fever had broken.

Mariella uttered a silent prayer of thanks and felt her tears flow faster. She'd never felt such relief in her life. She waited for them to stop and sat up in bed. She didn't want to scare her mother by leaving the room crying. Once she calmed, she crept out of the room and down the hall to tell her mother the good news.

Eva was in the kitchen frying eggs on the stove, while Estelle set the table. The dishes were done, the dirty clothes were gone, and the ashtray had been emptied. Mariella noticed how pretty and grown-up Estelle had become in such a short time, and she felt relaxed for the first time in days.

Mariella could smell ham crisping in the oven and her stomach growled. Estelle turned when she heard the floorboards creak under Mariella's step. She walked to Mariella and hugged her.

"I'm sorry we didn't clean sooner," said Eva. "Gavin didn't think you'd make it back until tomorrow, and we didn't want to disturb Lulu. It really was neat and clean before she got sick."

"Stop," said Mariella. "It's okay."

"Gavin's been fixing things, too," said Eva.

Mariella was happy to hear that it really hadn't been messy the whole time she'd been gone. Her eyes scanned the room, and she saw that someone had built end tables for the sofa. The screen door that had been torn was repaired.

They heard a knock at the door and turned to see Gavin and John in the doorway. Mariella and Eva ran into each other in their rush to open the door, and laughed.

"We'll let ourselves in," said Gavin, holding open the door while John wheeled himself over the threshold.

Mariella crossed the room to Gavin and hugged him for a long time. She held his face in her hands when she pulled away. He had heavy circles under his eyes.

"How are you holding up?" she asked.

His gaze dropped and then met hers again. His eyes were dark and troubled.

"Okay," he said. "Much better now that you're home."

"How are you down here during the week?" asked Mariella.

"I've been back and forth to check on Lu," said Gavin. "I also kinda hate it there now, so whenever my supervisor has an errand, I'm the first to volunteer. I do have to head back this afternoon, though."

"Thanks so much for checking up on them," said Mariella. "Lulu's fever broke last night."

"Thank God she's okay," said Gavin. Mariella saw her mother hug John and pull away shyly. It appeared that there hadn't yet been any formal proclamations of love between the two of them. Mariella stepped over to hug John when a painting on the wall caught her attention. It was her father's boat tied to a dock at sunset. She felt a lump rise in her throat.

John saw what held Mariella's attention. "I hope you like it," he said.

"How did you . . ." Her voice trailed off.

"Gavin took me down to the junkyard by the marina and showed it to me," said John. "I hope it's okay."

"What marina?" asked Mariella. "Here in Key West?"

The room got quiet.

Mariella walked over to the painting and put her hand on the picture. She was moved and didn't want them to see her emotion. Then anger rose. When did Gavin learn the boat was there? Why didn't he tell her he'd found it? Why had Gavin looked at her father's boat without her? She couldn't help but feel betrayed.

Eva cut the tension by announcing that breakfast would be ready soon, then left to check Lulu. Mariella turned and tried to catch Gavin's eyes, but he wouldn't look at her.

Soon Eva appeared with Lulu in her arms. Lulu wanted to sit on Mariella's lap, so Eva passed her to Mariella. While she fed Lulu, Mariella continued to try to meet Gavin's gaze, but he seemed to be avoiding her. He looked as if he felt guilty. She hoped that he'd just recently found the boat and hadn't had a chance to tell her yet, but the fact that John had painted and framed a picture of it suggested he'd known about it for a while. Had he known before going to Bimini? Why had he kept it from her?

When Lulu finished eating, Mariella placed her on Eva's lap and started clearing dishes. She walked to the sink, and in a moment Gavin was at her side with a pile of plates. While she filled the sink with water, he nudged her arm with his. She turned to meet his gaze. His brow was furrowed and he looked contrite.

"I was going to tell you . . ." he started, but was cut off when Lulu pulled at him to pick her up.

Mariella turned back to the sink and started washing the dishes.

"I'm so glad you're better, Lu," said Gavin, picking her up and tickling her sides. She wriggled and squirmed, but she clung to him.

"Hey, Gavin," said John, "I hate to say it, but you're gonna be cutting it close with the ferry if we don't leave soon."

Mariella turned to Gavin. He put Lulu down and looked at his watch.

"We do have to leave," said Gavin.

He put his arm around her, and kissed her cheek. Her hands were soapy and her heart was full of turmoil, so the best she could manage in return was a nod.

"God, I hate always having to leave," he said.

Mariella was mortified to feel the sting of tears burning behind her eyes. She avoided his gaze so he wouldn't see. She didn't want to make him feel worse, because she didn't even know whether she had a right to be angry, and she didn't want to cause him any stress after what had happened to that vet. Her frustration over not being able to talk to him made her hands shake. She finally choked back her emotion.

"Me, too," she said.

He hesitated a moment, then kissed her on the side of the head.

Then he was gone.

CHAPTER TWENTY-FOUR

The next morning, Mariella was back to work at the Hemingways' house, which was tense and quiet. Papa was holed up in his studio trying to find the muse. The boys played with trucks on the side yard. Pauline directed Jim on planting some new shrubs he'd picked up for the south lawn. Mariella scrubbed her fingers raw on the washboard, trying to get the stains of fish blood, salt water, and Bimini off everyone's clothing. Papa's Basque shirt and khakis hung on the clothesline like ghosts.

As eager as she'd been to get back, Mariella found herself daydreaming of happier times on Bimini, and conflicted over John's painting. She was frustrated with everyone, but didn't know whether she should feel that way. Part of Mariella realized that she was jealous that life had gone on in Key West without her. She wasn't as indispensable to her family as she'd thought and often told herself she wished to be. Part of Mariella was curious and angry that her family had shared something to do with Hal without her. She felt as if they were keeping something from her, and she resented it. She'd been spoiled by the leisure and privacy in Bimini, and now here she was—fingers red, dry, and swollen from the hot water, baking in the backyard sunlight, washing clothes, just one of the help again. She was tired because she had slept poorly, and she was angry at Gavin and frustrated because of their separation.

Mariella glared up at Papa's writing cottage, willing him to come down the stairs to stop and chat to break up the day, but the door remained stubbornly closed.

"Mariella!" shouted Isabelle.

Mariella rolled her eyes and wrung out the last of Pauline's bathing suits. She hung it on the line, wiped her hands on her apron, and went into the kitchen.

"You busy?" said Isabelle.

"Um, *yes*," she said.

Isabelle turned and put her hands on her hips. "Look at you, Miss Sassy. Housework beneath you now?"

Mariella groaned. "I'm sorry," she said. "I'm in such a funk today."

"I'd be in a funk, too, if I'd been fishing with Papa all summer and had to come back to work," said Isabelle. "Now, go on down to the dock and get us some fish for dinner." Isabelle squeezed Mariella on the cheek and turned back to slicing vegetables.

As Mariella walked out of the kitchen, grateful to have an errand, Papa pounded down the stairs. She felt her spirits lift when she saw him, but he passed by her without a glance. He was looking at a letter and almost knocked her over without apology. Once he was gone, she removed her apron, threw it on the table in the foyer, and let the door slam on her way out of the house.

Clouds had begun to cover the sun, though the air remained hot. The breeze picked up, and Mariella cursed it for not showing up earlier, when she was washing clothes. On her way to the dock, the streets were strangely quiet and empty. A newspaper blew across her path and stuck to the bottom of a sapodilla tree. Its headline screamed, "Unemployment Crisis," in big, black letters. She heard growling behind a fence and saw two stray dogs digging into each other with their teeth. She crossed to the other side of the road and turned down Virginia Street. She knew she was taking the long way, but she was in no hurry to go back to the house. She also had another motive: She wanted to see whether her dad's boat really was at the old marina.

Out of the corner of her eye, Mariella saw a homeless woman shuffling by on the other side of the road. She was wearing a dirty sleeveless shirt and a long ruffled skirt that once might have been pale blue, but now took on the colorless dinge of fabric worn beyond its life span. Her skin was deeply tanned and wrinkled. She was singing a song that came through on breaks in the wind. "Nobody knows the trouble I've seen." Mariella forced her eyes away and quickened her step.

When she got to the marina, she saw some junk boats to the side and couldn't believe she hadn't thought to check here before. Her mother had said the boat wasn't on Key West, but she should have checked anyway.

The rusty gate looked locked, but with a nudge, Mariella was able to scrape it open. The sound hurt her ears, and she flinched as the aging metal traveled through a well-worn path of its own coppery residue. She wiped flakes of rusted metal off her hands onto her dress and walked slowly into the yard.

All around her were the sad, broken frames of old boats with peeling paint, rusting propellers, and broken glass propped up by rusty barrels, or lying on their sides like the remnants of a terrible storm. Mariella saw one fishing boat leaning against an ancient Ford without wheels. The boat's name, *Lazy Days*, had new, unintended meaning.

Mariella saw a small skiff among the larger boats. It looked tiny among the old giants, and Mariella felt pity for it. She reached out and ran her hand over the edge of the bow, but pulled back as a splinter lodged itself in her ring finger. She bit it out and spit it on the ground, all feelings of pity replaced by annoyance. She smiled to herself for blaming a hunk of wood and bolts, but quickly sobered when she saw her dad's boat just ahead. She felt like she couldn't breathe.

The bottom of the boat was battered where it had hit the rocks, and its engine was gone. Her legs felt like lead as she tried to walk toward it. She could barely move them. She finally stopped trying and just stared at the boat.

ForEva.

Mariella didn't laugh at the name her father had chosen, the way she used to. She used to tease him about what a silly name it was. His elementary attempts at poetic language and romance had embarrassed her at the time. By the time she was old enough to appreciate a man who would endure ridicule at the dock for his love, he'd died. She had always regretted teasing him for it. She wished she'd told him that she wanted a man to dedicate a boat to her. She missed the time she had spent with him on it, and wished she could tell him about Papa and Gavin and her adventures that summer.

Then the name was mocking her. Not forever. Not at all. Nothing was. Mariella felt tears threatening to fall. Her eyes blurred, and she wiped them away with a violent motion as a sob rose in her throat.

Suddenly she wanted to get away. She couldn't stand looking at the boat anymore. She heard the gate scrape shut behind her, and turned to see a man with greasy white hair and an unlit cigarette behind his ear. He choked on a phlegmy cough and spit. He wore overalls and a soiled yellow shirt.

"Wait," she called.

He raised his eyes and smiled, revealing half a mouth of rotten teeth.

"I'm leaving," she said.

"Please stay," he teased.

She hurried over to the gate where he stood. He didn't move

out of the way, so she had to push past him. He smelled of body odor and moonshine.

"Got any part you need right here." He laughed.

"Piss off," she said without turning to look at him.

She heard the door creak shut and the lock fasten behind her.

August 15, 1935

Dear Mariella,

Always we make advances, then retreats. I don't want this to feel like war. I'll surrender everything. All you have to do is ask—and tell. Tell me why you're angry. Are you upset about John's painting because of what it means for them or what it means they had without you? Are you angry at me for showing the boat to John?

I understand.

If you want to know my secret, I'll tell you. I visit your father's boat often. I'm drawn there. Your mother had described it to me and John one night, and I found it when I was looking for spare parts to take back to camp. I've been back a few times since. I don't know what I'm looking for while I'm there, but I'll tell you that I found the boat while you were gone, and it connected me to you, so I wanted to keep going. I'll go with you anytime you want, if you want. I want to talk to you about it.

Our time together is forever interrupted with people. That's good. It's people we love and love to have around us, but it's bad because there are so many conversations we can't finish. So many things to talk about that never get covered. When I'm with you I just want you—quietly sometimes, hungrily others. I can't get in all the words and kisses and touches in our short time.

So it has to come through these letters. Little clips of what I'm trying to say to you, but don't think I'm saying well. I'm no writer, like that other one, but I sure know how I feel about you. I just can't get it to sound right on paper.

I hope you'll forgive me. I hope we'll get some time together soon.

I love you.

Yours,
Gavin

Mariella folded the letter back into its envelope and put it into her pocket while she walked up the ramp to her house. She felt better in some ways and worse in others. It was so frustrating to not be able to finish anything with Gavin. It was frustrating to have these conversations by mail when they needed talking out. She was still upset that he'd kept the boat's location a secret from her, but hated herself for being angry when Gavin had so much weighing on him.

When she stepped through the door, she saw that John was there. Lulu sat on his lap while he instructed Estelle on the guitar. Eva was in the kitchen preparing vegetable stew. Bread baked in the oven. It struck Mariella as a scene of perfect, domestic tranquillity, until she looked deeper and saw a poor widow, a legless vet, and fatherless children.

John looked up and smiled at her. She couldn't help but smile back. Lulu jumped off his lap and ran to Mariella for a hug. Estelle asked Mariella to listen to her play the guitar. She walked over to John, put Lulu back on his lap, and sat next to him on the couch.

The girls had gone to bed, and Eva fell asleep on her chair while they listened to Cole Porter records on the phonograph. John said he wanted to go home alone—he worried about Mariella walking back by herself—but Mariella wanted to stretch her legs and talk to John about Gavin.

The waning moon was overhead as Mariella walked John home. His strength astounded her. She offered to push the chair, but he insisted he wasn't tired. She lit a cigarette and they passed it back and forth, stopping when he wanted a drag. He spoke first.

"I hope you're not angry at your mom and me," he said.

"I'm thrilled for my mom and you," she said.

"I'm sorry if the painting upset you," he said. "I thought it would be a nice gesture so you and the girls didn't think I was trying to replace your father or push out his memory."

Mariella was quiet.

"I guess you felt left out," said John, taking the cigarette. The smoke hung low in the humid air, blocking John's face.

"I did," said Mariella. "I felt like I wasn't necessary."

"Everything good in that house—the reason it's lasted as long as it has—is because of you," he said. "You kept everything going to allow your mom time to grieve. You took care of the girls and your mom and the house. Now it's time to take care of you."

"But I feel like you all have something you're not telling me, or that you shared something without me, and I don't know how to get to it," she said.

Now John was quiet. He passed the cigarette back to her. The sound of cheering saved them from the awkward pause in the conversation. They were at the Blue Goose. Mariella looked into the crowd surrounding the boxers and saw Papa. He was refereeing a fight.

"Gavin said he finally felt like you were his and not Hem's," said John. "Is that true?"

"Yes," said Mariella, taking a drag of her cigarette. "Papa and I figured out what we are to each other."

"What's that?" asked John.

"Allied forces," she replied. John laughed and reached for the cigarette.

"Is Gavin part of the alliance now?"

"I don't know," said Mariella. "You can't keep secrets if you're in this alliance." She took the last drag of the cigarette, and stubbed it out on the ground. One of the boxers knocked the other flat out in the ring, and the crowd cheered. Papa clapped and jumped around like a child. Mariella and John resumed their journey in silence.

When they got to the house, they sat on the porch and shared a beer from the icebox, and another cigarette.

"You've got to know that he'll do anything for you," said John.

"I would for him, too," she said.

"Then be open to him," said John. "It's hard for us to trust people, and we need time to get it all out. You've got to try to understand that."

"I know," said Mariella. She did know, and was frustrated with herself for her snap judgments and impulse to anger.

A sharp gust of wind blew through the yard.

"I have to tell you," said John, "I'm worried about him up there on Matecumbe."

"I think he's worried, too."

"There's been a lot of talk about hurricane season up there lately, and how those guys don't stand a chance in their camps."

"But they have an evacuation plan," she said. "A train'll come down and take them up to Miami if a storm comes."

"That's what's supposed to happen," said John. "But Gavin's supervisor said certain men in charge up there aren't taking the hurricanes seriously enough. Guy named Ed Sheeran lived through the bad one of 1906, and he's trying to tell them, but he's not getting too far."

"They'll get them out," she said. "Besides, there are enough locals up there to know the warning signs of a hurricane. If their supervisors don't know one's coming, the natives will."

"I sure hope so," said John. "Of course, he's not worried about himself. He's worried about the guys with families who live in his camp."

Mariella thought of them. Gavin had told her of Lorraine and Henry Morrow, with their two kids, and several other families. He loved to eat with them when he was at camp so he could distance himself from the drunks. He loved to take the Morrow boy night fishing.

"When's he coming down to Key West?"

"Not till Labor Day weekend. He wants to get out of camp before the guys drink their paychecks away and get sloppy."

Mariella drained the beer but offered the last drag to John, which he took.

"On that note," she said, "I'd better get back. As usual, John, you're full of cheery thoughts to give me."

"I did it again, didn't I?"

"Yes, you always manage to," she said. "But I love you anyway."
Mariella leaned down and kissed John on the cheek.

"Be careful, Mari," he said. "Thanks for coming back with me."

Mariella walked home that night looking with new eyes at the
trees blowing in the wind. The sky was clear and she was grateful
they hadn't had any big storms yet that season. But she also knew
that they could come without warning, and often after days of
beautiful weather. She thought she'd write to Gavin that he should
come down to Key West if there were any hurricane warnings,
and they could all stay in John's little concrete house. It made her
feel better just thinking of it on the way home, but that night in
bed, she couldn't sleep.

August 17, 1935

Dear Gavin,

I was up all night worrying about you. I worried
that you have secrets you haven't told me; then I worried that I am driving you away with all of my turmoil. I worried that I won't see you soon enough, and
I worried that you won't want to see me after how
childishly I behaved.

Then I started worrying about hurricanes.

Yes, again, you can thank John for planting these
little worrying seeds, but he brought up some good
points about evacuation, and I just hope you have a
plan. But of course you do. You all are military veterans. You are organized and efficient, and the powers
that be would never forget those who gave so self-

lessly to their country all those years ago. And if they do, hop the first ferry and we'll ride out the storm in John's little fortress.

But enough talk of hurricanes. I don't want the wind to pick up my musings and spin it into something frightening.

On to some good news: Lulu's doctor thinks he knows what's wrong. Some kind of inflammation of the bowel. People with it are prone to fevers and stomach pains. He's started giving her shots of a vitamin to help with her anemia, and he's trying to determine the best way to treat her. Nothing much has changed, but at least we know a little more, and it does not appear to be fatal.

Anyway, you need to know a few things: 1) I love you, always, so you never have to worry that my quick temper means anything but that I am, in fact, immature, and have much growing to do. 2) I would prefer to be a Mrs. sooner rather than later, and I think I'm willing to get myself "in trouble" by you if that will expedite the process. 3) You are a selfless and beautiful person, and you make me much better just by being around you, so please, if you can, come see me soon.

I do love you and I miss you.

Ever Yours,

M.B.

August 20, 1935

Dear Mariella,

I'm counting down the days until Labor Day weekend. I'm skipping out after I get paid, and I'll be with you for three whole days. If you're not careful, I'll take you up on offer #2.

Love,
Gavin

CHAPTER TWENTY-FIVE

**U. S. Weather Bureau Bulletin
Saturday, August 31, 1935**

"Tropical disturbance of small diameter but considerable intensity central about sixty miles east of Long Island, Bahamas, apparently moving west-northwestward attended by strong shifting winds and probably gales near center. Caution advised southeastern Bahamas and ships in that vicinity."

Mariella was frustrated to be working on her day off, preparing the house for Pauline's Labor Day picnic, but at least she'd make extra money.

She stood in the dining room polishing the walnut table and chairs. The set was a fine piece from a Spanish monastery that Pauline had shipped with the great iron gate she'd turned into a headboard. Mariella ran her hand over the smooth, dark surface of the table, and imagined the Spanish monks who'd sat at it. The rag made a soft swishing sound on the wood as Mariella made great, sweeping circles. The first layer of polish obscured her reflection on the surface. The second swipe with the dry cloth pulled off the polish and returned her reflection.

Papa's whispered voice came in from the other room, followed by Pauline's. Mariella moved toward the door so she could hear them a little better.

"Come on," he said.

There was a low laugh, followed by the sound of a slap.

"Stop it. There are people everywhere."

"The boys and Ada are gone."

"The rest of them?"

"Jim's outside. Isabelle's at the market. Toby's working on the car."

"Mariella?" she hissed.

Mariella stiffened when she heard her name, and tiptoed back to the far side of the dining room with her stomach doing somersaults. She could still hear them kissing, but Pauline must have pulled away again.

"Stop."

It was quiet for a moment; then Mariella heard ice clink in a glass. Someone set the glass down on the table with force. She knew it was Papa.

"All excuses," he said. His voice was bitter.

"What—you expect to take me here on the carpet in broad daylight with the help moving about the house?"

"Excuses," he repeated. "That wasn't an issue last night, or the night before that, or the night before that."

"I had a headache."

"Bullshit," he said.

It was quiet again. Mariella heard sniffing and knew Pauline was crying.

"The doctor said another baby would kill me," she said.

"Then I'll use a rubber, for Christ's sake!"

"You know I'm Catholic!"

He snorted. "When it suits you."

Mariella cringed. God, he could be cruel.

"Bastard," said Pauline. Mariella heard Pauline run up the stairs.

She wiped off the last of the polish, walked into the kitchen, and threw the towels in the basket by the door. Mariella began washing dishes, troubled by what she'd heard.

She felt a hand on her back and jumped.

Papa.

She burned and knew she must have been red from head to toe.

"Hot in here," he said.

She felt his breath on her neck and could smell the booze. What was he doing? Her heart pounded, and she dropped the dishrag she'd been holding into the pot. She felt dizzy and had to break the tension.

"Can I get you another drink?" she stammered.

She felt him lean into her back. He reached around her and turned off the water she'd left running. A great soapy mass had grown from the top of the pot in the sink. He pushed farther into her back. Mariella stood frozen in a mess of fear and unwelcome desire. Finally he pulled away. She put her hands on the edge of the sink and didn't turn to face him.

A movement in the doorway caught her eye. It was Pauline.

My God, had she seen?

"I think I'll go to Josie's for a drink," he said.

Mariella didn't breathe until she heard the front door slam. Then she picked up the pot and dumped the soapy water down the drain. Pauline continued to stand there without speaking. Finally Mariella worked up the courage to look at her.

Pauline's chest heaved, and her eyes were swollen from crying. Her arms were crossed under her chest. She looked more defeated than angry.

Mariella managed to find her voice. "Would you like a drink, Mrs. Hemingway? Maybe some tea?"

Pauline shook her head.

"How about a snack?" said Mariella. "I could bring it out to you on the porch."

Pauline sighed and looked out the window. Mariella followed her gaze to the backyard, where leaves blew in the wind and clouds covered the landscape in shadows.

"Can I get you anything?" asked Mariella, eager for Pauline to either leave or yell at her instead of standing there in tense silence.

Pauline finally spoke.

"I want my marriage back."

Gavin didn't like the look of it. He smoked and watched the waves roll in toward the shore, large, slow, and deliberate. Usually the water lapped small and quick on the sand.

The recent article in the *Key Veteran News* about the possibility of the camps getting closed was also on his mind. It cited an article in *Time* magazine that the vets were a bunch of alcoholic derelicts. A group of them staggered by, hungover from drinking away their paychecks the night before, and Gavin rolled his eyes. Yes, many of them were drunks, but could you blame them? Bonus Marchers looking for work where there was none, shipped off to a lonely, mosquito-infested island to live in dirty tents and shacks and do dangerous work, seventy feet above shark-infested water, in tropical heat.

Gavin shook his head. He didn't want to think about Bonus Marchers, or Roosevelt, or shabby working conditions. He just wanted to get to Key West to see Mariella. He had missed the ferry last night because Sheeran wanted help securing floating construction materials. Sheeran didn't want to take any chances on losing thousands of dollars' worth of equipment with a storm on the way.

Gavin started back toward his shack in camp three to pack when something strange caught his eye. He walked toward the narrow road that ran between the gulf and the ocean to see what was moving over the pavement. As he got closer he saw crabs—hundreds of crabs—scurrying out from the ocean side of the straits of Florida, over the highway, and into the gulf side. First he smiled at the sight, but then it occurred to him that they were trying to get away from something. He looked out over the water and watched the huge waves lumbering into shore under a sky of high, wispy cirrus clouds. A car drove by, crushing crabs beneath its tires with a wet, crunching sound.

When Gavin got back to camp the air was buzzing. He stopped a vet whom he recognized as an artist for the *Key Veteran News*, and asked what was going on.

"Looks like we'll get to see a hurricane in the next day or so," he said, not masking his excitement. Then he disappeared into camp.

Gavin saw Sheeran hurrying over to the offices and ran to catch him.

"Bad news?" said Gavin.

Sheeran was sixty-five and out of breath. His forehead was creased with lines of worry, and sweat bled through his shirt.

"We're not getting missed on this one," said Sheeran.

"What can I do?" asked Gavin.

"Stay here and help me. We need to make sure our guys stay sober and ready for whatever comes our way."

"Maybe it'll miss us."

"Maybe it won't," said Sheeran. "And if it doesn't, well, I saw what happened in 'oh-six, and I assure you, you'd rather be at Argonne Forest. Now go start persuading some of the families to leave. I've got a meeting."

"Yes, sir."

Gavin was devastated that he wouldn't be able to get to Key West. He knew Mariella would be, too, so he ran to the post office to send her a telegram. It would be worse if he just didn't show up without sending word. After he sent the telegram, he headed over to the family shacks to warn them about the storm.

CHAPTER TWENTY-SIX

Key West
Sunday, September 1, 1935

Mariella helped Jim hold the boards to the window while Toby nailed them down. When they finished the side windows, they moved around to the front of the house and rotated duties.

Mariella started banging until she heard Pauline shouting.

She turned and saw Pauline coming up the walk with Gregory, Patrick, and Ada. The boys ran in the house with Ada at their heels to remove their church clothes, but Pauline stood in the front yard. Her face was dark.

"Is all this really necessary?" she asked. "The paper said it was just a tropical disturbance."

"Yes, ma'am," said Toby. "Papa plotted it out last night and said the barometer's dropping. It could be a bad one."

"Of course it has to come when I'm supposed to have a picnic," she said.

Papa walked out the front door. "You can forget your picnic."

"I've already bought all the food," she said. "Isabelle and Mariella have been working overtime helping with preparations."

"Well, now they're working overtime to help prepare for the storm."

"We can have a storm party," said Pauline.

"Yes, with Mariella's family," said Papa. "I told her to bring them over if it gets bad."

Pauline pursed her lips and crossed her arms over her chest.

Mariella looked from Pauline to Papa. She had told him that her family would be safe at John's. Did he deliberately say this to Pauline to provoke her?

"Now, if you're done with your little tantrum, I've got to see to *Pilar*," said Papa. "Mariella, come with me."

Mariella passed the hammer to Jim with her stomach roiling. Why was Papa using her as a pawn in his game with Pauline when she was already on such slippery footing?

Pauline stormed into the house mumbling about the boat being more important than she was, and something about a half-Cuban boardinghouse. Mariella's nervous energy turned to anger, and she stepped off the porch to join Papa.

The sky was gray, and the rain stopped and started in little bursts. The lighthouse had two red lanterns hanging one on top of the other. People up and down the street were out on ladders hammering boards over their windows and clearing their yards. Other than the noise of preparation, it was eerily silent.

As they walked into the boatyard, Mariella's stomach sank when she saw the flags flying, red on top and red with a black square underneath it. The storm was a certainty.

"Damn," said Papa, pointing at the flags. "I'd hoped my calculations would be off."

There was a crowd at the marina that morning. The line from the station house went to the gate. Papa marched to the front of it, with Mariella in his wake. She felt guilty passing all of the fisherman with a rich sportsman.

"Hey, man, can you haul *Pilar* out for me?" asked Papa.

The harbormaster scowled. "Look behind you, Hem. We don't have enough time to get them all out, let alone yours."

"C'mon, do me a favor."

"Your boat's for sport. Many of these guys make a living offa theirs."

"You don't have to make a big deal of it," said Papa. "I just got her fixed up. I can't bear it if anything happens to her."

"Don't do this, Hem. If I were you, I'd get some rope and tie her up. That'll keep her safe enough."

Papa grumbled and stormed off.

Under happier circumstances, Mariella would have teased Papa for trying to use his status to get favors, but she could see by his face that he was in no mood for it.

Papa cursed under his breath when he saw the line at Thompson's Hardware snaking out the door. They walked behind the register and found Chuck in the back.

"I need as much line as you've got. I've got to tie up *Pilar.*"

"Just about sold out," he said.

"Shit, Chuck. The harbormaster just told me he couldn't get her out of the water, and now you're telling me there's no rope. Help me out, here, man."

"I got some heavy hawser in the back I'll sell to you at cost, but it'll still cost you a fortune."

"I'll take it. How much?"

"Fifty-two bucks."

Mariella couldn't help but gasp at the price.

"I know," said Papa. "But I've put too much into her this summer to let her get destroyed in the storm."

Mariella tried not to judge. Papa just shook his head and started back to the sub yard.

Gavin's men finished placing the last of the loose boards in the back of the mess hall. He didn't like the way the walls were shaking, but there was nowhere else to put the wood. If left outside, it would fly like arrows in the wind gusts.

After that, Sheeran sent Gavin down to encourage the vets and their families to prepare for evacuation, while he tried to find out when his supervisor, Ray Sheldon, would be returning to camp. Ray was in Key West for the weekend on a honeymoon with his new wife, in spite of the storm warnings. Sheeran was outraged at how casually Ray treated the storm. Sheeran had told Gavin that his experiences with the hurricane of 1906 still gave him nightmares. That one had wiped out hundreds of guys laying the railroad.

Gavin was surprised that some of the vets were looking forward to the hurricane. They seemed of the opinion that if they survived the war, they could survive anything. Some of them were drinking—in spite of the fact that they'd received orders to stay sober—while others played cards. One of the guys had brought the camp's dogs and their puppies into the mess hall, but the puppies shivered against their mother, too spooked to play.

Gavin scanned the room and saw children huddled in corners with their parents. He told the families with access to cars to evacuate, but felt his panic rising when he couldn't find the Morrows.

Bracing himself against the wind, Gavin went out to the truck waiting in front of the mess hall and started driving back to camp three. As he traveled along the road, he felt the wind shaking the truck. The tide had reached the road and started breaking over the pavement. Gavin tried to fight off the terrible feeling he had that he would never see the people in camp five again, and pressed the accelerator. He knew he had to do everything he could to persuade the men in charge that all the vets and their families needed to be evacuated.

When he pulled into camp three, he went right to Sheeran,

but wasn't happy with what he found. Sheeran was watching the barometer with wide eyes, and rubbed his forehead.

"It'll be worse than I first thought," he said.

"The Weather Bureau hasn't confirmed it'll hit here," said Gavin. "And if it does, they say we've still got some time."

"I don't give a shit what the Weather Bureau says. My barometer's falling steadily, and it's reading lower than the barometers in Key West. I just got off the phone with the coast guard."

Gavin felt some relief that the storm might not hit Key West. He'd felt paralyzed all weekend without being able to get down there. John had sent a telegram that the girls were staying at his place, but that still didn't quiet Gavin's fears.

"Has the train been ordered?" asked Gavin.

"Ray Sheldon's ferry should have been here hours ago. Until he makes the call to Fred Ghent up north, we can't go anywhere, and goddamned Ghent is playing golf and no one can reach him."

Gavin ran his hands through his hair and started pacing. "My God, what can we do?"

"We can take care of our own as best we can."

"That's not good enough."

Sheeran looked at Gavin. He looked out the window at the pickup truck.

"Why don't you start taking the women and children up past Tavernier, where they'll be safer?" he said. "Their barometers are reading higher than ours, and you can probably get a few trucksful in before you need to get to shelter."

Gavin ran out the door, glad to have something to do that might help, but still worried about his friends. He drove back to camp five and, on the way, passed a truck carrying Ray Sheldon. He felt relief wash over him, but continued on his task, knowing that bureaucrats didn't always operate with speed. When he got to the mess hall the mood had darkened. No one drank or laughed anymore, and some of the women were crying.

Gavin reminded them to get ready for evacuation, but didn't announce that he'd be taking a truckful of people. He knew it would start a panic, and that wouldn't help. Instead, he walked over to the Wilsons, the first family he saw. Gavin told Mike Wilson to assemble his wife and children to go up to Tavernier. Mike exhaled a sigh of relief and clapped Gavin on the back. He hurried back to his wife, Eugenia, kissed her and his four kids, and pushed them out in the storm with Gavin.

The wind was blowing sand around, so no one could have ridden in the back. Eugenia and two of the biggest kids squished onto the seat next to Gavin. Two of the smallest kids sat on their laps. They all spoke very little, but their gratitude was conveyed on their faces. The baby sat closest to Gavin and kept putting his hand on Gavin's arm while he drove. Gavin felt a lump in his throat and silently prayed for their protection. He tried to smile reassuringly, but he had no assurance to give, so he kept his eyes on the road.

The wind and rain gusts were much worse than before, and the road was covered in several inches of water. Eugenia gasped and prayed, and the kids watched the storm with wide eyes. Gavin had to reach up to wipe the steam from the inside of the cab so he could see where he was going. He wondered whether it would have been safer to leave them at camp.

The nine-mile trip took three times as long as usual, but Gavin got them safely to the Tavernier Theater along the main highway. He helped Eugenia get the kids into the concrete building and turned to leave. As he was going, she hugged him and said, "God bless you." He was moved but tried to keep it together. He knew that if he lost it, he wouldn't get it back, and there were still many others who needed help. He nodded and returned to the car.

On the drive back to headquarters at the Hotel Matecumbe, the rain and wind died, but rather than making Gavin feel better, it filled him with dread. It was as if some great force over the water had sucked it all in and was about to spit it back out.

He saw Sheeran coming out of the building and heading to his truck. Gavin pulled up to him and rolled down his window.

"Well?" asked Gavin.

"They want to wait," said Sheeran. His voice shook. Gavin could see that he felt impotent. He was trembling in frustration.

"What? Why?"

Sheeran pointed to the sky. "Sheldon seems to think we're not going to get hit hard. He just cited the fact that the rain and wind were slowing. He's not paying attention to the barometer, which continues to fall. These gasps of good weather are just part of the bands of the hurricane."

"What will it take for him to make the call?" asked Gavin.

"He said they can have the train here within four hours of our call. He thinks we've got time. I think they just don't want a bunch of shiftless vets idling around up north. Sheldon said he'd be playing gin rummy at the hotel tonight if we need him."

"My God," said Gavin.

"I did hear Sheldon tell the clerk to call him if any more weather reports came in," said Sheeran. "I guess he thinks it could be serious enough to disturb his sleep."

"And there's nothing else we can do?"

Sheeran shook his head. "Just try to get some more of the women and children out. Then come on back to camp three and help me finish securing the construction equipment. There's nothing else we can do."

Gavin looked into the window of headquarters and saw Ray Sheldon laughing and slapping someone on the back. His new wife, Gayle, stared out the window. Her eyes met Gavin's. He could see her worry. He shook his head and pulled out to head back to camp five.

CHAPTER TWENTY-SEVEN

U.S. Weather Bureau Advisory
9:30 p.m., Sunday, September 1, 1935

"Storm center now 260 miles east of Havana and moving slowly westward. Hurricane-force winds likely. Vessels in Straits of Florida should use caution."

U. S. Weather Bureau Advisory
3:30 a.m. Monday, September 2, 1935

"Tropical disturbance still of small diameter but considerable intensity moving slowly westward off coast of north-central Cuba, shifting gales and hurricane-force winds at center. Caution: high tides and gales on Florida Keys."

The clerk listened to the meteorologist's report over the phone as he yawned. He hung up and woke up one of the staff to tell him the report and see whether they should call and wake up

Sheldon. Since it was almost morning, they decided not to wake him.

~~⤙⤚~~

Monday, September 2, 1935

Gavin sat up in his cot and decided to dress. He hadn't slept at all, and could no longer bear to lie in wait. He pulled on his work uniform and went outside without shaving.

The water was violent with whitecaps, and the sound of the waves slamming the shore filled his ears. The clouds sat fat and heavy fifty feet above the ground. It was drizzling steadily, and the wind blew without breaks. Gavin walked over to Sheeran's cabin and saw a light on in the window. He knocked at the door and Sheeran opened it. Sheeran had dark circles under his eyes and was wearing the same clothes he'd been in the day before. He waved him in and pointed to the barometer: 29.89.

It had been 29.96 last night. Normally the barometer rarely moved from thirty. A fall of that many points during such a short time meant trouble. Without speaking much, the men drove over to the headquarters at the hotel. It didn't seem as squally there, but Sheeran reminded Gavin of the rain bands that came out of a hurricane as it approached.

When they pulled in, the hotel owner, Ed Butters, was kissing his wife, Fran. He and his son were prepared to drive up to Miami for the day. Gavin thought it strange that they'd go and leave Fran, but then he thought that these people were natives to the Keys and surely knew when things were bad. It made him feel a little better, until the barometer started reading 29.87. Sheeran pulled Ray Sheldon into an office and closed the door. Gavin sat out with Fran and Gayle and listened as the voices got louder. Gayle put her hand on Gavin's arm.

"What do you think?" She was pretty and young, just twenty-seven. He could see her worry and wanted to assure her, but again couldn't find the words.

"Sheeran's been through this before," he said. "If he's worried, I'm worried."

Fran agreed. "I don't have a great feeling myself," she said.

Bonefish came in the door, bringing in a wind gust. Papers on the table near the door blew off and scattered. Gayle moved to pick them up.

"The lighthouse at Alligator Reef put up the hurricane flags," he said.

Sheeran walked out of the office with Sheldon.

"I'm calling Ghent," he said. Fern handed him the phone.

Gavin and Sheeran watched a freight train move into camp three. It held ten thousand gallons of water. The rain was coming down fast. Ghent was missing, and no one had been able to contact him. It had been almost two hours since Sheldon had called, and panic was setting in.

"Should we have them pump the water in the camp's tanks?" asked Gavin.

Sheeran looked at the rising tides.

"No," he said. "We might need water after the storm."

They'd started back to headquarters when Gavin remembered the Morrows. He turned and began running down the road as best he could in the wind.

"Where are you going?"

"I'll be back. Just want to check on a family."

Sheeran nodded and disappeared into the storm.

Gavin could barely see from the rain, wind, and sand slapping his face. He wiped his eyes with his wet sleeve and continued until he reached the rock on the side of the road near the Morrows' house.

Water from the gulf lapped the door of their house. The shack shook dangerously in the wind, and Gavin prayed they'd gone and found shelter up north. When he looked in the window he saw no one. He tried the door and it opened, and sure enough, the family was gone. He could smell the sour-sweet smell of the baby and knew they'd left not long ago. He didn't know whether he should be relieved or scared. All the way back to headquarters, he prayed for their safety. When he finally got to headquarters, Fran was pacing.

"Ed's coming back, and Sheldon sent Gayle north with some other civilians," she said. "The barometer's down to twenty-eight-point-nine."

Gavin looked out the window and saw a piece of roofing fly by. A riderless child's tricycle moved across the road in a wind gust and got stuck in a clump of bushes. He wondered how Mariella and her family were doing. He knew the barometer readings were higher in Key West, but his best hope was in John's fortress of a house.

Standing there, he resolved that this couldn't go on. He'd have to find a way to work in Key West. He'd use his savings to buy a boat. They'd start the business. He couldn't stand the separation from Mariella any longer.

Mariella hammered the last board over the window at her own house and stopped to massage her shoulder. Her ponytail was wet and stuck to her neck, and her father's old shirt was soaked through.

As much work as it had been, readying her house for the storm while her family stayed at John's was a relief. She needed physical labor to take her mind off her worry over Gavin's safety.

She heard a car pull up out front and walked around the side of the house to see Papa at the wheel of his Ford.

"Got something on your mind?" he asked.

She laughed. "Hmmm, just a little bit."

"Come on," he said. "Let's get your family and let them ride it out at my house."

"You came over here just to get us?" she asked, moved.

"Of course, daughter."

"I told you. They're all at John's—Gavin's friend. Over on Olivia."

"Are you sure it's safe?"

"It's a big blue cinder block."

"Above sea level?"

"Yes, sir," she said. The rain slowed, but the wind gusts were getting stronger.

"I'm done here," she said. "Can I help over at your house? I can't stand being caged in until I have to."

"Sure," he said. "Come on; I'll drive you."

As they drove down the street, Mariella chewed her nails. She bounced her knees up and down and fidgeted in the seat.

"Anything besides the storm bothering you?"

"I'm worried sick about Gavin."

"When did you last speak to him?"

"He sent a telegram saying he couldn't come down. Had to prepare the camps for the hurricane."

Papa was quiet. Mariella could see the lines of unease etched on his forehead.

"They'll send a train, though, right?" she asked. "Get the men up to Miami or somewhere inland?"

"Those men survived one of the bloodiest battles in military history," said Papa. "They'll figure this one out." His words sounded stiff and dishonest, and he wouldn't meet her eyes.

They pulled up to the house, and Toby was there carrying the deck furniture into the cellar. The boys ran out to greet them in little rain slickers and boots that made Mariella smile.

"Are you ready for the big storm?" asked Mariella.

"I'm not scared of some old wind," said Patrick.

Mariella looked at Gregory. He had his fingers in his mouth, and his forehead was creased with worry. He looked like a little Papa. She leaned down to pick him up.

"Did you know your house is the safest on the whole, entire island?" she asked.

Gregory shook his head from side to side.

"It's true," said Mariella. "And your papa will keep you safe."

Mariella put Gregory down on the lawn. "Come on. Help us put away your toys so they don't blow to Cuba."

Patrick and Gregory ran around the yard grabbing toys to take to the cellar. Mariella walked over to the peacocks.

"These?" she asked Papa.

"We'll bring them in later."

Mariella stepped onto the porch and picked up the table with the phone. As she entered the house, Pauline blocked her way.

"Please shake off before you come in here," she said. Mariella was taken aback by the iciness in her voice. She stomped and shook her hands, then wiped her feet on the porch before entering the living room. Pauline looked her up and down with distaste as Papa walked in behind her.

"Where are the others?" she asked.

"They'll be at a friend's house, and so will Mariella," he said. "I invited them all, but Mariella thinks they'll be okay."

"Well, since you're here," said Pauline, "go ahead and set the table. Isabelle cooked the roast I was going to use for the party, and I want to get in a good lunch in case dinnertime gets bad and we lose power."

Mariella made a move to go to the kitchen, but Papa put out his hand to stop her.

"No, she should go to her family now," he said.

"It's okay," said Mariella. "I'll help with lunch and then go."

Papa glared at Pauline. Mariella walked past her and into the kitchen.

The roast was warming in the oven. Mariella peeled potatoes while she brought a pot of water to boil. Once it was bubbling she threw in the potatoes, stir-fried string beans in oil, and sliced the meat. She could hear Papa and Pauline arguing in the dining room, but couldn't hear what they were saying. The boys ran through the kitchen, but Ada grabbed them by the arms and hauled them upstairs, instructing Mariella to bring their food up once Papa and Pauline were served.

When the potatoes were ready, Mariella mashed them with cream, butter, salt, and pepper, and made up the plates. Papa's voice was loud in the background, while Pauline's had lowered to a hiss. Mariella heard Pauline say her name and wondered whether Pauline was jealous that Papa had thought to bring her to the house.

Patrick and Gregory ran back in the kitchen from the hallway and into the dining room.

"For God's sake," said Pauline. "Ada! Get them upstairs."

Ada yelled for the boys from upstairs, and they stomped up and away from the storm brewing in the dining room.

Mariella walked into the room and set the plates on the table, silencing the Hemingways. Pauline slumped in her chair like a child, and Papa sat heavily in his.

"I don't know why you're still sulking," he said. "You've got your way. We're not going to Cuba to visit the Masons."

"Only because your boat is acting up," said Pauline. "Other-wise we would have gone."

"They invited us," he said. "I didn't want to be rude."

"Oh, please," said Pauline.

"And you're the only one with the problem."

"If it's my problem, it's your problem."

"Believe me," he said, "I know."

Mariella uncorked a bottle of red wine on the sideboard and poured what was left of it into their glasses. Eager to leave the room, she took the bottle into the kitchen and began to clean the mess. Mariella could hear that they were still arguing and finished cleaning as fast as she could. She heard the wind picking up outside the house and decided that she'd better get to John's before the weather got worse inside and outside of the house.

When she stepped into the dining room to tell the Hemingways, she felt the air quiver with the tension. It was deadly silent except for Papa's chewing noises. He cut bloody hunks from the roast, chewed them not quite enough, and washed them down with great gulps of wine. A drip of au jus ran down his chin.

"Shall we ask Mariella to join us at the table?" said Pauline. "Have a glass of wine, perhaps?"

Papa stopped cutting and looked up at Pauline. Mariella thought she would have died if she were on the receiving end of his look. Pauline gave it back like she had nothing to lose, since it was already lost. A fly landed on his meat and he didn't wave it away. They stared at each other for a full minute, or was it an hour? It was painful, but Papa looked away first.

"I'm just curious why the help gets more consideration than the wife," said Pauline. "Do you have any insight into that, Mariella? Because my husband doesn't seem to have any idea what I'm talking about."

Everything stopped. Mariella was afraid to move. The clock in the hall ticked loudly. Mariella's eyes darted to Pauline. Something changed in Pauline. She shrank in her chair. She wanted to take it back. It would have been better if Pauline had kept her posture, but the lion sensed the animal was wounded. He went in for the kill.

In a rush of linens and china, he lifted the whole table off the floor and tipped it over sideways, crashing it into the opposite wall. Mariella couldn't believe the display of violence, and was afraid to move. She looked at Pauline, who had jerked her chair back and had her face in her hands.

My God.

He crossed the dining room in a stride and gripped the arm-rests on Pauline's chair, putting himself inches from her face. Pauline began freely sobbing. She was sorry, so sorry. She loved him; how could he do this to her? She was just being ugly because she loved him so. And he screamed over it all, words that made no sense, words angry and boorish. He pushed his finger into her shoulder, hard, and Mariella was afraid he'd hurt Pauline. She could feel his violence, potent in the room. But the violence ignited something in Pauline and she stood up and began to yell a string of accusations at him about Jane and Jinny and Mariella and any other woman he'd been in contact with.

Mariella knew she had contributed to this mess and felt sick. She didn't know whether it would be best to stay and defend herself, or go. She wanted to defuse the situation and make it better, so she spoke.

"Stop, Pauline," said Mariella, her voice steady. Pauline stopped yelling and turned to Mariella. "You're wrong. Papa's never crossed any line with me."

"Don't tell me I'm wrong," said Pauline. "Since when does the help contradict me."

"Don't you speak to her that way," said Papa. "She's done nothing wrong. Your jealousy is making you ugly."

Pauline flinched like she'd been punched. All of her fears about being unattractive were validated. He shoved the knife in where it would wound her most, and Mariella knew the situation was now hopeless.

"Papa, please," said Mariella.

Pauline suddenly sneered. "Papa." She spit the word out. "Weak, like *your* miserable excuse for a father."

It was Mariella's turn to flinch. "What did you say?"

"Pauline—no!" said Papa.

"What—are you going to play Mariella's *Papa*?" shouted Pauline.

"Stop, Pauline, no!" shouted Hemingway.

"Her pathetic parents."

Mariella's hands clenched and she stepped toward Pauline. "How can you speak that way about my parents? You didn't even know my father. You don't know my mother."

"I didn't know him, but I know *of* him," said Pauline.

"Pauline, no!"

"What the hell's that supposed to mean?" said Mariella.

"Stop!" Papa was trying to push Pauline out of the room. Mariella couldn't understand what Pauline was saying and why Papa was trying to stop her.

"Your father was weak," said Pauline. She pushed Papa off her. "Weak like Ernest's father."

The room was silent again except for the ticking of the clock. Mariella looked at her for a moment before she understood. Her eyes filled. The secret hit her with gale force. The secret everyone knew but her.

Papa pushed Pauline into the kitchen and screamed at her to get away from them. Pauline sobbed and ran out into the hall and up the stairs. Ernest made a move toward Mariella, but she stepped back.

"Mari."

Mariella turned and ran out of the house.

The rain slapped Mariella's face in blasts, but it was the wind that most hindered her progress. A wave of nausea rose in her stomach. She put her hand against the banyan tree in the Hemingways' yard and retched behind it. She wiped the spit from her mouth with the back of her sleeve and started running. Soon she stood at the gate of the marine scrapyard. She could see her father's boat and tried to push the gate in, but it was locked. She banged it with her hands and groaned in frustration.

There had to be another way in.

Mariella ran along the outer perimeter of the fence until it switched to a smaller chain link. Behind a bush of pampas grass, she could see a tear in the fence. She put her face down and brushed past the grass, feeling its sharp blades scratching at her neck and pulling at her hair. She squeezed through the hole in the fence, stood, and wiped the mud from her hands.

It was raining harder now, and Mariella knew she should get to John's house, but she couldn't face them yet. She wanted to see the boat.

In a moment it was before her, leaning on its side whispering, *ForEva*. She walked up to it and placed both hands on it. The wood felt cold and soft, as if she could crumble it in her hands. She walked around the stern and looked at the empty space where the engine had been.

She started to think of all the clues she'd missed—his depression in the weeks preceding his death, the fishermen out of work because of the glut, his frustration over Eva's suggestion that he find another trade, his sudden death. Eva's meetings with the priest at St. Mary's, no more newspapers in the house, her mother's depression.

Gavin knew; John knew; the Hemingways knew. Key West knew. She recalled the deputy trying to keep her away from the boat that day, Nicolas pulling her, insisting she come away with him. Now she understood they hadn't wanted her to see because then she'd know that her father had killed himself.

Mariella shook her head. She felt like a fool.

A sudden gust blew a chunk of wood off the boat and into Mariella's leg. She flinched and reached down to touch her calf.

When she picked up her hand, blood covered her fingers. She had to go to John's house.

~~~

When she got there, Papa's car was parked out front.

She walked up to the door, and when she opened it, her mother and Mutt rushed to her. Eva grabbed Mariella and hugged her. She ran her hands over Mariella as if she needed confirmation that she was there and okay. Mutt sniffed her leg. Eva gasped when she saw the blood, but Mariella mumbled that it was just a shallow cut.

Papa and John watched Mariella. Estelle played dolls with Lulu on the floor, but watched the adults.

"Mari, I'm so sorry about what Pauline said," said Papa. "I can't ever fix this, but you've got to know how sorry I am."

"At least *she* told me the truth," said Mariella.

John looked down at the floor.

"Don't you understand," said Eva. "I just wanted to protect you."

"You had to know I'd find out."

"I prayed you wouldn't," said Eva, beginning to cry. "On my rosary every day I prayed for Hal's soul and for you not to find out. I asked God to at least make it so you wouldn't know. You were Hal's light and he was yours, and I don't know how he could have done that to you and to all of us."

Mariella felt the tears on her face but didn't wipe them away.

Eva continued. "And I felt so guilty, like I pushed him too hard. And I couldn't stand for you to find out, because I knew you'd blame me. And, God, Mariella, I can't stand to lose you, too."

Eva collapsed on the sofa and buried her head in her arms, sobbing. Mariella stared at the floor, unable to speak and unsure what to think. She thought maybe Eva was to blame, but then something inside her knew that it wasn't her mother's fault. There was something wrong inside Hal, the same thing wrong in Hemingway's father, and the vet, and every other person who'd taken his own life: a staggering inability to cope.

While Mariella thought of this, Estelle stood from her dolls and walked over to her.

"We needed you," said Estelle.

Everyone turned to her, surprised to hear her speak.

"To keep us going," said Estelle. "If you knew, you'd have been the same as Mama."

Mariella looked at her sister with new eyes and found her voice. "Did you know?"

Estelle looked at Eva and then at the floor. "I heard Mama talking to the priest," she said.

Mariella was filled with pity for Estelle. All along she'd known and kept it from Mariella to protect *her*, while she was tortured with the knowledge. Mariella wiped her tears with the back of her hand.

The sound of a chair scraping across the front porch reminded them of the storm. Papa stepped outside and brought in the chair. He put it in the bedroom and came back to the living room. He walked over to Mariella and put his hands on her shoulders.

"I have to go," he said. "Are you all sure you don't want to come with me?"

"They'll be safe here," said John.

Papa looked at Mariella, his misery palpable. She could feel his sadness and anger. She feared for Pauline.

"I'm glad she told me," said Mariella. "Don't hate her for me. I'm glad."

He looked at her for a moment and nodded. Then he was gone.

5:00 p.m.

The barometer read 28.42. The power had failed. The train hadn't been ordered by Ghent until after two o'clock.

It wouldn't get there in time.

There was still no sign of the Morrows, so Gavin rounded up more of the wives and children from camp three and loaded them into his work truck. He had a young vet take them north. The kids' eyes were as wide as the taillights Gavin watched disappearing into the storm. He said a prayer for them and hoped they'd make it. He knew they stood a better chance up north than they did on Lower Matecumbe. As they were leaving, Ed Butters pulled up to the hotel. Gavin saw Ed struggling to get himself and his son into the hotel, so he ran to help. It felt as if a thousand needles were pushing into his back, and he had trouble standing up straight. As he dragged them in, little sparks ignited in the air.

They fell in through the door of the hotel, and it took three of them to push the door closed. Gavin reached up and felt his neck. He pulled his hand away and looked at it, spotted with blood from where the sand had ripped his skin.

"What the hell were those sparks?" he asked.

"Sand," said Ed, wiping at his eyes. "The force of the wind's making it explode when it hits."

Fran stopped setting out the sandwiches she'd put together for the vets and covered her mouth with her hand.

"The wind—not the accelerator—pushed my car into town," said Ed.

Loud crashes could be heard outside, along with the steady sound of the rain and the hiss of the sand pelting the hotel. Gavin felt frantic inside, looking at the boards over the windows, imagining the vets huddled in the shacks that he knew wouldn't hold. The roof started banging, and Gavin looked up.

"It's gonna go!" yelled Bonefish.

Gavin dived over Fran and her son as the roof ripped away, and rain and sand poured in over their heads.

"To the car!" yelled Ed. Ed pulled Fran and their kids away into the storm. Sheeran found Gavin and told him to come with him aboard the dredge boat in the canal, where about thirty people from camp three were already waiting.

Gavin grabbed Sheeran's arm and then Bonefish's, and they started a human chain out of the hotel. Gavin couldn't open his eyes because of the sand. He put his head down and squinted to watch the ground as he moved to the dredge. The wind knocked them over, but they were able to right themselves and hunch toward the canal. The red tricycle that had been stuck in the mangrove smashed Gavin's side hard enough to knock the wind out of him. He put his hand on his side and tried to stand against the wind, but it kept pushing him down.

"Crawl, damn it!" yelled Sheeran, and the men clawed along the ground toward the dredge.

They passed the Butterses' car and heard the door slam. Gavin hoped all of the Butterses had made it in.

The wind screamed so loud it stung Gavin's ears. Under the howling, the sound of wood splintering and snapping caused him to turn around. He cupped his hands around his eyes to block the sand and rain and saw the hotel where he'd just been standing buckle, fold, and blow away like a house of cards. The side wall lifted, folded in half, and slammed into a nearby fire truck, setting off its siren. Splintered wooden beams exploded into the air.

A flash of lightning lit up the sky as a sharp wood beam flew past Gavin. It went through Bonefish's head with a sickening crunch, killing him on the spot. Gavin stared in horror as Sheeran grabbed his arm. The only thing he could think was that he didn't even know the guy's real name.

Gavin pulled out of Sheeran's grasp and reached for Bonefish's arm. He knew he had a family who'd want to bury him, and

Gavin wanted to find a place to put him. He tried to drag the vet over the sand and through sopping puddles, but he could barely stand himself.

Suddenly a wave crashed over him, pulling Bonefish away. Gavin's mouth filled with salt water. Sheeran jerked him to his knees.

"Get the hell under cover!" yelled Sheeran. "Now!"

Gavin looked once more for Bonefish, but couldn't see him, so he turned and let Sheeran pull him to the road.

They staggered low along the road, but rocks, shells, and flying debris hit them with shattering force. Suddenly another wall of water crashed over them, separating Gavin from Sheeran and pushing him toward the gulf. His feet found the ground and another wave crashed over him. He felt the seawater filling his mouth. He tried to find something to anchor himself to, but he kept spinning in circles.

His back slammed flat against the side of a stone wall. The water pushed into him and he thought it was the end, but the wave passed and he was covered up only to his knees.

While he struggled to get his bearings and find Sheeran, lightning flashed. He saw corpses of men he knew floating by. Mike Wilson. Al. Their bodies slipped by in a tangle of broken shacks and bed frames, construction equipment and coral.

Gavin saw a large group silhouetted against the sky, stumbling along the railroad bed. He knew it was the highest point on Matecumbe, and started wading through the water to reach them. The water was back up to his waist, but he pushed through to reach the railroad. When it got shallow, he crawled up the rest of the way.

The group he met was the hundred or so vets and their families who'd been in the mess hall at camp three. They pulled themselves along the railroad track.

He tripped in the water and ran into a woman.

Lorraine Morrow!

She was there with Janie and Teddy, and Janie was wailing. There was no sign of Henry. The wind pushed them off the track and the baby fell into the water. Gavin grabbed the infant before the water swept her away. He pushed Janie up through his shirt so her head rested against his chest and the shirt held her securely against him. He grabbed Lorraine by the hand and pulled her back to the railroad tracks. Teddy clung to the tracks and wouldn't move.

Suddenly Gavin felt rumbling. He thought the wind was about to rip the tracks off their ties. The crowd started shouting, and word reached him that the train had arrived. Gavin pried the boy's fingers from the tracks as cries of relief went up. The mass of people moved off the tracks to let the train through. Its front light was a beacon of hope to the weary, storm-battered group.

When the train stopped, the people started climbing in. Gavin put Teddy on the train and removed Janie from his shirt. He passed her back to her mother.

Lorraine cried and thanked him and disappeared into the car. Gavin helped lift a vet with a broken back on board the train and then climbed in himself, thankful for shelter from the battering storm. The car was filled only with soft whimpers as the wind screamed on outside. Gavin's face was raw from the blowing sand, and he was covered with bloody bruises from flying debris. His side where the tricycle hit him ached.

As the train started moving, a sudden gasp went up along the other side of the train car. Gavin turned to look over the heads of the people and through the windows, and saw a black wall rising over them. Before he had time to register the storm surge, he felt the car lift off the tracks and then start to turn. Gavin hung on to the rail at the doorway where he'd been standing until the pressure inside the car pushed him out. He tried to swim with the surge away from the train so he didn't get crushed, and made it to a clump of mangrove bushes.

He held on as the surge passed. The bush scratched him, but he knew it was his only hope for survival. He couldn't believe the train had been pulled from the track. He felt a fury rising in him against Sheldon and Ghent and all the bureaucrats who'd caused this, and thought that if he ever made it through the storm, he'd strangle them with his bare hands.

In every flash of lightning, Gavin's eyes met new horrors. A man impaled by a steel pole. A dead woman, the clothes blown off her body, tangled in the bushes nearby. A child . . . but he had to turn away from that. Henry. Oh, God, Henry.

He felt his chest tighten, and the sudden image of Mariella in this mess made him unable to breathe. He started mumbling a rosary to himself for her safety and that of her family and John. He knew he couldn't bear it if anything happened to them.

And all at once, it was as if a switch flipped and the storm went off.

The sky twinkled overhead. The moon lit the landscape with the gentle glow of a night-light. Not a breath of wind stirred.

The eye of the storm.

Gavin uncurled himself from the bushes and saw others rising around him. He staggered back to the train to help people out of it. He found Lorraine and the baby, but not Teddy.

"I can't find him," said Lorraine.

"Is it over?" yelled a man.

"No," said Gavin. "It's about to get worse."

"Why?" screamed Lorraine. "I thought God was havin' mercy on us."

"It's the eye," said Gavin. "We've got to find shelter."

"You've got to help me find Teddy," said Lorraine.

Gavin knew she had to find shelter quickly, but also knew he had to find Teddy—whether he was dead or alive. Gavin searched the landscape trying to find a shelter, but to his astonishment, there were no houses. An occasional wall or bent frame dotted the horizon, but almost everything had been flattened. He spotted a bus that had been parked by the hotel.

"This way," he said.

"Teddy!" she screamed.

Gavin grabbed her by the arms. "We've got to get you to safety or you're gonna lose the baby. I'll find Teddy once you're safe."

He put his arm around her waist and guided her to the bus. The sounds of people crying and retching over the corpses floating in the knee-high water were all around, but survival was paramount. They picked their way over fallen poles and through thickets of mangroves. When they made it to the bus, Ed Butters opened the door.

"Get in, for God's sake, before the storm's back upon us," he said. His face was pale and he was in a cold sweat.

Lorraine climbed into the bus, and Gavin passed her the baby.

"I'll find him," he said.

"Please," she sobbed. He turned and started to make his way back to the train.

He tried to run, but the obstacles on the ground and in the water made it difficult. His side ached as he climbed back through mangrove bushes and fallen palm trees. The idea of searching for Henry's body entered his mind, but he dismissed it. The living were the priority. He saw the overturned train cars just ahead and started calling the boy's name.

He stopped to listen, but instead of hearing a response, he heard a sound building under the silence. Suddenly the water around Gavin's knees dropped sharply. The noise started growing—a faraway howling and the sound of rushing water.

Gavin looked in the distance and saw what he feared.

The eye had passed and the edge of the hurricane was roaring back—the most powerful edge—preceded by a wave so large Gavin could scarcely believe his eyes. He felt the ground tremble beneath him and knew he had to find Teddy or the boy would be lost forever. Gavin ran to the railroad tracks, where he hoped Teddy would be clutching them, and to his relief he found him doing just that.

"Teddy." Gavin pulled at him, but he wouldn't let go, so Gavin had to uncurl Teddy's fingers himself. He finally got Teddy loose and started running with him back to the bus. He couldn't bear to look behind him. Gavin knew the water was nearly upon them and didn't want to see his death.

Teddy sucked in his breath as the howling grew louder. The wind started to push against Gavin's back as he jumped and crawled over mangrove bushes, shouting to Ed to open the doors of the bus.

When he reached the bus, he passed the boy in through the door. He heard a tremendous crash, and as he turned he was swept away in a powerful current.

Under the water, the noise of the wind was gone. It struck him how peaceful it was until a tree hit his bruised side. He felt his ribs crack. He opened his mouth in a cry of pain, and water rushed into his mouth, but he didn't fight it. He wanted to live in that stillness. The noise of the hurricane was so far away. He thought he'd take in the water and fill his lungs and escape the hell around him. He felt frantic for a moment, but then peaceful again.

As the water pushed him along, the hurricane started slipping away from his consciousness. Instead, he felt Mariella's body cradled into him on the bed in Bimini after the fight. He felt her warmth at his side in church. He felt the sand on his hands while he built a castle with Lulu. He saw Mariella's face, laughing, as he pulled her up from the floor when he'd flipped her that night, dancing. He saw her sweet face under her boy's baseball cap and felt her firm handshake.

He thought of his mother's coffin being lowered into the earth. Then his father's.

He saw the red bloodstain on the white snow.

He felt his father's hands on his on the baseball bat.

He tasted the butterscotch his mother bought him from the soda shop.

And then heard the sound of her lullaby.

Chapter Twenty-eight

Lower Matecumbe Key

Mariella stood in the cabin of the *Pilar*, her hands tight against the wood, willing the boat to move faster through the water. She wiped her face, but couldn't tell whether it was a tear or the salty seawater.

Earlier that day, survivors who'd made it down to Key West had given preliminary reports, but she and Papa didn't want to believe what they'd heard about the level of destruction. Papa had volunteered to take relief supplies in his boat, and Mariella jumped at the chance to help and wouldn't take no for an answer. He'd begged her not to go.

Mariella scanned the island coming into view. There were no buildings at all. None. But the little grassy mound nearby looked like Veterans' Key.

"This couldn't be it," she said. "Could it?"

Hemingway nodded. "This is it."

He slowed down the boat and motored to the dock, only it wasn't there.

It was as bad as they'd said.

She scanned the landscape and saw a barge and a boat, both heavily battered but upright, and wondered whether anyone on them was alive. She looked where the bridge once stood and saw people shell-shocked and walking around in various states of injury. There were uniformed National Guardsmen and what appeared to be Red Cross workers. Their faces were covered with masks.

As Papa pulled the *Pilar* up to a lone piling within jumping distance of the road, the smell hit. Mariella's eyes grew wide and she covered her face with her arm.

"Mari," he said. "This isn't a good idea. It's really bad."

"I'm getting out."

Papa sighed and reached for the piling. He passed Mari the wheel and climbed up to tie the *Pilar* to the piling. Then he hopped back down in the cabin and found an old towel. He bit one side, tore it in two, stepped over to her, and wrapped the towel around her face. Then he did his own.

Papa climbed out first on the wall of land where the roadbed used to lie. He reached back to help Mariella, and they set out.

The dead were mostly naked, the clothing having been ripped off their bodies and, in some cases, their limbs taken with it. Most of their faces were bloated beyond recognition, and flies buzzed in their eyes and between their legs.

Mariella looked up in the sky and wondered where the buzzards were. Then she saw one lying in a clump of gray-black, waterlogged feathers. At least they wouldn't start on the bodies. They were all dead themselves.

They picked through the mess of men and mangroves. Mariella and Papa came upon a tree and saw two naked, swollen women under a swarm of flies. Mariella had to turn away.

"Jesus," said Papa. "They used to work the sandwich shop at the ferry."

Papa moved ahead of Mariella while she tried to catch her breath amid the devastation and the odor. She was trying to be brave, but the horror was unimaginable.

She looked ahead and saw Papa stopped down by the water's edge, and was shocked to see him turn and vomit. After what he'd seen in his life, Mariella thought he'd have more of a stomach for this.

Then he met her gaze, and his look of panic filled her with a dread she'd never before experienced. She started toward him.

"Stop!" he called, putting up his hands. "Don't come any closer."

"What is it?' She continued to move toward him.

He wiped his mouth and rushed toward her, pushing her away.

"Stop," he said. "Go back!"

"No." Mariella pushed at him. He tried to hold her, but she broke free of his arms and stumbled over to the corpse.

There was a body floating lifeless in the water, its face covered with rope. It was its arm that stopped her short. On it, grotesquely enlarged on the bruised and mottled skin, were the numbers *11-11-18*.

She gasped and felt her heart beating in her ears.

She was vaguely aware that Papa had pulled her into his arms.

Several workers nearby came forward and tried to untangle the body from the coils of rope. Then she screamed and tried to move toward the corpse. Papa pulled her back, and she kicked and clawed at him. She fought him while he tried to drag her to the *Pilar.* He finally lifted her and carried her to the boat. Once they got to the *Pilar* he dropped her over the side and jumped in after her.

She tried to climb back out.

"Stop!" he yelled.

"Why?"

"Just stop." He held her face between his hands. She was losing strength. The fight was draining out of her.

"No, oh, Papa, no."

She finally gave up and let him hold her.

CHAPTER TWENTY-NINE

Mariella cried herself to sleep on the way back to Key West that day. When they arrived at the dock, the stragglers wanted details, but Papa ignored them as he roused her, pushed through the crowd with his arm around her waist, and led her to the car. He drove her to his home and carried her up to the sofa in his writing cottage, ignoring Pauline's questions and those of the staff.

"I'm going to John's," he said, while she stared into the room at nothing. The words barely registered. "I'll be back."

Mariella stayed in his cottage for six days. She allowed only Papa to bring her food. She didn't bathe or move from the couch unless she had to use the bathroom in the corner. She didn't cry; nor did she speak a word. She just tried to dig out of her pain and memories to a place where she was capable of making decisions.

Six days after he put her in the cottage, while the family sat at breakfast, Mariella walked down the stairs and into the dining room. She was pale. Her hair hung in greasy waves around her face. She was alarmingly thin—just a ghost of what she'd been— but her eyes were lit again.

"I want to go home," she said.

Papa stood and left his eggs and toast half-eaten on the table. The boys looked at each other, for once subdued. Pauline couldn't seem to bear to make eye contact with Mariella.

Papa drove her to her home, which, luckily, had survived the storm. When he pulled up, Eva was in the yard with Estelle, tending to the new flowers she'd planted. Lulu sat on John's lap, reading a book with him. When they saw Mariella, Lulu jumped up and ran to the car with her mother and Estelle. They swept Mariella away in a wave of tears and thanks to Papa. Mariella looked over her shoulder at him before she walked into the house and sent him her gratitude in her thoughts. She knew he could feel it.

Mark Bishop looked up as Mariella walked toward him on the dock. She wore Gavin's white shirt and dungarees rolled up to her knees.

"Hey, Mari."

She nodded, eager to speak but unable to find the right words.

"I'm very sorry to hear," he said, allowing his words to trail off over all the hard things. "Damn shame, what happened up there."

She stared at the water behind him, as serene as a lake, without the least hint of the violence that had recently passed over it. The sun winked off the surface, and small waves broke in a hush around the pilings of the dock.

She found her voice.

"Glad to see you sticking around," she said.

"Hell, I tried to leave but I just couldn't. I'll ride it out."

She looked at his boat and back out to the water beyond it. She reached for the stern.

"That's what I came to talk to you about," she said. "I've got an idea that might save both of us."

She was drowning here, on dry land.

Mariella lay in bed staring at the ceiling, listening to her sisters breathe around her. She couldn't stop shaking, tears wetting her pillow, sweat soaking her nightshirt. It was Gavin's shirt, and it still smelled like him.

How many days had passed since she'd come home from Papa's house? Four? Seven? Ten? She didn't know. All she knew was that Mark had thought her idea about the charter boat business might work, and that would save her. She had to get back to the water or she'd die. She might die anyway, but at least she'd do it where she felt at peace.

She tried to conjure Gavin's face, but all she could see was the bloated, lifeless corpse. The bodies with skin slipping off as the men tried to pull them from their watery graves. She felt the urge to vomit, but suppressed it.

Papa had been by the previous afternoon to give her a copy of the piece he'd written about his anger over the death of the vets. It was full of bitterness and contempt, and she couldn't help but read it again, her eyes seeking the most graphic places with morbid desperation. If she kept reading it, she might believe that what had happened really happened.

WHO MURDERED THE VETS? A FIRSTHAND REPORT ON THE FLORIDA HURRICANE
By Ernest Hemingway

Who sent them down to the Florida Keys and left them there in hurricane months?

Who is responsible for their deaths?

The writer of this article [Hemingway] lives a long way from Washington and would not know the answers to those questions. But he does know that wealthy people, yachtsmen, fishermen such as President Hoover and President Roosevelt, do not come to the Florida Keys in hurricane months. Hurricane months are August, September and October, and in those months you see no yachts along the Keys. You do not see them because yacht owners know there would be great danger, inescapable danger, to their property if a storm should come. For the same reason, you cannot interest any very wealthy people fishing off the coast of Cuba in the summer when the biggest fish are there. There is a known danger to property. But veterans, especially the bonus-marching variety of veterans, are not property. They are only human beings; unsuccessful human beings, and all they have to lose is their lives. They are doing coolie labor for a top wage of $45 a month and they have been put down on the Florida Keys where they can't make trouble. It is hurricane months, sure, but if anything comes up, you can always evacuate them, can't you? . . .

Who sent nearly a thousand war veterans, many of them husky, hard-working and simply out of luck, but many of them close to the border of pathological cases, to live in frame shacks on the Florida Keys in hurricane months?

Why were the men not evacuated on Sunday, or, at latest, Monday morning, when it was known there was a possibility of a hurricane striking the Keys and *evacuation was their only possible protection?* . . .

When we reached Lower Matecumbe there were bodies floating in the ferry slip. The brush was all brown as though autumn had come to these islands where there is no autumn but only a more dangerous summer, but that was because the leaves had all been blown away. There was two feet of sand over the highest part of the island where the sea had carried it and all the heavy bridge-building machines were on their sides. The island looked like the abandoned bed of a river where the sea had swept it. The railroad embankment was gone and the men who had cowered behind it and finally, when the water came, clung to the rails, were all gone with it. You could find them face down and face up in the mangroves. The biggest bunch of the dead were in the tangled, always green but now brown, mangroves behind the tank cars and the water towers. They hung on there, in shelter, until the wind and the rising water carried them away. They didn't all let go at once but only when they could hold on no longer. Then further on you found them high in the trees where the water swept them. You found them everywhere and in the sun all of them were beginning to be too big for their blue jeans and jackets that they could never fill when they were on the bum and hungry.

I'd known a lot of them at Josie Grunt's place and around the town when they would come in for pay day, and some of them were punch drunk and some of them were smart; some had been on the bum since the Argonne almost and some had lost their jobs the year before last Christmas; some had wives and some couldn't remember; some were good guys and others put their pay checks in the Postal Savings and then came over to cadge in on the drinks when better men were drunk; some liked to fight and others liked to walk around the town; and they were all what you get after a war. But who sent them there to die?

They're better off, I can hear whoever sent them say, explaining to himself. What good were they? You can't account for accidents or acts of God. They were well-fed, well-housed, well-treated and, let us suppose, now they are well dead. . . .

So now you hold your nose . . . up to that bunch of mangroves where there is a woman, bloated big as a balloon and upside down and there's another face down in the brush next to her and explain to you they are two damned nice girls who ran a sandwich place and filling station and that where they are is their hard luck. . . .

And so you walk the fill, where there is any fill and now it's calm and clear and blue and almost the way it is when the millionaires come down in the winter except for the sandflies, the mosquitoes and the smell of the dead that always smell the same in all countries you go to—and now they smell like that in your own country. Or is it just that dead soldiers smell the same no matter what their nationality or who sends them to die? . . .

You're dead now, brother, but who left you there in the hurricane months on the Keys where a thousand men died before you in the hurricane months when they were building the road that's now washed out? Who left you there? And what's the punishment for manslaughter now?

Who, indeed, Mariella thought.

She swung her legs over the edge of the bed and went out to the living room to her mother's chair. She sat with her knees pulled into her chest and looked out the window. The statue of Mary in the garden across the street looked back at her, her eyes sad, pitying, loving. Mariella was filled with an unexpected peace. She gazed back, trying to hold that peace until she could no longer keep her eyes open.

There was a commotion outside on the street.

Mariella's eyes jerked open. It sounded like a parade—but it was frantic and disorganized. The cigar man was sitting across the street. She saw him turn toward the commotion and then stand to get a closer look. The girls came out of their room, eyes thick with sleep. Eva followed, with worry all over her face. Mariella stood and opened the door. She stepped out onto the porch.

A gang of people moved down the street in a wave. Some of them jumped. They were screaming and laughing and crying. She saw Papa first—towering over the crowd, his face lit with the same smile she'd seen when she pulled up to the dock at Bimini all those months ago. Then she saw John, Nicolas, Mark Bishop, the Thompsons. Then Skinner, Isabelle, Jim, Toby.

What the hell was going on?

Papa was screaming her name—they all were.

She walked down the ramp with her mother and sisters close behind her. The sun was bright in her eyes, so the mass of people became a shadow. She put her hand over her eyes to shield the glare.

She heard his name before she saw him.

"Gavin!"

Lulu screamed and ran, pushing past Mariella. Mariella felt the air leave her lungs.

Then he was there and trying to run toward her in spite of his limp and his injuries. He was laughing and crying and screaming her name. She looked back at Eva—*My God, is he real?* Eva was crying and had her hands over her mouth. Estelle called his name.

"Gavin!"

Mariella was frozen.

Lulu reached Gavin first and tackled him. He grimaced, but he still beamed. He looked like he'd just returned from the war. He covered Lulu with kisses and carried her in his good arm as he continued toward Mariella.

Then Papa plucked Lulu out of Gavin's arm so he could get to Mariella faster. And then it hit her!

My God! He was alive! The soldier, the arm, the dead—it wasn't him! It was another Argonne vet.

My God!

She shot off like a gun and covered the block in seconds. Arms she thought she'd never feel again wrapped tight around her, pulling their hearts together, beating the same, forever.

EPILOGUE

Key West
July 16, 1961

It was eleven o'clock at night, two weeks after Papa's suicide. The people who had crowded the wall around the Hemingway House snapping pictures and sharing their stories had gone. Someone had left a bouquet of flowers and a shot glass. Someone else had left an old fishing reel.

Mariella clutched the letters to her chest as she and Jake walked toward the gate outside the house. She looked through the iron bars and remembered that day so long ago when she'd trembled at the front door, waiting for her first day of work.

Mariella's shaking hands prevented her from getting her key into the lock, so Jake gently reached for the key, opened the gate, and locked it behind them.

Jake had stayed with Mariella for these two weeks. He now knew everything about the year that Mariella met and fell in and out of love with Papa. He knew the story of his father wooing his mother, the fight his dad lost on Bimini, and the fight he won for his life in the hurricane. Mariella had told him how Gavin was rescued by Red Cross workers and placed in a hospital in Homestead, and didn't regain consciousness for days. How investigators from FERA, the Florida State's Attorney's Office, and the American Legion interviewed him about what he'd seen. How the National Guard burned most of the bodies because they could not be identified, and because their rapid decomposition compromised the health of the rescue workers.

Mariella had told Jake that at least 250 vets and four hundred civilians died in that hurricane. That only ten of the sixty-five children from the school on Matecumbe survived.

She told him that through Gavin's and others' testimonies at congressional hearings in 1936, the House passed a bill to award $217 a month to the deceased veterans' families, such as Lorraine and Teddy and little Janie, who had long since moved north to live with Lorraine's parents, never to be heard from again. She told him how the emotional scars from that time were potent and terrible, and left Gavin and the others never quite the same, though their new life on the water running charter boats seemed to restore Gavin a little more with each passing day.

She said the letters Papa and others had written her over the years would tell the rest. Especially the last letter, which she'd received three days ago. The letter he'd written just before he killed himself that didn't reach her until after he was gone.

Mariella walked around the side of the house listening to the chatter of the insects and the faint noise from the nightlife a few blocks east. Her memories rose around her like ghosts in the garden. She could see the silhouette of Pauline in the window looking out at the yard. She could smell Isabelle's bisque on the breeze. She felt the whisper of Jane Mason's dress the night she brought out the Green Fairy.

As Mariella approached the writing cottage, she could see that Toby had left on a light for her, just as she'd asked when she'd called him earlier that day. Toby, who'd spent all these years caring for the house and readying it for Papa or the boys' visits, was broken up bad, but said he'd be at Sloppy's tonight in tribute to Papa so she could have the house to herself.

Mariella stopped and stared up at the door, at the room lit from within, and felt tears well up in her eyes. God, how she ached to hear the click of Papa's typewriter in rapid fire, cutting through the screen door and the dark. How she ached to see him sitting at his writing desk.

She reached up to cover her mouth and waited for the emotion to pass.

"Mom," said Jake. "Maybe we should come back another time."

"No," she said. "I want you to read these here while I pay my respects."

He nodded and followed her up the stairs to the cottage.

Mariella took a deep breath and walked through the door and over to his writing table. It was empty. She motioned for Jake to sit and read while she walked the perimeter of the room, running her hands over Papa's books and stuffed game. She could hear the shuffle of the papers behind her, along with Jake's chuckles, gasps, and sighs.

Mariella ended up by the window that faced the direction they'd come and realized, for the first time, that she could see her house on Whitehead Street from this spot. And she was suddenly overcome by the feeling of Papa, as if he stood behind her, and she knew that he'd somehow be there, watching over her, always.

～⌒◯

December 31, 1940

Dearest daughter,

How do you and the family?

In the last couple months I published *For Whom the Bell Tolls*, got a divorce, and got remarried—though you know, no doubt, from the rags and gossip about town.

I thought of your wedding when I married Marty. It reminded me of when I gave you to that soldier, and how it was the best and the hardest thing I've ever done with a woman I love, and how I never felt better, because it was one of the only noble things I've ever done. My wedding was different, though, because of all the strain and hurt that preceded it. I vacillate between remorse and hatred for Pauline and sometimes wonder if you hate her too. I'll never forget her cruelty to you the night of that storm, though I know you were glad to find out.

But enough of that.

How's your little Jake? He must be nearly five— bugger was born nine months to the day after your wedding, or was it eight? He's the spitting image of Gavin, but I can tell he's got your personality. When I saw him last he stole my pocketknife and told me he'd use it to kill the fishies. My boys are crazy about him and want him to visit the Finca when they're here next.

How's Lulu? Your mom and John? I got Estelle's letter from Peabody. Her guitar instructor apparently gave her the highest marks in the class. She makes me proud, and I'll be happy to sponsor her as long as she wants to play there.

Still recovering from the Spanish Civil War. For the first time I felt like I was getting too old for this shit. I'm hoping the Finca will restore me while I grieve humanity and some old friends I lost, most notably, F. Scott. When I got word that he'd died of a heart attack earlier this month I nearly had my own. I didn't expect to outlive him. Thinking of him makes me sad and a little bit angry. With more discipline, a better tolerance, and no Zelda he could have been a great man. But all of that was under his control (barring the tolerance issue), so I shouldn't pity him.

And who am I to pass judgment on others on the subjects of drinking or women?

I'm counting on you to lift my spirits. You never let me give in to this self-pity and depression. Write soon to chastise me and lift me up. Send pictures of Jake. Consider coming down to Cuba for a visit.

Yours always,
Ernesto

P.S.: Holy shit, just saw the newspaper clipping you sent. Count Von Cosel—Key West eccentric—Jesus! He had the corpse of his beloved in his house for seven years before he was found out! I don't shock easily. That shocked the hell out of me.

July 21, 1951

Dearest daughter,

We are kindred souls, no doubt, to have lost our mothers on the same day—the same day. How is it that when they die, the fights, the harsh words, the manipulations and failings of these women die, too, and leave only those memories of scraped cuts attended, birthday parties, bedtime stories, and love—love like no one else will ever love you, love in spite of your shortcomings and sometimes because of them.

We are both orphans, with fathers dead of their own hands and mothers dead of age. It feels cold and lonely to have no generation above you to blame, to turn to, to respect. I'm not ready to be the top, and I suspect you aren't either, but what can we do?

I'll tell you what: We go on.

Life is a series of shit dumps. You get buried, crawl out, shake it off, and walk toward the next. Our fathers' actions begin to make sense to me on those terms. Suicidals are deemed insane, but didn't Einstein define insanity as doing the same thing and expecting different results? Perhaps those who persist at living are insane.

So again, Mari, tell me what's good. Talk me out of this. Tell me of the charter fishing business you and Gavin have done so well with that's supported you and your family; tell me of your sisters and their sweet husbands and beautiful daughters, and how John's holding up, and how the fights have been around town. Tell me the last best book you read. Tell me how well Jake's doing in school and sports and his new loves and heartbreaks.

Mary (the fourth) sends her love and tells me that your visit to us in Ketchum when the snow fell and you saw the flakes for the first time will forever live in her mind as her fondest memory. You and Jake running around in circles catching the white on your tongues—your brown bodies marking you as sun gods in this northern place, the snow unable to stick to you because of your warmth though it coated all the rest of us.

My fondest memory is of the first time you went to Spain with us and saw the bulls. In spite of the crowds and our companions it was only you and me and the bull and the bullfighter. I watched you as much as I did the bull, but I liked watching you more. I knew you were a true aficionado—you had the passion—when you wept before the bull was run through and had no words after. I remember when the bulls ran and you ran with them and made Gavin sit out so Jake wouldn't end up an orphan. I don't know if I've ever loved anyone as much as I loved you that day.

I'll think of that until I hear from you next. That will help.

Yours,
Papa

September 2, 1951

Dear Mariella,

I think of you every year at this time on the anniversary of the Labor Day hurricane. I think of you many other times of year, but on this day, in particular, you are with me all day—your strength and courage, your devastation followed by your elation, but mostly, I think of how I hurt you.

I never apologized to you. Oh, I know Ernest sent

my apologies, but I never spoke directly to you. You stopped working for us, I began to travel, and then my marriage began to unravel. I know you probably hate me, as you should, but please accept my deepest and sincerest apologies.

My anger and jealousy began their slow and definite erosion of me that summer. I have no one to blame but myself. I'm certain the end of my marriage to Ernest was justice for what I did to his first marriage. Like so many "other women" I was fool enough to believe that I was the man's *one true love*. We all know, of course, that Ernest's only true love is his writing. All of us exist in orbit around him when he needs to breathe from it, but it's to *it* he always returns—to *it* only that he's faithful.

But I digress.

I'm so happy to hear that your family is well and that you have managed so well. You are the strongest woman I know. I would have done well to pay attention to you more, watch your confidence, adopt your honesty, treat everyone as equals; perhaps it would have changed the way my life turned out.

Again, I am deeply sorry for the way I hurt you. I would be honored if you would write to me now and then to keep me up-to-date on your family and yourself. I will understand if you don't.

Very sincerely,
Pauline

May 6, 1959

Dearest daughter,

My heart aches for you. Your account of Gavin's death moved me to tears. How fortunate a man he was to have you all at his side when he died. Why cancers take some so young and not others never ceases to baffle me, but I know one thing: Gavin was the purest kind of man who led the best kind of life, so he will rest. I only pray that you will now that he's gone.

But of course you will.

I remember when you thought he'd gone after the storm. You allowed yourself to grieve for six days, then came out and took yourself home and prepared yourself to keep living. Then came the greatest day of my life—the day that gave me faith in God—when we paraded Gavin down the street to you, alive, resurrected, restored, so you could begin your happily ever after.

And the two of you: the legacy you've left and continue to provide. How you and Gavin lived your dream on your charter boats that now take up half the dock at the Harbor View and are captained by Mark Bishop and John and your sisters' husbands. My God, you are the fleet of Key West, and half the town has you to thank for its survival.

You know Gavin's body is gone, but you'll have him still. He'll be on the water with you when you're out fishing. He'll be in the air in the excitement of a boxing match downtown. He'll look at you out of his son's eyes.

I enclosed the picture that Mary took of me reading your letter. I didn't know she took it, but doesn't it just tell you about God and our relationship. My relationship with you, the only pure thing I've got, with God above us, approving.

I don't know much about God. Our relationship has been strained, at best. But I do know that God approves very much of you and of Gavin, and that you've had the richest kind of life. May he rest in peace.

Ever yours,
Papa

June 30, 1961

Well, daughter,

No doubt you've heard by now.

First, let me get all apologies out of the way. I'm sorry if I've hurt you. You're a true friend and I wish it didn't have to happen this way.

On better days, I thought I'd go to you in Key West and see if that place would resurrect the part of myself that had been, but I knew I'd just be bothered by a bunch of damned phonies and the ghost of my young, healthy, careless self.

So why? she asks.

Winter's been hard. Ghosts of dead wives (even if they're still living), unsettled sons, unquiet parents, friends loved and lost, critics, editors, poets, fishermen—

their voices have gotten so loud I can't hear my own—nor single them out to understand what they're saying. I went to Mayo to get help and they electrocuted me.

The voices stopped, by God, but so did mine. I can't write a word of fiction anymore. I can't even write the truth. If I can't write, I'm nothing.

This letter gave me hope—seeing these little black marks on the page that have sustained me all these years, at once depleting and restoring me. But when I tried them in my stories, they wouldn't come.

All that comes are the dreams in the night. I dream of the porpoise pod I told you about, and of Bimini, and of the Gulf Stream. I dream of fall with the great flare of life and color in the landscape before it blows away. I wish I had gone out at the peak, instead of waiting till the color was gone and only the dry, brown shell of what was once great remained.

Remember this: I'll be demonized and canonized because of this, but I'm no worse or better than any man. I'm not to be pitied—I've lived more lifetimes than any man deserves.

I do have to confess one thing to you, though. Remember that year—the year of the great storm— when all that summer you taught me that I had to stop collecting people and using them in my stories? You told me people were disposable to me. I fought you, but you were right, and you didn't want to be used. I told you I would never use you.

But I did.

It was in *The Old Man and the Sea*—the only thing I've ever been really proud of. It was the truest writing I've ever done. Santiago was the best man I ever wrote and the fish was the best fish and the hunt was the best hunt.

No doubt you think you are the boy. You are *like* the boy, because you are good to me and because I always wished you were with me. Because I never really thought a thing had happened until I told you, and I always said to myself, "I wish Mariella were here," like the lights on the boats in that Key West poem by the damned Stevens. But that isn't the whole story.

The sea—*la mar*—was the best sea I ever drew. She was the great beauty who held the old man aloft. Who gave and who took—but who always provided. Who nourished, challenged, and taught him. My girl, *la mar*—you are the sea. And your vast brilliance held me afloat longer and better than you can ever know. And I'm sorry to have used you, but your greatness and your goodness were too broad to ignore. And if I have a heart, it is yours.

Yours,
Ernest Hemingway

As Jake read the final words aloud, his voice was thick with emotion. He put the paper on the table with a trembling hand and looked into Mariella's eyes, and here, in this place, with Jake looking at her with eyes like Gavin's, and having heard her son read Papa's words with a raspy voice like her father's, she felt the chorus of all of the men she'd loved in the room, filling her with gratitude and whispering to her that she really had been given the richest kind of life.

ACKNOWLEDGMENTS

A book is never a solitary pursuit, and I owe my thanks to many for helping me in its completion.

First, and always, to God for giving me a story to tell.

To my agent, Kevan Lyon, and to my editor, Ellen Edwards, whose enthusiastic belief in me and in this story, and kind guidance in all matters of business and art, have been heartening and irreplaceable.

Also, to the Breakout Novel Intensive workshop leaders Donald Maass, Jason Sitzes, Roman White, and especially Lorin Oberweger, whose feedback and editorial assistance were invaluable. To my critique group at BONI—Dianna Barker, Mary Edelson, Karen Uhl, and Laura Vogel—I can't thank you enough for your help and support.

I'd like to thank the staff of the JFK Library and Collections in Boston. What I found in the letters, photos, and journals from that collection from 1935 were immeasurably helpful to my time lines, characterization, and domestic understanding of the Hemingway family at that time.

I'd like to thank my friends at www.ernesthemingwaycollection.com and at eHemingway.com. Also to Paul Tryon at Key West Pro Guides for information on deep-sea fishing; the wonderful staff of the Hemingway House in Key West; Ivan Lopez-Muniz, Sarah McCoy, and Alison Treppel for assistance with the Spanish language; Jim Leithoff for telling me how to shoot a rifle to get those shark-shooting scenes just right; Carter Gravatt for introducing me to the classical guitar music of David Russell, which helped inspire my writing; Karina and Jason Opdyke for putting *With Hemingway* in my hands at that book club, and filling in so many gaps in Hemingway's home life. I would also like to thank Michael and Melissa Bison for sending me a beautiful book called *Historic Photos of Ernest Hemingway*. It was so helpful in my renderings of character and setting.

To all the book clubs I met with for my first book, who encouraged me so warmly for this novel, I thank you. Special thanks to the Spalding Teachers Book Club and the Hidden Garden Book Club for their prepublication feedback.

To my early readers, Linda Andrus, Jami Carr, Sheri and Frank Damico, Alexis and Chris McKay, Vivian Mullen, Heather and Jeff Pacheco, Rich Reilly, Patricia and Rich Robuck, Adam and Alison Shephard, and Charlene and Robert Shephard.

To my anonymous soldier, whose generosity of detail, sensitivity, and honesty gave me so much for my characterization of Gavin and John.

To my husband, Scott, and my children, for allowing me to prattle on endlessly about Papa, dealing with my writer's highs and lows, and supporting me through this process; I love you beyond words.

And finally to my dear writing partner, Kelly McMullen, who helped me every step of the way through this process. For critique sessions at Hemingway's, Hardbean, and 49 West. For a hundred hours of late-night conversation that circled all the way around our lives, spirituality, relationships, process, and, always, the words. Deep, deep gratitude to you and to *nous*.

BIBLIOGRAPHY

Nothing gave me more insight into animating Hemingway than his own works. While I have a special love for each of his books, my favorites and the ones that most heavily weighted my portrayal of the author and the themes in this book are *A Farewell to Arms*, *Green Hills of Africa*, *A Moveable Feast* (newly released edition), *The Sun Also Rises*, and most important, *The Old Man and the Sea*.

Numerous biographies, articles, and Web sites about Hemingway, the Florida Keys, and the Labor Day hurricane of 1935 were also helpful, particularly in matters of time and place. They are listed below.

Baker, Carlos. *Ernest Hemingway: A Life Story*. New York: Charles Scribner's Sons, 1969.

Dryc, Willie. *Storm of the Century: the Labor Day Hurricane of 1935*. Washington, D.C.: National Geographic Society, 2002.

Hemingway, Ernest. "Who Murdered the Vets? A Firsthand Account of the Florida Hurricane." *New Masses 16* (17 September 17, 1935): 9–10. New York: Permission of International Publishers.

Hemingway, Gregory H., M.D. *Papa: A Personal Memoir*. Boston: Houghton Mifflin Company, 1976.

Historical Preservation Society of the Upper Keys. "*THE NATURAL HISTORY ROOM, Hurricanes Case, 1935 Labor Day Hurricane shelf*," www.keyshistory.org.

Kert, Bernice. *The Hemingway Women*. New York: W. W. Norton & Company, 1983.

Lynn, Kenneth S. *Hemingway*. Cambridge, Massachusetts: Harvard University Press, 1987.

Manning, Robert. "Hemingway in Cuba (Part Two)," *The Atlantic Monthly Volume 216, No. 2* (August 1999): 101–98.

McIver, Stuart B. *Hemingway's Key West*. Sarasota, Florida: Pineapple Press, Inc., 2002.

Meyers, Jeffrey. *Hemingway: A Biography.* New York: Harper & Row, 1985.

Reynolds, Michael. *Hemingway: the 1930s.* New York: W. W. Norton & Company, 1997.

Samuelson, Arnold. *With Hemingway: A Year in Key West and Cuba.* New York: Random House, 1984.

Scott, Phil. *Hemingway's Hurricane.* Camden, Maine: International Marine/McGraw-Hill, 2006.

Standiford, Les. *Last Train to Paradise: Henry Flagler and the Spectacular Rise and Fall of the Railroad that Crossed an Ocean.* New York: Three Rivers Press, 2002.

HEMINGWAY'S GIRL

Erika Robuck

A CONVERSATION WITH ERIKA ROBUCK

Q. What inspired you to write Hemingway's Girl? *Specifically, what drew you to Hemingway at this particular time of his life?*

A. I'm a longtime fan of Hemingway, and when my husband and I visited Key West several years ago, we took the tour of Hemingway's home on Whitehead Street. Our tour guide told us many memorable and interesting stories about the author that I had never known. By the time I made it to Hemingway's writing cottage I had that feeling writers get—a feeling like falling in love—that told me I would set my next book there. Several weeks later I had a dream that Hemingway and I were standing in the house in 1935, and he told me I had to write his book because he'd become irrelevant. I started *Hemingway's Girl* and never looked back.

Q. How did you go about doing the research, and what are some fascinating details you learned, which may or may not have made it into the final manuscript?

A. Research is one of the reasons I write historical fiction, and is one of my favorite parts of the writing process. It's a bit like detective work, and I never know what fascinating facts I'll find. Perhaps the most shocking story I found was that of Count Von Cosel, a man who exhumed the corpse of a young woman he loved; he kept her body in his home for years. As if the story weren't disturbing enough on its own, I was baffled to find that once the residents of Key West found out about it, they put her body on display for several days. Rather than feeling widespread disgust, many of the residents in town thought it was a romantic tragedy that he loved her so much. I had to include it in the novel as an example of how the boundaries of love can be broken by obsession.

Q. I found Mariella such an appealing character—struggling toward independence while assuming responsibility for her family. How did you come up with her?

A. I had the privilege of researching Hemingway's personal documents and photographs at the JFK Museum in Boston, where most of the Hemingway archive may be found. While I looked through hundreds of old photos, I came across a photograph of Hemingway on the dock in Havana with a marlin and a crowd of onlookers around him. In the photograph there were many poor fishermen, and a young Cuban girl with an intense gaze. She sat in my subconscious until I started reading about how Hemingway often called young women "daughter" because he had always wanted a daughter. Then I read about a young woman with whom he became infatuated later in his life, and Mariella was born in my imagination.

Q. I, for one, am so glad that Mariella and Hemingway never cross the line into physical intimacy. Can you explain your intention in exploring the forces that attract them, and in the romantic triangle you set up among Mariella, "Papa," and Gavin?

A. Mariella grew up on the docks and fishing boats of Key West, and in 1935 has just lost her father, the person closest to her. When she meets Hemingway at the dock, she is attracted to him because she has lost an important man in her life and because of their shared love of the sea. Hemingway is attracted to Mariella because he is growing to hate the life of privilege and pretense his second wife's money has helped make for him, and Mariella represents a woman who lives a good, honest life. Their relationship dances the line between flirtation and infatuation, but ultimately Mariella's strength of character firmly sets their relationship in a place of purity and mutual respect.

The dark side of their relationship is that Hemingway has a tendency to use others for his own purposes, in fiction and in life. Gavin, on the other hand, represents a man who treats others well, builds them up, and serves them. He represents the ideal man and the right path for Mariella to follow. When she sees him for the first time at Sloppy Joe's, the only path out of the crowd leads to him. That remains true throughout the novel.

Q. I had never heard of the 1935 Labor Day hurricane before reading your novel. Why did you decide to weave it into your story?

A. While researching Hemingway's life and writings, I came across his essay "Who Murdered the Vets?" I was moved by Hemingway's vehemence about the negligence on the part of those in positions of authority over the men who had served our country. This led me to do more research on the hurricane.

As a writer of historical fiction, it is my desire to illuminate little-known places or people in history. The Labor Day hurricane of 1935 was buried in history. The men and women who lost their lives were forgotten. I thought the issues of government negligence at that time would resonate with people of our time. I also wanted to honor the memory of those lost by including their stories in the novel.

Q. Would you discuss some of the choices you made in how you tell your story? For example, why did you decide to begin and end with action set in 1961, around the time of Hemingway's death? Why did you choose not to use Hemingway's point of view? And why did you make Mariella a widow when she learns of Hemingway's death?

A. In some ways, Hemingway's death was such a contrast to the bold life he led, and I knew I had to include a reference to it. I was surprised how many people didn't know he ended his own life, and while I didn't want to dwell on that, I did feel the need to tell it.

Mostly, however, I wanted my readers to remember him at his peak, on his boat, living in one of his most beloved towns. I also think that works of historical fiction that span multiple time periods show the interconnectedness of people across place and time, and that is an important theme in my work.

That said, putting words into Hemingway's mouth was intimidating enough. I didn't want to presume to know his thoughts, so I left him out as a point-of-view character. I did, however, finally give him a voice in the letters at the end of the novel. I hadn't planned on doing that, but after reading so many of his actual letters at the JFK Museum, I felt like I had his voice in my ear for weeks. One day, before I had even finished the book, I was overcome with the need to write the letters. The way they poured out felt like dictation. I'll take them as a gift from the muse.

As for Mariella, I chose to make her a widow in 1961 for a number of reasons. First, I wanted the reader to wonder throughout the book whether Jake was Hemingway's son or Gavin's son. Putting Gavin on the boat with Mariella and Jake at the beginning wouldn't have allowed me to plant that seed in the reader's mind. Second, I wanted to be true to the time. World War I vets like Gavin were exposed to gases in the war. He smoked. He lived a hard life in the sun and on the water. Life expectancy for men in the 1960s was sixty years of age. Gavin was a product of his time. Finally, I made Mariella a widow to show that no matter what happened to her, she continued to live and to live well. I wanted Mariella to be the strongest woman I could write, and I thought showing her as a widow on the boat with her son was a good contrast to her mother wasting her life, smoking on her chair, dependent upon others.

Q. *The Paris Wife by Paula McLain, a novel that imagines Hemingway's life with his first wife, Hadley, and* Hemingway's Boat *by Paul Hendrickson, a nonfiction study of Hemingway's relationship with his boat* Pilar, *were both* New York Times *bestsellers. What do you think accounts for the resurgence of interest in Ernest Hemingway?*

A. I've been thinking a lot about why the early nineteenth century has become so popular to contemporary readers, and I believe it has to do with war and economic depression. It's only natural that we look to the past in times of hardship, and since 2008 we have experienced a shocking economic decline, rising unemployment, and the effects of war. We look to identify with those who have lived through those times for comfort, for warning, and for guidance.

Ernest Hemingway is a somewhat romanticized product of those times. His life and death fascinate us, and his work continues to have relevance today.

Q. Do you think that Hemingway's work will stand the test of time, and still be considered an essential part of the American literary canon in fifty or one hundred years? How much do you think he consciously shaped his own literary legacy?

A. I do believe his work will remain an essential part of the American literary canon. His writings, from his Nick Adams stories in northern Michigan, to the streets of Paris in *A Moveable Feast*, to the waters off the Cuban coast in *The Old Man and the Sea*, capture men and women in intimate, raw, and often heartbreaking ways. Though he exposes those closest to him, he also exposes himself, his fears, his vulnerability, and his own faults through his characters. For every word he wrote he crossed out at least five words, and the words that didn't make the final manuscripts are every bit as important as those that did. He trusts his reader to dig in and find the deeper meaning in his clear prose, and because his work is so layered it endures.

Hemingway was widely thought to be a myth creator and a legend of his own making. I agree with that to some extent, but there is so much heart and truth at the center of his work that I believe most of it came from an honest place. I also think he was a larger-than-life person, and because the life he led was so different from the lives of most people, it's hard to identify with and accept.

Q. What would you most like readers to take away from reading Hemingway's Girl?

A. I tried to infuse the book with two main themes. First, I wanted to illustrate how using others for personal gain is predatory and corrosive. Hemingway used his friends in his fiction, Eva used Mariella for support, and the government used the vets for cheap, hard labor. Disaster or near disaster resulted from each imbalanced relationship.

Mostly, however, I wanted to show the magnificent scope of human resilience. I was astounded after reading the survival story of a man who was presumed dead following the Labor Day hurricane, but who showed up in Key West days later. I'd also read an account of a man and his son who lost almost twenty family members in the Labor Day hurricane but rebuilt on Matecumbe Key and continued to make a life for themselves there. These and other accounts of war widows or vets with post-traumatic stress, combined with stories from my own grandparents, the hardships they faced, and how they kept pushing forward, living life one day at a time and rebuilding their lives after tragedy, showed me the fierce longing and love for life that so many have. I wanted that message of perseverance to stand out above all else in the book.

Q. If you could have a conversation with Hemingway, or any one of the historically based characters in the novel, who would it be and what would you talk about?

A. Of course I would want to talk to Hemingway. I'd ask him whether he had any regrets about trapping so many of his friends and loved ones in the pages of his books. I'd ask him in which book he wrote his best self. Then I would encourage him to take himself back to the Keys on a fishing boat, where his demons couldn't reach him.

Q. Would you share some of your own life story, especially what led you to writing?

A. My grandmother was Irish and a great lover of stories. She always gave me books that most would have considered too mature for my age, and talked about them with me when I finished. She made me love reading.

My father also used to tell me and my brother scary stories on the way to school each day. He'd tell long, meandering tales of children exploring ancient trains or old schools, put in perilous situations, who always managed to outsmart the monsters and return home to safety.

My interest in writing developed in tandem with my interest in reading, beginning with short plays and poems, moving to songs and short stories, and finally to novels. It wasn't until I stayed home with my growing family that I was able to commit to novels, which has been almost a decade.

Q. What might we expect to see from you next?

A. I've always been interested in the writers of the "Lost Generation," like Hemingway, Fitzgerald, Joyce, and Eliot. In my Hemingway reading I kept finding references to how much Hemingway hated Zelda Fitzgerald, and this fascinated me. I felt as if she were winking at me from my research as a way to tell me we would meet later.

Once I started reading about Zelda and Scott Fitzgerald I got the same "falling in love" feeling I had in Hemingway's Key West home. Zelda Fitzgerald is a main character in my current novel, and I'm revisiting themes of the way people use one another, and the relationship of confession and atonement. Zelda's life is rich with tragedy and drama, and I'm completely caught up in the world of the Fitzgeralds.

QUESTIONS
FOR DISCUSSION

• 1. What did you most enjoy about *Hemingway's Girl*? Did you make an emotional connection with the characters?

2. At nineteen, Mariella tends to run with a rough crowd, and she indulges in behavior—drinking, gambling, petty theft—that would not have been considered ladylike during this time. Yet she holds fast to her own standards. Discuss her "moral code" and compare it to the moral code that the Hemingways and Gavin live by.

• 3. What do you think draws Mariella and Hemingway together? Do you think their relationship is more romantic or paternal, or something else? What do you think would have happened to her, and to their relationship, if they'd crossed the line into physical intimacy?

4. What do you think about Mariella's conflicted feelings for Gavin and Hemingway? What are the differences and similarities in the way Mariella views each man? Why do you think Mariella and Gavin choose not to have sex until they're married?

5. Mariella accuses Hemingway of "collecting" people by using them in his stories. She argues that he is taking away their dignity and demands that he never use her as a character. Do you agree with her? What do you think about Hemingway's admission at the end of the novel that the sea in *The Old Man and the Sea* is Mariella?

*6. Pauline is frequently angry and jealous over Hemingway's relationships with other women. Did you sympathize with her struggle to keep her husband's affections? Do you agree with Pauline's assertion that Hemingway's "only true love is his writing"?

7. The Key West community regards Hemingway with great respect and admiration, yet few of them know about his wild mood swings and tendency toward depression. How do you explain his emotional volatility? What do you think Jane Mason means when she says that Hemingway needs Mariella to be his friend?

8. Hemingway tells Mariella that he envies her poverty, claiming that he was "happy and true" when he was poor and living in Paris. What does this suggest about his current life in Key West?

9. How does Mariella's relationship with her mother, Eva, change over the course of the novel?

10. Why does Mariella's family keep secret from her the fact that her father committed suicide? Do you think they make the best choice? Does Mariella blind herself to the truth?

11. Both Hemingway's father and Mariella's committed suicide. How does the common experience affect their relationship?

12. Mariella constantly struggles to balance her commitment to her family and the search for her own happiness. Do you respect her for trying? Do you think a contemporary woman would make the same effort?

13. How did you feel about the treatment of World War I veterans at the Matecumbe work camps, and the veterans' propensity to drink and become violent? How does *Hemingway's Girl* portray attitudes by the government and the general population toward veterans during the 1930s?

14. Had you heard of the Labor Day hurricane, and its tragic consequences, before reading this novel? Compare the authorities' response to that devastating storm with the response of government officials to recent hurricanes and other natural disasters.

15. How does Erika Robuck's description of Key West in the 1930s compare to what you know of the island today? Which version most appeals to you?

16. Erika Robuck begins and ends the novel in the 1960s, around the time of Hemingway's death. Did you find this "framing device" effective? Would you have told the story differently?

17. Have you ever read Ernest Hemingway's novels? Which one is your favorite, and why? If not, has this novel inspired you to read his work?